THE GLEEMAIDEN

THE GLEEMAIDEN

Sylvian Hamilton

review

First published in 2004
by HEADLINE BOOK PUBLISHING

10 9 8 7 6 5 4 3 2 1

Cataloguing in Publication Data is available
from the British Library

ISBN 0 7553 0706 2 (hardback)
ISBN 0 7553 0917 0 (trade paperback)

Typeset in Janson by
Letterpart Limited, Reigate, Surrey

Printed and bound in Great Britain by
Clays Ltd, St Ives plc

Papers and cover board used by Headline are natural, recyclable
products made from wood grown in sustainable forests. The
manufacturing processes conform to the environmental
regulations of the country of origin.

HEADLINE BOOK PUBLISHING
A division of Hodder Headline
338 Euston Road
LONDON NW1 3BH

www.headline.co.uk
www.hodderheadline.com

This one's for you, Margaret

Cast of Characters

Abdul al-Hazred	Arab necromancer
Adeliza	Straccan's housekeeper at Stirrup, wife of Cammo
Aidan	Novice of Coldinghame
Ailith	Young woman of Waltham
Angels	Michael, Samael, Uriel. Knights of the White Brotherhood
Bartimeus	Monk of Cerneshead Abbey
Blaise d'Etranger	Knight, friend of Straccan
Brigid	Nun, prioress of Bedesdale
Cammo	Straccan's steward at Stirrup
Christina Aurifer	Young woman of Cromber
Countess Judith	Sister of Peter des Roches, widow of Earl Joceran
David d'Ax	Orphaned boy, kinsman to Blaise d'Etranger
Durand	Knight Templar, commander at Temple Bruer
Earl Joceran	Husband of Countess Judith
Emma	Sister to Ailith
Eustace de Vesci	Baron, traitor
Finan	Novice of Coldinghame
Fulk de Marseilles	Bishop of Toulouse, leader of the White Brotherhood
Garlanda	Countess Judith's laundress
Gaudy Company	Piper, Will, Tim, Pernelle. Travelling players
Giles	Cowman in charge of ox team
Gilla (Devorgilla)	Straccan's daughter
Hawkan Bane	Straccan's servant/companion
Hugh Tapton	Bailiff of Cromber Abbey

Isabel	Queen of England
Janiva	Straccan's betrothed
Joanna	Princess of Gwynedd, bastard daughter of King John
John	King of England
Kepp o' the Dykes	Water guide at Ravenser
Ketil and Edmund	Sons of Kepp
Lawrence Boteler	A crippled boy, pilgrim
Llywelyn	Prince of Gwynedd, husband of Joanna
Lucius	Monk of Dieulacresse, physician
Lucy Boteler	Lawrence's mother, pilgrim
Maître Deil	Bishop Fulk's secretary
Master Hare	Bell founder of London
'Mercredi'	Master of King John's intelligence network
Miles Hoby	Knight, friend of Straccan
Mungo	Monk, sub-prior of Coldinghame
Nicholas	Novice of Dieulacresse
Odo	Captain of archers at Stirrup
Osyth	Anchoress of Pouncey
Paul	Countess Judith's chaplain
Peter des Roches	Bishop of Winchester, friend of King John
Peter Martel	Straccan's clerk at Stirrup
Radulfus	Prior of Coldinghame
Ralf Tyrrel	Queen Isabel's champion
Raimond de Sorules	Gleeman
Richard Straccan	Knight, dealer in holy relics
Robert fitzWalter	Baron, traitor
Roslyn de Sorules, 'Sorrow'	Gleemaiden
Starling Larktwist	Spy
Thomas	Nuns' priest at Bedesdale
Tobias	Potter of Pouncey
Widow Trygg	Innkeeper of Locksey
Wilfred	Crippled pilgrim

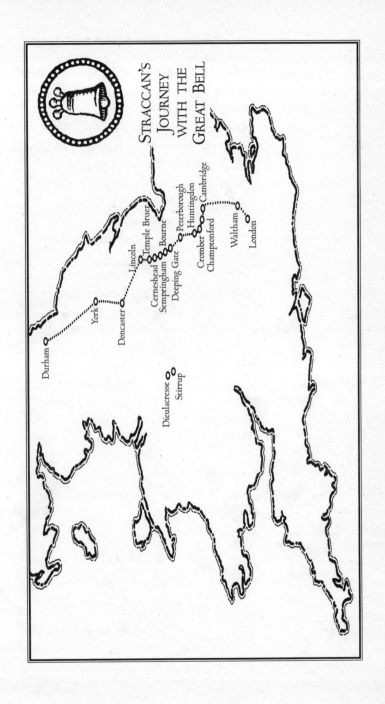

STRACCAN'S JOURNEY WITH THE GREAT BELL

Durham

York

Doncaster

Lincoln

Temple Bruer
Cerneshead
Sempringham
Bourne
Deeping Gate
Peterborough
Huntingdon
Cambridge
Cromber
Champtonford
Waltham
London

Dieulacresse
Stirrup

Chapter 1

Countess Judith kept her husband's head in a box. At night it perched on the pillow by her side, at meals it sat on the board by her plate, and her household feared it almost as much as they feared her. She talked to it, they whispered among themselves, and who was to say it didn't answer?

In life Lord Joceran had escaped his wife as often and for as long as he could. Eight years on crusade, two more as a prisoner of the Turks and every chance he got thereafter, until in the end he died, as all must. After that she had her will of him.

The head was all she had. True to form, the earl had been on pilgrimage when he died, in Spain. His body was buried there, and his squire had brought home the head, that being his lord's dying wish, to be entombed in the Benedictine abbey at Coldinghame, in the Lady Chapel he'd paid for; but his widow bagged it instead.

Minstrels sang of her great love and her grief, but if the truth were known Judith did not grieve. At last she had her husband where she wanted him. Hers entirely, at bed and board: under her eye, under her hand, under her thumb for the rest of her life.

As far as souls went, Judith had no fear. She had long since prayed Joceran out of purgatory and into paradise, and had no doubt that was her own eventual destination. The head would lie in the tomb with her, close-clasped to her breast, inescapably hers until all Christian bones and dust were summoned before God at the Day of Judgement. She was content.

Until the letter came from Coldinghame, from Prior Radulfus. She had never liked the man, a true Cuthbertian, barely able to be civil to a woman. A wicked, monstrous letter that forbade the coffining of the head with her body when she died, for Joceran had died an excommunicate and was still under the Church's ban.

It couldn't be true! But enquiry proved it, and it had come about thus: Joceran's squire, wishing to forsake the world for the life of a monk at Coldinghame, confessed to Prior Radulfus that his lord had slain a man in Spain on holy ground; not *in* a

1

church, exactly, but at its very door. The man was nothing, a peasant who truculently refused to get out of the great lord's way; it was so minor an episode that Joceran would have forgotten it had not a priest in wrath taken up bell, book and candle and cast him out from the family of God. And before he had the chance to buy his way back in, Lord Joceran was killed that very night, in an earthquake that shook the town. God's judgement, the townsfolk said, on the wicked foreign lord; though why God should take thirty innocents at the same time was a mystery.

What could be done? Judith crushed the letter in her hand, dropped it, ground it under her heel and ordered her household to prepare for a journey. She would ride her palfrey, she said, at which her ladies' voices rose in a chorus of dismay. At this time of year any journey, let alone such a one as she proposed, was most dangerous (no one dared say foolhardy). She had been ill, she had a cough and a pain in her chest; she was not as young as she once had been.

She brushed aside their concerns. Old she might be, but not feeble. No, she would not ride in a litter, nor would she write letters. She must go herself. Go where? They asked. To whom? To her brother, of course! Radulfus would have to listen to the Bishop of Winchester! It was unfortunate that Peter should be so far away, two hundred miles and more in London, but this was too urgent to be entrusted to messenger or letter. She must speak to him herself. Peter would make that insolent prior eat his words; if Judith had her way they would be crammed down his throat with the ill-cured parchment they were written on, but that was too much to hope for.

It was fine weather, dry and frosty; if it held, the journey south would not be too arduous. Good hunting weather. She would have ridden out herself, hawk on wrist, but for this unforeseen emergency; hunting was her favourite pastime. Peter's too, although he had few occasions for it since becoming so great a man – Bishop of Winchester, king's confidant, courtier, states-man, diplomat.

The last of the servants came running to the carts that would carry them in shocking discomfort to London. Father Paul, her chaplain, edged nervously out of the countess's line of sight and scanned their faces anxiously until he found the one he sought. There she was! Garlanda! He had feared she might not be coming. His leman, his love! A round, rosy countenance framed in stubborn curls that defied all attempts at straightening, merry

2

eyes and a merry mouth. She saw him at the same time, and winked as she scrambled into a cart. A flush of pleasure rose warmly from his throat to his brow, all else forgotten.

Judith's voice cracked like a whip: 'Father Paul, attend me!' His flush paled instantly as if a hand had wiped it off. Hastily, clumsily, nervously he mounted his mule and took his station at the countess's side. Her palfrey stamped, eager to be off. The bone of contention, the skull in its casket, was safe in her saddlebag – it went everywhere with her. She drew on her gloves, sniffing the crisp air like a hound, which she rather resembled; colour tinged her sallow cheeks as she shook the reins. Her cortège – ladies, men-at-arms, servants, cook, chaplain, physician and fool – moved off at a pace they could never keep up. Ride in a litter? Pah!

Chapter 2

S ir Richard Straccan reached the inn towards the end of a
bitter March day, chilled to the bone and bone tired, only
too thankful to reach shelter before dark. The stable was almost
full, which meant a dozen other wayfarers – pilgrims, judging
by the profusion of holy medals dangling from their bridles –
were already inside. He hoped there'd be some supper left.
Heaving Zingiber's saddle off, he checked the stallion's hooves,
rubbed him down, and left him munching contentedly in his
stall.

This inn was no different from the hundred others he'd
stopped at during the past year: a long, low, thatched building,
with the hall at one end, and sleeping quarters at the other
where all the guests lay down together in their clothes to get
what sleep they could. The cheerful noise of many voices and a
warm, moist gust of sweat and onions greeted Straccan as he
shoved the damp-swollen door open. At its tortured squeal a
brief silence fell as the pilgrims looked up from their suppers,
assessing the newcomer – tall and broad-shouldered, warmly
cloaked, face scarred, the hilt of a sword jutting up over his
shoulder: a knight. Still, it took all sorts, and with a matey
chorus of 'God save yous' they shuffled their bottoms along the
benches to make room for him, and resumed their interrupted
meal and talk.

When he'd finished eating, Straccan brought out a folded
piece of calf skin and opened it to display a drawing, inviting his
table companions to look.

'Anyone here seen anything like this? Anyone know where it
is?'

They bent over it, frowning at the curious rune-like symbol
– a vertical stroke with two branches on the right side, slanting
upwards. They pursed their lips and shook their heads with
the same blank lack of recognition he'd met everywhere, and
his heart sank.

'No . . . never seen that . . . no . . . Sorry, me lord.'

Another dead end. Sighing, he put the sketch back in his scrip.

4

It was all he had to go on, and after all these months it had got him nowhere.

Janiva, he thought, with a fresh pang to the ache of longing that never left him. *Janiva, where are you?* He could picture her so clearly in his mind's eye – her smile, the full-lipped oval face, red-brown braids lying over her shoulders, her green gown . . . When he closed his eyes it seemed he could even smell the scent of her sun-warmed skin, the sharp clean perfume of rosemary that she loved.

Impossible, unthinkable that he should never find her! Yet after so long . . .

More than a year had passed since Janiva's escape from her home village of Shawl, where she had been imprisoned on a malicious charge of sorcery. Her friend, the forester Tostig, had promised to take her to a place of safety, but had dared tell no one where lest they be forced into betrayal. They had ridden into the greenwood, and vanished. Straccan had been back to Shawl half a dozen times since then, hoping for word of them, but no word came, and Tostig had never returned. Everyone at Shawl thought him dead, and if he had perished, surely Janiva had too: by now their bones lay somewhere in the deeps of the forest, and would never be found. Tostig was a man of resource who knew the forest as a villein knows his strips, but outlaws, like wolves, hunted prey in packs; what chance would one man and a young woman have if they met with a band of armed ribauds?

The pot boy refilled Straccan's cup, and he drank and set it down. Had he been wrong to put his faith in the drawing? Sitting alone by the embers after the others had trooped off noisily to their pallets, he remembered the night his daughter Gilla had come barefoot to his bed.

'Father,' she'd said. 'I think I can find Janiva. I can scry for her.'

She had that gift: the ability to see, in water or flame, places and people far away. Scrying, it was called. Awed and uneasy, he'd watched while she stared into the candle flame and described what she saw – a high cliff face split by an outcropping of quartz shaped something like a forked branch and shining brilliantly white against the grey rock, a steep path leading to a terrace halfway up the cliff and a small stone house, clinging like a snail shell to the cliff face.

She drew the outline of the quartz mark for him. He sent copies to his agents, and to Templar commanderies and preceptories throughout the kingdom, where he had friends, certain that

5

someone would recognise it and tell him where to find it. Back then, at the beginning, he never doubted he would find her. Each morning he awoke with the expectation, *today, today*! But the days passed, and no one came forward to say, 'I know the place, it lies thus-and-so,' and weeks crawled by, and hope bled out.

After two months, wild with impatience, Straccan left his steward in charge of his manor, his clerk in charge of his business (he bought, sold and occasionally 'liberated' holy relics), and with his servant, Hawkan Bane, he took to the roads, showing the drawing at every vill and manor, every town, and asking every traveller they met. More than once, riding through a town, a market, a fair, he'd seen a green gown, a thick braid of russet hair, and reached for her, crying her name, only to see a stranger's startled face and know the bitterness of disappointment.

After six months he and Bane split up, to cover twice the ground and double their chances. Weather and roads permitting, they met or left word for each other in York. He was on his way back there now, weighted down with defeat after weeks lost following false leads, while expectation leached away and hope turned sour.

Given an enemy to fight, a tower to storm, some innocent to rescue or a relic to steal, Straccan was in his element. But *this* – this futile, unending riding from place to place, showing the damned drawing, asking the same damned question over and over . . .

He stared at the dregs in his cup. There was another thing – the guilty knowledge that this was all his fault, that the loss of Janiva and the suffering she had undergone was because of him. Two summers ago in Wales he'd challenged Lord William de Breos (whom the Welsh, who knew him best, named 'the Butcher') to battle on holy ground, violating Sanctuary. He made no excuse. He'd known full well what he did and how grave the sin; his intention was to kill, and the fact that things hadn't turned out that way made no difference. Afterwards he'd sought absolution, but his confessor held the matter too serious to pardon without consulting his bishop – an everyday, if costly, business, if it had not been for the Interdict.

For four years England had lain under the Pope's ban – its people cut off from the benefits and graces of Holy Church: no Mass, no sacraments, no bells, no burials in holy ground – all because King John refused to accept as Archbishop of

Canterbury a man whom the Pope was determined to force upon him. Caught between papal displeasure and the king's wrath, every bishop in England save one had fled into exile, and until the Interdict was lifted – which looked like being never – there were no bishops to consult. Until there were, Straccan must carry his burden of sin unabsolved, and he and all those dear to him would be the worse for it.

That was the trouble with sin, he thought morosely. It wasn't just the guilty who paid the price.

He touched the paternoster beads he wore under his collar, but felt no comfort, just desolation. Was this it, then? Time to give up and go home? Time to stop this fruitless waste of love and life and spirit. He had failed. It wasn't fair to his daughter or his people, and it was time he came to his senses. He would go to York, leave word for Bane to follow, go home, and take up his abandoned life. The joyless prospect stretched ahead, every bit as unappealing as his present situation.

God's precious blood, he swore to himself. What was he doing, sitting staring into a common clay cup as though he might find his answer there? *Go to bed, fool!* He banged the cup down on the board, startling the pot boy from his puppy-like doze in the warm ashes. What was the alternative? Was he to search the kingdom for the rest of his life until he grew gaunt with age, white-haired like some old madman from the tales of King Arthur's court, cursed to wear out his life on a hopeless quest?

Yes, if I have to!

It was late; the pilgrims were snoring, and as Straccan started to get up, yawning and ready for bed, the sleepy pot boy jumped up too.

'More ale, me lord?'

He lifted the jug, but Straccan turned his empty cup upside down to show he wanted no more . . . and stood like an image, staring, unbelieving, at the bottom of the cup, at the mark scratched in the clay.

Hauled from his warm bed and his wife's embrace, the innkeeper struggled futilely in Straccan's grip.

'Put me down, you mad sod! Let go! Oh, it's you, me lord – what's up?'

Straccan dragged the wriggling man to the dim light of a rush lantern hooked up beside the door, and shoved the little cup under his nose.

'Look, there! What's that?'

'It's a cup.'

'Not that! *That!* See? What is it?'

The man squinted at the cup's base. 'What, you mean the potter's mark?'

Chapter 3

Tobias the potter, staying at his sister's house in Richmond, was enjoying a lie-in – well, he had sod all else to do – when the stranger knight arrived on his enormous horse, with his enormous sword and his questions. Roused untimely from his pallet and shown one of his own cups, Tobias owned that yes, that was his mark, he scratched it on all his wares for luck; and yes, he knew the place the stranger wanted, it was his home, Pouncey. No, the stranger would never find it, it was a hidden place, Pouncey; and no, he didn't want to turn out in the cold. Look at the sky! It could still snow.

'I winter here, master. I don't go home till April.'

'I'll pay.'

Behind the knight's back Tobias saw his sister grimacing and nodding frantically at him, urging him with gestures to grab this heaven-sent opportunity. It had been a bad season. The shed outside where Nan normally kept her goats was stacked high with unsold pots and cups, as well as housing his donkey and cart, which meant the goats had to share the bedchamber. Nan had no objection on hygiene grounds, but the animals ate the straw pallets. Also Tobias's cart needed a new wheel, and the donkey was eating its head off, with fodder at a shocking price.

''Ow much?'

'How far is it?'

'To Pouncey? Forty mile.'

'A shilling a day.'

That was riches, but the potter was on to a good thing here and well aware of it.

'I'd like to help you, master, really I would, but I can't just leave all my stock here. S'pose it come to harm, then where'd I be?'

'I'll buy it,' said Straccan.

'What, all of it?'

'Yes, but only if you come *now*.'

'I ain't had me breakfast yet!'

9

'I'll hire a horse for you. Break your fast, and be ready when I get back.'

Three days later Straccan was staring up at the double-branched slash in the face of the great shelved cliff rampart known as Pouncey Edge. He'd never dreamed it could be so big. The cliff rose in three steps – the lower two well wooded – and was watered by narrow falls that cascaded from step to step to the river below. The upright stave of the vein of exposed quartz, silvery white against the grey-black granite, must measure full forty feet from top to bottom. The Edge seemed to scrape the clouds, and the granite bastion ran five miles from east to west. Gazing, awed, Straccan wondered how anything so vast could remain such a secret.

Tobias, who'd never ridden a horse before and reckoned distances by donkey, pouched his three shillings with a sense of disappointment. He'd been hoping for at least four, maybe even five, and didn't consider three adequate compensation for his sore backside. If he never saw another bloody horse it would be too soon. When he'd shown Straccan the well camouflaged beginning of the cliff path, he headed home, where his wife relieved him of the three shillings and set him to mucking out the pig. He wished he'd stayed in Richmond. Goats weren't as sticky as pigs.

The narrow path led upwards through stunted pines, an easy climb at first, but it got harder. Straccan, who spent most of his time on horseback, found it hard going, and by the time he emerged from the dwarfish forest that clothed the lower part of the cliff on to a rock ledge some forty feet wide, he was sadly out of breath.

It was bitterly cold and getting dark. There was a stone wall enclosing a winter-gnawed garden, and at the other end of the ledge a small stone house, built right against the cliff face. His throat was tight, and his heart thumping so hard it shook his body.

Twelve strides on shaking legs took him to the door, and as he raised his hand to knock, it was opened.

It wasn't Janiva. He stared at the tiny crone, shawled in a wolf pelt, regarding him with brilliant blue eyes that seemed far too large for her wrinkled-apple face. She smiled.

'You've come a long way, lad.'

'I'm sorry. I thought . . . You're not . . . She isn't here.'

'No, she ain't, if you mean Janiva. You'll be that knight of hers. Better come in, I suppose. It ain't much, but better than freezin'.'

He stepped inside, dismay and hope warring within him. 'Where is she? Please, my lady—'

'Osyth's my name, lad. Sit down and eat.'

There was a table and two benches. He sat down. There was a fire in a natural rock cleft which formed the back wall of this strange house, and a mouth-watering savoury smell rose from the pot hanging over the flames. Against the walls were two narrow box-beds heaped with quilts. There was food on the board – a honeycomb in a dish, a pile of little flat loaves, a round of cheese – but what made his heart leap almost into his throat was the jug on the table holding sprigs of bright-berried holly and trailing tendrils of ivy. Just so had he seen holly and ivy decorating Janiva's table at Shawl! She was here!

'Lady Osyth—'

'Later, lad, later.' She took a red clay bowl from the hearth and dipped it in the cauldron, setting before Straccan a stew fragrant with herbs, lavish with chicken, and glittering with little golden globules of rich fat.

'That'll warm your blood,' the crone said. 'Eat your fill, there's plenty more.'

'Where's Janiva?' Straccan asked. 'I know she's here.'

'She *was* here.'

The shock of disappointment lanced through him like a spear of ice. He jumped up, knocking the bench over backwards. Suddenly aware that he was cold through and through, cold to the bone, he stammered, 'W-where's she gone?'

'She was called to . . . well, to help some folk with their trouble. And if I tell you where, you'll go after her, and that won't help what she has to do. Leave her be to do what she must.'

'What trouble?'

'Morthwork, lad. You know what that is?'

He knew what it was all right. Sorcery, necromancy, the magic of ill! Fear for Janiva jetted acid into his empty belly, but before he could say anything more Osyth's tiny, wrinkled hand touched his, and instantly a spreading warmth coursed through his body. He looked down into her face. He'd never seen such eyes, so blue, so deep, so calm. He had no wish to look away. Under their tranquil gaze his fear, shock, disappointment and the iron-hard stiffness of the long journey drained out of him, leaving a wonderfully comfortable lassitude and sense of well-being. He had a job remembering what he'd been going to say, but with an effort, managed it.

'Is she in danger?' But the notion of danger seemed unreal, like a dream fading into forgetfulness.

'She's strong, she'll manage,' said Osyth. 'Understand, she *wants* to do this. Sit now, and eat before it gets cold.'

Obediently he sat, and the old woman sat opposite him, her elbows on the board and her chin resting on her clasped hands. Still the fathomless eyes held his.

'What d'you expect of her, I wonder?' the old woman said. He heard her clearly, and yet he hadn't seen her lips move, had he? 'Wife and lover, bed-mate, mother of your sons, is that what she would go to at that place of yours? What's it called, Stirrup? Funny name.'

'It was the rent,' Straccan found himself explaining. 'Back in King Edward's time the rent was a gilded stirrup, every Lady Day.' He felt a mild surprise at the inconsequential matter of their talk, but was far too warm and easy in his body to be concerned about it.

'Fancy,' said Osyth, refilling his bowl. 'Just one stirrup? Well, I s'pose your old king would have had a pair for himself after the first two years. Why don't you dunk some o' that bread in it, lad; it'll stick to your ribs better. What about your daughter, eh? What's she thinkin' o' this?'

'Gilla? She loves Janiva,' he heard himself saying. 'We want her to come home.'

'Been watchin' this place, your Gilla, ain't she? I've felt her. But it's shielded. She could see the rune, o' course, that's older'n me and stronger by far – I can't shield that – but she couldn't see Janiva, or me. What took you so long gettin' here?'

He told her something of the past year, the towns and villages, the false hopes, the false trails, the cold settling-in of despair. Odd – there was the taste of honey in his mouth, although he hadn't been aware of eating it, and he saw with surprise that his bowl and the platters on the table were empty, except for crumbs. He reached out a finger and touched the blood-red berries in the jug.

'Janiva put these here.' And only now did he realise: holly berries still red in March?

'Listen to me, lad. Janiva needs more than a man in her bed, more than house an' childer and to be called "my lady". She's come into her power since you saw her last. She ain't the same. She has work to do, and if your love'll be holdin' her back,

12

holdin' her down, then best you go back the way you come, now. Get on that big ginger horse and forget this place. Forget it, and go home.'

'No,' Straccan said. 'It's not like that at all. She's a free woman. She'll be no less free when she's my wife.'

'If that's true, you'll have to let her go sometimes. When she looks at you and says, "This I *must* do," are you man enough to trust her?'

He was drowning in a blue lake, and it was, as he'd once been told, a painless death. He was aware of someone clasping his hand, but he didn't want to be pulled out, he was quite happy where he was. A hand touched his forehead.

'Wake up, lad,' said Osyth. 'Fire and food've made you sleepy. It was a good idea o' yours, the garden. She'll like that. You'll do, I reckon.'

Straccan felt strangely light-headed, as though his thoughts had been picked out, scoured, and put back. He must have fallen asleep! He hadn't realised just how tired he was. Had he been talking about the garden in his sleep? 'How did you—' he began.

'Best you sleep here tonight,' the old woman said, brushing crumbs into the fire. 'Go home tomorrow.'

'But Janiva—'

'You been looking a long time. Let be, now. See to your own affairs. When she's ready, she'll let you know.'

'What d'you mean? How?'

'That I can't tell you. But she will.' She stooped and picked up a large jug from the floor. 'Make yourself useful, lad. The spring's at the end of the garth; fill this for me, will you?'

He took the jug and went outside. It was getting dark.

Wait a minute. He turned, looked back at the door, puzzling. What just happened? Time passed strangely in that little house. He'd been in there with the old anchoress for an hour at least, he *must* have been; he'd eaten a good meal and was warm all through, and yet the sky was no darker, and the shadows that lay across the garth were still in the same place as when Osyth first opened the door.

Countess Judith reached the northern outskirts of London – how it had spread since she was last there! – on Saint Alphege's day in the forenoon, and rested at the priory of Saint John the Baptist while her chamberlain rode ahead through the city and over the new bridge, the wonder of the

13

world, to warn her brother of her imminent arrival.

'Did you see him? What did he say?' she demanded when the man returned. Her gimlet stare bored into his skull.

'His Grace waits eagerly to bid you welcome, my lady,' her chamberlain replied, wooden-faced. What His Grace had actually said, with the look of a man whose blood has just run cold, was, 'My sister? Coming here? Now? *Merde!*' But the chamberlain was a diplomat at heart.

And indeed, when the countess and her retinue reached Southwark and Winchester House, the bishop's welcome left nothing to be desired. Her servants would have to sleep huddled together in the straw in the great hall along with the lesser beings who made up the bishop's household, but the guest quarters hastily prepared for the countess were fit for a queen; and queens, indeed, had stayed there. There was even a bathtub in the bedchamber, a novelty which confirmed Judith's worst suspicions: London was a sink of iniquity and decadence. She would have to keep a strict eye on her servants, lest they become corrupted.

Straccan met Bane in York on Saint Longinus' day, and they rode home together. Straccan spoke little, deep in his thoughts, and Bane knew when to keep quiet. They reached Stirrup on the eve of Saint Alcmund.

Gilla met him at the gate. Straccan hadn't seen her since the autumn; she was taller, and the slight, girlish body was rounding into the delicious curves of young womanhood. Her likeness to her dead mother took his breath away.

She wasn't surprised that he had come back without Janiva. 'I saw you coming,' she said, 'in the candle flame. Just you and Bane. But Janiva's all right, I know she is, and she *will* come, when she's ready.'

So Osyth had said, and now Gilla; and he must believe it.

The weeks Straccan had been away had seen plenty of activity at Stirrup. His steward reported all well: last summer's hay crop had been disappointing, spoiled by rain, but the cattle and sheep had grazed the new growth, the lattermath, and done well on it. The wool clip had been better than expected. Wheat and barley had recovered after the rains, and there'd been a decent harvest. They'd not need to buy any grain, and with wheat at three shillings a bushel and barley at two, that was a blessing, especially as they'd had to pay a high price for salt that winter, for with not enough hay, more beasts had been

14

killed and salted than they'd hoped.

Stirrup was a well-nigh self-sufficient estate, manor house, farmland, woodland and village; the workers all free, no villeins or bondmen. As free men they could of course bear arms. Indeed it was their duty to learn the rudiments of fighting in case the king should ever need to call on them, and Odo, the captain of the manor's small force of archers, an ex-soldier who hated to see good material go to waste, had trained men and boys in the use of pike and bow, as well as a useful bit of decidedly dirty unarmed combat, in case any fool should be taken unawares without even his knife to hand.

The manor house was an unconventional building on the same plan as the Roman villa that had once stood there. Stables, tack room, mews, storerooms, office, hall and chapel were arranged in a square enclosing a central yard, with the kitchen a separate building in the yard, next to the well. The main gate was guarded by a modern watchtower, and an old cracked bell gave warning of any approach.

It was an odd household, too, gathered by Straccan from many places and situations. His steward, Cammo, had been a prisoner chained on the bench beside him in a Saracen galley, years before. He had married Adeliza, Straccan's house-keeper. The clerk, Peter Martel, who looked after Straccan's business affairs in his absence, had served his father. Hawkan Bane had been locked in a pillory when Straccan first saw him, which might be thought an unlikely recommendation for a servant; but Bane had become more friend than servant and had been Straccan's companion in many unorthodox adven-tures.

In the office, his clerk greeted him as if he'd never been away, getting straight down to business. 'Glad you're back. Lord Hamo got a bit shirty about the price of that tooth of Saint Cecilia. He's not a happy baron.'

'Let him stew a while longer, Peter,' said Straccan. 'He'll grumble, but he'll pay. What about the relics from Cyprus? Did they come?'

'Yes. All there. I've put them in the book. The Countess of Gloucester wants a relic for the altar of a church she's building, something to do with Our Lady; she wants to know what we can offer. Oh, and Brother Lucius from Dieulacresse was here about the garden.' Peter put his pen between his teeth and riffled through the documents on the table with both hands.

Straccan beamed. The garden! 'Did he bring the plants?'

'A wagonload. Plants, trees, and special sacks of earth, as if we hadn't got our own. And a boy.'

'I didn't order a boy.'

'He's just lent. His name's Nicholas. Brother Lucius wrote it all down. I've got it here somewhere, how to plant and care for the things, but Nicholas was to see them settled in – as if they were colts, for Christ's sake!'

'Did he send the pear trees?'

'Pears, plums and a quince. He said if that grows it'll be a miracle, but you wanted it. Ha! Here it is.' Peter produced a list written in a monkish hand, and peered at it. 'What are cardoons?'

'God knows! Where's whatsisname, Nicholas?'

'Round by the orchard. He works, I'll give him that. Digging from dawn to dusk, planting, watering and suchlike. He goes to his mum's house at Falhollow to sleep every night. Brother Lucius wants him back, mind.'

The garden had been Straccan's idea; he'd consulted Lucius about it last summer, setting aside the ground in readiness for Janiva's coming. It was his gesture of faith that he *would* find her, and somehow, during that lonely year, its planning made her seem closer to him. Now he looked with satisfaction at the neat rows and groups of plants, and the spaded ground still waiting for its treasures. String and pegs marked new beds and paths, staked saplings shivered slightly in the breeze. It was a mild morning – March had softened in the last few days – and a fresh warm fragrance breathed up from the turned earth. At the boundaries of the new garden, stones had been stacked to build its enclosing walls. Perched on a stone, a robin waited to swoop on the worms exposed by Nicholas's spade.

'Did you do all this by yourself?'

The boy paused, his foot on the spade. 'Aye, master. Brother Lucius did the stuff wi' string and pegs, then he went home, an' I got on wi't.'

'It's good work. Would you like to stay at Stirrup and look after the garden?'

Nicholas smiled, pushing his thick dusty hair out of his eyes. 'Na, master. I be goin' to be monk. Tis what my ma wants, what I want too. Brother Lucius, he's too old and stiff for the bendin' an' diggin', but he know a powerful lot 'bout herbs and such. I'll be gardener at the priory, he promised. I allus loved the wonders

16

in the bud, and the green growin' things.'

His thick, earthy finger gently touched a leaf, much as a mother touches the face of her baby. Straccan could have sworn the leaf lifted itself to the boy's hand.

Chapter 4

The road from Bristol to Gloucester was always crowded with traffic to and from the port, and in these unsettled times, with rumours flying of rebellion and a French invasion, was busier than ever. Companies of knights and men-at-arms were on the move, grousing and cursing whenever they had to make way for the great long carts carrying wine, wool, timber and stone, hides, dried fish, live sheep, wheat, barley and pig iron. There were travellers returning from overseas or setting out on their adventures – monks, couriers, merchants, pilgrims, beggars – and abjurers too, poor sods, who to escape the gallows must tramp barefoot, escorted none too gently, to the nearest port to buy or beg passage into exile.

Some of the pilgrims and all the beggars were afoot. The three, a man and two boys, sitting at the roadside oblivious to the dust, might have belonged to either group, but on the whole their looks were against them: too unkempt, their clothes too ragged. Besides, the man looked sick, and the great carts lumbered slowly past, none willing to take a chance on them. The older boy, slight of build and sun-browned, looked to be thirteen or fourteen, the other no more than six years old. The man was young, tall and broad-shouldered, but it was all he could do to get to his feet, and when he did he limped. He had clearly been injured; there was dried blood on the leg of his breeches. The older boy bent to let the younger scramble on to his back. All three were very thin, dirty and exhausted, but it would be dark in a couple of hours and they must find a place to sleep – some straw in a shed if they were lucky, a hedge or dry ditch if not. Some shelter was essential; it was early April, still cold at night, and they had only the clothes they were wearing.

Back at the dock, when they had disembarked, the man had helped to load wine on to carts in return for the carter's promise of a lift as far as Gloucester. But they'd only travelled three or four miles when it became obvious that he was sick, and horror of contagion made the carter turn them off.

A woman riding a donkey trotted past and saw the boy carrying his little brother, as she thought. Moved to sympathy she reined in for a moment and called to the man, 'There's a hospice two miles on, pilgrim; they'll give you and your boys supper and a bed.' But he, using all his concentration to put one foot in front of the other and stay upright, didn't or couldn't respond. The older boy looked up, unsmiling.

'*Merci, madame.*'

Bloody foreigners! Frogs, by the sound of it. No wonder the fellow had no manners! Miffed, the woman heeled her donkey and trotted on. It began to rain, a brief but cold shower. The chances of a dry ditch receded, but at least it would lay the dust.

The little boy said, 'I'm so tired, Roslyn. Can we go there?'

'No, David,' said the other, who wasn't a boy, after all. 'If they're looking for us, they'll look in those places.'

The sick man stopped, swayed and mumbled something.

'What, Miles?'

'This is England,' Miles said. His head ached so cruelly that he found it difficult to think, let alone speak. 'Not bloody France. We're safe here.'

Roslyn raised a cynical eyebrow. 'You think? Best take no chances. We'll find somewhere to rest.' And to David: 'Will you walk for a bit?' Setting the child down, she took the sick man's arm over her shoulder, bracing herself for the weight. Like a couple of drunks, they staggered on, with the stumbling child clinging to Roslyn's tunic.

We can't go on like this, she thought. Frowning, she looked at the carts, great and small, trundling past, and the riders on horses, mules and donkeys. *Perhaps I can steal a horse.* Some folk afoot were towing handcarts. *Or one of those . . .* Some of these travellers would be stopping at the hospice the donkey woman had spoken of.

'Come on, Miles. Just a little further.'

Ten more steps, and ten, and another ten. A fat monk on a mule came up behind them. 'Get out of my way!'

But Miles was slow, and the monk, passing, stuck his foot out and gave the limping man a hard shove in the back. He went down on his knees, pitching forward on his face. David gave a loud cry of dismay, and as the monk urged his mule on, the child stood with small fists clenched, glaring after him. In the stream of travellers it was not possible to tell where the stone came from that struck the monk's back. He glared over his shoulder but jogged on.

Roslyn's reaction was strange. Instead of helping Miles she cried, 'David! No, David, don't! Look at me, at *me*, David!' and dropped to her knees beside the child, whispering to him, hugging him tightly with his head pressed against her so that he couldn't see the monk any more.

David tried to pull away. 'He hurt Miles!'

'I know, but you promised! No stones!' He struggled, but only when the monk was quite out of sight did she release him and help Miles up, propping him along as before. And so, painfully, they covered another mile.

As it grew dark they came upon a tumbledown shed, not far from the hospice, blessedly dry, a store for turnips and old hay. Miles's headache and throbbing leg gave him little rest, but he must have slept at some time for he never heard them whispering together, nor the girl leaving, and returning later pulling a small handcart. His dismay when he woke and saw the contraption would have been funny if it hadn't been serious.

'What's *that*?'

'Can you get up, Miles? I'll help you. We must be quick.' Quick, yes, before the owner of the cart woke and found it gone. 'Get in. I'll pull you.'

He baulked. 'In that? No! I can't!'

'Why? What's the matter?' They stared at him as if he was mad.

'You don't understand! It's a *cart*. I'm a *knight*. It's against my honour!' It was the most degrading thing that could happen to a knight; disgraced prisoners of war were transported in carts for folk to jeer at and throw turds. And he was right, they *didn't* understand.

Roslyn looked at him for a long moment, then gave a very Gallic shrug. 'As you please. David, jump in.' The child did so, and Roslyn took the shafts and moved off.

'Wait, Roslyn! Not so fast! I'll keep up. I can. I will, I promise!' But already the cart had travelled some way. Miles lurched after it, swearing. After twenty steps or so, he fell down. The cart stopped, turned, came back.

'David, help me get him in.'

As they dragged and heaved him – although thin he was big-boned and heavy, and ridiculously uncooperative – Miles began to cry, tears of weakness and frustration, tears of shame. At last he was in, sprawled on the planking; and losing no more time the cart set off again. David slid a folded sack

20

pillow under Miles's head. Tears made pale gullies down the little boy's dirty face.

'Miles! Oh Miles, don't die! Oh please, not you, not you too!'

Chapter 5

Bishop Fulk stayed to the end, long after most folk had grown bored and gone home. Not until the executioner's apprentices had raked out the embers and thrown the charred bones in the Garonne, lest any heretic should take them away to venerate, did Fulk sign his bearers to take up the chair and carry him back to his residence. As he jolted through the narrow streets of Toulouse his lips moved in prayer – not for the souls of the burned heretics, they were beyond hope of mercy, but for Christendom and the Faith, for Holy Church in her desperate struggle against the overwhelming tide of heresy, and for all godly men who fought the Church's enemies.

A dozen archers rode with the curtained chair, which was borne by eight carriers, and twelve spearmen marched with it, six to a side, in case anyone should be moved by the devil to try and kill the occupant. Their captain rode fully armoured, sword in hand, beside the chair, scanning doorways, windows, rooftops and alley mouths, alert for danger. Beneath his fur-lined robes the bishop wore ring mail from throat to groin, under his mitre was a steel skullcap, and within the curtained chair the hands loosely clasped in his lap rested on the hilt of a long-bladed dagger. These precautions might be thought unseemly for a man of God, but agents of Satan had tried seven times to kill him.

Fulk leaned back and closed his eyes; the smoke had made them sore. It had been a wearying day; it gave him no pleasure to watch human flesh char and sizzle like pork in the flames. He had done his utmost to save those wretches from their dreadful end, but like most of these cursed Cathars, sons of perdition, they had rejected the loving mercy of the Church and gone to Satan as blithely as any blessed martyr ever went to Christ.

At times the bishop almost succumbed to the sin of despair, for these heretics were like no others. The whole of the Languedoc was infected, from the highest-born nobility to the meanest serf. Villages, towns, whole cities believed themselves the only true Christians, and Holy Church the church of Satan. Generation after generation had been born, lived and died in heresy, and gone to hell. The Cathars had churches, bishops, priests – even women priests! They regarded the Holy Cross as a hateful and disgusting thing, the instrument of Christ's torture, the sacraments as worthless, and the Mass itself as sacrilege; for how, they asked, could a piece of bread, digested in the guts of the Catholic faithful and shamefully excreted, be the true body of God?

Deep-rooted, Catharism had grown out of the earlier Bogomil heresy and the perverted doctrines of the Manichees before that. The Cathars taught that the world and mankind had been created not by God but by Satan, and were altogether evil; that only the soul was of God, trapped in a fleshly prison from which it could only escape by leading a pure, chaste life. Marriage and procreation could only bring into the evil world more evil beings; therefore, they argued, Christ could not have been born from the womb of Mary. He was pure spirit and could never have assumed impure flesh, nor suffered physical death. There had been no incarnation and no resurrection.

In his litter, Fulk groaned at the magnitude of his task. No matter how many heretics burned, there were always more; their loathsome doctrine spread like the plague, sure proof that the last days were coming, as Saint John had written. Fulk would uproot and burn them, these foul weeds strangling God's garden, as long as breath remained to him.

But evil as they were, a stench in God's nostrils, these Cathars were as nothing compared to the monstrous affront to God, the living blasphemy that now threatened Holy Church and all Christendom.

The task of destroying *that* had fallen to him, and so far he had failed. It wasn't his fault, he had done his utmost, but here he stood alone against the tide of evil. Until help came, in the form of Lord Simon de Montfort's forces – please God, soon! – he would just have to keep trying.

There was shouting in the street. His bearers were slowing down. Fulk pulled the leather curtain aside and stuck his head out.

'What's the matter?'

The bearers stopped abruptly, amid yells and jeers and the high-pitched screaming of a terrified woman. Fulk beckoned his captain.

'What's going on?'

'Just another heretic, m'lord.'

23

The bishop leaned out for a better look.

He wasn't the only one held up. A pedlar with his laden donkey, a monk on a mule and a mud-splashed knight on horseback had also been brought to a halt, unable to get through the clot of people blocking the narrow street and egging on two rough-looking fellows wearing the blazon of a white cross. They were dragging a screaming woman from a house. She clung to the doorpost, but one had her round the waist while the other hammered at her bleeding hands with the haft of his dagger. A girl, seven or eight years old, clutched her mother's skirts, her face beslobbered with tears. A bystander tore the child away and flung her sprawling between the hooves of the knight's horse. The rider dismounted instantly to pick her up.

'Help us, sir, please! Please, help!' she cried, grasping the edge of his jerkin.

The knight laid a protective hand on her thin shoulder. 'What has the child done to be handled so roughly?' he demanded.

The men had forced the woman to her knees in the mud while one of them tied her hands behind her back. 'Nothing to concern you, sir. Heretics.'

At that the knight's face changed, all humanity wiped from it in an instant. Quite gently he detached the child's grip and pushed her towards the soldiers.

'I'm sorry, maid. I can't help such as you,' he said. 'God's work be done.'

A howl of approval went up from the onlookers. Muck and stones flew as the woman and her daughter were dragged away. The bishop's outriders began whacking at backs and bottoms with the flats of their swords, while the captain bawled at folk to make way. The crowd melted like grease, the knight remounted and rode on, the monk likewise, although the pedlar was having a spot of trouble with his donkey which had decided to sit down. With a 'One, two, three!' the chair bearers heaved up their load and trotted forward. Fulk let the curtain fall.

His secretary, Maître Deil, was waiting with the eager look of a man who had news and was bursting to tell it.

'He is here! He has just arrived!'

'He is late,' said the bishop sourly, taking off his mitre and rubbing the red dent across his brow. 'He was supposed to be here yesterday.' He took off the steel cap and turned his back for a squire to undo the straps of his mail shirt.

'The roads are bad,' Maître Deil said, but the bishop was

unwilling to be placated, and his face wore its look of discontent all the way to his private chamber, where a slot in the wall known to his household as 'the bishop's eye' allowed him to peer down into the hall without being seen.

'Which is he?'

'Near the door, by the first pillar. I have sent a servant to take him to the dormitory.'

Leaning against the pillar with his arms folded was the knight from the street. As the bishop watched, a lay brother approached and spoke to the knight, who followed him from the hall, limping heavily. The bishop scowled.

'He's a cripple! Could you find no fit man for the task?'

'Oh, hardly a cripple, my lord. And we have already sent three fit men,' Deil reminded him. 'With sorry results: two dead and one who will never fight again.'

'They didn't expect such fierce resistance. They didn't expect *any* resistance! It seemed simple enough.' The bishop tugged his lower lip between finger and thumb, mentally mourning the three good men wasted, two in their graves and the third left useless with but one arm. 'What in the name of God,' Fulk growled, 'makes you think this cripple can fare better?'

Deil hesitated. 'You know what the Faidits did to him—'

'Of course.' Fulk knew all too well. The Seigneurs Faidits, heretic knights dispossessed and on the run, showed no mercy to any captured crusader.

'After they let him go he refused to return to his domain. He ordered his wife back to her father's house and his daughter to a nunnery, and yielded his fief to his brother. Then he entered the novitiate at St Gilies, but after a year the abbot decided he was unsuited to monastic life. Since then he has not been fortunate in finding a place. Bad luck clings to him. He was – he still is – a fighter of renown. He is not to blame for what was done to him.'

'No, poor devil. But you didn't say he was a cripple.' He looked accusingly at his secretary. 'Holy Writ tells of men who made *themselves* eunuchs for the kingdom of heaven's sake, and nowhere is it written that they were cripples. I did not expect him to be lame.'

Maître Deil opened his mouth to protest, but seeing the bishop was determined to find fault shut it again and mutely handed him a damp towel to wipe the smuts from his face. His Grace was always short-tempered after a burning.

'You'll find no man more apt to the purpose,' he said when the bishop had wiped his face and hands. 'No one hates heretics more. Nor pity nor shame will stay his hand. And he knows England; he lived there for some years.' He poured a cup of wine; the bishop drank and held it out for more.

'Does he know why he's been sent for?'

'Not yet. Will you see him tonight, my lord?'

Fulk considered, tugging his lip again. 'Not now. Have someone stay close to him for a few days; note what he says, what he does. Someone discreet.'

Maître Deil raised a questioning eyebrow.

'You may be right,' Fulk said. 'But we must be sure. Pity and shame have no place in this mission.'

Two men, discreet to the point of invisibility, observed the new arrival continuously, and after three days made their reports to Maître Deil. Only then was the lame knight brought to the bishop's chamber, where Fulk spoke long with him, testing and probing, before getting down to the meat of the matter.

'Praise God, my son! You have been chosen to take part in a mission for Holy Church. A most secret mission.'

'I am honoured, my lord.' He didn't ask what the mission was; he would do anything, and they both knew it.

'I must have your oath of secrecy,' Fulk said, 'and your sworn word not to flinch from the task; to carry it out or die trying.'

'You have them.'

'Firstly, this meeting never happened. You understand? You will never speak of it, not even to your confessor.'

The lame knight bowed his head in assent. The room was growing dark. Fulk sat among shadows, the three tall candles on the table before him still unlit.

'When you leave here, ride to Fordelice,' he named a village some twenty miles north of Toulouse. 'Wait there until I send two others to join you. You will know them by this sign.'

His white, long-fingered hand with its great amethyst ring crept like a disembodied thing from the shadows to lift the lid of a casket standing between the candlesticks, and took out two lengths of white silk ribbon.

'Sew these in the form of a cross on your mantle. You know what it is?'

The lame knight nodded. 'The White Brotherhood.' He raised the ribbons to his lips and kissed them reverently before folding them away in his scrip.

'For this mission,' Fulk continued, 'your own names will never

26

be spoken. Instead you will be known by the names of angels of the Lord God.'

Taking a taper he lit it at the brazier and touched it to one of the candles. 'Uriel,' he said. 'The flame of God.' He lit the second candle. 'Samael, the severity of God.' He lit the third candle. 'And Michael, God's warrior.' It was an impressive piece of theatre. He looked up to see the lame knight's tranced gaze fixed on the flames and added softly, 'You, Messire Michael, will command.'

For a moment Michael's face was slack with astonishment, then he flushed and drew himself up, straight and proud.

'M-my lord,' he stammered, deeply moved, 'with all my heart I thank you. I thought there was no further use for me, but now—'

The bishop cut short his thanks. 'The three of you will ride to Bordeaux. Your quarry took ship for England there at the end of March. You will follow. Find him and kill him. Maître Deil will give you money for the journey. If you succeed, return here to me and your reward will be greater than you can imagine. If you fail, we shall not meet again, for then, of course, you will be dead.'

The lame knight nodded, his face impassive.

Fulk stood up and held out his pectoral cross. 'Swear your oaths on this. There is a fragment of the True Cross in it.'

Michael took it between his hands. 'I swear, upon the Cross of Christ, to carry out this task or die, and never to speak of it.' *Whatever it is*, he thought. *God helping me!*

'God and his son and all the saints are witness to your vow, my son. You are now one of the White Brotherhood, whose purpose is to destroy the enemies of God.'

Michael's face was exalted. 'I *will* destroy them, whoever they are!'

'*One* is especial,' said Fulk softly. 'Now listen. This is what you must do . . .'

God's warrior, the knight called Michael, left Toulouse that night, astride a much better horse than the one he'd come on and leading a laden rouncey, both from Fulk's stables. As he settled in the saddle and gathered the reins he remembered something.

'A woman and her daughter, heretics, were taken by men of the brotherhood the evening I arrived. What became of them?'

Maître Deil consulted his wax note-tablets. 'The girl was sent as bondmaid to the nuns at Montauban. The woman was released yesterday.'

'You let a heretic go?'

Deil shrugged. 'She had nothing of value to tell – no names. She wasn't worth the cost of burning, so in mercy my lord bishop ordered her eyes torn out instead, for while she lives there is hope her soul may yet be saved.'

'I shall pray for it.' Michael touched spurs to his horse and tugged the mule's reins. Maître Deil looked after him for a few moments, then shut the postern gate and hurried to the bishop's chamber.

'Has he gone?'

'Yes, my lord.'

'And the other two?'

'They have been summoned. They will be here tonight, or tomorrow.'

The bishop pressed his fingers to his aching temples. 'Deal with them yourself. Tell them no more than they need to know and send them to join Michael at Fordelice. And see that a courier leaves for Rome at once; the Holy Father must be kept informed. This time there will be no mistakes.' He clenched his hand on his pectoral cross, white-knuckled. 'God will not let this unspeakable blasphemy go unpunished. They will succeed.'

'What then?' Deil asked. 'If they return?'

'I promised a great reward,' Fulk said. So he had, and he meant it. What reward could be greater than a martyr's crown in heaven?

Chapter 6

'Judith, please! You really must leave it to me.' Bishop Peter des
Roches suppressed a sigh of exasperation. Negotiations on his
sister's behalf with Coldinghame – a skilfully balanced combination of bribe and threat – were at a delicate stage, and not helped by
Judith's habit of shooting off blistering letters to Prior Radulfus.
The bishop had been able to intercept them so far, but it had been
touch-and-go yesterday. He'd only managed to stop her courier, in
the nick of time, by closing London Bridge, causing a traffic jam
that brought the city to a standstill and Londoners' robust protests
in a storm about his ears. Their mayor was even bleating about
compensation, a piece of sauce that beggared belief!

Would she *never* go home?

She had nabbed him as soon as he was dressed this morning,
in the passage between his bedchamber and the stairs, eyeing
his costly clothes with disapproval. Peter des Roches was a
handsome man, which was to be expected, for he was close to
the king, and John would not tolerate ugly people around him.
Tall, florid, a little stout, the bishop was moderately splendid
this morning in a velvet so purple as to seem black unless the
light caught its gloss, and thigh boots of finest doeskin. He
looked like a prince, and only the small tonsure, almost hidden
in his wiry grey curls, proclaimed him a man of the Church.
Judith considered such display unseemly.

She stuck at his elbow as he walked, demanding, God help
him, that he excommunicate the prior of Coldinghame. 'What's
the good of being a bishop,' she ranted, 'if you won't use the
weapons God has given you?' The two women attending on her
looked harried, as well they might. It had long since dawned on
the bishop why Earl Joceran had spent so much time away from
home.

They reached the door of his private oratory. It wasn't the
hour for prayer, but any port in a storm.

'I will leave you here, my lady.' He opened the door,
expecting her to stand aside. 'We'll talk later.' But no, she
followed him inside, still talking. He heard a curious sound – a

29

squeak? A strangled yelp? – and the curtain of the privy in the corner swayed and bulged.

The bishop was annoyed. That was his private gong, and although he suspected that his body servants made use of it, Peter des Roches, irritated by his sister's presence, was in no mood today to live and let live. With an oath he whipped the curtain aside.

Only long practice helped him turn his involuntary laugh into a cough.

Over a woman's shoulder, the appalled face of the countess's chaplain gaped at him. The bishop couldn't remember the man's name, but hearing his sister's indrawn breath behind him couldn't help feeling a twinge of sympathy. 'Oh dear,' was all he said.

With a whimper of dismay, the chaplain's paramour scrambled off his lap, leaving her partner in a state of squalid disarray. Pallid with shock, the woman shook her skirts down and tried to dash past, but Judith, who had recognised her as one of her own laundresses, seized her by the hair and administered several stinging slaps, shrieking maledictions.

The din, of course, brought servants running, and their faces – avid, gleeful or horrified – peered in at the door.

Still sitting on the privy, the chaplain – *Paul, that's it*, the bishop remembered suddenly – had fumbled his clothes together and was bleating, 'Mercy, my lady, mercy!'

Judith shot him a look that might have frozen boiling oil. 'Fornicator,' she hissed, and striding forward, dragging Garlanda by the hair with strength fuelled by outrage, she seized the luckless chaplain by his ear. Towing both miscreants, she marched to the door. 'Out of my way!' The servants scattered.

Left alone at last in his oratory, the bishop didn't know whether to laugh or cry.

It was a sweet early May morning when a messenger came to Stirrup with a letter summoning Straccan to London, to attend the Bishop of Winchester.

'What does His Grace want?' Straccan asked.

'Dunno, me lord. He's at Westminster, and asks that you meet him there as soon as you can.'

'I'll leave tomorrow. Do you ride with me?'

'No, me lord, I've other errands. Better get on.' But his hopeful look in the direction of the kitchen wasn't lost on Straccan.

'At least eat before you go.' Straccan whistled for a groom, and having dismissed man to kitchen and horse to manger, went to find Gilla. She was in the garden with Nicholas.

'How long will you be gone?' she asked.

'It depends what he wants. Not long, I hope.'

But he felt decidedly uneasy. Why should King John's most trusted confidant send for him? Well, he'd soon know: if he and Bane left at dawn tomorrow, Tuesday, they should reach Westminster by Thursday night.

The three Angels rode to Bordeaux, where a knight of the Brotherhood had been killed, and in dying failed his appointed task.

It was their task now.

'Attract no attention,' Bishop Fulk had said. 'Arouse no one's curiosity. The devil has many agents.' So they avoided inns and hostels, even monasteries, and slept in their cloaks on the ground.

In the bright moonlight their shadows followed them as they set up camp for the night. The youngest, Uriel, had the job of tending the fire.

'Does he ... does he have *horns*?' he asked, turning the skewered meat to cook the other side. Reflected in his eyes, small red flames flickered.

'He's not Satan,' said Michael sombrely. 'He's flesh and blood, born from a woman's womb as we all were.'

'Then how shall we know him?'

'We are God's hounds on his trail,' Michael said. 'We shall know by the stink of the beast when we draw near.'

'And then?'

'We kill him, and bring back his head.'

Chapter 1

A dismal little penitential procession emerged from the gates of the bishop's palace at Southwark soon after dawn. Two men-at-arms flanked Garlanda, barefoot and in her shift, her head shaved of its impudent curls. She carried a massive church candle. Behind her came a man with a whip. The rain extinguished the candle, but it didn't matter. So early, on such a day, there were few to watch, but some are always ready to jeer at any helpless creature, to throw rotten fruit, eggs, or even stones although that was forbidden. Soon there was blood as well as rain and tears on her face.

The cobbles bruised her feet, and her arms were trembling with the weight of the candle when the first blow of the whip knocked her to her knees. There was laughter. On hands and knees she gazed wildly around, but saw no kindly face. No one helped her up. She was condemned, a fornicator; her sin the worse because her partner was a priest.

When the sinners were discovered and the truth came out, Lady Judith's wrath and disgust knew no bounds. Under her roof and unknown to her they had been lovers for more than a year! Heroic discretion had preserved their secret at home, but the long uncomfortable journey south was their undoing. It had allowed only two opportunities for mutual solace, and those had been hasty, nervous and unsatisfactory. Desperation and deprivation drove them to their fatal assignation in the bishop's privy. They begged for mercy in vain. Judith was adamant. Father Paul would be branded and flung bodily out of the bishop's gates, while his paramour was sent to the nearest brothel, where her misplaced ardour could be put to some use.

Father Paul was meanwhile locked up on bread and water. The countess took it upon herself to tell him of his sweetheart's fate, a salutary lesson that she thought would give him something to think about – as indeed it did, but not in the way she intended.

The messenger from Coldinghame brought a letter from Prior

Radulfus which sent the bishop hotfoot to his sister's chamber. He found the countess at her stitchery, with her ladies, while her newly appointed chaplain read improving extracts from a life of Saint Paul. At the bishop's entrance he stuttered into silence and covertly wiped the sheen of sweat from his brow.

'He has agreed, Judith,' des Roches said without ceremony. 'Radulfus has dropped his objections.'

'Has he indeed? What did you promise him?' his sister asked shrewdly.

'It so happens I had bait to dangle,' the bishop said, looking smug. The triumphant gleam in Judith's eye, he thought, boded little good for Prior Radulfus. She would never forgive him for the trouble he'd caused her. Des Roches felt almost sorry for the man, but not as sorry as he felt for Earl Joceran, who would wake at Judgement Day to find Judith still at his side.

With a glare that pinned her chaplain to the lectern, the countess signed to him to continue reading. His voice cracked with nervousness, swooping from soprano to baritone, and his blush spread from throat to tonsure. Des Roches recognised terror when he saw it. The horrible example of Father Paul's recent fall from grace must be ever foremost in the poor man's mind. The bishop had washed his hands of the ugly business; they were not his servants, and he could not deny Judith's right to discipline hers as she saw fit. Now he turned with relief from the sordid affair and its distasteful aftermath to his sister's departure. She insisted on starting for home at once. She couldn't wait to get there! God knows what the rest of her household was getting up to in her absence.

But in the preparations for departure, she didn't forget Father Paul. Her fury had cooled somewhat, tempered by her victory, so instead of having him branded as a fornicator, she left orders for him to be released after a month had passed, and sent on his way with twenty lashes to remind him of her magnanimity.

Des Roches saw his sister off, then ran upstairs to watch from the tower as her cortège clattered over the bridge. Not until it was entirely out of sight did he pull off his velvet cap and toss it into the air with an unepiscopal whoop of glee.

'Straccan! You lost no time. I didn't expect you before the morrow.' Pulling off his riding gloves, the bishop tossed them to one of the dozen – at least – pages milling around him, and drained the cup of wine offered by another upon one knee. 'Have they fed you while you waited?'

'Thank you, yes, my lord.'

Bishop Peter sank into a chair, where a brace of pages knelt to pull off his boots. Over the cup's rim his worldly, knowing eyes assessed Straccan. 'You've been away from home a lot recently.'

And how the devil do you know that? Straccan wondered.

'Forgive me for dragging you from your own affairs; I wouldn't do it without good cause. I believe we may help each other, you and I.'

Straccan kept his voice neutral. 'Indeed, my lord? How?'

'You remember William de Breos?' He waved away another cup-bearer, accepting instead a perfumed towel with which he wiped his face and hands. 'You drew steel on him – in Sanctuary.'

Straccan met the bishop's eyes. 'Yes.'

'In self-defence?'

'I challenged him.' *As you know damned well*, he thought. *What are you up to?*

'Breaking Sanctuary is a grave sin. And I understand you have not received absolution. It must weigh heavy on you.'

The ecclesiastical grapevine was nothing if not thorough.

'It does, my lord. My confessor felt it too great a matter for him. He said he must consult his bishop, but the bishop—'

'Is in exile,' des Roches interrupted. 'Of course. These are strange times. If a sinner needs a bishop, he must go to France or make do with me. In the regrettable absence of your bishop, Straccan, would you be willing to receive absolution at my hands?' He spread them, surveying them with some complacency, every finger gemmed, thumbs too.

There had to be a catch.

'Do you offer it, my lord?'

'With a fitting penance undertaken, yes.'

Ah! Here it comes. 'What penance, Your Grace?'

The bishop smiled. 'A simple task. It will keep you from your own affairs for a few weeks.'

'What task?'

'A matter of transport.' He laughed at Straccan's look of surprise. 'Unfinished business of my lord de Breos, which makes it curiously appropriate. I need a man I can trust to see the job done; you need absolution. Are you interested?' He stood to let a valet remove his crimson surcoat and slid his arms into a comfortable loose gown.

Straccan took a deep breath. This might sound like an answer to his prayer, but Peter des Roches was King John's man, and nothing to do with the king was ever what it seemed.

'Will you tell me about it, my lord?'

Des Roches motioned him to a seat. 'Some time before his downfall, de Breos ordered the making of a bell for one of his foundations. Since his disgrace and exile it has lain unclaimed – unpaid for, too – at the bell founder's yard in Southwark. The bell founder appealed to me, and as luck would have it I was able to find a home for his bell. It's to go to Coldinghame, in Scotland, where there is no Interdict and church bells still ring.'

The bishop sounded pleased with himself, as well he might. He had sought offers for the bell, and several of the more important houses of religion had elbowed one another aside in an undignified tussle to secure it. Strange that Coldinghame should emerge as the victor, seeing their bid was quite a bit lower than the rest, but no one knew the machinations behind that except Bishop Peter and Prior Radulfus. All that remained was to arrange for the bell's transportation from London. As the bishop said, a simple task – on the face of it.

'I don't understand,' said Straccan. 'Why pick me for the job?'

An oddly crafty expression crossed the bishop's face and was as swiftly gone.

'If you will get the bell as far as Durham, Coldinghame will send its own hauliers to take it from there. They're also sending some men down here to help load the bell and make themselves useful on the way north. It's a long, hard journey, even in summer. I want a man used to managing others, a man who'll take flooded fords and washed-out bridges as they come, who understands organisation and gets things done. I don't want the bell damaged or drowned in a river, stolen by a rival establishment or ending up over a cliff. If you'll take charge and get the bell safely to Durham, I'll absolve you of your sin.'

In the gallery over the tiltyard at Westminster, the queen and her ladies watched as her champion put the Spanish stallion through its paces. It was a magnificent animal, jet black, with faint silvery dappling like watered silk. Schooled to perfection, the animal was to be a gift for the king from his wife to mark the thirteenth anniversary of his coronation; the champion had been training it secretly for weeks. Half the women of the Court fancied themselves in love with Ralf Tyrrel, and those in the gallery stared hungrily at the rider's straight back and strong thighs, broad shoulders and head held so proudly with its cap of blue-black hair. Oblivious to the watching women, the knight was intent only on the horse.

Queen Isabel stared down at the pirouetting stallion. An observer would have thought that the rider had all her attention too, but in fact she didn't even see him; her thoughts were far away, on a man she'd not seen for eleven years – Hugh le Brun, the Lusignan lord to whom she'd been betrothed before the King of England snatched her for himself. How long ago it seemed. Long enough for her to have grown from twelve-years-old child to womanhood, to motherhood – she had borne John two sons and a daughter – but not so long ago that she had forgotten Hugh. Of late, with the king away so often, out of sight, out of mind, she thought of Hugh more and more.

The champion called to his squire, who came at a run, carrying a shield, and positioned himself at his lord's bidding behind the stallion. Some of the ladies stood to see better as the great horse stepped delicately backwards, stopped, and at some signal from its rider lashed out with both hind feet, hooves striking the very centre of the shield with a ringing crack, splitting it. Tumbling backwards, rolling away, the squire flung down the shield, while the women cheered and clapped and tossed down scarves. In the saddle the champion bowed, then set the horse to turning, left, right, and to prancing, flinging its front legs out in high style, while the audience laughed and clapped again, twittering like starlings.

'Isn't he magnificent?'

'The horse, darling? Or the rider?'

'Both of course.'

'They say the stallion was wild as a tiger, but Sir Ralf has tamed him like a dove.'

'One day he'll straddle a beast he can't subdue.'

'Don't you wish it may be you?'

'Don't we all, my pet!'

There was another ripple of laughter as they eyed the dark head and graceful body, laughter edged with excitement at the challenge of his indifference.

'Madame,' said one, seeing the queen was not listening, 'why has your champion never married? Surely he can't be a boy-lover.'

Reluctantly Isabel let go her pleasurable daydream. 'Sir Ralf? I don't know. Why don't you ask him? See, he has finished with the horse.'

Dismounting, Tyrrel came to the foot of the gallery, leading the stallion. He bowed deeply, and at a word from him the animal went to its knees, bending its head before the queen.

'Fie, Sir Ralf,' cried one of the women with a malicious trill of laughter. 'You are sweating! Is that a proper way to wait upon Her Grace?'

'He should pay a forfeit.'

'Ah, but what? What does he have that could please a lady?'

Teasing, lascivious, their eyes stroked his body as palpably as hands. He ignored them. They were whores. He could have any one, or all at once if he chose. It sickened him to think of these lewd sluts attending Isabel, their hands on her skin, bathing and dressing her, handling her hair, their filthy whisperings ever in her ear.

'Do the stallion's manners please Your Grace?' he called.

One of her ladies, giggling, said something behind her hand to the rest. The queen took no notice of them. She said, 'You have done well, Sir Ralf. My lord the king will be pleased.'

'Have you no favour for your champion, madame?' the giggler asked. 'We have stripped ourselves naked to honour him.' And indeed, the gauzy scarf she had thrown had left her breasts more than half bare. Tyrrel, infuriatingly, gave them not a glance.

Isabel drew a ribbon from her hair. It floated down, rippling like a blue silk eel. Tyrrel caught and kissed it, tucking it inside his shirt, looking up with a smile. But the queen had turned away, and was already leaving the gallery.

Spiders' webs and dead flies, straw and bird shit and a great cloud of earthy dust rose and swirled as the bell founder hauled the stiff sailcloth away to reveal an enormous bell. Man-high, and the same across its cavernous mouth, it lay on its side like a dull bronze elephant, slumbrous but somehow menacing. Bane walked slowly round it, lips pursed in a soundless whistle of admiration, while Straccan stared in amazement, shocked at its size – something des Roches had omitted to mention.

'What on earth does it weigh?'

'Fifty hundredweight,' said the bell founder with understandable pride. 'Give or take a few pounds. The biggest bell ever cast, she is. Tweren't her that killed him, you know.'

'Killed? Killed who?'

'The carter. When she fell. It was the ropes that broke, and the cartwheel that crushed him, but the men blamed my bell just the same, even though Bishop Peter himself said she was innocent. They blamed her, and they wouldn't touch her; just left her where she fell. Nor they won't help you, neither. They won't load her for you.'

'The bishop will send his own men,' Straccan said, beginning a mental re-evaluation of his 'simple task'. 'I won't need yours.'

The bell founder patted the dark, gleaming side of the bell as if it were the flank of a favourite cow. 'Nothing wrong with her,' he said. 'Beautiful she is, my Gaudy.'

'Gaudy?'

'Her name. Look.' He led Straccan round the other side, where the bell's vast mouth yawned. 'There, see?'

Above the rim was the word *GAUDETE*.

'Rejoice,' said Straccan. Behind him Bane gave a mirthless snort.

'Aye, and we did, too, when she'd cooled and came from the mould as sweet and true as we'd hoped. I paid every man a bonus. We all got drunk. A triumph, she is! Look, look here.' He pointed to the long, slim outline of a running hare, further round the rim of the bell. 'My mark,' he explained. 'That's my name. I'm Master Hare. Hare, bell, you see? Harebell.' He peered anxiously at Straccan to see if he had the wit to understand the play on words.

'Clever,' said Straccan.

'Aye! But when we started to load her,' he spread his hands expansively, 'what happened? This! Tom Carter dead, God assoil him, and his children orphaned. He was standing right beside the wheel, right where you're standing now, sir' – Straccan stepped hastily back – 'and when the bell came down the wagon was smashed and the wheel burst off and crushed him.' He crossed himself and stared bleakly at the bell and the splintered timber still to be seen beneath her. 'Not her fault,' he said with another comforting pat. 'Not your fault, Gaudy.'

'What now?' Bane asked, as they left the foundry.

'After I strangle my lord bishop, you mean?'

Bane grinned. 'Thought you might feel like that. It'll be a bugger getting that thing all the way to Durham. Though I don't suppose anyone'll try to steal it.'

Straccan sighed. 'Des Roches knew what he was doing. So did I, when I challenged Breos. There was no way this was going to be easy. Breaking Sanctuary is a serious sin; I was lucky not to be excommunicated.'

'What'll we do, then?'

'Go back to Westminster for our stuff, and go home for the time being. We can't get started until the men from Coldinghame get here. The bishop will send word when they do, and I'll come back then.'

'How long will it take?'

'God knows! It depends on the weather. And Hawkan, you'll have to stay at home this time. This is my penance; I must do it alone.'

Glad as he'd been to get home, he was already restless and not displeased by the prospect of the long, slow journey up-country. He needed something to do. And it was always possible that on the way he might hear word of Janiva. He had no idea where she'd gone, and he'd promised not to go looking for her, but that didn't mean he couldn't keep eyes and ears open, and hope.

The journey was tiring Countess Judith more than she would admit, but she stuck it out on horseback as long as she could before giving in. The solid downpour that began soon after they left Doncaster soaked her to the skin, and at last she capitulated to her women's pleas and took to the despised litter, making it clear that she was doing them a favour.

'Stop nagging,' she said testily, and yes, yes, perhaps she would rest for a day or two at York.

The abbot of St Mary's at York greeted her and, leaning on his arm, Judith surveyed her temporary quarters with a weary but still critical eye. At least there was no degenerate bathtub! The bed seemed firm enough, and a bright fire burned in one of those newfangled wall fireplaces. The guest master brought hot stones and wrapped them in wool to warm the bed. She let her saturated cloak slide to the floor and bade the abbot a brisk, 'Goodnight.'

Her women undressed her, brushed and braided her thin grey hair, and got her into bed, propped against a stack of pillows, a fur pelisse over her shoulders. Judith didn't believe in wearing a nightgown, that was for soft southerners, but having taken to her bed she made the most of it. Summoning her physician and complaining about everything from catarrh to constipation, she kept her weary women running with unguents, embrocations, potions and boluses, and had two fresh-killed pigeons split and applied like slippers to her cold bony feet, to draw the gout.

They prepared her nightly posset – the routine never varied – fetched her Mass book, her paternoster beads and the reliquary containing the earl's head, and set the candlestand beside the bed but not so near as to be any danger. Usually her chaplain would attend, briefly, at this time, to allay any concerns she might have over the welfare of her soul, but, well . . . Exultant as the countess was over her victory – she couldn't wait to see Radulfus's face – the sordid episode in Peter's oratory still rankled and her new chaplain was a flatulent bundle of nerves who jumped and farted whenever she spoke to him. She couldn't imagine why. She would dispense with his attendance tonight.

Finally she dismissed her last two women, and they withdrew to let their mistress say her prayers in private. Outside the chamber door they grumbled and yawned, tenderly rubbing their aching backsides and looking forward to shedding their wet clothes.

The scream bounced off the stone walls, rose to an incredible ear-splitting pitch and went on and on. For a moment the women froze, staring at each other, then both tried to get through the chamber door at the same time. They found Judith lying back against the pillows, candle-coloured with shock, gasping but uttering no more sounds, as if her scream had used up everything she had. Beside her on the pillow lay the reliquary – open – and grinning out of it was a face so hideous that it must surely be a demon!

'Jesus save us, that's never the earl, is it?' whispered Lady Maude, horror-struck, backing towards the door and crossing herself repeatedly.

Lady Alys, who was made of sterner stuff, ventured near enough to get a better look. Blackened, leathery skin was stretched tightly over the skull, and there was hair; there were eyes, shrivelled and fallen back in the skull, but still with a glint as if they were watching; and there were teeth, saints preserve us, what teeth! Great brown fangs! It certainly *looked* like a demon, but . . .

'It's an ape,' she said.

With a rattly sigh, the countess's head fell to one side and her eyes closed.

'Is she dead?' Maude asked.

Alys leaned over her. 'No, she's still breathing. Get the doctor back here, and send for the abbot, quick. She won't last long!'

Chapter 8

As the only bishop in England and the king's right-hand man, Peter des Roches was much in demand, and Westminster was seething with people: petitioners waiting to see the bishop, traders hoping to sell him something, messengers, emissaries with gifts and requests, the hard-done-by looking for justice, masterless men looking for employment, churchmen with complaints and demands. Horses were being led in and out of the stables as men arrived and departed. Bane led their horses away, and as Straccan crossed the yard he saw an old man dismounting stiffly, white with dust. There was something familiar about him.

'God ha' mercy! Blaise!'

Blaise d'Etranger was his friend, and had been his comrade in Scotland four years ago when the sorcerer Rainard de Soulis had kidnapped Straccan's daughter.

'Blaise,' Straccan cried again, shoving through the crowd to reach him. The tall old man turned his head, looking about for whoever had called his name. Straccan seized him in a dusty embrace.

'Blaise! God's precious soul, what are you doing here?'

He looked worriedly at his friend. The old man looked dreadful, dust limning his face with lines of age and exhaustion. His lips were mauve, his eyes sunken and his breathing ragged. He clung to his saddle with one hand and to Straccan with the other as his legs threatened to give way.

'I've a room and bed here,' Straccan said. 'Come and rest. Isn't Miles with you?' The young knight Miles Hoby had been their companion-in-arms in the same adventure, and had taken service with Blaise when it was over. 'Boy!' Straccan snatched at a stable lad's sleeve. 'See to Sir Blaise d'Etranger's horse.'

He slung Blaise's sword, saddlebags and baggage roll over his shoulder and supported his friend along a passage to the small mural room, barely more than a cupboard but blessedly private, thanking God it wasn't up any stairs. Taking Blaise across to the bed he sat him on it, lifting his legs and swivelling him round until he could lie back at full length.

'Rest there. There's a leech about somewhere. I'll find him.'

'No,' Blaise whispered. 'In my pack . . . a little flask . . . five drops, in water.'

Straccan found the medicine and a small pewter cup and slipped his arm under Blaise's shoulders, raising him to drink then easing him back on the bolster. Dipping a towel in the water jug he gently sponged the grime from the knight's face. The old man's breathing slowed and steadied, and the livid colour faded from his lips, leaving them pale. Presently Straccan realised he was asleep.

When he returned later Blaise still lay on his back on the narrow pallet, apparently asleep. His hands were crossed on his breast in monastic fashion, and his feet crossed at the ankles. So unmoving was he that it wanted only a hound beneath his feet, Straccan thought, and he might have been a figure on a tomb. He turned to leave quietly without waking the old knight.

'God save you, Richard.' Blaise opened his eyes and sat up.

'I'm sorry I woke you.' Straccan looked affectionately at him. With the dust of travel gone and some colour in his cheeks, Blaise looked a lot less dead.

'You didn't wake me. I was glad of the rest. How are things with you, Richard? Your little lass, is she well?'

'Yes, thank God. And you, how are you?'

'Nothing wrong with me.'

'What news of Hob?'

Blaise beamed. 'That boy soaks up learning like a sponge. He can read and write now, and he's a head taller than when you last saw him.'

The dumb serving lad Hob had rescued Gilla from Soulis when the sorcerer would have killed her; and afterwards, with Blaise at death's door and Straccan ill too, Hob had nursed them both with such skill that Blaise had taken the boy home with him to Cold-inghame, where the priory's physician had agreed to teach him the healing arts.

'He's happy at the priory?'

'Like a fish in water.'

'I was sorry to hear that your friend Prior Aernold had died.'

Blaise sighed. 'I miss him sadly. We were friends since boy-hood. And with him gone, I'm afraid I've become something of an embarrassment to Coldinghame. Prior Radulfus finds me an uncomfortable sort of tenant. Perhaps I shall go back to my own estate. When's supper?'

'Not long. We'll go to the hall when you're ready.'

Blaise rummaged in his baggage roll and pulled out a shirt, crumpled but clean. As his head emerged from it Straccan said, 'Where's Miles?'

The old man sat down abruptly on the bed, as if pushed. 'I don't know, Richard. That's why I came to London, seeking word of him. Hoping—' He paused, crossing himself, then added, 'Praying he is still alive.'

Straccan sat beside him. 'What happened?'

Blaise was silent for a while, gathering his thoughts. 'It's my fault,' he said at last. 'I sent him to France.'

'Why?'

'You know what's happening there? The so-called crusade against the Cathars in the Languedoc?'

'I've heard of the massacres at Béziers, Carcassonne . . .'

'My brother's daughter Giraude lived near Lavaur. Her husband was the Sieur d'Ax. There was a child, a little boy, David.'

'Lavaur . . .' said Straccan, dismayed. Lavaur had fallen to the Pope's crusaders a year ago. After the commander of the town's forces had been hanged and his sister thrown down a well and there stoned to death, Simon de Montfort's crusaders and Bishop Fulk's White Brotherhood set about exterminating the Cathars. Four hundred burned, while men of the Brotherhood rejoiced and sang hymns.

'I saw it coming,' Blaise said. 'I wanted to fetch Giraude and her family out before it was too late. Radulfus forbade me to go. He said I was too old! What he really meant was I mustn't be caught meddling with heresy again.'

'He's concerned for you.'

'He's concerned for the good name of the priory. It would look bad if it turned out they'd been harbouring a Cathar sympathiser for the past twenty years.'

'They're Cathars, your family?'

'No. Not that it matters any more. You know what Arnold Amaury said at Béziers, when they asked him how to tell heretics from Catholics: "Kill them all! God will know his own." They hanged the knights who defended Lavaur; they hanged Giraude's husband too. She and the boy, I thought, had been burned. It wasn't until November that I learned they'd escaped the sack of the town, God knows how! I sent Miles to find and bring them safely out of France.'

'When did he leave?'

'He sailed from Leith on the morrow of Saint Winefride, on a Templar cog. I know he reached Bordeaux, and I've heard nothing since. I've been to the Temple, but they've heard nothing either, except that all the Languedoc is awash in blood and fire. I should have gone myself. If harm has come to him, it's my fault.'

'Miles is no fool,' Straccan said. 'He'll bring them out.'

'God grant it!'

'Amen.'

They crossed the courtyard through a cold drizzling rain on their way to the hall for supper.

'Strange, isn't it?' said Blaise. 'There are Cathars everywhere: France, Spain, Navarre, Germany, even Italy. But so far, not here. I wonder why?'

Straccan trod in a puddle, splashing his legs, and laughed. 'It'll never catch on here.'

'Why not?'

'The weather protects us. People will stand for hours in the sun to listen to a hedge priest ranting, but they won't hang about in the rain.'

They took their places at one of the lower tables. At the high table the bishop was entertaining guests: at his right hand sat the Mayor of London, Henry fitzAilwin, and at his left a good-looking man in plain, well worn hunting leathers. As Straccan sat down the bishop raised a hand in greeting and spoke to one of the servers. Presently a covered dish from the high table was set before Straccan. Heads turned to see who was so honoured, and the mayor looked curiously at him.

'Who is that man, my lord bishop?'

'Richard Straccan. And by God's nails, I believe the old fellow beside him is Blaise d'Etranger! Haven't seen him in years. Thought he was dead.'

The mayor shrugged – he'd never heard of either man – but the bishop's other guest stared long and hard. D'Etranger! Every knight and companion-brother of the Temple knew that name. Cast out from the order, suspected of sorcery, accused of heresy, tortured, imprisoned for years until purged of his sin, Blaise d'Etranger had retired to a Scottish monastery twenty years ago. Nothing more had been heard of him until three years past, when he stumbled somehow upon Rainard de Soulis's plot to kill the king, and managed to bring about the downfall and destruction of those involved. Most of them, anyway. The witch Julitta de Beauris had got away, and Soulis's Arab sorcerer, a really nasty piece of work, had seemingly vanished into thin air. As for Straccan, hadn't he been responsible (some said to blame) for uncovering the plot? And hadn't d'Etranger, that old warlock, acted Merlin to Straccan's Arthur?

Aware of being watched, Straccan looked up and met the steady, assessing stare.

'Who's that at the bishop's left?'

Blaise shook his head.

'Don't you know?' said the man at Straccan's other side, with a pitying look for his ignorance. 'That's Ralf Tyrrel, the queen's champion.'

Chapter 9

L ondon was not so big nor its inhabitants so many that they did not recognise the great men of Church and state, even when they chose to ride without attendants, with hoods pulled well forward and mantles drawn well up to hide their faces. Stallkeepers and shoppers alike gave the rider on the black gelding no more than a glance as they pressed against the stalls to let him pass in the narrow alley. What Robert fitzWalter, lord of Baynard's Castle, was doing on the wrong side of the river without even a squire was none of their business.

Not everyone was as sensible.

'Spare a ha'penny, me lord,' whined a beggar, rising, an unlovely apparition, from the cobbles almost under the horse's nose. 'Ha'penny, fourthing, me lord, for the love o' God—'

'Bugger off,' growled the rider. But the beggar, limping alongside, dared to grasp a stirrup. Slipping his foot loose, the rider planted it squarely in the beggar's chest, sending him lurching backwards into a kennel, where he landed with a squeal of dismay and a splash. His clutching hand, however, had also caught the edge of the rider's mantle, tugging it down just enough to show his face – only for an instant, but long enough.

With a furious glare the rider pulled his mantle up again and rode on, cursing all impudent beggars.

''Ard luck, mate.' Two more of the mendicant fraternity appeared, as such creatures did, from nowhere, and helped their comrade out of the kennel, malodorous and dripping. The nearest stallkeeper lobbed a horse turd at them.

'Clear off, or I'll set my lads on you with clubs! And don't come creeping back unless you want your heads broken! We don't want your sort here.'

The wet beggar legged it down the road after his rescuers, forgetting, in the heat of the moment, to limp. Around the corner, in the shelter of St Olave's buttressed wall, they stopped to get their breath. The wet beggar squeezed ineffectually at his sodden tatters.

'It's not like I'd got any spares,' he complained in a nasal whine. 'Wet things don't arf bring on my rheumatics. No call for that, was there? 'Ell mend 'im, the sod!'

'What you want to go and grab at 'im for? Lucky 'e dint run you down. Don't you know oo that was?'

'No. I ain't from round 'ere. Oo was it, then?'

'Robert bleedin' fitzWalter.'

'Oh. 'Im.'

Robert fitzWalter was a big, hearty-looking man anyone would think as dependable as English oak, unless they happened to notice his eyes. Small, light-coloured, anxious, they were never still, scuttling like mice from face to face in company, wondering what each man was thinking of him – as if he didn't know. *FitzWalter the coward, fitzWalter the traitor, fitzWalter who surrendered the castle of Vaudreuil to the French without even a fight . . .*

That had been ten years ago, but he'd never lived it down. He saw it in men's eyes every day. Not that it mattered now. Soon, very soon, things would be different. They would regret every insolent stare, every jibe, when the Great Enterprise came to fruition and Robert fitzWalter was the ruler of England.

His fellow conspirators were waiting for him at the meeting place, a riverside whorehouse where no one would expect great lords to congregate. He had chosen carefully, picking only the disaffected, those with grudges against the king, those up to their ears in debt to him, those who felt cheated of lands, heiresses or wardships they felt should rightfully be theirs. On the stair he paused, listening to the voices from the room above. There was no need to see the speakers; each could be identified by his favourite oath.

'By God's body,' boomed a bass voice: Eustace de Vesci. 'Nay, but by God's teeth . . .' That would be Mowbray. 'God's eyes, my lords,' as Montbegon joined in, and 'God's cods!' from de Ros. Arguments going back and forth, heating and cooling and heating again, and from time to time a new voice would add its opinion – 'Never, by the face of God!' or 'God's reins, what next?'

Had they all come? Listening, fitzWalter missed one voice among the many. Was Tyrrel not there? Or was the queen's champion simply silent while the rest yapped?

He strode in, pulling off his gloves, and they fell silent at his entry.

'My lords.' His eyes flicked from face to face. Tyrrel wasn't there. 'You know why I sent for you. The Welsh under Llywelyn are in open rebellion and the king must take the field against them. The Normandy campaign's postponed; all are called to muster at Chester in mid-August. There will never be a better time. The Welsh won't fight a battle; they hide in the hills and pick the English off as we pass. When a stray arrow rids us of John, no one will think it anything but the misfortune of war.'

Mowbray stood up. 'Can we be sure of the man?'

'He's been well paid, and promised more when the job's done.'

'What if he talks?' That was de Vesci, who really should know better.

FitzWalter smiled. 'Don't worry, my lord. He'll say very little with his throat cut.'

'I don't like it,' said de Ros. 'You can't trust the Welsh. Especially not Llywelyn, he's as many faces as a barrel of coin. And what of his wife, eh? What of the Princess of Gwynedd? Christ, man – John's own bastard – d'ye think *she'll* betray her father?'

'The Princess Joanna knows nothing of this,' fitzWalter said impatiently. 'Llywelyn may be a slippery bastard but he's no fool. She's watched and warded. She minds her child and her embroidery, like any other woman.'

'Mind you don't underestimate her,' said de Vesci, who, married to a king's bastard himself, knew the breed rather better than fitzWalter did. FitzWalter ignored him.

'When will we know the king's dead?' Montbegon asked.

'I'll have true word within twenty-four hours. The young king will be at Lambeth; we'll proclaim him at once.'

'London won't like it,' de Vesci said.

'London will lump it,' fitzWalter said. 'I'll have a thousand pikes in the street before word spreads.'

'And the queen?'

'She'll be kept out of the way until it's all over. We don't want her kin in Angoulême claiming a share of the pie.' It was *his* pie. He could practically taste it: all England under his control, its king a child of four, moulded to his will. And if necessary there was always the other boy, Richard, a toddling two-year-old, even more malleable. 'Isabel will be closely warded,' he said. 'No communication with anyone. By the time they hear about it in France, young Henry will be crowned, the Interdict lifted and John rotting in his tomb.'

They talked and argued a while longer before leaving, singly, spacing their departures so as to attract no notice. FitzWalter watched from behind a shutter as each man mounted his horse and rode away. None of them was followed. The street outside was deserted, save for a leper sleeping in the shelter of a horse trough.

He picked up his gloves, but put them down again when he heard footfalls on the stairs. 'You're late,' he said sourly as the queen's champion ducked in through the low door.

'I couldn't get away earlier. I saw de Vesci on the bridge, looking damned pleased with himself. What did you promise him?'

'None of your business. You'll get what *you* want as long as you do your part. Don't cock it up, Tyrrel. The queen must be kept close.'

'Leave the queen to me.'

'Be ready, then. I'll send word as soon as I know John's dead. Where will you hold her?'

'Ravenser.'

'That godforsaken place?' FitzWalter laughed. 'Good. That should be safe enough. No visitors, mind. We don't want some crafty bugger marrying her – and don't *you* get ideas about it either.'

'A pity,' Tyrrel said, 'that you have a wife, my lord, or you could marry her yourself.'

He'd thought about it. There were various ways to dispose of a wife, but Lady Gunnora was a formidable woman; nothing short of murder would rid him of her, and that would bring down the wrath of her powerful de Valognes kin upon his head. No, let Tyrrel keep the queen secretly until he decided what to do with her. If the cocky bastard had his way with her so much the better. Shamed, dishonoured, she'd find no following. There'd be no 'queen's party' to undertake a rescue, no heroics over Tyrrel's whore.

He waited a bit longer after the champion left before mounting his horse. As he passed the horse trough, the leper, a noisome heap of rags, stirred and shook his clack-dish. FitzWalter tossed him a penny from a safe distance.

'God save ye, me lord,' rasped the leper. From behind his mask, bright eyes watched as the last of the conspirators rode away; the hand that groped in the muck for the coin, though dirty, was whole, unmarked by any disease. Scrambling to his feet, after a quick look round to make sure no one was watching, he stowed the mask in a pocket and turned his mantle inside out; reversed, it became a beggar's smelly, patched cloak. Thus transformed, its wearer went – *slunk* would be more apt – about his business.

49

Behind a bony, weary horse, the cart bounced along the rutted road, jolting the sick man cruelly. Inside, it stank of chicken shit and feathers, but Miles no longer felt ashamed of his disgrace. He neither cared nor knew where his helpless body lay. They had avoided Coventry – its steeples and smoke were behind them now – but in the hot, red-litten dreamscape of his fever, Miles was still in France, hiding from devils and searching for something . . . someone . . .

'David.' Miles's cracked, dry lips shaped the word, but no sound came. At his side the little boy wetted a bit of rag from the water bottle and carefully, tenderly, squeezed a trickle of water into the sick man's parched mouth. The cart gave a great lurch, and Miles cried out in pain, conscious – only for a moment – of where and who he was before sliding helplessly back into hell . . .

He hadn't realised the extent and ferocity of the war until he reached the Languedoc. Sacked towns and villages, still smoking, reeked of death; cartloads of prisoners, women and children as well as men, peasants, farmers, villagers, shopkeepers, defeated knights and men-at-arms all in together, trundled the roads to their deaths. The smoke of burning houses and burning heretics was everywhere. He breathed it in as he rode; it blackened his skin. He would never forget the stench.

In this strange land heretics and Catholics had long lived side by side in mutual tolerance, but when the crusaders came to slaughter the Cathars, and the faithful took shelter in their churches, they were cut down all the same. No one was safe.

Miles found the Tour d'Ax sacked and deserted, and the town of Lavaur a ruin, thinly peopled with terrified survivors who fled at the sight of any man with a sword on a horse. But he had found an old woman who'd served in the d'Ax household, and she told him the boy and his mother had escaped and fled to Portet. At Portet he was told they'd gone to Balbonne, or perhaps Montgey. At Balbonne no one knew of them.

Still hopeful, he went on to Montgey, where he was told they were dead, David and Giraude, his mother. The town was a charnel house; corpses still lay unburied in houses, in the streets, in the churches where they had thought themselves safe. A starving little blackguard tried to cut his purse, but Miles caught him, gentled him like a frightened dog and gave him bread. The lad had seen a boy – slim, dark, fourteen or so – take a living child from among the corpses. He had to find the child. He didn't know what else to do. It could have been David.

'Where did they go?' Miles demanded. The boy spread his hands, denying any knowledge. But, if he was asked to guess, milor . . .

'Guess!' Miles took a coin from his purse. The boy snatched it.

'Montségur,' he said. 'That's where all the heretics go, if they can. It's safe there.'

'They're not heretics!' But the boy had ducked under Miles's arm and was away.

In the cart, the sick man shifted and moaned, thinking himself again on the road to Montségur . . .

Montségur was in the mountains, a hard road, and as he climbed he began first to shiver and then to sweat. It was the ague of the district, acute and recurrent, and he had been too ill to fight when a robber stole his horse and his weapons. He had lain long by the roadside when the two women found him.

To his horror, they were heretics – Cathars – and most shocking of all, priests! Women priests! Crusaders and men of the White Brotherhood were everywhere looking for them, but they nevertheless managed to take care of Miles, despite the constant risk of capture, torture and death. As the holocaust continued they moved from one hideout to another. He remembered a woodcutter's tent, a shepherd's hut; he was carried in a litter when he couldn't walk, and once in a coffin. And so he came to Montségur, impossibly high atop its mountain.

And David wasn't there. A little boy, they said – no one knew his name – had died just a few days earlier.

He had no memory of the next few days; the fever overwhelmed him. They nursed him, those gentle, frightened heretics, and when he was a little better and could get up, he helped care for others. There were many sick; it was the fever season. In his delirium a man babbled of the children's sanctuary at Montperil. 'Where's Montperil?' Miles asked, but they were silent and hurried him away; and when, later, he looked for the man, he had died. No one would speak of Montperil.

As soon as he could, he took to the roads again, on foot, in the snow and the butchering winds of the Pyrenees. And at last he found Montperil.

The mountain stronghold was a refuge for Cathar orphans. No road led there, and so far the crusaders and the Brotherhood hadn't learned of it. Since the war began, children had been passed like parcels along lines of safe houses to Montperil. There was said to be a secret way through the mountain, so that if the enemy came the besieged would all just melt away in the night and leave an empty tower. It was their most hidden place, their last redoubt.

David was there, and Sorrow.

Roslyn de Sorules was her name. 'Sorrowless,' he had said and smiled, when she told him. 'I'll call you Sorrow, for short. There are other Roslyns, but only one Sorrow.' She was a singer, a wandering musician, a gleemaiden, whose master had been killed, along with David's mother and a hundred others, in the massacre at Montgey. That was where she had found David, among the dead.

When he told them who he was – that David's kinsman had sent him to bring the boy to safety – David had refused to go without Roslyn and she would not let him go without her, so they all left together, early in February. They were given horses and weapons, and warned there would be danger – they knew that anyway but didn't expect trouble from the White Brotherhood. They weren't heretics; each wore prayer beads and the crucifix. Nevertheless, the men who attacked them had the white cross sewn on their mantles . . .

'Miles, you must try to eat something.' The cart had stopped. Roslyn crouched at his side with a wooden bowl in her hands. 'I have eggs,' she said. 'They will do you good.'

He had been in France, on the road outside Foix where the first ambush happened . . . Bewildered, he stared into the girl's face. 'Sorrow? Where are we?'

'I have asked the way. It is not far, your friend's manor. Ten miles, maybe. We will get there tomorrow. Can you sit up? You must try to eat. It is beaten eggs, see? It will slip down.'

But he turned his face away and closed his eyes.

Chapter 10

The salty air smelled of fish. The youngest Angel had never seen the sea. He'd been told it was vast and blue, and had imagined a wide, table-top-smooth expanse of water, the colour of the Holy Virgin's robe. Instead, his eyes were stabbed by thousands of shards of sunlight, a myriad dancing points of burning light that almost blinded him. He had a precarious sensation of standing at the edge of the world.

Seabirds stalked the shore, stabbing their beaks into the malodorous tide-wrack, and wheeled overhead in dizzying loops, calling urgently. There were more boats than Uriel had thought to exist, most with the eye of God painted on their prows; and large ships, all swaying with the motion of the sea so that the wreaths of bells on their masts chimed in continual accompaniment to the gulls' screaming. Where the water lay shallow, several wretched abjurers stood waist-deep, arms outstretched, vainly begging for passage. A priest gabbled prayers and swung his censer, sprinkling a new boat with holy water and blessings.

The sea was more than vast; it was eternal. It stretched to the horizon, where it met the sky, and there was no land anywhere out there. Although he stood on firm ground, Uriel felt as if at any moment he might be blown away across that unending blaze of diamond daggers until he fell off the edge of the world. He sat on a bollard and stared unhappily at the ships. The idea of getting on one of them, eye of God notwithstanding, and setting out upon the terrifying sea made him feel ill, and he was ashamed lest the others guess his fear.

Beside him, Michael spoke: 'There's nothing left of the hostel but ashes and rubble, but I found the owner. He says they took passage on the *Star of the Sea*, bound for Rouen – Hoby, the boy and a young woman. Hoby was wounded in the leg. The *Star*'s here now, and bound for Rouen once more. We shall sail in her. God is with us.'

The others nodded. They expected no less, for, after all, they were about his business.

A steady south wind carried the vessel to Rouen, an unusually swift and smooth passage. The shipmaster gave thanks to the Blessed Virgin and Saint Paul, who had brought the *Star* safe to port once more despite the deplorable state of her bottom and the three unchancy passengers whose presence made him uncomfortable. Although the Angels wished to draw no attention, the very fact that they kept to themselves, repelling friendly or plain curious approaches from fellow passengers, meant they were noticed.

They spoke little, even to one another. They ate together, shunning the communal board, and prayed kneeling on the deck like monks. That alone would have attracted attention. Men who prayed so hard and often must have secret sins on their consciences, and the shipmaster was glad to see the back of them at Rouen.

There they learned that their quarry had tried to find a ship bound for Scotland, but had made do with one for Bristol. The Angels turned away from the dozens of ships in the busy harbour and walked along the shore, past rows of fishing boats and dark nets draped to dry. They found a man willing to carry them to Bristol, but now the wind, perversely, blew onshore, and they must wait. Wrapped in their mantles, they lay down in the lee of the boat, until in the grey light just before sunrise the skipper prodded them awake with his foot. The wind had changed, and unless they wished to swim to England they'd better shift their great carcasses now!

Huddled in the stern, cold, wet and queasy, the Angels watched the coast of England appear, a dark smudge looming through the thin fog on the horizon.

Summoned by the clanking of the watchbell and Cammo's shout, Gilla ran to the gate, expecting to see her father and Bane. But no. Outside the gate a dilapidated two-wheeled cart, drawn by a bony ancient horse, had come to a halt.

'Beggars, by the look of 'em,' said Cammo. 'If you want to give 'em food or anything, young mistress, best not let 'em in the yard.'

The driver jumped down, a ragged, dirty boy, fourteen or fifteen years old. Running quickly to the offside wheel, he shoved a wooden wedge under it, although from the way the poor horse stood, head hanging, legs splayed, sides heaving, it was utterly blown and couldn't have pulled the cart another yard if a fire was lit under its belly.

'Demoiselle, milady, is this the house of milor Straccan?

54

Miles is his friend. Miles is sick.'

Gilla stared at the boy and the cart. 'Sir Miles Hoby? In there?'

The boy plucked up the tattered flap at the back of the cart. Inside, on a heap of smelly sacks, lay a man – filthy, gaunt, heavily bearded – but Gilla knew him.

'Miles!' And to the boy: 'We must get him inside. Cammo, bring the cart in. Fetch Adeliza.'

'A moment!' The boy – who was he? Why were they so ragged? – knocked sharply with his fist on the tailboard. 'David!'

A head poked through the flap: a child's dirty face, a matted thatch of curls and big dark eyes blinking in the sunlight. Seeing Gilla with the steward, a large man, looming at her shoulder, he gave a cry of terror and burrowed back inside the cart. The boy called to him reassuringly, and let down the tailgate.

'It's all right, David. Come, come to me.'

With a quick, mistrustful glance at Gilla and Cammo, the child scooted on his bottom to the edge and dropped into the arms raised to catch him, burying his face in the boy's neck and clinging like a monkey.

Gilla reached to touch Miles's forehead; it was hot as a bakestone, and the stink of stale blood and pus and the sour sweat of fever rose from his body. His eyes were closed, and there were hectic patches of colour on his sunken cheeks.

'Richard,' he muttered.

'It's Gilla, Miles. Father's not here, but he'll be back soon.' She turned to the boy. 'What happened to him?'

'He was wounded – his leg. It doesn't heal, and on the ship the fever started.'

Ship? Never mind, there would be time for the story later. She must get Miles into a bed, see the wound, clean it; she knew something of plain nursing and the care of wounds – every gently born girl, even when convent-raised, was taught them and could stitch flesh as competently as linen – and this lad, and the little one, needed a good meal, a bath and their beds. At her call a groom came running to unharness the exhausted horse and coax it to shuffle to the stable, while two serving men grasped the shafts of the cart and drew it in through the gate.

'Get a litter for Sir Miles and carry him to the bedchamber. Adeliza, we need hot stones in the bed and hot water to wash him.' To the boy she said, 'Will you go in with him? I'll have a bath made ready for you. Shall I take the little one?' She held up her arms, and the frightened child, striking out at her, knocked off the boy's knitted cap.

At Gilla's startled exclamation the boy-no-longer – the girl – pushed her braids back from her face and said, 'Safer to be a boy on the roads – not much, perhaps, but a little.'

Not until Miles was asleep, with Cammo's son watching at the bedside in case he woke, could Gilla see to the needs of her other unexpected guests. While they bathed, and their clothes were being pummelled in the washtub, Adeliza found a shift and gown for the girl, and a tunic to fit the boy. Rather than alarm the child with more strange faces, she brought warm milk from the kitchen herself for him, with good red wine for the girl, pease pottage and bacon, bread to sop in honey and sweet preserved fruits. When she'd served them she sat with Gilla on the bench beside the girl.

'I don't know your name,' Gilla said.

'Roslyn.'

'Miles called you something else when we put him to bed.'

'Ah, that.' She dabbed at a spot of honey on the child's chin and gave him her finger to lick. 'He calls me Sorrow.' Her eyes flicked past Gilla towards the screen at the door. Gilla looked round to see who had come in, but no one was there.

'Sorrow? Why?'

'I am Roslyn de Sorules. Miles says there are many Roslyns, but only one Sorrowless, and he calls me Sorrow.'

'When did you last eat?' Adeliza asked. They had tackled the food like famished animals.

'We had the dole at a nunnery,' Roslyn said, frowning, reckoning back. 'Not yesterday. The day before, I think, or perhaps the day before that. Yesterday I stole some eggs. Miles was too sick to eat, but David ate them.'

Lulled by their voices, the little boy had fallen asleep. Full of warm milk and pease pottage, he lay on the cushioned bench with his head in Roslyn's lap. A stray curl stuck to his flushed cheek.

'Is he your brother?'

Roslyn laughed. 'No! He is well born, this little one. His mother was a noble lady and his father a knight, a lord, the Sieur d'Ax.'

'Where are they?'

'Dead. Soldiers hanged his father, killed his mother.' She spat in the straw. 'Lord Simon's men.'

'Who is Lord Simon?' Gilla asked.

56

Roslyn stared at her, astonished. 'You haven't heard of Simon de Montfort?'

Gilla shook her head. She knew nothing of Pope Innocent's crusade against the Cathars of southern France; such tidings hadn't reached Stirrup, and the nuns at Holystone had never spoken of it.

'He leads the Pope's crusade against the Cathars,' said Roslyn.

'What are Cathars?'

'Heretics.'

'David's parents were heretics?'

'I don't know what they were. I found him at Montgey after the town was destroyed, underneath his mother's body, soaked in her blood. She hid him. A soldier ran his pike through her; it broke, but beneath her it pinned David to the ground by his tunic. He couldn't get out. I heard him crying. She wasn't quite dead when I found them and lived long enough to tell me his name. David says they were hiding for a long time – ever since his father was killed – running from town to town, hiding from Lord Simon's men.'

'God save us,' said Gilla, crossing herself. 'What happened then?'

'I had friends. They helped us. They hid us and passed us from place to place, until we reached Montperil, in the mountains.'

'But Miles . . . How is it you are with him?'

'He was looking for David. Someone, a kinsman, sent him to the Languedoc to find him. He found us at Montperil. David wouldn't leave me and I wouldn't let him go, so Miles brought us both away.' She looked from Gilla to Adeliza, then back at the bread which she was dunking in honey. 'Will he die?'

'He is very ill. I've sent to Dieulacresse for Brother Lucius, the physician. How was he wounded?' She was worried by the condition of Miles's leg. The deep sword-cut above his knee was full of pus, with tight swelling and dusky inflammation spreading up his thigh. Adeliza had poulticed it with all-heal.

'We were at Bordeaux, trying to find a ship to take us to Scotland. We spent the night at an inn on the waterfront and were asleep when a man burst into the room. In the dark he slashed at Miles's leg instead of his neck. It was too dark to see, but I could smell him, the ribaud. I could smell his sweat, and I had my dagger.' She patted the long knife in a sheath at her belt, no mere eating knife but a killing tool.

'It was harder than I thought – to kill a man. The first stab hit a rib, but the next found a soft place. By the time people came to see what all the noise was, he was dead.'

Gilla's hands shook as she refilled Roslyn's cup. 'A robber . . .'

Roslyn shrugged. 'Perhaps. But not the first. The first was at Foix; we were ambushed on the road just outside the town. Just one man, but a knight, well armed. Miles killed him.' Her teeth flashed in a quick grin. 'He is good, Miles. He fights like a . . . like a wolverine! The second time was at Portet. It was another knight; he came at us on the forest road with a lance. He killed our horse. Miles wounded him. He should have killed him – I told him so – but he let him live. We took his horse and left him there. Perhaps he died, after all.' She saw Gilla's horrified expression and tried to explain.

'It is war, demoiselle. Men killing other men – de Montfort's soldiers searching for heretics, heretics ambushing and killing the soldiers. And there are the deserters, hiding in the hills and forests, and outlaws. But the men who attacked us were knights of the White Brotherhood. They wore the white cross. I saw it stitched inside their cloaks when I cut their purses.'

'You stole their money?'

Roslyn looked surprised. 'Of course!'

'What is the White Brotherhood?' Adeliza asked.

'Men who have sworn to hunt down heretics.'

'But Miles isn't a heretic,' Gilla said. 'Why should they want to kill him?'

Roslyn picked at the edge of her bread trencher. 'I don't know. Demoiselle, he mustn't die!'

'We will pray to God and the saints for him.'

'God and the saints?' said Roslyn, with a twist to her mouth. 'You think they hear?'

'Don't you?'

The girl shrugged. 'If they hear, I think they cannot care.' She lifted David's small body without waking him. 'May we go to bed now, David and I?'

'Of course.' Gilla got up. Adeliza had made up the bed in the little mural room off the main bedchamber so that the little boy wouldn't be disturbed if they had to tend the sick man during the night.

Gilla came into the chamber with her arms full of blankets to find Roslyn had opened the shutters and was leaning out of the window, looking down into the yard. Curled up like a puppy in the middle of the bed, David slept; he hadn't moved since she laid him there.

'You'll be cold with the window open,' Gilla said.

Roslyn glanced at her, a flash of deep blue eyes quickly veiled again. '*Merci*, demoiselle, but I am not used to sleeping indoors, shut in.'

Gilla put the blankets on the bed, smiling down at the sleeping child. 'Shall I bring a pallet for David? We can lift him on to it; nothing will wake him now.'

'No. He will sleep with me. He has bad dreams.'

And that was no wonder.

'Yes, of course,' Gilla said, aware of the girl's ... Was it hostility? Not really. Wariness, reserve. 'You're safe here.'

Another guarded blue glance. 'You are very kind. I hope you are right.'

When Gilla had gone Roslyn lay down beside David, pulling the blankets over them both and curving her slight body round the child's back. The young lady was wrong: there was no safe place. She had seen women and children slaughtered in churches, priests at their altars and nuns in their cloisters, infants in their mothers' arms. Wherever she turned, she saw more dead souls than living. She shivered as a draught gusted down from the window, but if an enemy entered the yard below she would hear, and if danger threatened from within the house she and David had a way out.

So far at least, this place held no apparent threat, and untroubled by the people living there now its ghosts went about their own affairs.

In her arms David twitched and cried out. Tears slipped from under his eyelids as he endured his dreams.

Once upon a time, there had been a castle ...

In his dream, David saw it again in sharp detail: the white stone walls and turrets blinding in sunlight, the winding stairways and cool, echoing passages, the bower where his mother and her maidens sat sewing, the stables where his father was almost always to be found among the beautiful horses, the white mares and stallions that the Sieur d'Ax bred and loved, as his forbears had done for five generations since the great Rodrigo Diaz, whom men called the Cid, had given Vincent d'Ax, his comrade-in-arms, two mares and a stallion of the bloodline of his great warhorse Babieca.

There had been a white colt, born on David's fourth birthday, which was to have been his own.

The bad men came to Ax with the first snow in the winter of

David's fifth year. His nurse Tatanie and their chaplain Father Jacques tried to delay them while David's mother got him to safety; she told him not to make a sound as she carried him down into the undercroft and along a damp, dark passage smelling of rats which opened out, at last, into a cave on the hillside below the Tour d'Ax. Above them, in the light of the setting sun, the castle looked all bloody. Hidden under the gorse bushes, they could hear the screams and prayers of people David had known all his life. He could hear them now, in his dreams, screaming as they died.

Not everyone was killed. David's father and his knights were driven down the hill like cattle, chained despite their wounds, stumbling, falling and trying to hold one another up. Those too injured to walk were dragged in a dung cart. David's mother cried then. It was the only time.

The bad men didn't hurt the horses. David and his mother watched from their hiding place as the animals were led away, the colt among them; it had snuffed the air and looked towards the place where David lay, and whickered as if puzzled to be leaving him there.

His mother crouched over him, shielding him with her body lest the bad men see them and shoot, but no one did; and after dark, while behind them the castle burned and collapsed, they crept away. The fog of dust and rubble that rolled down the hill enveloped them, so that they must cover their mouths and noses in order to breathe, but it also hid them from the eyes of the bad men. They walked all night in the snow; when David's legs gave out his mother took him on her back like any peasant woman. They kept clear of the burning villages and avoided any sort of road that horsemen might use.

The white colt had had blue eyes. It would be a well grown young horse now. He wondered if it still remembered him.

For a month David and his mother hid with other refugees in the hills, but hunger and cold and fear of the bad men's patrols drove them at last to a town, to Portet, where an old woman who had been a servant to the d'Ax family took them in and hid them from the bad men.

Instead of the castle there was now a very little house, just two rooms, the upper, where everyone slept, reached by a ladder. Instead of the Sieur d'Ax's servants, knights and men-at-arms, instead of his mother's ladies and damsels, there were just Tante Fabrisse and her goat, who lived in the downstairs room with them. The old woman made much of David, calling him her lamb and her dove, and kissing his hands as all his father's people used to do.

Then the bad men came to Portet. Tante Fabrisse's son came at night, at the risk of his life – for he was a known Cathar – to warn them that crusaders were coming and to urge them to go with him to his farm outside Montgey. The old woman would not go. She had lived in the small house for forty years, she said, and she would die there rather than leave. But when the bad men came, the old woman – along with twenty-seven other suspected heretics – was dragged to the market place and burned in a barrel.

There were no horses on Pierre Bonhomme's farm, but there was a donkey, as well as sheep, goats and hens. The house was long and low with no upper floor; the animals came in at night to one end of the kitchen, and the homely smell of manure pervaded bedding and clothes alike. David had grown out of his clothes – his bony little wrists stuck out a good two inches from his sleeves and his mother had cut the feet off his hose – and the rough, scratchy fabric which was all Pierre's wife could provide rubbed his skin raw.

The crusader who found his way up the winding, barely perceptible track to the farm wore a white surcoat with a red cross tacked to one shoulder. He was a deserter, looking for food and loot. He had a sword and a mace, and he kicked the door in and stood in the doorway with the low winter sun at his back. He looked young. He had spots and a fluffy beard, and he squealed like a pig when Pierre's son Marc drove the pitchfork into his belly.

There were other places after that – towns, villages, farms. David wished they could stop running but knew he could never go home. The white castle was gone; his father and his brave knights had been hanged like dogs, and the bad men would kill him and Maman too if they found them.

There were always people ready to help them when they heard the name d'Ax. 'They loved your father,' Maman said, 'and they love you.' As spring turned into summer, and summer to fall, they were passed from place to place, hidden in farm carts among turnips and in merchants' wagons among their goods. The abbess of the convent of St Marie Madelaine at Montgey was cousin to the Sieur d'Ax, and gave them sanctuary.

'Mother Justine has sent for help for us,' Maman said that night, when they lay in bed in the abbey guest house – a real bed, with a mattress and pillows and soft blankets. 'Someone will

61

come, my darling, to take us out of this cursed country and over the sea to a safe place.'

'When?' David asked.

'The abbess's messenger must get there first. It will take many weeks, but we can stay here until then.'

Two days later the crusaders attacked Montgey, and sacked and burned the abbey. David and his mother ran out with the nuns and the abbey servants, and the townsfolk who had taken shelter in the abbey church. Knights with swords and men-at-arms with pikes herded them, and outside the abbey gates archers were lined up to shoot them down as they came. David and his mother were caught in the press of screaming, terrified people, pushing and struggling. Some fell and were trampled. The bells of the church were ringing in triumph as the crusaders closed in to finish them off.

To David's surprise his mother went down on one knee, took his hand and kissed it. Then she drew her mantle around them both and crouched over him, hiding his small body under her own.

He couldn't see. The bells were deafening, a hundred devil blacksmiths hammering on anvils, but they couldn't drown the screaming, the horses neighing, men cheering. Maman's body jerked. She gasped and whispered, 'David, don't move.' The hot wetness of her blood soaked him.

The screaming went on for a long time, and when at last all was quiet he whispered, 'Maman,' but she didn't answer; and when he tried to move, he couldn't, held fast by his mother's stiffening body and the binding shroud of her blood.

Chapter 11

G illa wiped Miles's burning face with a cold damp towel, and at the cool touch he opened his eyes.

'Be careful. He throws stones,' Miles said hoarsely, struggling to raise himself on his elbows.

She pressed him back – he was weak as a baby – and pulled the coverlid up again as a fit of shivering shook him. He went on muttering, but the only word she could catch was 'stones'.

'Hush now, be still.' She wrung the towel out in cold water and laid it across his forehead. 'Who throws stones?'

Miles sighed. 'David. Be careful, he's . . .' His voice dwindled away into mumbled nonsense. His body shook with the hard rapid beating of his heart. His breathing was laboured, the fever flush darker tonight; even his lips looked dusky. His eyes were bright and sunken, his face skull-like. What little flesh he'd still had on his bones when he arrived was melting away almost as she watched.

Gilla dabbled her face with the cold water to keep herself awake and once more silently begged God, his Son and every saint she could name to spare Miles's life. It was four days since he had turned up with the little boy and Roslyn de Sorules, like beggars at the gate. Together she and Brother Lucius had dealt with his wound, applying hot poultices of honey, and to her relief the tautly swollen leg had responded well; its shining redness had subsided and the foul matter had been drawn out, along with scraps of dirty cloth that the sword point had carried into it. The wound was healing, so why this fever? Why this rapid, shallow, difficult breathing? With her ear against Miles's chest Gilla could hear every breath rattling as if there was water in his lungs, and the brown sticky sputum he coughed up was streaked with bright blood. Brother Lucius came each day, and each day looked graver. Despite all they could do, she feared they were losing him. The monk would return tonight. He said Miles must be bled, to ease the strain on his heart.

Tiredly she rested her head on her arms at the bedside. *Janiva would know what to do*, she thought. And the thought sharpened, clearing the fog of tiredness from her mind. *Yes, Janiva knows . . .*

Roslyn's voice broke into her thoughts; she hadn't heard the gleemaiden come in. 'Gilla? Shall I stay with him now? David is sleeping. You should try and rest.'

Gilla got up. 'I will. But there is something I have to do first.'

She took a lighted candle from the stand, and went along the passage to Bane's room. For this, she must be alone. The room was little more than a cupboard, holding just his bed and a chest, and no one would disturb her there. She shut the door, put the candle on the chest and sat on the edge of the bed.

'Holy Mother,' she whispered, as Janiva had taught her, 'ward me now.'

She stared into the flame.

Her breathing slowed as her concentration deepened. For a little while nothing happened, then the flame, which was burning steadily, fluttered and swayed then stilled again and slowly expanded to fill her vision.

The trance deepened, the flame became a ring of fire, and there, hazy at first but clearing as she leaned towards it, she saw Janiva, thinner than she remembered and wrapped in a brown mantle with her hair hidden under a coif like a nun's.

'Janiva,' she said silently, mind to mind. 'Janiva, I need your help.'

At the tinny clang of the watchbell Roslyn ran to the window and looked down into the yard, to see two riders dismounting. A boy led their horses away – from Gilla's description of her father's stallion, Roslyn recognised Zingiber, and knew his rider to be Miles's friend. The other would be his servant, Bane. As she watched, the steward came hurrying out to greet them, and they passed out of her sight into the hall below.

A few moments later she heard someone coming up the stairs at a run. The curtain at the stair head was dragged aside, and Straccan came in, bringing with him a fresh smell of rain, horse and leather that Roslyn found clean and exhilarating in the stuffy room. He hadn't stopped to fling off his mud-splashed cloak or take off his boots. Later, she noticed the scars, but in that first moment she thought only, *How tall he is, and how sad.* Then, for an instant, that other sight of hers, the curse she'd lived with all her life, glimpsed a shadowy form at his side, a young woman in a blue gown, and knew her to be Gilla's mother, they were so alike. The shade laid her hand on his sleeve, brushed her cheek lovingly against his shoulder, and he knew nothing of it. Then he

64

came to the bedside, and the fragile form was gone.

He didn't seem to see Roslyn, just groped under the coverlid to grasp his friend's hand. Miles lay propped against pillows to ease his breathing, his eyes glittering like glass under half-closed lids, but at Straccan's touch he turned his head.

'Richard . . .' Miles's voice was a feathery whisper, scarcely to be heard.

'I'm here, Miles. I'm here, brother.' Tears brimmed in his eyes as he looked at the wasted face. Holding Miles's hand between his own he knelt beside the bed and bowed his head so that his tears blotted the coverlid.

'Galen wrote,' the old monk said, drawing his lancet from his pocket and testing its edge on the horny heel of his thumb, 'in his great work *De Ingenio Sanitatis*, that the patient should be let blood on the unaffected side, from the basilic vein, while Avicenna recommends the saphenous vein; but in this case both the patient's lungs are affected, and I am not at all sure that phlebotomy is the right course of action. He is already so weak.' He tapped the lancet in his palm, considering. 'But who am I to argue with the great doctors of medicine? My son,' – to Straccan – 'get the bowl. We will draw eight ounces from each arm, and satisfy both authorities. Master Bane,' – to Bane, who was hovering at the stair head wanting to be useful – 'will you tell them in the kitchen to boil a great cauldron of water? We shall need it later.'

Straccan held the bowl as the dark blood ran into it. He felt slightly sick at the sight; wounds he could deal with, but this deliberate letting of blood was something that made his teeth clench. From the small room off the bedchamber he could hear David crying – a desperate, terrified sound – and the soothing murmur of the French girl's voice, comforting him. She had been here with Miles when he came in, but he had hardly noticed her – a thin-boned, dark-haired girl with wary eyes. A gleemaiden, his steward said. He wondered what strange chance had brought them together, she and Miles, and the child, and how she had managed to bring them here with Miles so ill.

When eight ounces had been taken from the left arm, Brother Lucius bound it up and turned his attention to the right. When it was finished Miles lay against his pillows pale as parchment, but his lips were less blue, Straccan thought, and the hammering of his heart less frantic.

'Now,' the monk said, frowning at his pulse-glass with his

fingers on Miles's wrist. 'There's one more thing we can try. I brought a sack of herbs with me. We will poultice him, hot and hot on his chest, all night long if we must.'

Throughout the evening they laboured over Miles, applying hot poultices one after another as fast as they cooled. Gilla quietly replenished the candles, and fetched bread and broth from the kitchen for Straccan and Brother Lucius. There was nothing more for her to do; she retreated to a stool in the corner, to wait. Janiva had promised she would come.

The untouched broth grew cold as the night wore on, and it seemed to Straccan that despite the tall stands of candles the shadows were thickening around the bed.

'God, of your mercy, Christ, of your mercy . . .' he prayed, aware also of the monk murmuring prayers, even as their labours continued without pause: dipping the towels, wringing them, raising the patient to wrap them round his wasted body, covering him warmly to keep the heat in as long as possible, while the next poultice, and the next, and the next were prepared and applied.

The candle-clock had burned down to the midnight ring before Gilla sensed the change she was waiting for. A clean, bright scent of rosemary freshened the exhausted air of the sickroom, and Straccan looked up, startled, from his seat by the bed. Gilla experienced an odd lurching sensation, as if she were falling head over heels – and it was done. Janiva was there within her, sharing Gilla's mind, seeing with her eyes, using her body and hands, and speaking through her lips.

It was Janiva who touched Straccan's hand, and said, 'This I *must* do.'

At those words, Osyth's words, Straccan's hands closed on Gilla's arms, gripping them so hard that she flinched, and he let go, appalled to think that he had hurt her. 'What is this? What are you doing?' he demanded, but then he saw— No, it was impossible! He couldn't believe it! For an instant he saw Janiva's face, then Gilla's again, but it was Janiva he saw looking at him through his daughter's eyes.

'Ssh,' she said softly, and laid a finger across her lips. Shaken to his heart but remembering his promise to Osyth, he made room for her at the bedside, and dared say no more.

Through Gilla's eyes Janiva looked at Lucius, and to him it seemed that his soul was naked under that searching gaze; but in him she saw only compassion, innocence and an abiding wonder at the mysteries and marvels of God's world. She smiled at him, satisfied. No harm would come to any in that room through Lucius.

'Open the shutter,' she said. Straccan obeyed. She bent over the bed and placed her hands on Miles, one on his brow, the other over his heart.

Gilla could feel the power flooding into her as Janiva drew it up from the living earth, and from Gilla's own body as well, from blood and bone and life, power too strong for her to handle alone. It coursed along her veins like painless fire as, through her hands, Janiva poured that power into the energy-paths of Miles's body, murmuring the spells that would strengthen him, and tracing with her fingers on his flesh the runes of healing and life.

The candle-clock was just a puddle of wax in its dish when at last, exultant, Gilla felt Miles's life-tide turn under her hands.

Cool air flowed in through the window. 'It's sunrise,' said Straccan, surprised – the night had seemed eternal – but the pale light at the window, he was sure, could not alone account for the stealthy withdrawal of the shadows that had gathered around Miles's bed.

Janiva was gone.

Gilla swayed, suddenly bereft; empty, cold, shaky, she was thankful for her father's arm circling her waist, supporting her against his warm body. There were tears on his face, and Brother Lucius was on his knees, praying.

She was so tired. 'Father . . .'

'Sweetheart, are you all right?'

She nodded, and even that much was an enormous effort.

'Janiva was here,' he said, and she nodded again. '*How?*'

It was even more of an effort to speak. 'She had to be asleep before she could leave her body; that's why it was so late. Then, as long as I was willing, she could share mine, and use me to heal Miles. Is he all right?'

'Yes, look!' Straccan passed his hand across Miles's face, bringing it away wet. Miles's hair was wet; sweat stood like blisters on his brow and rolled, glistening like oil, down his face and neck. His dark flush was fading.

'God be praised,' said the monk, scrambling to his feet. 'He is breathing easier already. We must keep him warm; I'll build up the fire.' He suited action to words. 'See, he sleeps. Nothing could be better for him now than healthy, restorative sleep. With

God's blessing, he has been spared, to take up his life again.'

Gilla sagged against her father, and but for his arm would have fallen. He picked her up – light, beloved weight – and carried her to bed. She didn't move or open her eyes as he pulled the blankets up. He touched her hair, stared helplessly at her sleeping face. What had he just seen? Magic? A miracle? Were they the same? His own legs felt weak and he was too shaken to think about it now; there would be time for that later.

'Sir Richard, your daughter . . .' The monk's voice behind him was hesitant.

Did Lucius understand what had happened? *If so, it's a bloody sight more than I do*, Straccan thought. 'What, Brother?'

'It's a rare gift she has, but a dangerous one. Be careful, my son. There are some who think such gifts are not of God but Satan. For her sake – and your own – bid the maid take care.'

Chapter 12

P eter Martel scratched on his wax tablet at Straccan's dictation. 'From Richard Straccan at Stirrup, near Dieulacresse, to Blaise d'Etranger at the Priory of St Mary at Coldinghame. Know that Miles Hoby is come safely out of France with your kinsman, the boy David d'Ax. The boy is well . . .' Straccan's voice trailed away. He gazed unseeing out of the window, wondering what to have Peter write next.

'Brother Lucius says Miles won't be fit to travel for a moon at least,' he said. 'But if I tell Blaise how ill he's been, he'll worry overmuch.'

'Don't tell him,' offered Peter. 'Just say he's been sick and is better of it, and he'll be on his way with the boy as soon as he's full able.'

'Good. Write that.' He saw Gilla cross the yard to the kitchen, David at her heels. The child still woke them all at night, trapped and screaming in the terror of his dreams, and he hid whenever a strange face appeared, but he had become much attached to Gilla, and submitted meekly to Adeliza's daily attentions with soap and comb. Good feeding and regular washing had begun to transform the grubby foundling into a very attractive, sturdy little boy, and had put some flesh on the slender bones of Roslyn de Sorules as well.

What did Miles call her? Sorrowless? What kind of name was that? Straccan knew from Gilla how Roslyn had found David trapped under his mother's body, but the gleemaiden never spoke about herself: not where she came from nor who her family was, nor how she came to be searching among the corpses at Montgey.

Frowning, Straccan returned to his dictation. He hadn't wanted to pester Miles with questions – his friend's recovery had been slow, with one or two setbacks that had frightened them all – but although thin as a hayfork, with no more appetite than a kitten and still abed, he really was on the mend at last.

Across the yard he saw Adeliza appear at the kitchen window,

69

setting a tray of honey cakes on the window ledge to cool. A moment later Bane passed, snatching a couple of cakes on his way.

'Finish the letter with my loving greetings, and I pray God he keeps in health,' Straccan told Peter. 'Find someone to take it to London, to go north by sea. I'm going to try and tempt Miles to eat something.'

Nipping smartly past the kitchen and pilfering two more cakes from the tray as he did so, he found the invalid sitting up, wearing a guilty expression.

'Have you been trying to get out of bed again?'

'Well, yes,' Miles confessed. He looked embarrassed. 'I hate using that piss bottle! It's against my honour. I wish they'd let me use the jordan.'

'They' were Roslyn and Adeliza, who adhered strictly to Brother Lucius' orders. Miles was not to get out of bed for another week, and then he might sit in a chair, warmly wrapped, for no more than an hour in the morning. He would find himself much weaker than he expected, the old monk said. True, his stars were more auspicious now, but to overdo things at this delicate stage of his recovery could kill him yet.

Miles didn't believe a word of it. The piss bottle stood beside the bed, and the lidded jordan half a dozen steps away in the corner by the window; at present his sole ambition was to reach it.

He eyed the honey cake suspiciously. 'Adeliza said no solid food yet. If she comes in and catches me—'

'The quicker you eat it the better, then,' said Straccan, sitting on the edge of the bed and stuffing his own cake in his mouth. 'And make sure there's no crumbs,' he added indistinctly, with his mouth full, 'or she'll have my guts for garters as well as yours.'

'Been meaning to ask,' said Miles when he'd finished. 'How's the old horse?'

'You won't know him. Rest and good feeding have done wonders.'

'I thought he'd drop dead long before we got here.'

'Where on earth did you get him – and that dreadful cart?'

'Sorrow stole them. She's very good,' Miles said admiringly. 'She stole food for us, you know. Eggs, bread, milk. Even money! I don't know where she got the cart; she wouldn't say. We landed at Bristol – I couldn't find a ship to take us to Scotland – and walked all the first day. But I was sick. I couldn't keep going. God knows where she got the bloody cart! She pulled it with me inside all the next day.' He looked up at Straccan, shamefaced. 'I swear, Richard, there was bugger all I could do about it! We slept at the roadside, and when I woke up next morning she'd got the horse as well.'

'How did you come by her?' He was curious. He had scarcely noticed her at first, beyond the briefest courtesies, being so worried about Miles. But lately her slim figure was catching his eye more often. Gilla had found a bolt of crimson cloth in the storeroom and she and Adeliza had made a gown for the gleemaiden. Now, vivid as a flame, and with her dark hair and golden skin, it was impossible *not* to notice her. She drew all eyes. Not that she tried, he thought. But she moved like a fawn, and the dagged hem of her gown danced about her slender ankles. *Jesus*, he thought guiltily, *I've been alone too long*. He dragged his attention back to what Miles was saying.

'She was there at Montperil, with David. He wouldn't leave her, nor she him. They'd been together for some time, ever since she found him among the dead, when she was searching for her master.'

'Her master?'

'He was a minstrel, a gleeman,' Miles said. 'Raimond de Sorules. She was daughter and apprentice both to him. He was killed in the sack of the town where David's mother died.'

Seeing Miles felt like talking, Straccan asked, 'How did you find them?'

'First I went to Lavaur. The Sieur d'Ax and his family lived near the town, but their castle had been sacked . . .' His eyes stared into memory as he recounted his travels, his misfortunes, the twists and turns of his search and his eventual arrival at Montperil. From time to time he stopped to drink from the jug of watered wine beside him and when he got to the three attempts on their lives on the way to Bordeaux, Straccan interrupted.

'What *is* this White Brotherhood?'

Miles explained. 'The Bishop of Toulouse is their leader. They have only one purpose, to kill heretics. That's what's so queer, Richard: anyone could see we weren't heretics.'

Straccan laughed. 'What do heretics look like?'

'Well, the Cathars wear black, for a start, or dark blue. No colours. And they would *never* wear this.' He tugged at the thong round his neck, under the shift he wore abed, and pulled out his crucifix. 'This is abhorrent to them. They wouldn't be seen dead wearing it. And we each wore one.'

'Maybe they were just robbers, after all,' Straccan suggested.

'Outlaws wouldn't care if you were Cathars or Catholics or tree-worshippers.'

'No,' said Miles. 'All three times, the attacker had the white cross on his mantle. I saw it on the last one when the fire started.'

'What fire?'

'At that rathole of an inn, at Bordeaux. The room caught fire. Till then I couldn't see who I was fighting; it was pitch dark in there. I don't know how the fire started; there was no candle. It just suddenly went *whoof*! The whole place burned down. We were on the top floor. I shoved Sorrow and David down the stairs and got everyone else out of their beds. They all got out, except the sod who'd tried to kill me. He went up in flames. He was dead by then, of course. Sorrow stabbed him. Serve him bloody well right!'

With her arm up to the elbow in the water, Gilla knelt by the river's edge where the bank overhung the water. It was a favourite place of hers; the first primroses grew there, and kingfishers nested in holes in the high bank on the other side. The river wasn't very deep, and slender brown fish hung not far below the surface, barely swaying in the gently moving water. Behind her she heard footfalls in the grass. David. She didn't look round. She'd seen him following her, thinking himself unseen.

A stone fell, landing right beside her. Not large, but not a small pebble either. If it had hit her, it would have hurt.

'Don't do that, David.'

'I wouldn't've let it hurt you. What are you doing?'

Gilla sat up, wiping her wet arm on her kirtle. 'Trying to catch a fish,' she said, 'the way Hawkan does.'

'I can do that.' David settled beside her, belly down in the grass. 'Roslyn showed me.' A brown wet-velvet shape nibbled softly at the slim white fingers waving temptingly in the water, thought better of it and darted away.

'Roslyn is a better name than Sorrow,' Gilla said. 'Sorrow sounds sad.'

David ignored that, as with a flurry and a splash his arm curved up from the water, flinging a small flapping fish on to the grass. He looked at it doubtfully. 'He's very small. Must we eat him?'

'No,' said Gilla. 'Put him back.'

Reprieved, the fish swam away, and the children lay on the

bank peering down into the water. The smooth stones on the river bed looked near enough to touch; Gilla tried to grasp one marked with a white blaze like an arrowhead, but it was beyond her reach.

'How deep is it?' David asked.

'Up to my waist.'

'Can you swim?'

'No. Can you?'

'I don't know.' He jumped up, and before she could stop him let himself fall forward into the water.

'David!' Gilla was in after him instantly, seizing him round the middle and shoving him up on to the bank. 'Why did you do that? Now we're all wet!'

The boy sat laughing as she scrambled out after him, wringing water from her skirt and her hair.

'That was stupid,' she said.

'I just wanted to see if I could swim. It was cold. Don't fish feel cold?'

'I don't know. Don't ever do that again; you might drown! Now we'll have to go and get dry things on.'

'No.'

'Don't be silly.' She reached for his hand, but still laughing, he backed away. 'Well, I'm going. My gown's soaked. Stay wet if you want to.'

He was so quick! She didn't see his arm move, but a stone whizzed past her cheek and struck the tree beside her, falling at her feet. The stone had a white mark like an arrowhead. On impulse she bent and touched it. It was hot.

She looked up. David was gone.

Chapter 13

By the feast day of Saints Mark and Marcellian, Miles had achieved his ambition and managed to walk to the jordan. True, on his way back to bed his legs had folded and he'd fallen, but that hadn't diminished his sense of triumph. Bane had cut him a stick to support himself, and he'd kicked the piss bottle under the bed.

'I'll come downstairs tomorrow and see you off,' he told Straccan, still panting from his efforts. 'And if you're following the old Roman way north you can look for me to catch you up in a week or so.'

'You should go home by sea,' Straccan said, dismissing the wildly optimistic 'week or so' without comment. 'It's a long hard ride to Scotland with a child along.'

'David's no trouble. It was a long ride to Bordeaux too, farther than from here to Scotland.'

'I'm not going for a holiday; it's penance. I'm not supposed to enjoy it. Bane's not coming with me and I don't think you should either.'

Miles looked contrite. 'I forgot. Perhaps we will go by sea.'

'What about the girl?'

'Sorrow? What about her?'

'Do you mean to take her to Coldinghame with you? I think Prior Radulfus might take a dim view.'

'Well, to tell you the truth, Richard, I don't know *what* to do about Sorrow.'

Roslyn sat on the river bank, just where – although she didn't know it – David had jumped in the water to find out if he could swim. It was a quiet place, out of sight of the manor, where no one was likely to come upon her, and there were no ghosts to distract her.

Round her neck on a thong hung a small bone flute. She'd found it that morning, concealed under a napkin at her place at table in the hall. There was no one to thank; only servants were present, tidying away pallets and blankets and setting up boards and trestles. It was early, breakfast hadn't yet been brought across from the kitchen, and without waiting for it she'd slipped out of the hall and across the yard, hoping guiltily that David wouldn't catch sight of her and follow. She had few opportunities to be alone, and she needed solitude now.

Someone wished her to have this gift privily, so she must take it in the same spirit, but she longed to know who it was had guessed her aching need for something, anything, that she could play. Her own flute had been sold to buy food for David at Montgey after her master's murder. He had died trying to save his harp, smashed by a crusader's mace. She'd found his broken body after a long search through the dead, his arms around the shattered frame of the harp Queen Eleanor herself had given him in his youth. Never had there been a sweeter voice than the harp Minoulet, lost now for ever, and mourned, even as she'd mourned her master.

Père Raimond . . . She missed him as she would a limb. For nine years he had been her teacher and father both, and she could barely remember the time before that. Her life had begun on the day he bought her.

Raimond de Sorules paid one Paris livre for the starveling urchin. He'd heard her singing in the market place, seen her scrabbling in the kennel for the rotten fruit thrown at her by those who thought it funny, and he followed her home. The mother was only too willing to be rid of her.

He scrubbed her in the horse trough at his inn. When he'd got the dirt off, most of it, washed her matted hair and de-loused her, he stood the small, trembling body on a barrel and walked around it with a critical eye, frowning at the raw weals on her knobby back and the bruises and bug bites on shins, ribs and arms.

The stable man sold him a pot of smelly salve. It stung, and tears rolled down her face, although she made no sound. He put one of his own shirts on her, far too big, but it would do for the time being. A length of twine served to girdle it so she wouldn't trip on the hem, and the innkeeper's wife, sorry for the big-eyed waif, plaited her hair in one long, thick braid and tied it with a twist of wool.

That night she ate her fill for the first time in all her seven years.

He made a nest of pillows for her in his bed. Seeing the stark terror in her eyes, he set the great hard bolster firmly between them, but she didn't sleep. Nor did he, and all that night, in the darkness, he could feel her desperate stare.

The stream sang quietly to itself. Père Raimond was dead, and his ghost had no place here. If the spirit of Raimond de Sorules was still earthbound, Roslyn thought, surely it wandered the bright roads of France, and played and sang at the courts of queens and princes. He would prefer that to the sterility of the Church's heaven.

She examined the flute. It was made from the leg bone of a large bird – a swan or perhaps an eagle. At last she put it to her lips. It had a sweet, slightly breathy voice, unlike any other she'd known. All instruments had their own voices, no two alike. She fingered through a scale, then the notes of a complicated little melody, an echo of the river's music.

She settled her back against the bole of a tree. She should have plenty of time. Everyone would be busy today, for on the morrow Sir Richard was leaving for London.

Leaving!

Who could have thought that the words of those silly love songs were true? This pain was real, like a hand squeezing her heart. She had never felt like this before. Why now? Why him? A knight! It would have been funny if it didn't hurt so much.

After tomorrow she would never see him again. *Be thankful, fool*, she told herself. *When he has gone, this pain can begin to wear away. No matter what the foolish songs say, no one ever died of love.*

She began to play. It seemed that the stream paused to listen, and the trees leaned towards her. Sunlight sifted through their branches, and she fancied that among the quivering leaves gleamed the green-gold laughing faces of the tree-sprites; or perhaps it was no fancy.

The people of Stirrup without exception, from Straccan's clerk Peter, an educated man, to Daft Harry who looked after the pigs, believed passionately in luck, both good and bad. Unabsolved sin, especially so grave a sin as breaking Sanctuary, could only bring bad luck to the sinner, and by extension to his kin, his household and his whole estate. So far the manor reckoned it had got off lightly. A cow had gone dry, a horse had gone lame, and the cowman's little daughter had fallen down the well. By the grace of God she'd been hauled up alive, but it was a warning. It followed that the lord of the manor's penance and subsequent absolution would remove the impediment to good fortune and set things to rights, bringing good luck to them all. They were delighted to see him set forth at last, and congregated at the gate to be sure of it. A little aside from the rest, Roslyn de Sorules and David watched too.

Sir Richard would have his daughter's company as far as the convent at Holystone, where she had spent her childhood. One of the other boarders, Millicent, was to be married, and Gilla was to be maid of honour at the wedding. Straccan led her palfrey out and waited to help her mount. He set his hands on her waist to lift her, dropping a kiss on the top of her head which now came as high as his breastbone. Mother of God, she was growing up!

From the bedchamber window above came a feeble shout. Straccan looked up at Miles and raised his hand in farewell. The morning light showed the young man clay-pale and very thin. The shirt he wore, one of Straccan's, hung from the bony points of his wide shoulders like a tent; but all the same he was on the mend. Brother Lucius was certain of it.

Straccan put his foot on the mounting block and swung up into the saddle. He wasn't taking Zingiber for this tedious plod up the country. He'd chosen Apple, a grey palfrey, and led a small stout nameless rouncey for his baggage. Gilla touched heels to her mount and rode out under the gatehouse arch. He followed. He wouldn't look back. He never looked back; it was bad luck.

He looked back. Everyone else was waving, but Roslyn had turned away. The early sun, rising above the east wall, haloed her like a martyr in a church window.

They reached Holystone in the afternoon, riding down to the nunnery from the low hill to the west. The convent's fields, crop and pasture, spread around it like a patchwork mantle in shades of green, and smoke was rising from all the kitchen chimneys. Villeins working in the fields straightened their backs to stare at the riders, grinning and shouting a welcome when they recognised Gilla. Near the gates they caught up with a group of lay sisters towing sleds laden with greenery, wild apple blossom and fresh rushes.

'Tis Gilla!'

'Come for the weddin', my duck?'

'Your turn next, eh?'

Gilla laughed, blushing, but the words wrung her father's heart. Her friend Millicent, the bride, was the same age as Gilla.

He should have arranged a marriage for her by now. He resolved to set about the matter as soon as he had finished his penitential journey.

Late that evening he stopped, sitting on a milestone to eat the bacon, bread and cheese Adeliza had packed. When the rouncey tossed its head and whickered, and both horses tilted their ears towards the scrub across the road, Straccan's hand was instantly on his sword hilt and he jumped to his feet, but it was only a dog – a bony dog, so dirty that its original colour couldn't be guessed. From beneath a hawthorn bush, the dog fixed him with a hungry stare from one eye. The other was closed, clotted with old blood, and flies kept trying to settle on it, making the animal twitch its head.

'Here, boy!'

Straccan fished a chunk of bacon fat from his dinner and lobbed it. The dog darted forward and snapped it in mid-flight so fast that he blinked. There was the creature, under its bush again as if it had never moved, but swallowing. Its balding, whip-like tail stirred the dead leaves, and a pink tongue lolled. He could swear it was grinning. He sighed and threw it the cheese. Followed by what was left of the bacon.

It was getting dark. There was an inn he knew, half a mile ahead. When he got up the dog slunk away into the brambles and didn't follow. Thank God for that.

He left early next morning. After a mile or two Apple snorted and stopped. Straccan and the horses looked back. The dog was following. It came no nearer when he halted, but sat in the road and shuffled the dust with its scabby tail. He rode on, and the dog trailed after him.

Chapter 14

L ike flies round fresh dung, beggars swarmed at the gates of the Bishop of Winchester's great house on the south side of the Thames. Dole of broken meats and gravy-soaked bread from the tables within was handed out every night after the bishop, his guests and household had dined. None went away empty, but anyone who ate as fast as he could and went back for more seldom got away with it. The almoner never forgot a face. It was only on his night off that there was any hope of cheating, but woe betide any fool that dared try; the beggars themselves would sort him out.

They had done so tonight. Their victim, a stranger in Southwark, hobbling round the corner as he carried off his second helping, dropped it and went reeling, gasping, from a punch in the belly. Tripped by a crutch thrust between his ankles and prone in the mud, he got as good a kicking as the regulars had ever enjoyed administering. Even the dogs had a go at him, snapping at his skinny legs as he tried to crawl away, ripping his long, bunchy, clerkish gown and squabbling over the pieces.

His chastisers scrabbled at him, snatching anything worth having – his sandals, his cloth bonnet – they'd have had the gown off him as well, but as one tore off the bonnet a cry went up.

''E's a priest! Look at 'is 'ead.'

They saw the stubbly tonsure and melted away with their booty into the clotted shadows, leaving their victim sprawled in the rain, bruised and bleeding.

It was some time before the quondam Father Paul stirred, groaned and got painfully to his feet. For a few moments more he stood swaying, dizzy and confused, trying to get his bearings. With a sudden gasp he thrust his hand into a pocket in the voluminous skirt of his gown, and sighed with relief to find he had not been robbed of its contents. Stumbling, lurching, he made his way along the river bank towards the stews, baths and brothels whose ground rent contributed a surprising sum to the bishop's non-judgemental and tolerant coffers. Garlanda was there, somewhere behind one of those doors, one of those shuttered windows. Shouting his leman's name he hammered on one door after another, kicking for good measure and throwing stones at the shutters when the doorwards refused to admit him.

'Bugger off, mate. We're shut. Even 'ores got to sleep.'

Tears, blood and mud masked his face, and worse when at last a shutter was flung back and the contents of a chamber pot were decanted on to his upturned hopeful countenance. Eventually, tired of the noise, the Bunch of Figs sent its burly doorwards out to put a stop to it. There was no knowing which of them dealt the blow that cracked his skull.

Bleeding from the ears, whimpering, and dying, although he didn't know it, he crawled through the dark empty alleys until he came to an open gate. A rift in the clouds let the moon light a refuge, a big yard and a shed under which stood a long cart piled with straw. He squirmed into it, pulling straw over himself so that no one would see him. He'd be safe here tonight; in the morning he'd try again to find his lover, and when he did they would flee and be married in France, where no one would know him for a renegade priest. They would need money, but through the thick layers of cloth he touched his pocket again, and was comforted.

He felt dreadfully ill, but he supposed he'd feel better by morning.

The Bishop of Winchester was at his Southwark house, and Straccan, who had gone first to Westminster, arrived late, having bribed the bridge gatekeeper to let him through after the bridge was closed for the night.

He was shown into the bishop's private chamber, where des Roches, looking tired and ill-tempered, was supping alone, dictating letters between mouthfuls to a pair of clerks. To Straccan's surprise, des Roches dismissed the clerks. It was such an extraordinary privilege to speak with the great man alone that he was immediately on his guard.

'Sit down, man. Have you supped?' The bishop waved a hand at the dishes before him. 'Help yourself. Everything's ready for you; the bell will be loaded at first light. You can be first across the bridge and out of London before the streets get busy.'

'What about the team from Coldinghame?' Straccan asked.

Des Roches gave a derisive snort. 'Team! Just the sub-prior and two novices. Fat lot of use they'll be. Now look, Straccan.' He set his elbows on the board. 'Nothing must go wrong with this business. You get the bell to Durham safely, and I'll not forget it. You'll find my goodwill worth having.'

Straccan looked enquiringly at him. 'It's just a simple matter of transport, isn't it, my lord? Or is there more to it than you mentioned before?'

Des Roches chewed his lower lip and pushed a dish of dried apricots towards Straccan. 'I have a . . . personal interest in the matter,' he said presently. *Here it comes*, thought Straccan. 'You see,' the bishop continued, 'my sister's husband died abroad, on pilgrimage . . .' And he launched into an account of Earl Joceran's misfortune, and his devoted widow's wish to be buried with her dead lord's head.

Straccan listened, fascinated.

'So the lady has her way at last,' he said when the bishop had, apparently, finished.

'Ah – well. No, not yet. My sister wasn't a well woman, not well at all, but try telling her that! Her physician tried, and she sent him off with a flea in his ear, but he was right: the long journey was too much for her. I implored her to stay here until she was stronger, but no, she must go home. She got as far as York, and there she discovered that her husband's head was no longer in its casket. It had been stolen, and this left in its place.' Des Roches reached under the table into a cupboard, and set a small round hairy object among the dishes. It was the size of a newborn child's head, but uglier than most.

'Jesus! What is it?'

The bishop glowered at it. 'Some sort of monkey.'

Straccan picked it up. It sat in the palm of his hand and leered at him.

'It's dried, like those mummified things that turn up in the Egyptian desert,' he said, examining it. 'It must have been a shock for your sister.'

'It was. And the shock, after the journey, was too much for her. She died at York.'

'I'm sorry.'

The bishop sighed. 'She was past seventy. How far past she never would say, but she'd had a good run. Her body was coffined at York and sent on to Coldinghame. And there it waits, above ground, for the monks can't bury it until the missing head turns up. She made sure of that.'

She had. She had bequeathed her lands and fortune, half to her brother and half to the priory, on condition that her body and her lord's head were entombed together according to her wish. If this should not be done, for whatever reason, the whole lot would go instead to the Cistercians at Mailros. The will was valid and unchallengable. Abbot Robert de Longchamp at York, with his prior and no less than six of the obedientaries, had witnessed it. Lapped in lead, Lady Judith awaited her obsequies, and failing the head neither Bishop Peter nor Prior Radulfus would see a penny.

'Abbot Robert sent that bloody thing to me,' des Roches said, flicking a finger at the monkey's head. 'Does it look like it's laughing to you? Does to me.'

'I suppose it does,' said Straccan, who felt a bit like laughing himself but hid it well. The monkey's eyes were like raisins, and its thin lips had shrunk away from the unpleasantly large brown teeth. 'When do you think it happened?'

'The substitution? Abbot Robert said Judith was certain it happened while she was here at Winchester House.'

Straccan set the little head down carefully, wiped his hands on the tablecloth and picked up a quail. 'Why did she think that?'

'While she was here she dismissed her chaplain, a lewd fellow who was caught in the carnal act with his concubine. She had the woman sent to the Bankside stews, and turned Father Paul off without wages. A trifle harsh, perhaps, but it was her household to order as she pleased.'

'You think the chaplain stole the head?'

'My sister was certain of it,' the bishop said. 'She cursed him on her deathbed.'

'But you haven't found him yet.'

'No, but I will. I think he'll ask a ransom for it – why else steal it? And anyway, it's hard for a priest to disappear; they tend to stick out among common men.'

Straccan finished his meal and stood up. 'With your leave, my lord, I'll get some sleep.'

'Of course. Oh, one other thing . . .'

Straccan paused at the door.

'I've some relics here, part of the spine of Saint Gudula and some ribs, to go to Waltham and Cambridge. You might as well take them, Straccan; you'll be trundling right past their gates. Doesn't matter who gets what, as long as they get three bones apiece. My secretary will pack them up. You can take them with you in the morning.'

Straccan was at the bell founder's yard soon after dawn, but the bell was already on the wagon when he got there, and the slow business of harnessing the oxen – twenty-two of them – carried

82

on while the master carter came to greet him, doffing his cap and sizing him up with an experienced eye. *Just how much of a bloody nuisance will you be?* that eye wondered. Straccan answered it by demanding how many spare wheels and axles were to be carried, and where the bloody hell were they?

Two young men in Benedictine novice garb were helping harness the animals. They appeared to be wearing leg irons, but nevertheless seemed very cheerful as they worked. Straccan turned his attention to the cart. Its flatbed was mounted on eight iron-shod wheels, and above these the great bell Gaudete, shrouded in sailcloth and roped to the thickly strawed wagon bed, towered like one of the small domed mosques Straccan had seen in the Holy Land. It didn't look as if anything, oxen or even elephants, could hope to get it moving. The master carter was shouting at someone about the spare wheels and axles. Spare iron tyres and shoes for the oxen were further necessities, Straccan thought, and if there wasn't a smith in the company he'd have to hire one.

As he walked round the wagon his eye was caught by several small shiny things tied to the ropes that bound the bell. He scrambled up on to the cart to look. Pilgrim badges – the cockleshell of Saint James, the ampoule of Saint Thomas – and there were scraps of coloured rag and bits of old parchment too – prayers, by God – tucked underneath the ropes.

The smoke of a cook-fire rose from the adjoining yard. Straccan pushed open the gate and looked in. The yard was full of activity: tents had apparently been set up overnight and were now being dismantled and packed away; there were men and women, children too, three mules, a couple of dejected pack-horses, and several small two-wheeled carts parked with their shafts stuck up in the air. A woman at the cook-fire was ladling breakfast pottage into bowls for a dozen or more people who grinned and waved and called greetings when they saw Straccan.

'God save ye, me lord!'

'Fine day, sir!'

Straccan called the carter over. 'Who are all those people?'

'Oh, them. Them's pilgrims, me lord,' the man said, staring glassily past Straccan's shoulder with a look that said 'Nothing to do with me, squire' louder than words.

'Pilgrims.' He might have known. 'What are they doing here?'

'They're coming with us.'

'Who says?'

'Brother Mungo.'

'Where's Brother Mungo?'

The carter jerked a thumb in the direction of the bell founder's cubbyhole. With a thunderous expression Straccan strode over to it.

Brother Mungo, Coldinghame's sub-prior, with two sturdy young novices, Aidan and Finan, had come from Berwick by ship to London to escort the great bell back to their monastery. The young men, cheerful and willing volunteers, had never been farther from the convent than their very local home villages. At first they were alarmed, and then excited by the size and splendours of London. Indeed, its temptations had quite overcome them: they were caught sneaking back to their lodging at Winchester House after a disreputable foray into Bankside, an experience bought at the cost of ten lashes apiece – cheap at the price, they reckoned.

Although condemned to wear irons and subsist on bread and water until well clear of London, and with the rough frieze of their habits sticking painfully to their bloody stripes, they had helped load the bell in the foundry yard as soon as dawn gave enough light. It was a dangerous job, lowering the huge bell on to the cart, but they clapped on to ropes and heaved with all the goodwill in the world. Their backs might be sore, their ankles galled, but they'd be the envy of the dormitory when they got home.

The sub-prior, a man afflicted with the unfortunate combination of a yellow complexion and bright ginger eyebrows, looked up from the map laid out and held down with iron wool-weights on Master Hare's table.

'The pilgrims? What about them? They are glad to travel with us, for protection on the road.'

'Where are they going?' Straccan asked. Probably to the Holy Rood at Waltham. Thirteen miles. Two days, with luck.

The monk looked puzzled. 'To Saint Cuthbert, of course. Bishop Peter gave them his blessing yesterday. They won't be any bother, I'm sure.'

'They'd better not be,' Straccan growled. All the way to Durham! Des Roches reminded him of Cammo, his steward, who also didn't believe in giving a man one job if he could manage two or more.

Mungo was staring past him with an expression of disgust.

'Don't let that fleabag in here!'

'What?'

'Your dog.'

Straccan spun on his heel. The dog was just a few feet behind him, scratching with enthusiasm.

'It's not my dog.'

The monk picked up a wool-weight, and yelped in annoyed surprise as Straccan struck it from his hand.

'Leave it alone!'

Gaudy rode high above their heads. A complicated web of ropes encasing the padded sailcloth cover lashed the bell to the cart, itself strengthened with iron bands. The carter cracked his long whip over the backs of the oxen and uttered encouraging howls. The beasts lowered their heads and strained forwards. Slowly, reluctantly, the great wagon began moving, and the supply wagons and the rest of the company fell in behind.

Chapter 15

Oxen couldn't be hurried. Given good weather and something more or less recognisable as a road, they could haul their burden no more than nine miles in a day, while five was as much as one could hope for over the broken, holed, boggy tracks that made up most of England's highways. But the Great North Road, following the line of the old Ermine Way, was better than most, at least for thirty miles or so beyond London. Unless it rained, and it didn't look like it, the bell should reach Waltham the day after tomorrow.

The Romans had laid the Ermine Way a thousand years ago, and although long stretches of it were now lost to flood and forest, its stones plundered to build walls and foundations, a hawk's eye would still see the pale, sure line running north, broken here and there only to reappear further on, mile after mile, all the way to the border of the wild Scots' land and even beyond. Some folk thought it ran to the edge of the world.

The bell and its escort, carts, pack animals and gaggle of pilgrims, put Straccan in mind of a band of cheap mercenaries – undisciplined, unsightly and noisy. The sub-prior rode ahead, with the two novices one each side of the bell cart, while Straccan ranged up and down the length of the column, and the pilgrims brought up the rear. One, better off than the others, rode a donkey; the rest – one poor fellow dragged himself on crutches – plodded along, some carrying their baggage on their backs, others pulling little handcarts with their babies and children within.

At first, as they crossed the bridge and marched through London, with folk flocking out of shops and alleys and hanging out of windows to see them pass, the pilgrims had sung hymns, the quavering music scarcely to be heard over the shattering din of the cart's iron-shod wheels on the suffering cobbles. As the morning passed, the oxen plodding stolidly and uneventfully on, the pilgrims fell silent and dropped behind until they were out of sight; but mid-morning, when the bell wain halted at the roadside, they caught up again, busying themselves with bread and cheese and ale. Women fed babies, children chased one another with piercing squeals and those unused to walking took off their shoes and tended their feet.

The tallest and most tattered pilgrim to Saint Cuthbert, who had appointed himself leader by virtue of having been there before, had contrived to fashion a banner and daub on it a figure of the saint wearing a bright yellow halo and a misogynistic scowl. Bearing this, the staff's end resting in a leather cup attached to his belt, Luke marched before the others and planted the banner beside the road while they dined in its shadow.

There was no sign of the man on crutches, but by the time they'd finished their dinners he could be seen toiling along in the distance.

'Why don't 'e ride in one of the carts?' someone asked. 'Plenty of room and comfy too, in with the beasts' fodder.'

'Carter offered, but he's made a vow to go all the way afoot.'

'Poor sod,' said the first speaker.

Several among the company shared his sympathy, and when they halted for the night Wilfred found himself on the receiving end of small kindnesses: strips of cloth to pad the armrests of his crutches, soup kept hot for him, a damp rag to wipe the dust from his mouth and eyes.

The beasts were unharnessed, and hobbled or tethered to graze; water was brought for them, and the first day of Gaudy's journey was over.

Straccan saw to his horses, set up his small tent and put his saddlebags and gear inside. When he'd done the rounds of the makeshift overnight camp, with a word for everyone and trying to fit names to faces, he returned to his tent, shucked off his boots, unbuckled his belt, stretched, yawned and shook out his bedroll. All things considered, it hadn't been a bad day. Uneventful, dull even, which was all to the good. If boredom was the worst he would have to endure on this penitential journey, he'd be getting off lightly.

At least, thank God, he'd been too busy to think about . . . well, magic.

Like most men – sensible ones, anyway – Straccan feared and mistrusted magic. But, good or evil, it was a fact of life, and even sensible men couldn't always avoid it. He in particular couldn't avoid it as the woman he loved and hoped to marry was a witch.

Janiva . . . Where was she? What was she doing? Helping folks in trouble, Osyth had said, and that trouble had to do with morthwork. He crossed himself. Sorcery meant danger. Whatever she was doing, wherever she was, there would certainly be danger. And in some place where she was in danger she had left her sleeping body, put it off like an empty shift, to come to Miles's aid. Far-journeying, Gilla called it, but she didn't know how it was done. Suppose someone, an enemy, had come upon Janiva, apparently asleep, helpless, while her spirit was far-journeying?

She knows what she's doing, he told himself. 'She's strong,' Osyth had said. And even if he knew where she was, he must leave her alone. But he ached to hold her in his arms; only then could he know she was safe.

With a sigh, he took up the small chest containing Saint Gudula's relics and sat down to pick out the three bones he was to deliver to Waltham Abbey on the morrow. Sliding his fingers gently through the sheep's-wool packing, he felt the irregular shapes of the small bones – knobbly vertebrae, slender ribs – and something hard and round that was neither part of a spine nor a rib. He pulled it out.

The wizened face of the mummified monkey grinned at him. The bishop's damned fool of a secretary had packed that as well.

Chapter 16

S trong men make the worst invalids, and now that his strength was returning, albeit in a somewhat tiptoe fashion at first, Miles wanted to go down to the hall for dinner.

'I shall get up today,' he announced. 'I shall get up and dress and eat downstairs like a Christian. I've had enough of bed.'

'That monk says you must lie abed another week,' Roslyn said. She was sitting, cross-legged like a tailor, playing chess with him on his bed, while David, on the floor beside them, played at knights with little figures Bane had crafted from twigs and straw.

'Brother Lucius is a good fellow, but he underestimates the Hoby powers of recovery. Where are my clothes?'

'What about your beard?' David asked.

Miles rubbed his chin. He hadn't shaved since leaving Rouen. 'I'm sure I can borrow a razor,' he said.

The child eyed him doubtfully. 'Are you going to fall down again?'

'I hope not, imp!'

It was a near thing, all the same. The solid stone steps felt like jelly under his feeble legs, and by the time he reached the table sweat had soaked through his shirt, and he subsided palely into a chair with a gasp of relief, vastly pleased that he'd made it but secretly dismayed at the effort it cost him. The next day he was shocked to find his sword so heavy that his arm trembled when he held it up. He felt as he had when, as a small boy, he'd tried to wield his father's sword but with both hands could hardly lift it.

He would talk to the smith. He must strengthen his arms; they were as weak as a maid's.

The smith obligingly produced half a dozen iron bars of different thicknesses and weights, and Miles began a series of exercises, starting with the lightest bars and practising every day. Every day, too, he walked, morning and evening, as far as he could, until his legs felt like seaweed; then he would push himself to walk further next time, returning to the hall for dinner, ravenous.

There was no dais in the hall, no high table. If Straccan

89

needed to address his household he would stand on a bench or on the board itself. Trestles and boards were set up in a T, family and guests at the top, and the rest of the household down the tail of the T, at which twenty could sit with elbow room, thirty if squashed up.

'Who cooks for you at home?' Adeliza asked Miles. She was delighted at the return of his appetite, and had organised something of a minor feast in celebration.

'Our meals are sent over from the priory kitchen. Good plain fare, with treats on feast days,' said Miles. 'But I'll miss your cooking when I go home.' He looked along the board at the pies and puddings, and the gleaming breasts of roast duck and chicken. 'This is a fine feast.'

David looked up, eyes bright. 'A feast should have music!' There had always been music at the castle he sometimes dreamed about.

'Why, we can do music, my love,' said Adeliza. 'Fulbert has a tabor, and Bane has a bagpipe.'

'If Sorrow still had her flute, she'd play for us,' Miles said. 'But she sold it somewhere along the way, to buy food for us.'

Roslyn said, 'I have another.' She looked at the eager faces along the board, wondering *Who gave it to me? Was it you, or you?* And *Was it him?* Well, what if it was? He was gone now. It was a casual kindness, nothing more. *But he looked back*, her treacherous heart reminded her. *He did look back!* And the ache under her breast that came whenever she thought of him loosed its grip as she took out the flute. 'Would you like me to play?'

David clapped his hands. 'Play, Roslyn! Play for us!'

The hall erupted into activity, tables cleared away and benches dragged into a circle, with a stool in the centre for the glee-maiden. Someone was sent at a run to the farm cotts, and presently a dozen more folk came hurrying for the entertainment; by the time they were all settled they numbered twenty or more.

Roslyn took her place in the centre, and bowed to David.

'Young sir, what would you like to hear?'

David banged on the table with his spoon. ' "Puddings and Pies"!'

She began to play. 'Puddings and Pies' was a merry, gambolling tune that set feet tapping until the listeners could no longer bear to sit but pulled the benches back to make room and danced around the player, sending the fresh straw flying under their heels. At last they collapsed, scarlet and out of breath, and began calling out names of tunes, while Roslyn played snatches of each.

In Adeliza's lap, David was losing the battle to stay awake. There were bits of straw in his curls, and she gently teased them out. His eyelids drooped, and opened again, and stayed closed at last. He was only still when asleep. From cock-crow to cock-shut his day was one of constant activity: under everyone's feet, always asking questions, in the kitchen, in the stable, in the smithy. Sometimes he still woke crying, from God knew what dream-terrors, but not so often now. Cradling him in her lap, delighting in his solid weight and warmth, and the sweet scent of his flesh, Adeliza marvelled at the change in him, from terrified starveling to joyous innocent. The whole manor would be sorry when Miles was full well again, and must take David away.

Seeing the sleeping child, Roslyn played a lullaby. The hall could not have been more still if it had been empty. At Adeliza's feet Bane sat in the straw, hugging his knees, and never took his eyes from Roslyn.

Chapter 17

Straccan was dragged from a deep sleep by the sound of screaming. His body reacted before his mind caught up, scrambling out of the blankets, snatching up his sword and shucking off the scabbard before he was fully awake. The screaming went on but had begun to crack and splinter, and there were other voices, excited, frightened. He tore at the tent flap and burst out into darkness.

A sudden flare of light as someone lit a torch showed the screamer – a woman in her shift, mouth stretched wide – and someone on his knees over a dark huddle on the ground, a man's body. Straccan reached them, swearing as his foot skidded in a pile of ox dung.

'Is he dead? Who is he?'

The kneeling man looked up, and the torch lit the worried face of Brother Mungo.

'His heart's beating,' the monk said shakily. 'He's the cowman – Giles, I think.'

'Bring that torch over here,' Straccan called. One of the novices, Aidan, Finan, he didn't know which, brought the torch and held it over the man while Straccan searched for a wound, and finding none, turned his attention to the head. There was a lump at the back of the skull.

'What happened?' Straccan turned to the woman, who had stopped screaming and begun to take an interest.

'I just come out for a pee and fell over him,' she said. 'Ain't he dead, then?' She sounded disappointed.

'No. Did you see anyone else?'

'Just Brother here,' she said, with a jerk of her chin at the sub-prior.

'I heard her scream and ran out to help,' the monk said, getting to his feet. The whole camp had heard her scream. Some in shirts, some in shifts and some with blankets clutched round their nakedness, they had come from their tents and shelters, bringing more lights. The man on the ground grunted and opened his eyes.

92

'Me beasts,' he said, sitting up suddenly. 'There was some bugger in among the beasts!' And he threw up all over himself.

'Aidan, Finan, pick this poor fellow up and take him to our tent,' said Brother Mungo. 'Put him on my pallet— Ah, better give him a wash first.'

'Good idea,' said Straccan, relieving Finan of the torch. 'I'll be along in a minute.' He headed for the oxen hobbled behind the camp, a darker mass in the darkness.

In the candlelit dimness of Brother Mungo's tent, the cowman was enjoying being the centre of attention. 'I 'eard somefing,' he said, when Straccan came in. 'The beasts was uneasy-like, you know? Snorting and stamping. I got up, and saw some bugger creeping round among their legs. I said, "Oi!" I dunno what 'appened then. My 'ead don't arf 'urt!'

Holding a candle close to Giles's face, the monk peered into his frightened eyes, and then setting the candle down gently felt Giles's skull, with an odd listening expression as if he expected to hear the bone crack.

'No crepitation,' he murmured. 'Your head's not broken, but you'll have headaches for a while.'

'Got one now, ain't I!'

A worried-looking young lad pushed his way into the tent. 'All right, Dad?'

'No I ain't bloody all right! Do I look all right?' But he gave the boy a rough hug and held on to him.

'You saw someone,' Straccan said.

'That's right.'

'How? It's a dark night, no moon.'

'Well, I dunno, but I saw . . . Yes! There was a torch, stuck in the ground. That's 'ow I saw 'im – I yelled at 'im, and it went dark again. What 'appened?'

'He dashed the torch out and hit you with it,' Straccan said. 'I found it.' He held up the charred stump. 'Did you see his face?'

'No. Just a shape.'

'Well, whoever it was, he was trying to lame the beasts. I found this too.' Straccan held out a short-handled knife with dried blood on its slim blade. 'He must have dropped it when you called out. I found two of the oxen limping.'

Giles surged up from the pallet, wincing at the hammer blow of his headache. 'Lame my oxen? Why would anyone do that?'

'I don't know. It looks as if someone doesn't like you.'

Giles thought for a bit. 'There's Sam Atwood – 'e wanted this job. 'E wasn't too chuffed when I got it. But no, 'e'd never 'urt the beasts.'

'Put a night watch on them from now on,' said Straccan. 'You and your boy. Just in case whoever it was tries to finish what he started.'

He returned to his tent but got no more sleep during what was left of the dark hours. The cowman's question kept him wakeful. Why would anyone try to lame the oxen?

The queen was in her bower. The perfumed room was very warm, heated by two charcoal braziers, and hung with some of the bright tapestries that the king's mother, Queen Eleanor, had brought to England, depicting – what else? – scenes of love. The murmurs and chirpings and occasional bursts of song of many small birds filled the chamber; there were small bright-plumaged birds in cages everywhere.

'Madame,' said one of her women with a sly smile, 'your champion is here.'

Tyrrel entered the bower, bowing very low. 'Madame, will you give me leave to go to my manor at Locksey? Affairs there need my attention.'

The radiant smile that still curved her lips as she turned to him had been for her pretty finches, not for him, but he didn't know that, and his heart beat faster.

'But of course, Sir Ralf.'

One of her women said, 'Whatever shall we do without you, Sir Ralf?' and the rest of the empty-headed sluts giggled. He waited to be dismissed, but Isabel had turned back to her birds; she had one perched on her finger, and was coaxing it to peck a morsel of cake from between her lips.

The finch took flight, and clung to the bed curtains while the women squealed and twittered.

'It is so sad,' Isabel said with a deep sigh. 'They die. They last no time at all. Some only a few days.'

She took no further notice of her champion as he backed, bowing, to the door. Indeed, she had already forgotten him.

The whore was cheating, showing off to the dark eye that watched her through the judas hole. On the other side of the wall the king's spymaster, known as Mercredi, nodded appreciatively at the deft way she palmed the true dice and substituted the false. A pity to waste such artistry when it wasn't needful. She could have lifted her client's purse entire

94

and anything else she fancied – his belt with its handsome Welsh-knot buckle, his dagger, the silver clasp at his collar, the gold ring on his finger – hell, she could strip him stark naked and he wouldn't notice.

It wasn't so much the wine he'd drunk, although he'd drunk a good deal. Enough, perhaps, to make the drug unnecessary, but you couldn't take chances in this business. Mercredi watched as she snapped her fingers before the man's unfocused, glassy grin. No reaction. With practised efficiency she rifled his pockets – nothing there – and turned her attention to his scrip. Nothing there either, except his money, which she didn't touch. She paused for a moment, frowning, then unbuckled his belt and slid it through her fingers. A nod of satisfaction, and from the secret pocket in its lining she eased out a flat oilskin packet.

Clever girl! Wasted on this job, Mercredi thought, but where else could he use her? She was young and still pretty, but with that appalling Bankside accent it wasn't possible to place her anywhere other than in a kitchen or stew. She slid aside a panel in the wall and thrust the packet through.

In his cramped, airless office – a secret cubbyhole between two bedrooms in this quayside brothel – Mercredi examined the seal on the packet and set to work with a heated blade. The letter wasn't long. His lips pursed in a soundless whistle as he read it. He copied it quickly, refolded and rewrapped it, expertly re-affixed the seal and tapped on the panel. The whore took the packet and put it back in her client's belt, buckling it round his girth again.

'Wazzat?' he said thickly, opening glazed eyes and groping at her bosom.

'Nothin', me duck,' she crooned. 'You 'ave a nice kip. You won't miss your ship, I promise. I'll wake you.'

Mercredi rolled and sealed his copy of the letter, and rang the bell for one of his boys. As usual, two turned up at a run, each trying to elbow the other aside and bag the errand. The bigger won. Half a dozen urchins kept their souls in their bodies in his service, running errands and taking messages. He paid them – very little – and gave them a dry place to sleep, but that was more than any of them could have hoped for otherwise.

'Take this to Winchester House; give it to the bishop's secretary, no one else.'

The lad took the letter, tucked it out of sight under his ragged shirt and turned to leave, bumping into a new arrival, a ragged, pungent beggar who had climbed the stairs as quietly as a cat.

Unsurprised, the boy ducked under the beggar's arm and ran down the stairs two at a time.

Mercredi leaned back in his chair and looked at his visitor with disapproval. Starling Larktwist was one of his best agents and possessed a natural talent for deception coupled with a surprising intelligence, but he had an unfortunate predilection for muck. 'Did you *have* to come like that?'

The man looked down at his tatters. 'These are me working clothes. Your message said come at once.'

'Anything to report at Baynard's Castle?' Mercredi asked.

'FitzWalter ain't come out all day. De Vesci and Percy went in. Still there when I left.'

Mercredi made a note on his wax tablet. 'You won't be going back there, Larktwist. I've another assignment for you.'

The ragged man looked interested. 'What?'

'The man you saw last week at fitzWalter's meeting, Ralf Tyrrel. He's asked leave to go to his manor at Locksey, near Cambridge. There's a horse for you at Bishopsgate. Go to Locksey, talk to people, see who comes and goes. Your contact is the landlord of the Yellow Hawk in Cambridge, William Dewer. If Tyrrel leaves Locksey, tell Dewer and follow.'

Larktwist sniffed. 'What about money?'

Mercredi pushed a purse across the table, and Larktwist secreted it somewhere among his tatters, scratching as he felt the migration of a tribe of lice from armpit to groin.

Mercredi frowned. 'Locksey's a small place; you can't pass as a beggar there, and they'll drive lepers out, so get yourself cleaned up. Look respectable – if you can.'

'Course I can,' said Larktwist, affronted. He knew how to mix with nobs, if the need arose. He hitched his rags about himself with dignity and turned to leave. 'Trust me.'

'A touch of refinement wouldn't go amiss.'

'You want refinement? Easy! I'll be as refined as a nun.'

As he reached the door Mercredi said, 'And Larktwist . . .'

'Yes?'

'Stick to him.'

'Oh, I will, sir. Like shit to a blanket.'

Chapter 18

A cometary tail of human misery and optimism trailed behind
the bell. More pilgrims had joined them on the road, some
lame, a few blind; and a group of barefoot sack-clad penitents
had seized the chance to tag along as far as Waltham, lashing
themselves with little whips as they trudged and loudly confess-
ing their sins to all and sundry.

On the evening of the second day the square tower of
Waltham abbey church was sighted, and a dusty cheer went up
from the pilgrims, who quickened their pace to close the gap
between them and the bell. Tonight they would sleep at
Waltham Holy Cross. Tomorrow they would pray in the abbey
church, see – and perhaps be permitted to kiss – the relics, and
thus spiritually fortified, begin the next leg of their journey.

Gaudy trundled through the town with a din of iron-studded
wheels on cobbles, fetching folk from their suppers to see what
all the racket was. The oxen were loosed to graze in one of the
abbey's water meadows, while carters, smith and cowman set up
camp. Pilgrims and penitents were given the hospitality of the
abbey's hospice, Brother Mungo and the two novices welcomed
into the community for the night, and Straccan, having chosen
two vertebrae and one rib of Saint Gudula from the chest, went
in search of the sacristan.

Inside the splendid, cross-shaped church the miraculous Black
Rood hung over the west door, veiled now, of course, because of
the Interdict. None in all England might gaze on the crucified
Christ while its king persisted in his wicked flouting of the Pope.
Under the pall that covered it the black stone crucifix was
encased in a latticework of silver, rich with gems. Since its
miraculous discovery in the time of King Canute, the rood had
had a history of marvellous cures. It had healed King Harold in
the days before the Norman bastard seized the kingdom; healed
him of a palsy that had held him bedfast for a year. In gratitude
Harold had built this church, and ever since, pilgrims had
flocked to it with prayers and offerings, until the abbey was one
of the richest in the land.

When the delicate little bones of Saint Gudula had been deposited in a fine gilded copper reliquary and safely locked away, the sacristan invited Straccan to dine and sleep in the abbey's comfortable guest quarters. Thinking of his hard bedroll, he was tempted but stood firm. He was a penitent like any other, and soft lying had no place in this journey.

The sacristan walked with him to the west end of the church. The great doors, which stood wide open all day, were closed now for the night, but folk could still come and go by the wicket door cut in one of them. A few pilgrims had chosen to spend the night near the rood and were busily spreading their bedrolls, out of the draught. The sick on their litters, unable to move, had to put up with it. As Straccan picked his way through the prone bodies he saw a young woman kneeling on the worn flags under the rood, staring up at it, her lips moving soundlessly. It was so cold in the church that her prayer was visible, each word a little puff of mist. As he approached with the sacristan, she made an end, crossed herself and got up. The hood of her mantle fell back, revealing hair as fair as moonlight.

'Still here, Emma? It's near dark. I'll get someone to take you home,' said the sacristan, looking about and beckoning to one of the canons, who was replacing the burned-down candles.

'I should be honoured to escort the lady,' Straccan offered, but the everyday courtesy met with a surprising response: sudden fear widened the girl's eyes and she stepped back.

'No!'

'It's all right, Emma,' the sacristan said. 'Brother Ailred will walk home with you.'

With a nervous glance at Straccan the girl drew her mantle closely around her and followed Brother Ailred out through the small door.

'What was that about?' Straccan asked. 'I just offered to take her home and she looked scared out of her wits.'

'Don't be offended, Sir Richard. She has reason to fear. Just a year ago her sister Ailith was taken on her way home from this church, and never seen again. Twins, they were, as like as peas in a pod.'

'What d'you mean, "taken"?'

'Their father had died not long before and they were unhappy because there could be no masses said for him, because of the Interdict. They took it in turns to come, each evening, and pray for his soul. It was Ailith's turn. It was about this time of evening, growing dark, when she left here. When she didn't come home

Emma raised the alarm, and their neighbours turned out to search for her, but found no sign. A beggar-boy said he saw a man stop and speak to her, and that she went with him as if she knew him. But Emma said her sister knew no men, and wouldn't have done that. Whatever happened, she was never seen again.' He sighed. 'Now Emma comes, each evening, to pray for her sister's return, or if she is dead, for the peace of her soul.'

A sad tale, thought Straccan, as he headed for the camp. But no doubt the missing girl had a secret lover, and had run off with him.

It took eight days to reach Cambridge, eight days that put ten years on Straccan. If to begin with he'd thought his penance light, he knew better now. There were the carters, who stuck to the rules of their guild with dogged determination: only so many hours driving in a day and not a minute more, dinner at noon and supper at dusk, and to each man his allowance of ale – good ale – or else. There were the oxen, who seemed to know they were two short and to resent it, who must be fed and watered and pastured and never hurried, and who proceeded at the pace of the slowest and knew to the minute when it was time to halt, and halted then no matter where they were, even in the middle of a ford. There was Brother Mungo, a Jeremiah anticipating disaster at every turn, who managed, without even trying, to magnify every difficulty, making the carters uneasy and the mules skittish. There were the pilgrims, oh God, there were the pilgrims. And there was the dog.

Long before they reached Cambridge Straccan found himself the reluctant judge-arbiter in all disputes. Despite telling the pilgrims their affairs were none of his, they persisted in asking his advice and bombarding him with their complaints and demands for redress and/or retribution. The days resolved themselves into a series of halts, minor accidents, altercations, decisions revised again and again, problems and quarrels that escalated into fights. He confiscated the pilgrims' daggers, leaving them just their eating knives, but it was surprising the amount of damage they could inflict on one another with those. There was always somebody bandaged. And at every halt, and even while on the road, there was an unceasing chorus of protest and complaint.

'No 'ard standing 'ere, sir!'

'Pull to the roadside, then, and stay there tonight.'

'Sir Richard, you don't give us time for our orisons.'

'Pray faster, brother.'

'Sir! Woodbine's cast a shoe!'

'Halt! Where's the smith? You, Tom, set up your forge.'

'Sir! Another bloody axle's broke!'

'Halt! Bring up another one.'

'Sir, the beer barrel's leaked into the flour!'

'Halt!'

'Sir! Bowlegs's baby's got spots!'

'Oh God!'

He'd seen nothing of the dog since leaving London and had actually forgotten it until it turned up again on the third night after leaving Waltham Holy Cross. The company had halted outside the village of Durslea, descending on its small church like a plague of locusts to pray and leave offerings at the obscure shrine of the even more obscure Saint Wilphege – a local saint not recognised ('yet' said the villagers) by Rome. It was a well kept church, maintained by the lord of the manor and housing in some splendour the tombs of his forbears. The life-sized image in marble of the present lord's grandfather, Philip d'Espere, lay at peace with crossed ankles and hands clasped in prayer upon a low table-like tomb. Straccan, kneeling before the altar for a quiet word with God, heard a prolonged sound, like dried peas falling on the stone floor.

''Ere,' said a grubby child reproachfully. 'Your dog's widdlin' on Sir Philip!'

'It's not *my* dog,' said Straccan crossly. Nevertheless, he looped his belt round the creature's neck – it was grinning, he was sure of it – and towed it out of the church, flinging a penny to the scandalised child. Outside the church he let the dog go, and it trotted off as if it had affairs of importance somewhere close by. Straccan went back to the camp, only to be interrupted in the middle of his solitary supper by an indignant delegation of the cowman, his boy, the two carters and the smith.

'Me lord, your dog's pinched our dinner!'

He followed them to the cart under which the criminal sat, panting around a mouthful of dusty feathers and scaly yellow legs. Its tail gently thumped the ground when it saw him.

'It's not my dog,' he said.

In the morning things started as they were to go on. Hotly pursued by a laughing Brother Finan, the dog fled with the Benedictines' breakfast bacon clamped in its jaws and squeezed in under the bottom of Straccan's tent just as he was pulling on his boots. The novice poked his head through the flap.

'Beg pardon, sir. Your dog—'

'It's not my dog!'

'Oh? Sorry, sir, but—'

'What?'

'Can we have our bacon back?'

Straccan fixed the dog with a severe glare. 'Put it down,' he said. Rather to his surprise it obeyed, and stepped back wagging its tail. He picked up the dusty, beslobbered, fatty hunk of meat and offered it to Brother Finan, who wiped it on the skirt of his gown and bore it away.

The dog looked reproachfully at Straccan. He stared back and began to laugh.

'All right, you win!' He was lumbered with it. Resigned to the inevitable, he took the dog down to the river and gave it a bath. Clean at last, it proved to be white, with reddish ears. Shockingly bony with long legs and the overlarge feet of a young dog, a hound, it was no more than a year old, he reckoned, and its feet not mutilated as demanded by Forest Law; lost from someone's hunting pack, and now in spite of all denials, *his* dog.'

He'd have to give it a name.

A hesitant voice, a woman's voice, cut in on his musings. 'Sir . . .' She was small, thin, old. No, when he really looked at her, she was probably only in her twenties; she had lost her front teeth and was so tanned by wind and sun that she looked much older, but her eyes were still young, the colour of bluebells, and fixed imploringly on him.

He bowed. 'Your servant, mistress.'

'Sir, will you let us join your company? We are bound for Durham, to Saint Cuthbert, and a monk at Waltham told me you are going there.'

'Come if you wish, and welcome,' Straccan said. 'How many are in your party?'

'Just me and my son. I am Lucy Boteler, his name is Lawrence.'

'Do you have horses? Or a cart?'

'No, I walk. I will keep up. We will not trouble you.'

There were twenty or more folk following on foot now, in the vast dust cloud raised by the carts. Not all were pilgrims; several were just travellers glad of the security offered by the large company, and at every stopping place some left to go their ways and a few more tagged on.

'Where is your son?' Straccan asked.

She pointed at her bundle, or what he'd thought was her bundle, on the ground a few yards behind her, wrapped in her cloak. As he looked, it moved, and a small sound, a child's whimper, came from it. Straccan walked over and turned the cloth back.

'God have mercy!'

It was a child, four or five years old, skeletally thin, the skull's outlines sharp under the yellow skin, the eyes fever-bright.

The woman folded the cloth back further. The child lay on his side, his withered legs, mere sticks with hugely swollen knee-joints, drawn up against his belly. At the base of his spine was an ulcer Straccan could have put his fist in.

'I carry him on my back,' the mother said. 'I am strong, and he weighs next to nothing. We will keep up, I promise.'

'You can't walk all the way to Durham with him on your back.'

She glared fiercely at him. 'If that's what it will take to move Saint Cuthbert's heart I can; I will. I'll *crawl* if I have to!'

The boy was dying, Straccan could see that. He should be in his bed at home, or in a convent infirmary where he could die in peace, not dragged around the country like this, from saint to saint.

'It will kill him,' he said bluntly.

'You can't say that! You don't know! Our priest knew a man who took his son to Saint Cuthbert. They slept by his tomb every night for a week and on the seventh night the saint appeared to the boy and he was healed!'

There were stories like that about every saint's tomb, but that didn't mean it couldn't happen. Straccan had seen a miracle; who was he to say there couldn't be one for this child?

'Giles!' he yelled, turning away from the boy.

The cowman came at a trot. 'Sir?'

'You can make a bit of room in your cart for this child, can't you?'

Giles, on the point of indignant refusal, looked at the boy and at the mother, and changed his mind. 'Room enough,' he said gruffly. 'Only a tiddler, ain't he?'

As Mistress Boteler set the boy down on Straccan's pillow in the cowman's cart, Straccan watched her face, ravaged with anguish and love. What else could she do? If his daughter were dying, if leeches and medicine had failed, wouldn't he do as Lucy Boteler was doing, carry her from shrine to shrine in search of a saint's compassion?

102

Chapter 19

At the clang of the bell Brother Paulus laid aside his toasting fork with a philosophical sigh and padded down the steps from the porter's room to the wicket door in the great gate of Dieulacresse, the gate being shut and bolted for the night.

There were three horsemen, plastered with the dried mud and dust of long travel, but it was not supper nor beds for the night they sought, only directions to Stirrup.

'Stirrup? Sir Richard Straccan's manor? Just keep to this road, sirs. You'll come to the river; there's an old broken stone cross that marks the ford. Three leagues more and you'll come to Stirrup. But if you seek Sir Richard, he's not there.'

'You know him?' All three of them kept their hoods pulled forward, and Paulus, as inquisitive as he was garrulous, couldn't see their faces no matter how hard he tried.

'Bless you, sir, of course. Sir Richard is a benefactor of our house. You must have heard of our treasure, our relic? The jawbone of Saint Andrew? It was Sir Richard's gift.' He would have gone on extolling its virtues, but the stranger interrupted.

'Perhaps you know of a young man, a knight, wounded in the leg. Is he there, at Stirrup? There may be a young lad with him and a child, a boy.'

'I couldn't say, sir, but our infirmarian will know. He's been several times to Stirrup lately.'

Brother Lucius, summoned from sleep to the guest hall, was conscious of a certain reluctance to answer these men, which he did not understand. But the travellers said they were friends of Sir Miles; it was a worthy thing, surely, to bring friends together, and his patient – still weak and suffering the boredom and frustrations of convalescence – would be glad to greet his friends. Although, he reflected when back in his bed, that grim, grey, lame knight was not the sort of man he'd have thought to be a friend of young Hoby.

The three made camp by the ford and the broken cross. It had fallen long ago and was speckled with lichens and moss. Uriel gathered wood and lit a fire in the shelter of the stones.

The smoke made him cough. He didn't like England; it was damp and misty and hardly anyone spoke French. From his saddlebag he took a pie he'd bought earlier in the day, and bit into it. It did nothing to raise his opinion of the country.

'What if Hoby's no longer there?' he asked.

'We will follow,' said Michael. 'God will guide us to him.'

The other two slept while Uriel kept first watch, gazing into the fire and thinking of his home. He hoped Hoby would be at Stirrup – God, these English names! The sooner they found him, the sooner he could go home, resume his name, regain his honour . . . thrown away, and all for a faithless woman. In Toulouse the bishop's secretary had offered to revoke his sentence of banishment for murder and restore him to his estates, and had even promised him the Church's blessing and great reward for serving God in this secret matter.

'Don't you know better than to blind yourself with firelight?' Michael's harsh voice cut into his thoughts, and he looked up, blinking, blinded indeed by his long staring into the fire. Darkness hid his guilty flush.

'Get some sleep,' Michael said, putting more wood on the fire. 'I'll take the next watch.'

Uriel pulled his mantle round him and lay down. He watched as Michael settled with his back to the fire, his sword across his knees. A stern, forbidding man who spoke no more than he must, what sin could have made him undertake this duty? And Samuel, who seldom spoke at all, what had he done? Each of them was outcast from his own place and people, hoping to buy redemption by this service to God.

Uriel yawned and closed his eyes. God willing, he would not be long in this miserable island. The English deserved it.

David bolted upright in bed, eyes wide with terror. 'Maman! They're coming!'

It was the third night in a row that he had been restless, muttering in his sleep. Now that Miles was out of danger, they had changed places; Miles slept in the mural room, while Roslyn and David shared a truckle bed in the bedchamber. With Straccan and Gilla away from home, they had the room to themselves, and for the last two weeks David had been sleeping better, it was no longer a nightly commonplace for him to wake screaming. But now he did, panicky, struggling, his arms tangled in the sheet.

Roslyn held his trembling body in a tight hug. 'David, what is it?'

'They're coming,' he panted. 'I saw them! Bad men, three of them, with swords!'

She didn't waste time with useless comfort, or with reassurances. 'How near?' was all she said.

'I don't know. Not far.'

She was dressed in moments, not in her gown but in the ragged boy's clothes she had worn on the road. She could hear Miles getting up as she hurried David into his clothes and latched his shoes. 'Don't worry, *p'tit*; we'll be gone before they get here.'

Miles came out of his room, half asleep, yawning, clutching a blanket round his middle and carrying a candle. 'What's the matter? Bad dream? You're dressed!'

'We're leaving.' Roslyn took David's hand and tugged him towards the stair head.

'What? Now? It's the middle of the night!'

'The bad men are coming,' David said.

'What men? Do you mean the Brotherhood?'

'Who else?' Roslyn snapped. She pulled a satchel, ready packed, out from under the bed and slung it over her shoulder.

'It can't be! How do you know?'

'David says so. I believe him.'

'Sorrow, it was just another nightmare.' Miles stuck his candle on the pricket and turned to the child. 'Wasn't it, old son?'

'*No!*' As if David's yell had caused it, the air in the bedchamber became suddenly hot and dry, as if a great oven door had opened to let a wave of fierce heat pour into the room.

Roslyn seized David by the shoulders and shook him hard. 'Stop it!'

'What? Is *he* doing that?' Miles demanded, and as the heat intensified he backed away. 'Oh God!'

'David! Don't!' Roslyn cried. Flames sprang from the matting at her feet. She stamped on them. 'Stop it!'

'I'm sorry! I'm sorry!' With the boy's terrified wail the heat was gone as suddenly as it had come. Roslyn held him close, a small, desperate boy sobbing his heart out against her breast.

'Did he do that?'

Over David's head Roslyn glared at Miles. 'What do you think? Miles, they followed us. We have to go *now!*'

'But this is England! They won't dare do anything here!'

'Don't be a fool! You've seen what they do. If we go, they will leave the manor alone and come after us.'

'No!' At David's panicky cry the heavy, weighted curtain at

the stair head billowed and thrashed, and the brazier – luckily unlit – rocked and fell over, tumbling cold charcoal and ashes on the floor. Roslyn cried out as coals and ash lifted from the floor and flew at her, a strafing storm of small sharp missiles and dust. She clapped her hands to her face; blood ran through her fingers.

Shouting, 'David! Stop!' Miles pulled Roslyn to him, shielding her with his body. At his shout the onslaught stopped, just as it had before.

'What's going on?' Bane came up the steps two at a time. 'What was that crash?'

'The knights of the White Brotherhood,' Roslyn said. 'They are coming here.'

Bane paused on the brink of asking 'How do you know?' and thought better of it. If Roslyn said the men were coming, he believed her. He looked at the fallen brazier, the scorched mat, the mess of coals and ash everywhere, and Roslyn with blood running down her cheek. 'What the devil happened?'

'Never mind! We're wasting time,' Roslyn said.

'They can't be the same men,' Miles protested. 'They're dead. Well, two are for certain, and I doubt the other survived.' He ran a hand through his tousled hair. 'Bane, I'm sorry. I never dreamed they'd follow us here. Sorrow's right; we must go. We'll need horses, and I need a sword.' He darted back into his room and began pulling on his clothes.

'You must have really pissed them off for them to come all this way after you,' Bane said. 'Is it vengeance, d'you think? For the ones you killed?'

'No,' said Miles. 'It's not me they want, nor Sorrow. It's David.'

'David?' Bane said incredulously. '*David?*' At that, flames sprang up the curtain; in a moment it was ablaze from bottom to top. With a curse, Bane leaped at it, wrenched it from its rings, rolled it up hard and stamped it underfoot, blowing on his scorched fingers and swearing. 'Shit! What the hell's happening here?'

'I didn't mean it,' David whispered.

Roslyn stroked his hair. 'Hush, it's all right, *cher*. No one's hurt.'

He reached up to touch her face. 'You're bleeding. I did that. I won't, I *promise* I won't do it again.'

'I'm all right. Come.' She took his hand and started downstairs. Miles clattered after them, buckling his belt. Halfway down Roslyn stopped and faced him. 'Miles, you must stay here. You'll just slow us down.'

'She's right,' said Bane. 'They'll stand a better chance without you.'

'I can't let them go alone! It's against my honour! I'll be all right!'

'They won't go alone,' Bane said. 'I'll go with them. I'll take them to Sir Richard; he'll know what to do about your white bastards. Have you got everything you need, Mistress Roslyn?'

Roslyn hesitated only a moment, then with a quick smile touched his arm. 'Yes, thank you, Master Bane.' Her hand on his sleeve was as light as a leaf, yet Bane felt it like a brand through leather and cloth.

'We'll get a good start tonight,' he said. 'There's a full moon. As for you, Sir Miles, you're needed here. Someone's got to defend the manor, and I reckon that's your job.'

Chapter 20

At Cammo's urging the village emptied in less time than it took to say a paternoster. Men, women and children, with their dogs, goats and one very unwell pig, trooped in at the gate, which banged shut behind them, the great beams shoved into place to hold it fast. The two lesser gates, six-inch-thick solid oak reinforced with iron, were shut and barred, and pikemen positioned there. On the watchtower and the walls, Miles and Odo stationed their archers, and at the main gate all eyes watched the crest of the road from Dieulacresse for the first glimpse of the enemy.

Those who normally came in to work every morning, in stable, forge or kitchen, got on with it; fires were lit, and Adeliza and her helpers set to work preparing enough food to go round. Cammo hid the silver. Peter hid the relics. Hall and yard swarmed with wildly excited children, making bloody nuisances of themselves.

'There's trees not so far off. They may try to bring up a ram,' Odo said. 'But we can pick 'em off like pigeons if they get up to that sort of nonsense, no bother.'

'More likely one will parley here at the gate while the others ride round to test for weak spots,' said Miles. He had positioned some of the women on the walls as well, wearing leather jerkins and men's caps; they giggled a lot and they couldn't actually pull a bow, but the enemy wouldn't know that, and the manor appeared to be in an excellent state of defence.

'We'll keep them talking as long as we can,' Miles said. 'The longer they're farting about here, the further Bane and the others will get. Once they're off the highway, this lot will never find them.'

The watchbell clanked dolefully. Miles could see three riders, small in the distance, coming fast. Bane and his charges had a few hours' start, but their horses couldn't match the pace of these. He must buy as much time as he could.

'Bad cess to 'em,' Adeliza said, setting down a jug of ale and scowling at the oncoming horsemen. 'Poor little lad, and him just getting over it too. Why can't they leave him alone?'

Buggered if I know, thought Miles. But whatever the reason, it had been David, not him, that the man at Bordeaux meant to murder. In the night, in the cold foetid darkness of the inn's upper chamber, the attacker had hacked with his sword at the bed where David slept – where David *should* have been sleeping had he not crawled in with Sorrow for warmth. Miles, coming later to bed in the dark, had fallen exhausted on to the nearest pallet – David's – and slept there, waking an instant too late as the sword stroke that should have cut off David's head cut deeply into his thigh instead. The would-be killer knew where the boy was meant to be. Miles wasn't his target.

David seemed to be a very ordinary little boy. Except for the stones and the fires. He didn't throw the stones, they just *happened*. And he certainly didn't light the fires, but they happened too, whenever he was badly frightened, whenever he or Sorrow or Miles was in danger. He wasn't ordinary at all.

There had been a few people at Montperil who had known David's father in the peaceful days before the crusade. It was queer, the way they behaved towards David – asking his blessing, kissing his hands. What was it they called him? Miles frowned, remembering. '*Logos*' – that was it. Whatever that was.

The riders halted less than a bowshot away and spoke together for a moment, then one rode forward.

'Is Miles Hoby here?'

Miles shouted down, 'I'm Hoby. What d'you want?'

'We have no quarrel with you or your people. You have a child there, a boy you brought out of France. Give him to us and there will be no bloodshed.'

'Go to hell!'

'He's no kin of yours. If we have to fight you, your people will die. Is that what you want?'

'Better kill us quickly, then,' Miles yelled. 'I've sent for the sheriff; he'll be here soon.'

Odo followed this up with an arrow that landed neatly at Michael's feet.

Michael drew back hastily and went into a huddle with his comrades. Keeping at a safe distance, as Miles had predicted, the other two then made a circuit of the walls, with the archers along the top keeping arrows pointed at them all the way.

From their vantage point on the walls the defenders watched the two men ride down to the village and dismount, unsheathing their swords, kicking doors open and searching each house. Then they mounted again, and one rode slowly through the orchard towards the river and out of sight of the manor, while the other galloped back to join Michael before the main gate.

Nicholas had spent the night at his mother's house, a privilege for which he had permission from the priory while working at Stirrup. Some time before midnight he got up to tend his mother's sick calf and saw in the moonlight Master Bane, with the boy David and the young woman who played the flute, riding very fast on the road from Stirrup. He waved, but they didn't see him.

In the morning he set out for the manor. He always enjoyed the three-mile walk, and looked forward to the work that awaited him. He wondered where David had gone; they had become friends, and the boy had offered to help him today, outlining the herb beds with smooth stones from the river. Perhaps he'd be back later in the day. Whistling, happy, Nicholas walked on.

There was a man on a horse. Not going anywhere, just stationed sideways across the road, almost as if waiting for him. Perhaps he was lost and needed to ask the way. And so it seemed, for the man called to Nicholas.

'You, boy! Do you know Stirrup?' He spoke English in a funny way.

'Yes, sir, that I do. I work there.'

'Is a small boy there, who has six years?'

'That's David, but he's gone.'

'Where has he gone?'

'I don't know, sir.'

To Nicholas's amazement the man drew his sword and, leaning down from his high saddle, held the point against his chest.

'Where is he? Tell me, or I'll split your heart.'

With sudden horror Nicholas knew that this must be one of the bad men David had talked about, men who tried to kill him before he came to Stirrup.

'I don't know,' he said, backing away, half-turning to try and make a run for it.

'They're going,' Odo called down to Miles. 'The third one just joined 'em, said something, and they're riding off like the devil was after them. I hope he is, and may he catch 'em, too.'

Why had they gone? Miles wearily climbed the tower steps

again and stared. The three were almost out of sight, riding hard, in the right direction too, damn them. 'Keep vigil,' he said. 'They may be back.'

But the afternoon crawled past, and they didn't come back.

The watchbell clanked and clanked, jerking Miles from his uneasy sleep in the gate guard's cubbyhole. The day's activities and his exhaustion had brought home to him, as no words of Roslyn's could, that he was in no condition to travel yet. But as soon as he could, he'd follow.

'Is it them?' he shouted.

'No,' Odo yelled back from above. 'It's Brother Lucius, afoot, with some poor soul stretched over his saddle.'

Adeliza came running as the gate squealed open, and the old monk led his mule inside. Tears streaked his dusty face. The body lying across the saddle was Nicholas, and he was dead.

They laid the lad's body on a table in the hall, and the people of the household gathered round, grieving and appalled.

'God and his son forgive me, I should not weep,' Lucius said, fisting tears from his eyes. 'His soul is more surely with Christ now than any I have known. My heart rejoices at it; it is the pitiful flesh that weeps.' He fell to his knees beside the makeshift bier. 'Lord, Master, I know he is with you, but for us who loved him, it is hard – hard.' His tears dripped on to the boy's unmoving breast. 'God will welcome him, who so delighted in his creation.'

'There's no wound,' Miles said. 'You would think he slept. How did he die?'

Lucius got up from his knees.

'He was smothered. See . . .' He turned the boy's head to the light and pointed at the pale smudges of bruising round mouth and nose; then, gently raising Nicholas's eyelids he said, 'See the red spots in the whites of his eyes? These I've seen in others who died this way, or were strangled. Nicholas was killed by a man's hands. And that man knelt upon his body, see . . .' He drew the tunic up to show dark bruises over the sharply prominent ribs. 'And pinioned his arms.' There were purplish marks of fingers, clear, on the boy's thin arms. 'He could not have fought much. Half starved all his life until he came to the priory, his strength was small.

'I rode here today because I was concerned about those men:

111

they came to the priory last night and said they were your friends. Sir Miles, forgive me, I told them you were here. But afterwards I had ill dreams, and came to see if all was well. I found Nicholas's poor body beside the road. And now, God help me, I must tell his mother.'

Chapter 21

The narrow streets of Cambridge were thronged with people – it was market day – and the queen's champion and his two body servants made slow progress through the press of folk in the market place. His squire he had sent ahead to his stronghold of Ravenser, to give warning of his coming. He must go there first; there were preparations only he could make. When all was ready he would return to his manor at Locksey and wait to hear from fitzWalter.

A fellow with a dancing bear held up his progress for a little while, and on the far side of the square some sort of entertainment was going on: costumed players strutting on a ramshackle stage, a few planks laid across a low cart. Almost unaware of the noise and activity, and certainly unaware of the nondescript little man following him, he rode in silence, lost in thoughts of the queen.

No word had ever been spoken between them of their feelings – none knew better than she the peril – but seeing him in her chamber, unexpected, unprepared, just for a moment he was sure she had looked at him with her heart in her eyes.

His own heart had leaped to meet hers, but that was all. Her women, John's spies, watched her like hawks for the least indiscretion, avid for the chance to drag her to shame, dishonour and death. He must be even more careful than she, lest their passion betray them. They could do nothing while the king lived.

The wind blew in gusts, driving clouds of eye-stinging smoke into the streets, rattling shutters, sending shop signs whirling and banging, shaking the canvas sides of traders' booths and coating meat and fish, laid out for customers to buy, with dust.

Starling Larktwist could see Tyrrel's head and broad shoulders above the crowd; he wasn't difficult to follow and he wasn't trying to hide. So far this had been an easy job, hardly worth his talents. Tyrrel had spent the last two days at Locksey, riding into Cambridge each day with Larktwist following at a discreet

113

distance. On the first day the champion had visited his tailor, saddler, wine merchant and swordsmith. Yesterday Larktwist had followed him to the riverside wharves and warehouses, where the champion gave a heavy purse to the captain of a cog while men loaded barrels into a cart, barrels leaking a pinkish powder. Half an hour in a pub and a few rounds of drinks bought him the information that the stuff, whatever it was, was going to Tyrrel's castle of Ravenser, and Tyrrel himself was bound there on the morrow. After dark Larktwist had gone back to the wharf and scraped up some of the powder, stoppering it in a little phial for his contact, the landlord of the Yellow Hawk, to send to Mercredi in London.

The champion and his men had reached the entertainment. The players were giving a mystery, and had rigged their stage to depict hell, earth and heaven. The planks were earth, with a sailcloth awning above, painted to depict blue sky and white clouds and underneath the cart a smoking brazier represented hell. Satan was on stage. He wore two masks. The one on the front of his head smiled sweetly, but the other, on his arse, was shuddersome. Art or chance had managed to give the painted, modelled features a look of sneering, unholy triumph; the mouth showed a hint of teeth and a wet, lolling tongue eager to lap up souls, while the eyes conveyed an infinite contempt.

Satan pranced back and forth on the little stage, in cunning costume to match the masks: at the front he was a bishop, robed and mitred, smiling benevolently as he raised a hand in blessing; then, quick as a whip, he would turn to show his naked back and goatish, hairy legs, twitching a thick, rat-like tail aside as he bent and thrust that other face, his true face, towards the shrieking audience.

The Blessed Virgin, apparently standing on a small cloud, was lowered from heaven by means of a rope with much creaking and jerking, but the audience was very willing to be pleased, and cheered her descent. She wore a blue mantle and had long golden hair, and that was all that mattered. When she reached the stage, she set about the devil with a wooden sword, while he squirmed and squealed for mercy to no avail. A trapdoor opened, and she kicked him into hell to tremendous applause.

The players – there were four, Larktwist saw, God, Jesus, his mother and Satan – lined up to take their bow. Two thirds of their audience did a bunk before God could come round with the hat, but Tyrrel flung a handful of good ringing silver, more than

114

the players could normally hope to earn in a month, and the Blessed Virgin scooped up the coins and winked at him before ducking out of sight behind the curtain.

The queen's champion rode on, and at his back his men exchanged knowing looks.

Everything that could go wrong, did. The last three days had been a nightmare. Provisions were found to be mouldy, carts broke down, oxen went lame or began scouring, the pilgrims bickered and came to blows. Straccan's rouncey had cast a shoe, Rob Bowlegs sat in a wasps' nest, and the smith burned his hand badly when shoeing the horse. It wasn't possible to stop other wayfarers from tagging along, and one of them made off with the donkey, another charge on Straccan's purse.

There was also increased military activity: knights, singly and in groups, strings of horses, men-at-arms with their commanders, bands of excited volunteers, cartloads of supplies, labourers, ditchers, carpenters and general dogsbodies, and king's messengers at full gallop. The Normandy campaign had been called off – it was all anyone talked about – and King John's resources were now being devoted to putting down the rebellious, treacherous Welsh.

'It's war,' said Brother Mungo with gloomy satisfaction, as the bell wain toiled up a hill.

'Jesus save us,' cried Millie Fisher. 'Are the Scots coming?'

'Probably,' said Mungo, causing a perceptible wave of panic.

'It's the Welsh,' Straccan bellowed, standing in his stirrups. 'Listen, you lot! They're not coming here! They just want their country back. They've asked us to leave but we're still there and they've had enough of us!'

'Infernal cheek,' huffed the master carter, who had political opinions. 'After all we've done for them.'

'Like what?' yelled Luke Bannerman, who had a Welsh mother, a short temper and a ready fist.

'Well . . . civilisation,' said the master carter. 'Soap. Nit combs. That sort of thing.'

Luckily – in a manner of speaking – as a cartload of barrels drew level with the bell wain, their lashings chose that moment to part, releasing an avalanche of casks, fortunately empty, which leaped and bounced and thundered down the hill, effectively putting a stop to further developments.

Brother Mungo was the only one hurt. As he turned his back to yell a warning, a barrel bowled him over, and he rolled downhill among the rest, novices and pilgrims pelting after him, half gleeful, half afraid of what they would find. He had merely bitten through his tongue, and found speech difficult for several days. If there had been a patron saint of barrels, Straccan might have bent a penny to him.

Lucy Boteler had made her son as comfortable as possible in Giles's wagon, settling Lawrence on his stomach supported by wool-stuffed pillows, so that as the wagon rolled along, the springy wool cushioned him from the jolting and he could see out through the laced-back sailcloth flaps. His mother walked at the cart-tail, talking to him.

Someone had parted with a precious pilgrim badge from the shrine of Saint Winifrede of Shrewsbury, pinning it to the canvas where Lawrence lay, and someone else had given Mistress Boteler a tiny phial of Saint Thomas's Water for the boy. He had swallowed it obediently, and not long after was able to take a little broth.

Straccan reined in alongside. 'God save you, mistress. How is Lawrence today?'

In her thin dusty face, the eyes were young and very blue. She had been beautiful once, he thought; and then, as she cast a loving look at the child, *She is beautiful still.*

'Somewhat better, sir, thank you. He ate some broth.'

'That's good,' said Straccan, pleased and surprised. He'd expected to be burying the boy before now. 'God save you, Lawrence.'

The boy's face was just visible between the open flaps. His eyes were as blue as his mother's. To Straccan's astonishment, at his greeting Lawrence's lips tucked up at the corners. If it wasn't quite a smile, it was a good try.

With painful slowness, they ate up the miles. At fords and bridges, the bell and its followers held up the progress of other travellers for hours. They had always tended to straggle, not just fore and aft but sideways as well, and with the increase in traffic it was necessary to keep them well over to one side of the road.

One thing followed another. At Champtonford the great wain bogged, and all the oxen's straining efforts failed to break it out. Borrowing three more pairs of oxen from the nearest manor wasted the best part of the day and cost a shocking twopence a head, the manor's bailiff not being one to miss a chance like that. Scarcely were they on their way again when it was discovered that the crippled pilgrim, Wilfred, was missing, and Straccan had to go back and look for him. He found Wilfred in a ditch, minus his crutches and uproariously drunk, and by the time they got back it was dark, the day had been wasted, only three miles covered, and everyone was thoroughly fed up.

And during the night it came on to rain.

It poured steadily until just before dawn. The tents leaked, wetting bedding and sleepers. The covered carts leaked, soaking all the supplies. The straw packing around the bell was saturated, adding weight to the great cart; the oxen, as soon as they started to move, noticed the difference, resented it, and baulked every few yards. And although the rain stopped and the sky cleared, there was little chance of getting things dry. Wet bedrolls and clothes were draped from every cart, in the hope that sunshine and the rising wind would dry them; and even the novices, usually unsquashably cheerful, were damp and subdued.

The next morning started just as every other morning on this truly penitential journey. Straccan still had his breakfast in his mouth when it began.

'Sir Richard, the oats are ruined.'

'Sir, the salt's all washed away.'

'Sir, Luke Bannerman says someone's pinched one of his shoes!'

'Sir Richard, your dog . . .'

The dog reluctantly gave up the remains of the shoe – beyond repair – and Straccan added the cost of a new pair for the bannerman to his rising list of expenses.

They actually managed to cover a mile before the next calamity.

'Sir! Sir! Millie Fisher's left the baby behind!'

'Tell me you're joking!'

'No, sir. Sorry, sir. She laid him down when she'd fed him, while she and her man packed up. She thought he put the baby in the cart, and he thought she did.'

'I'll go back for it. Keep going, don't stop. I'll catch up.' He touched spurs to Apple's sides and headed back the way they'd come, the damned dog running alongside, overjoyed, barking like a fool.

But it was the dog that found the baby, thank the saints, just where his mother had laid him, still fast asleep in a natural mossy cradle under the raised roots of a noble beech. He woke as Straccan lifted him, eyeing his rescuer with dark blue eyes, and crowed with delight at the rocking rhythm of the horse's hooves.

So far so good, only half an hour lost; the bell and its train of carts and hangers-on should have kept up a reasonable pace this fine dry morning.

He smelled the smoke and heard the clamour before he came in sight of them. What the devil was going on? They'd gone no more than half a mile and were stopped all anyhow along the road; carters, smith, pilgrims and monks all panicking about flinging buckets of water on to the bell wain, from which smoke was still rising.

He thrust the baby at its mother, who was more interested in the fire than in her now-squalling offspring, which she took, shook – as if it were a bottle of medicine – and clamped to her breast, plugging its yells with her nipple. Straccan dismounted and ran to the cart, relieved to see no flames. At least they had acted promptly, and thank God the river was at hand! The straw packed around the base of the bell was charred, the towering sailcloth-wrapped dome scorched and streaked with soot, but the smoke was diminishing.

Straccan scrambled up on to the flatbed and edged around the bell, tugging at its blackened ropes, transferring a good deal of soot and charred straw to his hands and clothes, and receiving the contents of a bucket full in the face as he swung down to test the lashings where they passed under the cart.

'Oops! Sorry, sir!'

'Never mind. Keep it coming; we don't want it breaking out again.' He caught at the sleeve of the nearest man – it was the smith. 'Give me a hand underneath.' They crawled under the cart and began testing the lashings.

'Seems sound enough,' said the smith. 'All right your side, is it?'

Straccan grunted assent. 'What happened?'

'Search me! We were rolling along nice as you please when Brother Finan noticed the smoke. It never really got going, thank God – too damp. If the wagon bed had caught fire we'd really be in the shit.'

'But how could it start in the first place? You were on the move, there were no cook-fires going, no sparks. What the hell happened?'

'I dunno. Just one damn thing after another, ain't it?' They crawled out and stood up, wet and filthy. The smith looked uncomfortable and lowered his voice. 'Is it true what that monk says, that the bell killed a man in London?'

Straccan let out an exasperated snort. 'No!'

118

'But a man *was* killed?'

'It wasn't the bell, Bishop des Roches said so.'

The smith looked unconvinced. 'Brother Mungo—' he began.

Straccan cursed Brother Mungo, silently but with passion. 'Don't you believe the bishop knows best?'

'Well, I s'pose—'

'He blessed the bell before it left Southwark, didn't he? And everyone making the journey with it. You were there.'

'Yes, but—'

'But what?'

'There was that business with the oxen, right back at the beginning, and ever since then there's been one thing after another. We oughter be nearly to Peterborough by now, instead of here. The bishop may have blessed it, but it don't *feel* right.' He leaned closer to Straccan, so that no one else might hear. 'Did you ever think, Sir Richard, that maybe Old Horny don't want that bell to get there?'

Straccan's hand closed in a painful grip round the muscled hardness of the smith's arm. 'Did Brother Mungo say that?'

'Well, not exactly—'

'Keep that thought to yourself, smith, or take yourself back to Southwark and explain your reasons to the bishop!' He let the man go and clambered back on the flatbed, shouting to get everyone's attention. 'Well done, all of you! Now in the name of God let's get moving!'

Something turned under his foot. He bent and picked it up – a tinder-horn, blackened and split, stuffed with bits of charcoal and moss. He stirred them with his finger. Tiny sparks glowed, faded and glowed again.

It certainly looked as if *someone* didn't want the bell to get there.

He was still thinking about it when, after locking the horn away, he stretched himself on his still-damp bedroll at last. He'd taken the laming of the oxen to be an act of malice by a rival with a grudge against the cowman, but he'd been wrong. Last night someone had put that incendiary in the bell wain, where, if it hadn't rained, it would have smouldered sullenly for a while before setting fire to the straw – by which time the fire-raiser would have been back in his tent or cart, innocently abed. Chances were that by the time the fire was discovered it would be too late; the cart would have been destroyed. But it *had* rained, and not until the morning, when the cart was underway and the wind had risen to tease the smouldering moss to sparks and flames, did the fire start.

Who was responsible? Despite the bishop's resourceful solution, a man had died because of Gaudy's fall. What if the dead man's kin, with a grudge against the bishop, were trying to scupper his plans for the bell?

When it came to grudges, there were other possibilities. His mind turned to the Countess Judith, and to Father Paul, her ill-used chaplain, and his light o' love. The chaplain knew the terms of her will. If the bell didn't reach Coldinghame, Lord Joceran's head would never lie with his lady in her coffin – always providing the head turned up. Des Roches believed the chaplain had stolen it, to ransom, but perhaps the theft was simple revenge. If the head was lost and the bell failed to reach its destination, all Lady Judith's plans would count for nothing. In purgatory or paradise, her soul would never rest. Now *that* would be vengeance.

The scent of cooking woke Roslyn. Rolling over, she saw Bane squatting by the fire, and David opposite him, sitting cross-legged eating a sausage on a stick, laughing and talking. They got on well, those two. The sun was half out of bed, a great red orb squatting on the eastern horizon, and the scent of sausages made Roslyn's mouth water.

'Sleep well?' Bane asked, handing her a sausage speared on a hazel twig. 'You snored.'

'I don't snore!'

'Oh? Must've been David.' David giggled, and Bane reached across the fire and poked him in the ribs.

When they'd finished eating, Roslyn took David to the stream and washed his greasy face and hands, and then her own. Returning to the fire she combed her fingers through her tangled hair – she'd lost the ribbon on the ride yesterday.

'Do I look all right?' she asked.

Bane studied her. 'The words "hedge" and "backwards" come to mind.'

'*Merde!*'

Bane fished about in the multiple pockets sewn inside his jerkin and produced a comb. 'Here.'

Surprised, Roslyn took it. 'Thank you.' She combed her hair, separated it into strands and braided it. 'I don't suppose you have a ribbon?'

Wordlessly Bane delved in his saddlebag and came up with a

piece of string. 'I've been meaning to ask,' he said, as she wound the braid round her head and fastened it in place with a wooden hairpin. 'Where did you steal that dreadful cart you turned up in?'

'It was at the roadside. The man had gone for his breakfast.'

'Just like that?' She nodded. 'How did you get his nibs to go along with it?' He put out the fire.

'Miles?' She laughed. 'Ah, that was harder than stealing it. He said he could not lie in a cart, like turnips. He said it was against his honour.'

'He would.' Bane began packing his cooking gear.

'So I put David in, and left Miles to follow on foot.' She fiddled with the hairpin, pulled it out and jabbed it in again with an impatient ferocity that made Bane wince. 'We did not have to go far,' she said. 'He was quite ill by then. When he fell down I went back for him. Next day I found the horse.'

'Roslyn, look!' A yellow butterfly had alighted on David's hand. His face was rapt, and wonder lit him like a lamp.

'How long have you been looking after him?' Bane asked.

'A year— No, more – it was May when I found him at Montgey.'

'Lucky for him.'

'For me, too.' Her eyes, usually so guarded, were soft as she looked at the child.

'Put a crimp in your own plans, though, didn't it?'

'My master was dead. Without him, I had no plans. We were on our way to Toulouse, to compete in Bishop Fulk's festival of music.'

'Toulouse? Isn't that a dangerous place?'

'For heretics, yes, but we were not Cathars. The bishop loves music. He was a maker of songs himself before he entered the Church. It is a famous festival! Every year troubadors from all over France are there. The great prize is a cup filled with gold pieces, and there are purses of gold and silver, and rings for lesser singers.'

'So you hoped for a purse of gold.'

She flashed him a look of scorn. 'I spit on the purses,' she said, and spat between his feet with practised accuracy. 'Raimond de Sorules would have won the great prize. There is – there was – none to equal him!'

'You play very well yourself.'

'Bah! You have only heard me play the little flute. I can play the harp, the rebec, the lute, the cittern – anything! My master

121

had a harp – oh, such a harp! Minoulet was its name. Queen Eleanor gave it to him when they were both young; he was her lover,' she boasted, and remembering the tales he'd heard of Eleanor of Aquitane, Bane believed her.

'How did you team up with him?' he asked, heaving his saddle on to the horse's back and buckling the girth. Roslyn mounted her mare, and he lifted David up behind her.

'He bought me,' she said. 'When I was very young. He was father and mother to me for nine years, until they butchered him, like a calf, and smashed his harp to pieces.' Bane saw her eyes shine with unshed tears. 'He tried to tell them who he was, where we were going. Bane . . .'

'What?'

'When will we meet with Sir Richard?'

'It depends where he's got to. Two or three days.'

'Those men, they will come after us. They are very dangerous.'

'I'm quite dangerous myself,' said Bane.

Chapter 22

Sir Ralf Tyrrel unlocked the bedchamber door, removed the key, went in, and closed it behind him, locking it again. Then he turned, leaned back against the door and nodded, satisfied.

They had prepared this one well. It didn't seem to see him. It stood in the centre of the room, wearing a mantle of blue silk and a coronet of pearls. He watched it for a few moments, then stepped closer.

'Turn round.' It obeyed. 'Yes, like that. Now, be still. Don't smile.'

It gazed dreamily past him, the pupils of its eyes enormous. Its lips moved, but no sound came from them.

'Don't speak,' he said softly. 'Don't move.'

He walked round it. New-washed, the perfumed hair shawled its back – not as pale as *hers*, of course, but blonde. He lifted a tress and let it slip, cold and heavy, through his trembling fingers. He could hear the creature's soft, rapid breathing, feel the living scented warmth, *her* perfume, radiating from its body.

'Stay there.' He circled the room, snuffing candles, until just two were left to halo its hair, like a saint's. Carefully he removed the coronet and loosened the cords of the mantle, which fell to the floor with a swish and rattle of silk and gems. It was naked underneath.

He took it by the shoulders to push it, quite gently, on to the bed, and knelt beside it on the coverlid, reaching to snuff the candle flames. As always, darkness worked its magic: the hair he wrapped around himself, the silken limbs he stroked, the lips that opened under his were *hers*. In the darkness he took her, sobbing, 'Isabel!'

He opened his eyes in a dawn light less kind. At his side the creature lay on its back, flushed, open-mouthed, snoring softly. A strand of brassy yellow hair stuck to its damp cheek and across its swollen lips. It smelled of sweat.

Sickened, he rolled away from the hot touch of flesh as it stirred, mumbling something indistinct. It would wake at any moment. He must be quick, before its eyes opened. He could

123

not bear that this grotesque caricature of his love should speak.

The mantle was where it had fallen, beside the bed. He drew the thick golden cord from its collar, keeping his eyes on the creature with the fascination of disgust, the way a man keeps his eyes on a fat spider on the wall while reaching for something, anything, with which to smash it.

When it stopped wriggling, he drew his dagger.

The steward came into the chamber when all sounds had stopped. The champion, wrapped in the bed's fur coverlid, was whimpering and shivering, as if he'd been pulled from the river.

Since Cambridge, the travelling players had had nothing that resembled luck and this afternoon's performance at Poley had been pathetic.

'A halfpenny, three fourthings and a button,' said Piper in disgust. 'Not enough to get pissed on.' He shook the collecting bag and turned it inside out, displaying its emptiness to the others. They stared silently at him. He hated it when they did that. What did they expect?

'What d'you expect?' he yelled, flinging the bag down and stamping on it. 'I can't magic coins out of purses.'

'We shouldn't've stopped there,' Will said. 'I said we shouldn't've stopped there, didn't I? Didn't I say it?'

Tim said nothing, just went on staring. Piper sighed. 'Anyone else got any money?'

They turned out their flat purses and pockets. Piper counted the ragged wedge-shaped pieces, halfpence and fourthings. Fourpence halfpenny. Could be worse. Too late to push on now for Picklingham; they'd have to make do with stale bread and lard tonight, but tomorrow they could buy bones to make a stew, and onions to flavour it, and they had dried peas and a little flour left to thicken it. If they were careful the stew would do for the next day as well, Piper thought.

They were still staring at him.

'Don't look at me like that. It's not my fault. We'll do all right at Picklingham tomorrow; we'll give them the play of Adam and Eve.'

'Don't be daft,' said Tim. 'How can we do Adam and Eve without Eve? In case you've forgotten, we're short of a woman since Pernelle buggered off.'

'She'll come back,' said Piper. 'She left all her stuff, didn't she?'

'She took the bloody money,' Will said. 'There must have

been at least three shillings there.'

'She'll be back,' said Piper again. 'Meanwhile, Tim can do Eve in a wig. Stuff padding down his front—'

'I'll stuff something up your arse,' said Tim hotly. 'I'm not doing Eve! She has to kiss Adam! Anyway, we still need four players – Adam and Eve, and God and the Serpent.'

'Will can do God *and* the Serpent. They're not on stage together.'

'I won't play Eve! Last time I played a woman – Bathsheba, it was – I got *offers!*'

Will grinned and made an obscene gesture, for which Tim would have punched him if Piper hadn't seized his fist.

'Stop that! What'll folk think if God's got a black eye? There must be something that doesn't have a woman in it.'

No one came up with anything. The three men sat in glum silence on the tailboard.

'D'you really think she'll come back?' said Tim, after a while.

'Look,' said Piper. 'If she went with that fancy lord he'll throw her out when the novelty's worn off. Where else is she going to go?' He scowled. 'I told her no whoring! We're actors, not tail-renters. And anyway, it's too late to do anything now. Where could we find an audience at this time of day?'

Tim cocked his head. 'What's that?'

'What?'

'That noise. Something's coming.'

Presently they all heard what Tim's sharp ears had picked up first, the tank-tank-tank of ox bells and a rumbling noise, getting louder, and voices raised in discordant song. Looking up at the crest of the low hill behind them they saw a pair of oxen come into view, and another, and another, followed by a lot more, and, eventually, a heavily reinforced long cart, carrying something like a giant's beehive swathed in canvas.

After it, over the hill, poured what looked like the lost tribe of Israel: carts, horses, mules, people. Some of the people were singing, and not all were singing the same tune.

A rider came cantering downhill ahead of the oxen, a big sword at his back and a red-eared white hound running at his horse's heels.

'God save you, masters,' he greeted them. 'Is it far to Pickling-ham?'

'Two leagues,' said Piper, watching the oxen's slow progress. 'You'll not get there before dark, not at that pace.'

'Have to camp here, then.' The horseman surveyed their

surroundings, assessing the advantages of the site – reasonably level ground, a shallow river, rough grazing – and waved a signal to the carters. The oxen slowed and came to a ponderous halt, with much blowing and snorting. It was within a few minutes of knocking-off time, and they knew it to the second.

Tim stared at the enormous beehive thing towering over them. 'What's that?'

'That, lad,' said Piper, gazing raptly at the crowd – by God, there must be thirty or forty people – 'is an audience! Bang the drum!'

Tyrrel climbed the spiral steps of the juliet tower like a crippled old man, bent, tortoise-slow; his feet, as he lifted them one after the other, heavy as iron. As always, after an indulgence, he felt weak and unwell, and the sweat that soaked his clothes smelled goatish, rank. It would be a day or two before he was himself again, a month or two perhaps before the need grew desperate again. The intervals between these ... episodes were getting shorter. It had been a year between the first and the second. Then eight months, then six ...

The tower had been abandoned long ago, but he'd had it put back in repair to house his prisoner. There were two floors above the undercroft, each a large, round, single room. The prisoner lived in the lower chamber, and the upper chamber, accessed from within the other by a ladder, was his workroom.

For a prisoner he was well treated. He had a bed and blankets, and a table where he could sit to read and write. It gave his guards (there were always two on duty, day and night) the creeps to see the old man writing in his book, his lightless ophidian eyes staring at nothing while his pen went *scratch-scratch* – pause, dip – *scratch-scratch*. The brown skeletal hand hardly seemed to direct the quill; indeed, one of the guards swore he'd seen it write of its own accord while the old man lay on his bed. They were not even sure that he slept. He certainly didn't eat enough to keep a rat alive, although food was carried to him every day.

It was almost a full year since Tyrrel had last climbed these steps. At the top he unlocked and opened the door. The heat inside the red-litten chamber was stifling. The fire was never let out. At times it was fed with fuel until it roared, and its eerie glow shone from the single round window at night like an evil moon. The vitiated air had a metallic smell, and a hanging lamp with four wicks gave a sullen light which threw deformed

126

shadows on the walls. There was a cacophony of sounds: the rhythmic creak of bellows and the bubbling, whistling and hissing of various vessels coming to the boil. A slave heaved at the bellows, a black man, glossy with sweat; and another, his hands wrapped in rags, shuffled the pots around, shifting some from the fire's heart and moving others into it. Each slave wore an iron belt fettered by a long chain to a ring set in the floor, and neither looked up when Tyrrel entered.

In a cage on the wall a mangy monkey screeched and scratched. In cages on the floor rats and toads hunched in misery. The bloody light of the flames flickered on the stone walls, and the servants of the fire cast monstrous shadows.

'Where is he?' Tyrrel demanded.

One of the slaves, salaaming, said, 'He sleeps, *sayyed*.'

'Wake him!'

The slave knelt down and shook what looked like a heap of rags under one of the long, scarred, scorched tables. It whined. Tyrrel kicked it.

'Up, dog!'

The slave helped the bundle of rags to its feet – an impossibly thin, impossibly old man, mummy-like, his skin loose and dry like a snake's about to be shed, although what might struggle from that chrysalis of skin was not to be thought of. He wore the robes of a desert Arab, stained and scattered with scorches and burn holes. His black eyes glinted at the champion, and one claw-like hand with long, thick, twisted fingernails crept out from his robe like a loathsome great insect, touching lips, brow and breast.

'Well?' Tyrrel demanded. 'Is it done?'

A slave repeated the question in the old man's foreign tongue, and relayed his reply. 'You are too early, *sayyed*. At the dark of the moon—'

'I want to see it. Show me.'

The other black picked up a long pair of tongs, but the Arab squealed and jabbered, waving his hands.

'He says it must stay in the fire, in the heart of the fire; the heat must be kept constant at this time, *sayyed*, or all will be to do again.'

Tyrrel scowled. 'But it will be ready then? That is sure?'

The Arab spoke again, and again the slave translated. 'He says it will. And he reminds you of your promise.'

Tyrrel's lips twitched. It might have been a smile. 'Oh, I remember. We have a bargain. When I have the elixir he may go

127

free. Get on with the work. I'll come again at the dark of the moon.'

As he left the chamber the Arab's eyes followed him with hatred, and when the door closed behind him the sorcerer spat in the ashes on the hearth, and with his crooked finger wrote signs that would have frightened the two slaves, had they still had eyes to see.

The players gave their audience *Sir Fulke fitzWaryn*, a bawdy romp in which the notorious outlaw (Will, in shabby green) tries to seduce a modest maid (Tim, luridly painted, in a straw wig and under protest), but is challenged and defeated by her irate father (Piper): a very moral play, hastily cleaned up a bit, seeing there were monks in the audience, but with plenty of slapstick and foolery. They were cheered to the echo and invited to supper, and when Piper took the hat round he collected just over a shilling.

After supper, as the pilgrims and all settled down for the night, Straccan strolled over to the players' carts, gave Piper a penny and offered the players a shilling a week and their meals, plus whatever they could extract from their audience, if they were willing to travel with the bell to its destination.

'Durham?' Piper looked doubtful. 'Don't they speak another lingo up there? How can we make a living if they don't understand us?'

'It's not that different,' said Straccan, crossing his fingers behind his back and hoping it was true. 'And you can always mime.' He wanted these players. He'd seen the effect of the players' clowning on his company's sagging morale; they'd rocked and wept with mirth, he'd even laughed himself. If there was entertainment to look forward to each evening it would take their minds off ogres, fairies, outlaws and wolves; even, God grant it, curses. Despite his efforts the whole company had heard some garbled version of Gaudy's history from Brother Mungo, who ought to have known better. The women were nervy, the men short-tempered, the carters mutinous and murmuring about curses, and Straccan feared that just one more calamity would result in them dumping the bell and going home. It was also unfortunate that for the past few days the dog – he still hadn't thought of a name for it – seemed to have taken a dislike to the bell. Mungo called it 'a portent', and the carters had taken to forking their fingers in the sign against the Evil Eye whenever the dog howled at the bell wain.

It was doing it now! It had jumped up on the wagon bed and

was scratching at the canvas cover, worrying at it with growling determination. It had clawed a rent in the tough canvas and torn out some of the straw padding. There must be a rat in there.

'Get down! Get off that,' Straccan called. It looked at him and whined eagerly, wagging its tail; then seeing that Straccan wasn't going to help, resumed its efforts. Straccan clambered on to the cart and dragged it off by the collar. Luckily most of the company was already abed, in carts or tents.

Keeping hold of the dog's collar he returned to Piper.

'Well?'

'It's a decent offer,' Piper said. 'But our company's not complete. We need a new woman; the one we had ran off in Cambridge.'

'That's up to you,' Straccan said. 'I won't pay any more, but she'll get her food.'

'Fair enough.'

'What do you call yourselves?'

It was a sore point. They'd argued about it for months. 'Piper's Men' didn't sound all that impressive, and Pernelle had objected to the 'Men' bit. 'Piper's Company' sounded more important; Piper was all for it, but the others weren't keen. 'The Players' could be anybody. They were stuck for a name.

Staring embarrassedly at his patched boots, Piper muttered something like, 'Haven't decided yet.'

'How about "The Gaudy Company"?' Straccan suggested. One after the other, the players' faces broke into wide smiles.

Chapter 23

Bane didn't look all that dangerous. He was not much taller than Roslyn and scrawny in spite of an appetite like a giant's. He wore a short sword in a scabbard at his back, a small bow and quiver at his shoulder and a visible dagger at his belt, but in addition he had secreted about his person several knives which he had made himself – small, wicked blades set in flat, roughened wooden hafts, easily slotted into boots or breeks or sleeves or even inside a cap; and the lace that fastened his jerkin could double as a garrotte.

'There's a pilgrim hostel a mile along this road,' he said. 'Shall we sleep there tonight, or lie out?'

'It's dry,' said Roslyn. 'Let's stay outside.'

'Are you sure? There'll be a real bed.'

'Who knows who has died in it? Better outside.'

Bane looked curiously at her. 'As you will.'

He hadn't been surprised to discover that she could tickle trout, snare a rabbit, and knock down a pigeon or a fat partridge with a stone from a slingshot, as skilfully as he could. Between them they kept the pot full, but bran and oats for the horses were less easy to get. Bane's talents at disguise were used to the full; no one would recognise him in the sunken-faced, stooping, elderly man who bought oats at a farm one day, and the sprightly, chubby-cheeked, pot-bellied, much younger fellow haggling over the price of bran at an inn the next day. At inns and villages, Roslyn and David stayed out of sight.

Joanna clenched her teeth and held her head high. She mustn't cry. Long ago her father had told her, 'Princesses never cry,' and she would never do anything to disappoint him. Besides, they would all see her tears. She was the Princess of Gwynedd, and no matter if her heart was ground in the dust, she wouldn't let anyone guess how much it hurt.

They had quarrelled again, she and Llywelyn, and when she couldn't bear his savage words any longer she had gathered her pride around her like armour, turned her back on him, and left him alone in their bedchamber. He had not come after her. He was a great lord and proud, and they had injured each other. She had said bitter things, driven the knife of her words deep, and she too was proud. From this day there was no going back. Nothing would ever be the same.

Yet she loved him. She had thought he loved her.

Back then, when they first met, he probably did.

Her tearless eyes had the inward, unseeing look of remembering, and in memory she was back at Ludlow, just fourteen years old, when the Prince of Gwynedd came to court the King of England's daughter.

John let them talk, dance, ride, hunt together. Then, after a week – in which she had fallen head over heels in love – he came to her chamber before the evening's feasting had begun, and asked her, 'Do you like him, Joanie?'

She had said, 'Whatever you think best.'

Her father took her hands and stared into her eyes – green as his own. 'No, Joanie, love. It's for you to choose. This would be a useful alliance, I'll not deny, but if you don't like the man, then that's an end to it. I'll steer his eyes elsewhere and keep my girl.'

Like him? His thrilling voice, his strong, tanned hands, his eyes, so dark they were nearly black, bright with laughter, excitement, and when he looked at Joanna, admiration. When he took her hand in the dance, when his thigh pressed hers as they rode side by side, a sweet shock of desire lanced through her body. *Like* him?

What had she said, webbed in the glamour of first love? 'He's beautiful!' And saw her father's worried expression change to one of relief and pleasure.

'Be sure, Joanie,' he said, and hugged her.

Now memory stabbed her with longing for her father, the dear, familiar smell of him, the scent of his skin and clothes, known and loved all her life. She wished she were a child again, to take her fears to him and be comforted on his lap, in his arms; her small world set to rights.

Her first duty was to her husband, she knew that. But if he took up arms against her father men would die and the poor folk would suffer. If she said nothing, she betrayed her father. If she sent warning – always assuming she could, for she would be watched now more than ever – she betrayed Llywelyn. John would come with a host; Wales would be laid waste, its prince imprisoned, perhaps even executed, for treason.

Unthinking, her feet had led her to the chapel. At least in

there she could be alone, for the space of a prayer.

Bane set traps each night and checked them at first light, sometimes thereby adding a squirrel or a rabbit to their daily fare. Returning to their campsite this morning, a fat rabbit hanging at his belt, he heard David cry, 'Bane! Bane!' and a man's laugh, and another's curse. Christ, they'd been found!

He made for the hollow where they'd slept, stringing his bow and nocking an arrow as he ran, and came upon not the three knights but two ribauds, one – still laughing – grasping the reins of their horses, the other holding Roslyn, one great hand over her face and mouth, an arm around her waist, hoisting her up off the ground so that her kicking feet had no purchase. David, winded and crowing for breath, sprawled in the cold ashes of their fire, where one of the men had kicked him. Bane saw Roslyn's long knife lying on the ground, but by the blood soaking her attacker's breeches, she'd managed to slash him in the belly before he got the dagger away from her.

Get the one with the horses first – the other one's got his hands full.

The feathered shaft seemed to sprout from the outlaw's eye. The man stood for a moment as if nothing had happened, then gave at the knees and fell, dragging the horses' heads down with him by their reins wrapped around his hands. Just as well; they might have run otherwise, spooked by the smell of blood.

The other man, fully occupied with the struggling Roslyn, hadn't noticed his partner's collapse, and by now David had his breath back and had got to his knees in the ashes, his small white face a mask of fury.

Before Bane could nock a second arrow, stones were flying. One struck the outlaw's elbow. He yelped in pained surprise and dropped Roslyn, who rolled away from his feet, scrabbling in the grass for her knife. Another stone smashed his mouth, breaking teeth and filling his mouth with blood that ran down his chin. Where were they coming from? David wasn't throwing them; he was just kneeling there, glaring at the ribaud, his hands gripped together, white-knuckled. And anyway, there *were* no stones in the grassy hollow.

'Bitch! Whore!' The outlaw made a grab for Roslyn's hair, and at the same moment that Bane's second arrow pierced his throat, Roslyn drove her knife up under his ribs. He went down like a felled ox, falling to his knees, then on to his face. His legs twitched, and he lay still.

Roslyn was swearing like an archer, in French and English, as she sheathed her knife and knelt in front of the boy.

'David. David!'

David put his thumb in his mouth. Tears ran down his face, but he made no sound. Roslyn gathered him in her arms, rocking backwards and forwards on her knees as if she held a baby.

Bane bent and picked up one of the stones. It was a big, smooth river pebble, real and solid as, well, as stone; greyish, heavy – and hot. He dropped it quickly and wiped his hand on his breeches.

'Let's go,' he said. 'They may have friends.'

Flies were already droning and crawling on the dead men's faces as Bane liberated the horses from the first outlaw's clutch. They mounted, Bane taking David up in front of him. 'Hold on, soldier,' he said.

The boy closed his eyes and sucked his thumb, and his other hand gripped Bane's belt.

'I'm sorry,' he whispered.

'What for?'

'The stones. This time . . . this time I wanted them to come. I made it happen.'

'Don't worry about it,' Bane said. 'You have to use whatever's handy if someone's trying to kill you.'

'But I promised. When I hurt Roslyn, I said I'd never do it again.'

'Well, this time you didn't hurt her, did you? You saved her life.'

'Is it all right, then? To do a bad thing, to help someone?'

'I don't know about that. But your father was a knight, wasn't he? And you'll be a knight too, when you're grown. And it's a knight's duty to protect the weak, especially ladies.'

Anything in skirts less weak than Roslyn de Sorules Bane hoped he'd never meet, but this sophistry seemed to satisfy David, and after some consideration he stopped sucking his thumb.

Chapter 24

Locksey was a large village, big enough to support an inn, of sorts. It wouldn't do for noble folk, who would claim hospitality at the castle anyway, but Starling Larktwist – unrecognisable as the neatly dressed, respectable, eminently refined doctor, forced to stop there when his horse went lame – found it suited his purposes very well.

His gelding's inflamed frog had prevented him following Tyrrel to Ravenser, but as the champion was expected to return to Locksey shortly, Larktwist had made the best of things. As soon as he let slip his calling, he was welcomed with open arms – literally, in the case of the widow Trygg, who had managed the inn since her husband's death the previous year.

Reclining luxuriously in the widow's feather bed, his head pillowed on her generous bosom, the doctor wasn't really paying attention as she extolled the virtues of the late Trygg, until a word snagged his attention.

'Dragon?' he said, sitting up. 'What dragon?'

'Oh, it was 'orrible,' said the widow, pulling him down again. 'You'll catch cold, my lovely, sittin' up like that wi' nowt on. Come 'ere!' And she pulled his head down between her mountainous breasts.

'What dragon?' he persisted, in no danger of catching cold although suffocation was a definite possibility.

'The dragon Sir Ralf brought back from the Scots' land. Thought to tame it, 'e did, but twas against Nature. Oh, it used to give no end of trouble! Its breath killed the leaves on the trees, and the stream where it drank was poisoned too. The fish all died, and poor folk that drank from it, they sickened and died too, my Trygg, for one. Everyone in the vill 'ad to use the lord's well up the castle, aye, an' pay for it!'

Larktwist managed to come up for air. 'A real dragon?'

'Oh yes. Kept it in the east tower, 'e did. We could see its fire, at night, through the window up the top, all red and burning, and we could 'ear it 'issin'.'

'Is it still there?'

134

'Bless you, no, pet! Sir took it away to Ravenser. Ooh, that's nice! Do that again.'

'Why would anyone want a dragon?'

She put her lips close to his ear and nearly deafened him with the volume of her whisper. 'For the gold!'

'What gold?'

'Dragons can make gold, of course. 'Ere, you married?'

'Um, unfortunately, yes,' lied Larktwist, thinking, *Dragons? Gold? Jesus!*

'Pity. Be good for the inn, to 'ave a doctor on tap, as it were. 'Ere, sometimes I get this pain in me back . . .'

'Roll over,' said Larktwist. He was going to have to report this. Mercredi would think he'd lost his marbles. 'I'll massage it for you.'

He was sure he could hear hammering. It sounded as if someone was building a scaffold. No, it was someone battering at the inn door. Larktwist sat up, and so, when she'd caught her breath, did the widow Trygg. Feet came thundering up the stairs, and the bedroom door was kicked in. A massive man in Tyrrel's livery strode to the bed and grasped Larktwist by one ankle. Two men-at-arms crowded in behind him, grinning like apes over his shoulders.

'You. Come with us. Sir Ralf wants you.'

'Why? I've done nothing!'

The sergeant-at-arms pulled him off the bed and let him fall to the floor. 'Bring 'im,' he snapped at his men.

'I'm a free man! You can't—'

The widow Trygg, clutching a very inadequate blanket, thrust herself between Larktwist and the soldier.

'Don't 'urt im!'

'Won't need to, so long as 'e does what 'e's told,' said the sergeant. ''Ere,' he added, eyeing the widow's rosy nudity with an understandably lascivious grin. 'Fancy a spot of 'ow's yer father? I can come back later.'

'In a pig's eye!'

The men-at-arms hauled Larktwist upright. He hung in their grasp like a wet shirt.

'Where's your stuff?' the sergeant demanded.

'My stuff?' Larktwist looked around vaguely. His clothes and boots were scattered across the floor in a trail from door to bed. He still had one sock on.

'Your doctoring stuff.'

'Oh!' He had a medicine box, of course he had. He'd won it

playing dice with a travelling quack who called himself Simon Superbus. It had all sorts of things in it, mostly foul-smelling. What they tasted like he shuddered to think. He had no idea what they were for, but so far he'd had no complaints, probably because he hadn't hung around long enough to get any.

'Is that why you've come for me? Someone's sick?' *Sweet bleeding Jesus, what have you got yourself into now, Starling?* he asked himself. He was going to be taken to the castle, an opportunity unlooked for and far beyond his remit. That was spy's work. He wasn't a spy. He just followed people, reporting where they went and who they met; he'd done it for years and took pride in it, but to be a real spy, an agent-in-place, was a different kettle of fish entirely. Different scale of pay. Different level of risk. As he scrabbled into his clothes he mentally weighed one job against the other, and as they dragged him downstairs decided that the first chance he got, he'd be out of there.

If he lived!

He tried to find out, as they lugged him through the village and over the drawbridge, across the bailey and into the garrison quarters, why his skills were required, but the sergeant said nothing until they were in the garrison dormitory. It was like garrison dormitories everywhere, ill-lit, cold and smelling of socks. On a pallet in a corner, beneath the feeble light of a wall lantern, a prone figure lay under a blanket.

'It's the captain,' said the sergeant.

'What's the matter with him?'

''Ow should I know? That's what you're 'ere for.' The sergeant snapped his fingers and the two men holding Larktwist let go. One of them gave him a shove towards his patient.

He crouched beside the pallet and prodded the blanketed mound. A hand appeared and pulled the cover aside, revealing a pallid, sweaty face.

'You the leech?'

Larktwist nodded. 'What's wrong with you?'

A finger beckoned him closer. He leaned forward. The captain whispered in his ear.

'Really?' said Larktwist, interested in spite of himself. 'Let's have a look.'

The captain cast a glance of agonised embarrassment at his comrades. 'Not with them here!'

'You heard him,' Larktwist said. 'Outside!' Muttering, with backward glances, the sergeant and men-at-arms trooped out.

'And shut the door behind you,' Larktwist shouted. It slammed.

He unhooked the lantern. The captain raised the blanket. Both of them peered underneath it.

'Cor!' said Larktwist.

'Can you do anything?'

Larktwist sniffed. He could do *something*, of course. Whether it was the right thing or not was another matter. But in for a penny, in for a pound.

He opened his box and studied the contents while the captain watched anxiously. Then he picked up a long needle. The captain made a small whimpering sound through clenched teeth.

'Don't worry,' Larktwist said. 'This won't hurt a bit.'

Two days later, when the champion had returned from Ravenser and the captain was well enough to get up, the steward brought Larktwist a purse from Sir Ralf and congratulated him on a job well done.

'All in a day's work.' His success had astonished him, but they weren't to know that. Almost everyone on the manor had consulted him about something or other. He'd done very well out of them during the past couple of days and was mixing a further supply of his best-selling item, a bit of everything in his box stirred into vinegar and sweetened with honey. He tucked the purse in his bosom and resumed stirring.

'Er . . . what was it ailed him?'

'I never discuss a patient,' said Larktwist primly, straining the mixture into a jug. The steward hovered at his side, watching as he poured it through a cow's horn into a bottle and shook it vigorously, his thumb over the top. Then Larktwist tasted it. It made his eyes water.

'What's that?' the steward asked.

'My universal specific,' Larktwist said solemnly.

'Your what?'

'Good for everything.' He opened the box and put the bottle away among the phials and pots. 'Coughs, colds, bellyaches, diarrhoea, constipation, melancholy, piles, boils . . .' He eyed the steward covertly during his recital. Whatever ailed the man was sure to be in there somewhere. 'Toothache,' he continued, 'sore eyes, sore feet, the stone, rupture, red water, black water, worms, baldness . . .'

'What about—' The steward looked furtively at the others in the hall and whispered hotly into Larktwist's ear.

'Did it?' Larktwist asked, interested. 'When?'

'Last night, and again this morning.'

'Lucky I'm still here, then. This is the very thing.' He held up the bottle, and the steward reached for it.

'Uh-uh,' said Larktwist, snatching his hand back. 'That's fourpence.'

'Fourpence? That's robbery!'

'Please yourself.' He made to put the bottle back but the steward grabbed his wrist.

'All right! Fourpence. There you are.' He counted out pennies and halfpennies and clutched the bottle to his breast. 'Do I drink it all at once?'

'Drink it? God, no! You dip it in. Just before . . . ah . . .' Scarlet-faced, the steward hushed him with desperate gestures. 'Well, you know. It'll smart a bit, mind.' He shut and locked the box. 'I'll be getting along, then. The widow will be keeping the bed warm for me.'

'What d'you mean, getting along? Sir Ralf's very pleased with you.'

'Is he? That's nice.'

'You're a useful man to have around.'

'Well, yes, but—'

'Our garrison surgeon died last week.'

He didn't like the way this was going. 'He did?'

'So you're coming to Ravenser with us.'

Chapter 25

'You shouldn't have killed him,' Michael said. 'There was no need.'

'He was nothing! A serf,' Uriel protested.

'A serf of Straccan's manor. And Hoby said the sheriff was on his way there,' Michael said. 'If that was true, there may be a posse after us by tonight.'

Uriel flushed. 'I didn't mean him to die. He was a weakling. They can't be that far ahead, with the child to carry, and Hoby's not with them.'

Two leagues from Stirrup they'd got wind of their quarry. A swineherd had seen them: two horses, man, woman and child. What's more, he knew the man, a servant of Sir Richard Straccan, Bane by name. They'd been heading south-east. Where to? Well, that was anyone's guess, but this was the road to Derby.

'Who is the woman? His mother?' Samael asked. Michael looked at him with surprise; he spoke so seldom.

'I don't know. His mother escaped with him when his father was taken. There were rumours that she died at Portet or Montgey, but her body was never identified.'

'Why did Hoby bring them to England? Are they kin?'

Michael frowned. Samael was asking too much. Tell them no more than you must, Bishop Fulk had said. 'That's not our concern. We were not sent to kill Hoby or the woman, whoever she is, unless we have to. We are here to kill the boy.'

Why? Samael wondered, unthinking obedience shaken for the first time by a tremor of curiosity.

The roads were unusually busy. Servants and stable boys at every hostel they came to had been run off their feet since dawn attending to bands of knights and men-at-arms, cartloads of supplies of all sorts and groups of tramping labourers, all heading north-west.

'For Chester, at the king's command,' a young knight volunteered when Michael bought him and his dusty companions a round of drinks. 'It's war, at last.' The knights cheered, and applauded by banging their cups on the table. A lot of ale splashed about but no one seemed to mind.

'War?' Michael said. 'With King Philip?'

'Not this time.' The young man laughed. 'We're going to teach the Welsh a lesson. Treacherous little buggers,' he added indignantly.

'We are looking for some friends,' Michael said, signalling the innkeeper to bring the jug round again and heroically swallowing the sour brew when it came. 'A man, a young woman and a small boy, with two horses. Have you passed any like that on your way?'

No, they had not. Not that they would have noticed.

They would keep to the road, make for Derby, ask at every hospice and alehouse, every priory gate, every priest's cottage. Sooner or later someone would have seen their quarry. And there seemed little fear of pursuit, for with the whole country mobilising for war, the king's officers, sheriffs and coroners, would be far too busy to waste time on such trivial matters as the murder of a serf.

They rode out of the hostel yard, Samael and Uriel in front, Michael bringing up the rear. He frowned as Uriel rowelled his horse with unnecessary savagery, thrusting past Samael and galloping ahead, showing off, heedlessly scattering goats, hens and folk afoot, bowling over a toddling brat that sat in the mud and bawled, fortunately unhurt. Its father shook his fist after the rider, and people shuffled sullenly aside to give passage to the other two.

Uriel turned at last and rode back to his companions, laughing, jostling Samael's horse without apology, spoiling for trouble. Samael said nothing, but Michael saw his jaw muscles jump as he clenched his teeth rather than start the shouting match the young man obviously craved.

Michael kneed his horse alongside Uriel's and fetched the knight a heavy blow across the face with his forearm. 'Mend your manners,' he snarled, as blood burst from the astonished young man's nose. 'Were you taught none as a squire?' And, as Uriel opened his mouth, 'Not a word! You'll keep silence the rest of this day and ride at the tail. Get behind!'

The young fool was a liability, the worst sort of well born lout. Rash, stupid and brutal. Three men had been chosen for this task and three might well be needed to complete it, but if Uriel didn't toe the line from now on, he'd send him back to France.

★　★　★

At Chester, on the roof of the castle keep, Robert fitzWalter and Eustace de Vesci gazed out over the landscape at the rows of tents, fluttering banners, stacks of pikes, loaded sumpter wagons and men who had answered the king's call to arms: thousands of men, and more arriving every day.

FitzWalter leaned on the crenellated parapet and watched an ant-like line of covered wagons crawl past the castle.

'When will the king come?' de Vesci asked. Broad-shouldered, tall and lean, dark of skin and hair and clad in black, he was a wedge of night beside the scarlet-clothed fitzWalter.

'A week. Perhaps less.'

'And the couriers? When will you send them?'

'They left this morning.'

The Great Enterprise had begun. Nothing, fitzWalter thought exultantly, could stop it now! Couriers had been dispatched to the Welsh princes – to Llywelyn, Gwenwynwyn, and the smaller fry with their impossible names, Maelgwn ap Rhys, Madog ap Gruffydd, Maredudd ap Rhobert – detailing the disposition of the host. When the king crossed into Gwynedd, at a pre-arranged signal those he trusted close to him would withdraw, leaving him to the enemy. A letter had gone to the queen at Woodstock, sealed – apparently – with the king's private seal, commanding her to join him at Nottingham; and word had gone to Ralf Tyrrel at Locksey, telling him when the queen would leave Woodstock. As soon as king and host crossed the border into Gwynedd, fitzWalter would ride to London and seize the young princes.

No, nothing could stop it now.

Behind the flimsy privacy of her bed curtains the princess of Gwynedd lay awake, listening to her waiting-women snore. The wives of princes were never alone. Even in her bedchamber she had two attendants, in case she should call for wine or for a hot stone for her feet, or even for music, if she was unable to sleep. And there were few she could trust. Her knights, although sworn to her service, were first and foremost Llywelyn's men, and her women resented her, their prince's foreign-born wife, bastard daughter of his enemy King John.

She had carried the letter hidden in her sleeve all day, waiting for an opportunity to pass it to the one man of whose loyalty – to her – she was certain, her food taster, Peredur. Not until the evening meal did the chance arise: there was a new fool, a gift to the prince from the French king, and while all the court rocked with mirth at his lewd antics she slipped the little roll of parchment from her sleeve into Peredur's hand. No one noticed. God willing, he would reach the king in time to stop him setting out for Wales.

The letter told her father that if he crossed into Gwynedd, his own lords intended to murder him. She had overheard Llywelyn and his brother discussing the plan. Tears slid down her cheeks and blotted into her pillow. By warning her father, she betrayed her husband. She loved them both. Between them, they were tearing her apart.

Another day lost.

Straccan sighed. 'There was a wheelwright at Cromber. Aidan, take my horse. Go back and fetch him.'

As the novice scrambled into Apple's saddle and galloped back towards the town where they'd spent the night, Straccan stood staring morosely at the bell wain, tilted to the right but kept from collapsing further by props, and at the lopsided wheel. If Aidan hadn't noticed the wheel's wobble when he did, it would have come off and the wain would have overturned, bringing down the bell. Aidan and Finan, walking alongside, taking turns to carry Mistress Fisher's baby, would have been crushed.

'Shall us unpack then, sir?' the bannerman asked.

'Might as well,' said Straccan glumly. 'We won't be going anywhere today.' He heard the tide of grumbling spread as they set up their grubby tents and shelters again, but turned his back on the unlovely sight and scowled again at the bell wain. The pieces of the lynchpin lay at his feet, and he lifted his foot to kick them aside . . . paused, and picked them up instead, scraping thoughtfully at the fractured ends with his thumbnail.

It wasn't unknown for a lynchpin to crack, but it was uncommon.

Of course, when the pin had been sawn through to start with and gummed together with wax, it was just a matter of time . . .

He looked up sharply at the sound of hooves. Six, no, seven riders, armed with pikes and bows. They stopped when they reached the camp, and one dismounted, saying something to the smith. Voices rose angrily, and the other horsemen dismounted. Straccan strode over to them.

'What's the matter?'

'Sir Richard,' cried the smith. 'They want to search our camp! Tell 'em they can't! I'm not 'avin' them muck up my tools!'

They were wearing livery, and their leader was a middle-aged

142

leathery-looking man with the badge of some lord in his cap.

'By whose authority?' Straccan demanded.

'Well,' said the man with the badge, 'I'm Hugh Tapton, bailiff to the abbey of Cromber, so I suppose that's my authority. Good enough?'

'Who's the abbot?'

'Ah, now there you've got me. There's no abbot just now – the Interdict, you know. We make do with the prior until the king permits us to elect a new abbot. Whenever that may be. You in charge of this lot?'

'Yes. I'm Richard Straccan. What d'you want?'

'No trouble, Sir Richard, but there's a girl missing from the town.'

'What girl?'

'Thomas Aurifer the goldsmith's daughter, Christina.'

'Why come here?'

'You were there last night. The town's been searched. Now we're looking further afield.'

'Then go on, bailiff, do your office, but see your fellows behave. There's a very sick child in the third cart – no one's to touch him.' Although every morning he expected to be told the boy had died, Lawrence Boteler was still alive. 'No shoving my pilgrims around, no pinching the women's bottoms, no tampering with their stuff, understand? We're on an errand for His Grace the Bishop of Winchester, and these pilgrims are under his protection. I'll be right here watching, and I won't miss a thing. Get on with it.'

The carts were searched thoroughly, even the little hand-drawn ones, and the bailiff's men looked very closely at every female face in the company, but no bottoms were pinched, and they were forced to admit at last that there was no goldsmith's daughter there.

'Run off with some squire, like as not,' said Brother Mungo.

Tapton scowled. 'Keep your loose tongue clamped, monk! Christina Aurifer's a good maid. You'd do well to pray for her, rather than defame her.' He put his foot in the stirrup. 'I fear the worst,' he said. 'Two years ago another young woman vanished and was never found. And this one is much like her.' He swung up into the saddle.

Straccan caught at his bridle. 'Like her? How?'

'Very fair,' said the bailiff. 'Hair as bright as Our Lady's own.'

Like the girl at Waltham.

'Wait a bit,' said Straccan. 'She may not be the only one.'

Chapter 26

Christina opened her eyes in the cushioned, lurching, dimly lit space, and found herself still in the nightmare.

Daylight filtered reluctantly through the heavy brown canvas; she heard men's voices, horses' hooves and the rumbling wheels of the jolting wagon, and smelled horses and dust. She tried to move her arms and legs, but it was useless – she was still tied hand and foot.

She had no idea what had happened to her. The last thing she remembered was getting out of bed and opening the bed-chamber shutter – but why would she do that? No one opened shutters after dark. She tried to concentrate, although it made her headache worse.

It had been the middle of the night, she in her bed and her parents in theirs, her mother's tire-woman wuffling softly on the truckle bed at their feet. From the loft above came the snores of the apprentices; her father always sent them to bed first and took away the ladder so they couldn't sneak out at night.

She had been asleep, and someone had called her name. Someone outside. She got up and opened the shutter, and remembered nothing more until she woke in the wagon.

Saint Thomas! Holy Mother! Help me!

She began to struggle against her bonds, crying out weakly. And as before, hands grasped her shoulders, held her head, forcing the neck of a flask between her lips, filling her mouth with sickly-sweet syrup that she must swallow or choke, thrusting her helplessly down again into the red-black petals of the dream that enfolded her.

The common room of the Swan at Darley smelled of smoke, sweat and onions, and was full of people. Half a dozen archers in the sheriff's livery hogged the fire, dicing for first go at the inn's one and only trollop, while their captain lay full-length, asleep, on one of the tables, among crusts, spilled ale and gravy. At the other table eight assorted travellers spooned their pottage, too hungry for conversation, and in one corner a pedlar dozed,

144

sitting on his pack, a small white dog in his arms. A serving girl, rosy with heat and mirth, was packing another wayfarer's saddle-bags with provisions, giggling and flirting good-naturedly as she did so. In went bread, cheese, a sinister-looking coiled black sausage, hard-boiled eggs and a block of ham, smoked and hard as wood.

'Got any raisins?' the man asked. There was nothing remark-able about him; he wasn't very tall, and wore a plain grey cloak over brown riding leathers, but he *did* have a nice smile and hadn't tried to grope the girl, which, come to think of it, was remarkable enough.

The Swan's rain-swollen door jerked open, stuck halfway, and yielded to a solidly placed kick. The archers looked up from their dice at the tall, grey-haired man, a knight by his mail hauberk, his sodden cloak dripping into the puddle already there and his high boots clarted to the knee – the inn yard, after two days' rain, had the consistency of soup.

Michael stood in the doorway for as long as it took to eye everyone in the room, then came in, swinging the heavy wet mantle off his shoulders. The other two Angels followed him, Uriel dragging the door shut behind him. Once in, their wet cloaks hung up to drip, they said nothing, just stared at the diners, who fidgeted uncomfortably and one by one got up to vacate the benches for their betters. The archers resumed their play. They were the sheriff's men and weren't getting up for anyone.

The man in the grey cloak had faded inconspicuously out of the picture and into the kitchen. The girl picked up a jug and approached the new customers.

'Ale, lords?'

'Wine. What food have you?'

'Pottage, if you're in a hurry. If you can wait there's a coney pie in the oven, and ducks on the spit.'

'We'll wait.' He felt in his purse and held up half a penny. 'We are looking for a man; he has a young woman and a little boy with him. They have two horses, one grey, one brown. Have you seen them?'

'Not to notice, m'lord. It's been that busy.'

The tall knight put the halfpenny back in his purse. One of the others, a young man, handsome in a hard-eyed, hard-mouthed fashion, seized her wrist.

'Are you certain? The boy has six years.'

A funny way of speaking, she thought – a Frog. She tried to

pull her arm away but he twisted it, making her yelp with surprise and pain. Several heads turned, scowling, but no one dared interfere.

'Leave her alone,' said the tall knight impatiently. 'Ask them.' He jerked his head towards the archers, who nudged one another and prepared to play dumb. Rubbing her wrist, where red finger marks already bruised the skin, the girl slipped out of the room into the kitchen, where she found the man in the grey cloak helping himself from a barrel of raisins.

'They stopping for dinner?' he asked.

She nodded. 'Bloody Frogs! You the one they're after?'

'Could be.'

'They asked about a woman and a little boy.'

'My kids,' said Bane. 'We're in trouble.'

'What did you do?'

'I was just minding my own business when this deer came bounding out of the forest into my backyard, with an arrow in its side. Dropped dead at my feet. The verderer wouldn't believe me. I knocked him out, got my kids and ran for it. They'll put a rope round my neck if they catch me.'

She massaged her aching arm. 'What can I do?'

He beamed. 'Good girl! When they've had their dinner, can you tell them that maybe you *do* remember us, and I was asking about the road to London?'

She laughed. 'I'll do that, gladly.'

'Bless you.' He gave her a squeeze and a quick, light kiss, picked up his saddlebags and slipped out the back door.

The stable was dark, quiet, and smelled comfortingly of horses and hay. The Angels' horses, fine big geldings, were stalled, their noses in their mangers and their saddles and gear on the rail at the back. At the foot of the ladder to the hayloft he whistled. A small boy looked down from above, and grinned.

'Hello, Bane.'

'Hello, yourself. Where's Roslyn?'

'Here.' She was behind him – he'd heard nothing – with her long dagger in her hand. 'We saw them ride in. What are they doing?'

'Eating. I'll fetch the horses.' He had left their horses out of sight behind the dovecote. 'Get David. We'll leave the road and cut across country to Croxton, and south to Peterborough from there.' By his reckoning, the bell would pass through Peterborough before they got there; they would pick up its trail and catch up with Straccan somewhere between Peterborough and Deeping

146

Gate. 'We'll ride through the night.'

'They won't follow until tomorrow,' Roslyn said, sheathing her knife.

'They're eating. Doesn't mean they'll stay the night.'

'They'll have to. I cut their girths and stirrup leathers and threw the irons in the midden.'

It was late as they rode away from Darley, with the first stars pricking holes in the darkening blue sky.

'We'd better not stop until we reach Temple Tutton,' Bane said. 'There's an inn there where we can rest for a while.'

'No,' said Roslyn quickly. 'No inns. Under the stars is better.'

'What's wrong with inns?'

She glanced at him. 'Have you ever seen a ghost?'

He crossed himself. 'I saw a vision once, but no, no ghosts.'

'Sometimes,' she said softly. 'Sometimes I do.'

'Oh.' There was a thoughtful pause, then Bane said, 'How d'you feel about haylofts? I prefer them myself.'

Larktwist reined in, uttering a long whistle of surprise and hoping he didn't look as dismayed as he felt. This was the usual reaction of anyone seeing the fortress for the first time. The archer riding beside him glanced at him and grinned.

'Ravenser,' he said, unnecessarily.

The fortress stood on an island surrounded by waterlogged bog thick with reeds, with no apparent means of getting to it; boats were no use, and there was no visible causeway. At the western end of the island stood an old-fashioned round juliet tower with a conical roof, and at the other end a square donjon. The juliet had been built during the bloody reign of King Stephen, when God and his saints slept. Any brigand could build a tower in those days and make a living from plunder and wrecking.

It was an earlier Tyrrel, one of William the Bastard's bully boys who, having seen the island monasteries of Ely and Ramsey, spotted the possibilities of Ravenser. Three hundred years earlier the little Benedictine convent on the island had been sacked by the Danes, who slaughtered the monks and nailed the prior to the church door. Their vengeful ghosts were believed to haunt the island, and it had been abandoned except for sheep and their unfortunate shepherd, the only man who knew the secret of access. Tyrrel kept him for his knowledge, made the island his headquarters, built the juliet tower with the stones of the convent, and terrorised the marshland for seven

147

years before dying, undeservedly, in his bed.

A later Tyrrel abandoned the juliet and built a modern square donjon at the other end of the island, with a curtain wall all the way round and a gatehouse. Grown rich on booty, he added a two-storey wing to the donjon, where he enjoyed privacy for his specialised pastimes. This suited the present Tyrrel well enough and he had made no alterations, although the monks' ancient church, hard by the juliet tower, had now fallen into disuse, and one of the upper chambers of the donjon was used instead on the rare occasions when a priest from the abbey at Cerneshead turned up to say Mass. Since the Interdict he hadn't bothered; if any of Ravenser's people needed his services they had to go to him.

The company halted at the edge of the mere. Shading his eyes from the sun Larktwist saw a shaggy-haired figure come out of the gate and walk straight into the mere until the water came halfway up his legs. Instead of sinking, he kept coming, weaving to left and right through reeds and clumps of willow, until he reached them. His skin and clothing were much the same colour as the mud, and Larktwist noticed a wavy blue tattoo on his forehead. Without a word he turned and started back. The company formed a double file and fell in behind him on the sunken causeway.

'Who's that?' Larktwist asked the man riding at his side.

'Kepp o' the Dykes.'

'I hope he knows what he's doing.'

The man hawked and spat into the water. 'Fam'ly secret, ain't it. Had it from his dad, an' his dad from his granddad. Been here for ever. Bloody webfoots.'

'Why not just mark out the path?' Larktwist suggested.

'What, so anyone can just walk in? Use yer brains! Sir Ralf likes it this way.'

Riding under the portcullis Larktwist noticed the crossbow-men on the gatehouse roof with a sinking heart. Things had not gone according to plan. First, because of his horse's lameness, he'd been stuck at Locksey when the champion rode on to Ravenser, and now he'd been brought to Ravenser bloody Tyrrel was back at Locksey, getting up to God knew what.

He'd done what he could to let Mercredi know the situation. Before leaving Locksey he'd sent a message, through his contact in Cambridge, under guise of ordering supplies to replenish his medicine box. He'd needed them anyway, having doled out whatever was asked of him: purges, aphrodisiacs, cough cures and washes for sore eyes. If they hadn't done much good they'd at least done no harm, although one of the men-at-arms, who'd wanted something to gee up his amatory prowess, spent the night groaning in the privy instead of in his doxy's arms, but luckily blamed it on the fish he'd had for dinner.

The champion's squire and servants had remained at Locksey with him, only men-at-arms being sent on ahead with the new leech. The sumpter carts, packed, as far as Larktwist had been able to see with weapons, wouldn't begin to arrive until the morrow; and at least he'd been able to get that much information to his chief.

Word of their arrival and the anticipated coming of the lord of Ravenser had brought his villeins from farms and cotts with their dues of fruit and vegetables, flour and cheeses, honey, pigs and sheep, straw and fodder. The guide was kept busy all day leading wagons and handcarts back and forth across the causeway. That would be a sod of a job in winter, Larktwist thought. He took himself out of the way, climbing the steps on to the curtain wall, from where he could see the whole island and the surrounding marsh. What a place! He'd planned on slipping away at the first opportunity, but he'd never manage to keep to the secret path, and anyway, if he tried to sneak out of the gate he'd end up as full of crossbow bolts as a hedgehog had spines.

The mere seemed endless, and the vast expanse of sky made him feel small and helpless; the wind could blow him away as easily as a dead leaf. He turned his attention to the island. There was the usual clutter of buildings in the bailey – kitchen, bakehouse, brew house, well house, armoury, smithy, stables, water cisterns; and down the other end of the island, beside the juliet tower, an ancient stone church – all that was left, although he didn't know it, of the convent's buildings. The donjon wasn't all that impressive, but on this island it didn't need to be. It was inaccessible anyway.

'You the new surgeon?' One of the crossbowmen had come up behind him and was offering a mug of ale and an ingratiating smile.

'I'm a leech,' said Larktwist with a hauteur that was starting to come naturally. 'That's a cut above your common surgeon.'

'Oh,' said the guard, disappointed. 'Only I've got this boil . . .'

Chapter 27

In the morning Larktwist explored his temporary – God willing – abode. No one challenged him as he wandered about the bailey, and some gave him good day. He seemed to be accepted as on the strength. He had a look in the stables, checked his horse's hooves and pinched an extra helping of oats for it, poked his nose into forge and kitchen, and gradually, unobtrusively, made his way to the other end of the bailey, to the church and the juliet tower.

He tried the church door; it wasn't locked, but the church had been stripped and was now a storehouse for firewood and sea coal, great piles of which were stacked against the walls on either side of the door. A dead mallard lay spread out in one corner, and the bird shit, feathers and coal dust scattered over the flagstones were marked by recent footprints. An oblong on the floor showed where the altar had once been, and there was no glass in the high narrow windows. A low arched doorway at the back opened on to a narrow, damp stairway leading down. Treading gingerly, he descended the slippery steps.

The crypt was much older than the church and had been the original place of worship for the Benedictines who had made their home on the island. When the church above was built, this subterranean chamber became the charnel house and burial place of the monks; their stone coffins were piled along the walls, and behind a rusted iron gate ancient bones, green with mould, were heaped higgledy-piggledy. Massive stone vaulting curved overhead, the stone altar, cracked and chipped, was still in situ, and there were empty niches in the walls where figures of the saints had once stood. It looked as though renovations were under way: half-burned torches lay on the floor, and stone blocks were stacked against the wall. Some of the niches had been filled in, but the job was unfinished.

It was damp and dark, the only light coming down the steps from above. Greenish slime covered the floor and rose halfway up the walls. After a very quick glance round, Larktwist, shivering, mounted the steps much faster than he'd descended. A gust of wind blew in through the open door, stirring the debris and ruffling the dead bird's feathers. Uneasily he clutched the amulet he wore round his neck. The place gave him the creeps. He backed towards the door without taking his eyes off the stairway entrance. Shadows seemed to be massing the other side of the arch, as if darkness was pushing its way up the steps from below.

Losing your grip, Starling, he thought crossly. There's nothing there, for God's sake!

A grating screech echoed through the chapel, rebounding off the walls. His heart gave a what-the-hell's-that? thump, followed by an urgent get-the-hell-out-of-here hammering, and his legs didn't wait for him to think about it.

As the door banged to behind him, the raven on the roof gave another derisive screech and flapped away. Swearing, Larktwist threw a stone at it. He thought he'd missed, but there was an affronted squawk and a black feather drifted down. Feeling better, he stuck it in his cap for luck.

The sumpter carts from Locksey were lumbering over the causeway in the wake of the guide. When they reached the island, Kepp turned aside, waiting until the way was clear, and while they went on into the bailey he splashed back to lead the next lot across. As the carts drew up, servants erupted from every doorway to unlace the flaps and carry things inside. One cart continued past the storerooms, past the donjon, and drew up in front of the wing. The only entrance was ten feet above the ground, reached by a wooden stair, and the steward and his wife – who, as far as Larktwist knew, was the only woman on Ravenser – came hurrying down as the cart stopped. The driver unlaced the cover at the back and pulled down a ladder. The steward's wife clambered up and disappeared inside the wagon. Larktwist saw the canvas side shiver and bulge as she moved about within, and then she appeared again at the cart-tail, climbed part-way down the ladder and turned to help someone else, someone wrapped in a concealing cloak. But the wind, flattening the material against the wearer, outlined breasts, hips – a woman. She seemed unsteady on her feet, and would have fallen if the steward and his wife hadn't been there to steady her. Each took one of her arms, propping her up as they assisted her towards the stair.

Suddenly she broke away from them, giving the steward's wife a shove that sent her sprawling, and staggered towards Larktwist, stumbling and falling against him. His arms automatically went round her. She was very young, very beautiful, and her pupils were so dilated that her eyes looked black.

He thought she said, 'Help me!'

'What?'

She slid through his grasp and fell to her knees, not in supplication but because her legs had given way. The steward, right behind her, pulled her to her feet; she crumpled again, and with a curse and a glare at Larktwist, he picked her up. With his wife fussing at his heels he carried her up the stair like a child. Her long fair hair fell over his arm and trailed on the steps, and one arm hung limp. Sunlight winked on the paternoster beads wound around her wrist – blue stones, gold, a costly trinket, Larktwist thought. She must be the champion's private bit of squeeze.

Back in the hall he found several of the crossbowmen, off duty, dicing for halfpence and fourthings at the table. Larktwist brightened. Life wasn't all bad. Taking a few fourthings from his pouch he shook them suggestively.

"Ow'd you play this game, then?' he asked, looking as simple-minded as he could. The players glanced at one another, grinning, and budged up along the bench to make room for him.

'I'll show you, my son,' said the sergeant, with a welcoming leer.

There's one born every minute, Larktwist thought, not forgetting to add a pious *Thank God!*

'Where've you been?' the sergeant-at-arms asked.

'I wanted to pray. I pray every day,' he said piously. 'But the church is empty. You got a chapel somewhere?'

There was a sudden silence, then everyone spoke at once.

'You want to keep out o' there . . . It ain't safe . . . the roof . . . You could get hurt . . .'

'Oh. Right.' Catch him going back in there! Odd, though, the roof had looked fine to him.

King John reached Nottingham in mid-August, intending to set out for Chester a few days later to lead his host against the Welsh and crush them for good, but he had scarcely dismounted when the courier from Wales threw his plans into chaos.

At God knew what risk to herself his daughter's letter told him that there were traitors among his barons, men whom he had favoured, who had sworn allegiance to him but who now intended to draw back from him in the thick of the battle, leaving him for the Welsh to kill. More, she named them!

152

FitzWalter, de Vesci, Mowbray, and this one, and this one, and that: the monstrous list of Judases went on.

' 'Lights!' he shouted, and boys came running to light the candles set about the room. The shadows fled, but John felt chilled to the bone. The peril had been so close. But for Joanna he would have ridden to his death. Thanks to her he would destroy these traitors before they could destroy him.

They could not know of her warning. He would summon his barons, guilty or innocent – for how could he know which was which? – to attend him in Nottingham, to consult with them about matters that had come to his notice concerning the campaign. The innocent would curse and complain but would obey. The guilty would hear alarm bells ringing. What would they do? Confess and beg mercy? Betray others? Bluff it out? Flee the realm?

He spread Joanna's letter out and read it again. She begged him to show mercy to her treacherous husband and the lesser Welsh princes for their part in this plot, but not even for her sake could he do that. They must pay the price of treason. They had sworn never to bear arms against him, and to guarantee their loyalty they had given him their sons as hostages. Here, now, at Nottingham, were twenty-nine Welsh boys of noble blood, the youngest no more than ten years old, and one of them, Gruffydd, Llywelyn's own bastard son.

John crushed the letter in his hand and groaned. He loved his daughter dearly, and what he must do would surely break her heart.

He gave his orders, and sat down to dinner.

The new abbey church of St John at Peterborough, encased in scaffolding and with builders swarming over it like ants, rose daily a course or two nearer to heaven. Stone dust hung in the air like mist. For two years the din of creaking winches, carpenters hammering and sawing, masons with mallets and chisels, labourers mixing mortar and whistling or singing as they worked had competed with the monks' singing. A giant web of ropes and safety nets surrounded the scaffolding, and long, alarmingly flexible ladders bent and swayed under the weight of the men who swarmed up and down them like monkeys. On the morning of the feast of Saint Tarsicius, the prior stood watching the work, admiring the beautiful creamy stone blocks, when a stumbling, dusty man led a limping, lathered horse through the main gate, and would have fallen but for the monk's swift step and steadying arm.

Both horse and rider had the anxious expression common to exhausted creatures, whether four- or two-legged, and Prior Alrede noticed the letter case bearing the royal arms strapped to the saddle.

The man leaned for a moment on the prior's arm, then straightened and braced himself. Red-rimmed eyes looked out from a face grey and stiff with dust.

'My horse . . .' he wheezed, but the prior had already signalled to a groom to come and lead the drooping animal away.

'It will be cared for. Come inside and refresh yourself.'

The messenger shook his head. 'Lend me a fresh horse, brother. I have a message for your abbot, but I cannot stay.'

'Abbot Akarius has been dead these last three months,' the prior said. 'You may give your message to me; I am Prior Alrede. Who are you, sir knight?'

'Hubert de Pomfret, a royal knight, the king's man,' the courier said, but he didn't look proud of it.

'I hope His Grace does well,' the prior murmured politely, not giving a toss whether the king did well or ill. Let the devil look after his own.

'He does not,' Hubert said. 'He has never done worse ill.'

The prior frowned. 'Why, man, what do you mean?'

'His Grace has hanged the Welsh boys, the hostages, at Nottingham,' Hubert said. 'A worse thing he never did. The youngest was ten years old, my own boy's age.'

'*All* of them?' the prior asked, grey as ash.

'At the last moment he spared Prince Llywelyn's son. Twenty-eight he hanged, and sat at dinner while they died.'

When the weary messenger had ridden on with his dreadful tidings, Prior Alrede called the community together, all sixty monks and the novices, lay brothers and servants of the house, and in a voice unsteady with shock told them what had happened.

'God have mercy!'

'Christ have mercy!'

'God have mercy on their souls!'

The prayer burst forth from mouth after mouth, as shock spread from face to face.

'What can we do?' the sub-prior, a Welshman, asked, tears streaming down his cheeks.

'We can ring the bell,' said the prior.

'But father prior, the Interdict . . .'

154

'We will ring the bell. Their souls will not go unheralded. I'll answer for it. Go!'

The bell's slow, grieving notes rang out over the town, following Sir Hubert as he galloped towards Huntingdon on a fresh horse borrowed from the abbey stables, to spread his sorry tidings. Presently the men and women of the town began arriving at the abbey to learn the reason for the ringing, and stayed to weep and pray.

'Why does the bell ring?' Straccan shouted as the great wain rumbled through the town gate. He hadn't heard a church bell since the Interdict began four years ago.

'By order of the prior, for the souls of the Welsh hostages,' the sentry shouted back. 'Hanged by the king at Nottingham, yesterday.'

Chapter 28

L arktwist couldn't sleep. His pallet was hard and damp, which wouldn't normally have bothered him – he'd slept on worse – but the idea of being surrounded by water and marshland made him profoundly uneasy. Around him the garrison snored and farted. How could they sleep, when the bloody island might sink into the bog? He was sure he could feel the donjon being sucked slowly downwards. It would sink in time. Maybe tonight.

He couldn't stand much more of this. He flung back his blanket and sat up. No one moved. He hadn't taken off his clothes; now he picked up his shoes and tiptoed past the two rows of pallets.

The door opened on to a winding stair. Up or down? He pulled his shoes on. The night watch would be about somewhere, probably with a jug of ale and perhaps, if his luck held, with a pair of dice as well. If he was going to be stuck on this bloody island for a while he might as well make a profit.

He went down to the hall. Cups and bowls were scattered over the table but no one was there. Sounds came in through the unshuttered windows – voices, thumps, someone coughing. The main door was unbarred and opened on to the top step of the flight that led down into the bailey.

Although past midnight it wasn't really dark, and there was something going on. Another cart had arrived, and was drawn up by the juliet tower. Larktwist had thought the tower abandoned, but now a door gaped open at its foot, the opening lit by a torch on the wall inside. Two fellows were unloading barrels and stacking them at the top of the steps beside the door, and another man came out of the church carrying a basket of coal on his back, which he took into the tower, emerging presently with the basket empty and returning to the church for more. A red glow lit a window up near the top, under the pointed roof.

Fire!

Dark shapes, man shapes, moved back and forth past the window, and the ruddy glow intensified. With a sudden fierce hissing, flame-shot smoke belched out from vents under the roof. One of the men below looked up and crossed himself. They finished unloading and began to carry the barrels inside, one by one.

A sudden downdraught sent a gust of smoke along the bailey; the fumes made Larktwist's eyes burn and left a metallic taste in his mouth. The fiery glow flickered and flared, and the hissing noise rose and fell and rose again, swelling to a shrill shrieking whistle that stopped, abruptly, as the glow of the fire diminished.

He remembered the widow Trygg's dragon. Nonsense, he'd thought. Now he wasn't so sure.

But in the cold light of morning it was easier to remember that Saint George had slain the last dragon, and according to Holy Church there were none left in England. Therefore the smoke and fumes simply meant that there was one hell of a fire kept burning in the top chamber of the juliet. When he wandered casually in that direction after breakfast, the door was closed and the window shuttered, but – he narrowed his eyes and stared hard – there was a wavy distortion in the air around the pointed roof, a heat-shimmer, although in the sunlight he couldn't see any smoke around the almost invisible vents.

A light, fitful breeze lifted puffs of dust – pink, yellow, black – from the tower steps, dispersing it over the mere. It didn't seem to be doing the marsh much good; the reeds were brown and dead-looking, the willows sere and yellow. The widow Trygg, Larktwist recalled, said the dragon's breath had killed trees.

He glanced at the gatehouse. The sodding crossbowmen were at their posts, and one was definitely keeping an eye on him. He also saw the captain of the night watch trotting down the keep steps, heading for the gong at a rate that spoke of urgency. Tilting his cap forward over his eyes Larktwist strolled nonchalantly after him.

'It worked, then.' He settled himself in neighbourly fashion on the hole beside the captain, a sufferer from chronic constipation who had asked him for a purge and got rather more than he bargained for.

'It's worked all right,' the captain said, between groans. 'This is the third time I've been in here since breakfast. What in God's name was in that pill?'

Buggered if I know, Larktwist thought, but all he said was, 'Many rare herbs. Look, I need more supplies; or I'll run out, and then where will you be? I need to go to the nearest town and stock up.'

The captain strained, puce for a moment, and subsided again. 'Make a list of what you want, and I'll see it's sent for.'

'I ought to go myself,' Larktwist grumbled. 'You can't trust anyone else to get it right. Pills like I gave you, for instance – just a touch too much of the vital principle and your bowels could turn to liquid and be lost.'

The captain blanched. 'I can't let you leave. It's more than my job's worth.'

'No skin off my nose,' said Larktwist cheerfully. 'They're your guts.' He adjusted his clothing and left, whistling.

A rickety handcart was drawn up in front of the stable, and two ragged-arsed, barefoot boys, eleven or twelve years old, were shovelling stable muck into it from a monumental heap by the door. One nudged the other when they saw him approaching, and Larktwist's sixth sense, honed by years of experience of dodging dangers large and small, stopped him in his tracks, so that the 'accidental' shovel-load of dung missed him by inches. The boys hooted with mirth, grinning at him across the steaming cart.

Larktwist grinned back. 'Do that again and you'll be eating that stuff for dinner.' Moving with a turn of speed they hadn't expected, he grabbed each boy by an ear and twisted, not savagely but enough to make his point, and when he let go they didn't run off. The civilities had apparently been observed, and friendly relations could commence.

'You new here?' the older of the two demanded.

'That's right. Oy, what's this?' The boys gasped as he took a halfpenny from behind one lad's ear, noticing as he did so that they each had a blue tattoo, like the guide's, on their foreheads. It looked like an eel. Must be something local. He'd heard strange tales of the marsh dwellers from the men-at-arms. Webfoots, they called them, and believed they had strange powers. They could 'call' the creatures of the marshes, eels to their nets, ducks to their arrows; whistle up the marsh lights to lead their enemies to certain death; and find their way through the swamps by hidden paths and sunken trackways known only to a few.

'Funny place to keep your savings,' Larktwist said. 'Oh look, here's another.' Repeating the performance with the smaller boy, who stood transfixed with wonder. 'What's your names?'

'Ketil,' said the elder boy. 'He's Edmund.'

'Live here, do you?'

'We live at the Dykes.'

158

'What's that, a village?'

'Lord Ralf's farm.'

'D'you do this job every day?'

Ketil wiped his nose on the back of his hand. 'Most days.'

Over the next few days he made a point of meeting them, listening for the squeal of their cartwheels just after dawn, sharing food he pilfered from the kitchen, gossiping, swapping tales of the marvels of London for their comprehensive knowledge of Ravenser and the surrounding country. They listened and chattered as they shovelled, while Larktwist sat on a trestle kicking his heels. He told them of the lions and other strange creatures kept penned up in the king's great tower in London, and they told him about Old King Snake – 'as big around as *this*,' said Edmund, stretching out both stick-like arms – who lived in the marsh and hunted sheep, and sometimes unwary travellers, at night. He told them of the heads and quartered bodies spiked on London's fine new bridge, and they regaled him with tales of the water goblins, who stole babies from careless mothers, to eat, and sometimes left their own frog-like infants in their place. He told them the streets of London were paved with gold, and they told him about the wizard in the juliet tower.

'Wizard? What wizard?'

They had filled the cart and were devouring their customary 'wage' of kitchen leavings before dragging their load away.

'The old man up there. The infidel.'

'Infidel?'

'Lord Ralf's wizard. He keeps him chained up, up there.' Ketil pointed at the juliet. 'That's where he does his magic stuff.'

'What magic stuff?'

Ketil looked around cautiously before answering. 'That's where he makes the gold.'

Gold? Again? 'I thought it was dragons that made gold,' Larktwist said. The boys looked at him with superior scorn.

'Don't be daft. You'd never get a dragon up there. There ain't room.'

A groom, offended by the sight of the lads sitting on their cart, eating, threw a horse turd and yelled at them. 'Hey, webfoots! Get yourselves back to the Dykes before I take me belt to the pair of you!'

Ramming the last of their bread and dripping into their mouths, they nodded goodbye to Larktwist, took up the shafts of the cart and dragged it, wheels squealing painfully, to the gate, pausing by the tiny cell-like chamber where the guide spent his days and nights. The guide popped out, carrying two fish on a string, which he handed to the younger boy.

As the guards waved them through, the dinner horn sounded, and there was a general stampede towards the donjon. Larktwist took a few steps, glanced back over his shoulder and stopped. The cart was screeching its way through the gate, but the guide . . . The guide had returned to his cell and was shutting the door.

'You in the family way?' someone asked, elbowing him aside. 'You're in everyone else's bloody way!'

'Sorry. Forgot something.'

He ran to the steps and up to the curtain wall, and watched as the boys dragged the cart down the slope to the water's edge and into the mere, and on to the hidden causeway unaided.

Passed down from father to son, eh? He thought, and went grinning to his dinner.

That night more barrels arrived and were carried into the tower, and the fires flared again in the topmost chamber, and smoke and fumes leaked from the vents above, to be torn away by the wind. Birds died, the boys had said, when the wizard's fires burned – the mere would be littered with their floating corpses.

He had a bad feeling about this. Infidel wizards were hardly commonplace, and he'd encountered one three years ago, in Scotland, when he'd been compelled to act as servant to a dangerously idealistic young knight called Miles Hoby. Larktwist was no hero, never had been. His mother had warned him to look out for himself, as no one else would, and never to volunteer, and he never had; but in spite of his reluctance he'd been part of the small group of men, led by that other sodding hero Sir Richard bloody Straccan, who had discovered and thwarted a plot to kill the kings of both England and Scotland. A plot that depended on the black arts of an infidel wizard, the ancient Arab Abdul al-Hazred. Al-Hazred had escaped. And now here was a Saracan wizard, working – making gold, if the Widow Trygg and these lads were to be believed – for Sir Ralf Tyrrel.

He *had* to get off this bloody island! He hated to admit it, but he'd be quite chuffed to see Sir Miles, or even Sir Richard, riding to his rescue just about now.

There was never a knight around when you needed one.

160

Chapter 29

P rior Alrede clambered, puffing, on to the plinth of the
nearest tomb and, perching precariously with one sandalled
foot on the impassive stone features of Lord Ferrers, anxiously
scanned the people packed in the nave. Was that Straccan?
Between the fat woman in blue and the beggar? The sour-faced
sub-prior from Coldinghame, Mango or whatever his name was,
had described a tall, wide-shouldered man in travel-soiled grey
garb, dust in his hair. As if aware of being watched, the man
looked around, and the prior saw the scarred cheek and nose,
and was sure.

Above the crowded nave the great slow deep bell boomed its
sorrowful tidings while the people wept and prayed, and still
more came pushing in through the great double doors which
stood wide open. Even the aisles were crowded, and Straccan,
with one hand on his belt pouch – this was an opportunity that
Peterborough's cutpurses wouldn't pass up – reacted instantly to
the tug at his sleeve, seizing the tugger in a punishing grip before
realising it was a monk.

'Sorry, brother! I took you for a thief.'

A warning rumble near his feet made the prior look down. A
thin white dog, hackles a-bristle, bared its teeth at him. He
shifted his feet nervously and smoothed his rumpled habit.

'Ah, your dog . . .'

'Quiet, you,' said Straccan, and the dog subsided.

'I am Alrede, prior of St Peter's,' the prior said, looking hard at
him and seeing not a dusty, tired, rather shabby man but a
solution, an answer to prayer, a godsend. 'I believe you are the
knight escorting the great bell for His Grace of Winchester?'

'I have that honour.'

'May I talk with you, a few words in private, Sir Robert?'

· 'Richard,' the godsend corrected. 'Richard Straccan.' The dog
pressed against his leg and whined softly, eager to leave.

'Sir Richard, of course, of course,' said the prior hastily,
mentally kicking himself. Names were not his strong point, but
he knew they were important; people disliked it when they were

161

miscalled. It wasn't the best beginning. But needs must! He ploughed on. 'Sir Richard, there is a matter – a very important matter – on which I would value your advice.'

Ten to one it's about some relic or other, Straccan thought tiredly, following Alrede through doors and along passages, trailed by the dog, to the prior's comfortable, spacious chamber. There he accepted a cup of excellent wine and sat down to listen to the prior's important matter. He was right, it was about a relic, but not quite what he expected. Prior Alrede didn't want to commission him to 'liberate' one from another church or act for the abbey in a purchase. The monks had a problem. They had borrowed a relic, the Caul of Saint Peter, a year ago from the abbey at Cerneshead, and its return was now overdue.

'Through no fault of ours,' the prior said earnestly. 'We have tried to return it, twice, and each time we have been set upon, and only by the grace of God and Saint Peter did we manage to save the Holy Caul and bring it safely back here.'

'Who's stopping you?'

'Monks from Croyland,' the prior said. 'May the foul fiend run away with them! They claim the caul is rightfully theirs, which it never was, and demand that we yield it to them. We have no fighting men; all who owe the abbey knight-service have answered the king's summons and gone to Chester, to fight the Welsh.' He paused, sighed, crossed himself and continued. 'I sent an escort of five monks with the Holy Caul – I had no reason to expect trouble – but there were no swords to protect it, and Croyland's monks knew this. They lay in wait and attacked our brothers with staves and slingshot!'

Despite his tiredness, Straccan was interested. 'Have you told Cerneshead what's happening?'

'Of course. But they have no knights either. And unless the caul is returned by Michael's Mass we will lose the manor of Nelby, which was given as security for the loan.' Much of the fine stone for their new church came from quarries at Nelby and they could not afford to lose it.

'In a sense, we are under siege,' the prior said. 'Spies from Croyland watch our gates. If any brother of this house sets forth he is in peril, and there is no hope of returning the caul in time to save Nelby. Sir Richard,' he looked at the godsend earnestly, 'you are in a position to do this abbey, and Saint Peter, a singular service.'

I'll just bet I am, Straccan thought. He knew what was coming.

'Brother, um . . . Mango told me you are heading for Lincoln,

162

by way of Deeping Gate and Borninger. Sir Richard, you will pass five miles from Cerneshead Abbey. Croyland will never suspect you are carrying the caul. Will you take it?'

The relic was in a flat pewter box about six inches square, itself in a plain, scuffed leather case. He could feel it pressing into his ribs, inside his shirt, as he walked down to the bell camp. Five miles out of his way was little enough, and the prior had promised prayers for him and anyone else he chose to name for the next year. He was still unabsolved and couldn't afford to pass up prayers.

Supper was in preparation and his belly was grumbling; he had declined the prior's offer of a good supper, feeling it had no part in a journey of penitence. The Gaudy Company's stage had been set up, and the players were gathered round their cook-fire dishing up the meal. He thought dismally of the stale bread and hard cheese which was all he had left in his saddlebags. Anyway, the horses came first, and he trudged to the picket line to see that all was well with them. His rouncey had picked up a stone that afternoon, but luckily he'd noticed before any damage was done; now he checked their hooves again, rubbed their soft noses and ears, gave each an apple and fetched more water from the river.

He stopped at the cowman's cart to ask how Lawrence did. The boy had a slight fever; flushed and restless, he would only lie quiet on his mother's lap. She was coaxing him to take sips of water, tilting the cup to his lips, stroking his damp hair, humming a little tune over and over. Each time she stopped humming he tugged at her sleeve to make her start again. His eyes were sunken and dulled.

'I would go to the abbey church, to bend a penny to Saint Peter for him,' Lucy Boteler said, 'but I can't leave him.'

'I'll do that for you, gladly,' Straccan said. 'If you'll measure his length for me, I'll light a trindle for him myself.'

She fished in her belt pouch for a hank of sewing thread and measured the child from crown to heel, snipped the thread, coiled it into a little ring and dropped it in Straccan's palm. That thread, coated with wax and folded upon itself, would burn long, carrying the prayer to the Saint at God's side. 'May God be good to you, sir, you and all you hold dear.'

'Amen.'

'There they are!'

163

Bane reined in and leaned forward, resting his forearms on the pommel of his saddle. Beside him Roslyn shaded her eyes against the low sun and stared across the river. She had been dreading this ever since they left Stirrup.

In the meadow the other side of the Nene was an untidy sprawl of tents and overnight shelters, clusters of people grouped around fires, carts great and small, picketed horses and mules and a herd of oxen surrounding an enormous wain on which stood the great bell Gaudy. Small in the distance, a man clambered on to the wain and began moving around the bell, tugging at the ropes that held it.

Even from this distance, she couldn't mistake him, and the scourge-cord round her heart that had never quite gone, tightened again.

'There's Sir Richard,' said David.

Satisfied with the lashings – he tested them night and morning now, and at odd times during each day's journey – Straccan leaped down from the wain and headed for his tent and meagre supper – not part of his penance but the consequence of his own forgetfulness. He should have laid in fresh provisions before leaving Peterborough, but what with one thing and another—

'Sir?'

He spun round on his heel, saw Bane's face, and his bones turned to water.

'Gilla—'

'She's all right I swear!'

Behind Bane he saw Roslyn and David at her side. 'Mistress Roslyn,' he said with a bow, wondering what in the name of God they were doing here and why she was dressed as a boy. The shock of the unexpected sight of Bane, the heart-lurching dread of bad news, still flared in his belly and fizzed along his veins. 'And David.'

'Sir,' said the little boy, standing very straight, his head tilted back to look up into Straccan's face. 'I am sorry to be a trouble to you.'

Straccan's lips twitched at that, and he bowed with grave courtesy. 'Sir,' he returned. 'It's an honour to render what aid I can to the kinsman of my good friend Blaise.'

David's solemn face flowered into a smile of delight, and the slender girl at his side smiled too. It was, Straccan realised, the first time he had seen Roslyn de Sorules smile.

'You'd better come to my tent.' He led the way, and then remembered the bread and cheese which was all he had to

164

offer them. 'Go inside. There's water for washing in the jug. I'll get you something to eat.'

Over bowls of rabbit stew and bread, which Straccan had scrounged from the Gaudy Company, Bane told him about the White Brotherhood and their pursuit of David.

'It's him they want,' he finished. 'Sir Miles said so. Don't ask me why! We missed them by the skin of our teeth at Darley, gave them the slip there and laid a false trail for London. But they'll realise they've gone wrong, sooner or later, and they won't give up.'

'Blaise talked about the White Brotherhood. They hunt down Cathars.'

'We are not Cathar,' said Roslyn, wiping the last of her stew from the bowl with her finger and licking it. 'And David is no heretic.'

'Even if they were,' Straccan said, 'why should these men go to such lengths to track down and kill a child? Mistress Roslyn . . .' She looked up and he remembered that wary look. 'His mother still lived when you found him. She told you his name. Was that all she said?'

Roslyn frowned. 'She said, "He is the *Logos*." '

'*Logos*?' said Bane. 'What's that?'

'That's all?' Straccan asked. Roslyn nodded.

'What's it mean?' Bane asked again.

'I don't know,' Straccan said. But he'd heard the word somewhere.

He gave up his tent to Roslyn and David; tomorrow he'd find other accommodation for them, a tent or room in one of the carts. He and Bane dossed down under the smith's cart.

It had been a bad day, and there'd be no sleep for him tonight. The hanging of the hostages had shaken him, as it would shake the entire realm. *God, have mercy! Twenty-eight helpless boys!*

He'd shoved the caul under his pallet, and the hard edges of the case dug into his back through the thin padding. So far there'd been no sign of Croyland's Benedictine bandits, but he'd bet his boots they'd find out about Prior Alrede's scheme one way or another, and trouble with the Church was the last thing he wanted! He had trouble enough as it was, wondering who in his train of pilgrims was trying to bugger the bell!

As for David . . . what had his mother meant by 'the *Logos*'? The word flickered at the bottom of his mind, and a memory took shape and swam to the surface. A church . . . a priest . . . somewhere . . . He had it! The Mass of the eve of Christ's birth, in Cyprus, years ago. The church, brilliant with candles and packed with crusaders as the holy hour of midnight approached . . . the old priest, tears of joy on his withered cheeks, retelling in a voice that trembled with emotion the incredible miracle of the Nativity . . . The joyful cries of his friends and companions . . .

'Christ is born . . . *Christus natus est* . . . He is born! He is born!'

He remembered it vividly now, could even smell the hot wax and the incense and his companions' sweat. But he still didn't know the meaning of *Logos*, or why it brought that scene to mind.

Now Blaise's young kinsman was his responsibility, and in Miles's absence he would have to get the boy to Coldinghame. They must travel at Gaudy's pace until Durham. Once the bell was off his hands he would take David to Scotland, but meanwhile the wagon train was probably the safest place for him. If these men of the White Brotherhood should come, what would they do? Attack the bell's retinue on the road? Hardly likely. Attack the camp at night? Possible, but risky. There were more than fifty men and half a dozen women travelling with the bell now – and several children close to David in age. How would they know which was which?

And then a monstrous thought surfaced, driving all else from his mind. What if they made sure of the one by slaughtering all? Like the Holy Innocents, the children of Bethlehem, murdered at King Herod's command because he didn't know which one among them was the threat to his power.

Chapter 30

'**G**od's holy entrails!'

Robert fitzWalter tore the king's letter in half and flung it on the brazier, where the parchment curled and blackened and the heavy black seal began to melt.

It was all up! John knew. The letter commanded fitzWalter to meet the king at Nottingham, together with 'certain of our barons that we may be assured of your loyalty', and the courier who'd brought the message had orders to return with him, setting out on the morrow. The Great Enterprise lay in ruins.

He struck the table with his fist. There would be no march into Wales now, no convenient death of the king at the hands of the enemy: the campaign had been called off. He could hear the shouting and trumpet calls outside, horses neighing, wheels rumbling, all the chaotic din of an army preparing to break camp and move out. Behind him the door banged open and he whirled, sword half out of its scabbard, but it was Eustace de Vesci.

'He knows!' De Vesci thrust his own letter in fitzWalter's face. 'He's not coming! The campaign's off; he's told everyone to go home. He's ordered me to Nottingham.'

'And me.'

'God's precious body! Who's the Judas?'

'Use your head, man,' fitzWalter growled. 'Who's the only hostage not dangling from a rope's end at Nottingham?'

'Llywelyn's bastard. Are you saying the prince of Gwynedd himself betrayed us?'

'Who else? To save his son's life.'

De Vesci flung his own letter down. 'He can't prove anything.'

'When did that matter to John?'

'We can deny it!'

'Are you going to the king?' fitzWalter asked. They stared at each other, one pale, the other darkly flushed.

'Are *you*?' de Vesci demanded.

'And put my head in the leopard's maw?'

'Where will you go?'

167

'As far from John as possible.'

'He has a long arm.'

'Not long enough,' said fitzWalter. There was no time to lose. In the morning the courier would be waiting, and when he failed to present himself at Nottingham the king would send men to take him. If he could get to London one of his own ships would take him to France before John knew he'd gone. The French king had no love for him, but still less for John. Philip would welcome him on the time-honoured principle that 'The enemy of my enemy is my friend.'

'What of the others? Mowbray, Montbegon—' de Vesci began.

'Forget them. They'll either try to convince John of their innocence, or they'll cut their losses and run. It's each man for himself.'

'They'll implicate us.'

'Let them. There's no proof.'

'What about Tyrrel? We should warn him.' De Vesci looked even more worried, if that were possible.

'I know you and Tyrrel are cronies, but sending word to him now will put the noose round our necks. Anyway, it's too late. By now he will have the queen.'

The captain of Isabel's escort was understandably nervous. For the queen to travel with a mere half-dozen knights was unheard of, but it was the king's command, she had said when he urged her to take more; a small escort would travel faster and attract less attention, and she and her lady-in-waiting would ride astride, as they did when hunting, to make better speed.

They had stopped briefly, dismounting to bait the horses, at Stonely, when they saw a troop of riders coming towards them. The queen's knights drew their swords, but Captain de Lacy, squinting against the sun to see the banner, cried, 'Red and blue, Ralf Tyrrel's colours!' There were audible huffs of relief as the men sheathed their swords again.

The champion rode at the head of ten men-at-arms. They slowed as they approached, and Tyrrel reined in, dismounted and bent his knee to the queen.

'Sir Ralf,' she said, 'why are you here?'

'My lady, you must come with me. The enemies of the king are near. They mean to abduct you, to force the king to yield to their demands. You must not be taken.' He drew from inside his mailed gauntlet a rolled parchment bearing a green seal and

168

offered it to Captain de Lacy. 'Here is the king's order.'

De Lacy glanced at the royal seal, cut the ties and scanned the brief lines. 'It is as Sir Ralf says, madame. You and Lady Maude must go with him. My men and I are ordered to join the king with all speed.'

Isabel laid one slender, jewelled hand on Tyrrel's arm. 'Sir Ralf, where is the king?'

'On his way to deal with the rebels, my lady.'

'And my children?'

'Safe at Windsor, madame.'

'Where will you take me?'

He lowered his voice so that only she could hear. 'To my stronghold of Ravenser, until the king comes for you.' He offered his clasped hands for her foot, to help her into the high-cantled saddle. His hands were as steady as a mounting block, but the beating of his heart was like thunder.

The great lords of England, with their knights and men-at-arms, archers and crossbowmen, carts of weapons, fodder and other provisions, horses, mules and oxen began slowly dispersing from Chester to all parts of the realm, some glad to be going home, others grumbling, cheated of blood and booty. Wales would suffer no invasion after all, not this year at any rate, but its treacherous princelings would never forgive the murder of their sons; there would be a reckoning yet.

While the two leaders of the aborted revolt fled – fitzWalter to France to pose as a pious martyr persecuted by a godless excommunicate, and de Vesci to Scotland, where his father-in-law King William could not refuse him shelter – others involved in the Great Enterprise set about bluffing and buying their way back into John's unchancy favour. Despite the slaughter at Nottingham, panicky barons – loyal and disloyal alike – rushed to offer sons and daughters as hostages so long as they themselves were spared. Richard d'Umfraville handed over four sons and a castle, regretting the castle most of all; he could always get more sons. Earl David of Huntingdon, from whom John demanded the castle of Fotheringay, dug in his heels and offered a son instead.

Meanwhile, at Nottingham castle the king dismissed his household knights, seeing with good reason treachery in every familiar face, retreated to his private apartments with none but mercenaries to guard him and sent out his two most trusted mercenary captains, one to guard his children, the other to escort the queen from Woodstock to the safety of the royal fortress at Corfe.

'Open in the king's name!'

'Who's there?'

'Royal knights! King's men!'

The captain of the guard at Woodstock put his eye to the peephole and recognised the king's favoured mercenary captain, Philip Ulcotes. He sent a boy running to fetch the chamberlain, and signalled to the gatehouse. The portcullis began its slow, jerky ascent to admit Ulcotes and his men.

'Where is the queen?' Ulcotes demanded, as soon as they were in the bailey.

The chamberlain looked surprised. 'The queen? But you're too late; she's gone.'

'What d'you mean, gone? Where is she?'

'She's on her way to Nottingham, to the king, of course. He sent for her. She wouldn't wait for her chariot; she left everything, just took six knights and one waiting-woman!'

'When did she leave?'

'Yesterday. Why, my lord, what is it? Is something wrong?'

Oblivious to all this, ignorant of the enterprise, its collapse and consequences, the great bell Gaudy and its attendants, like a snail surrounded by ants all covered with mauve dust, crawled from Peterborough to Deeping Gate, thence to Bourne, and from Bourne to Sempringham, skirting the Fens on the ancient packed clay road that ran beside the Romans' great Caer Dyke.

The bones of Saint Gilbert at Sempringham had brought pilgrims flocking to the priory and had even affected attendance at Becket's shrine in Canterbury. Gilbert was a new saint, a novelty that hadn't worn off yet, and Straccan's pilgrims were delighted to have the chance to pray at his tomb and buy relics – threads from his clothing, dust from the shrine, water in which his corpse had been washed. The master, another Gilbert, and Prior Adam welcomed the pilgrims and offered the hospitality of the priory's guest quarters, but several of them decided to sleep on the floor around the shrine, and Mistress Boteler spread her pallet there, cradling her son in her arms all that night.

The rest of the bell's retinue set up their tents and shelters with the swiftness of long practice, nipped into the priory for a quick pray and a blessing, and returned to the camp for supper and entertainment. Tonight the Gaudy Company was to present *The Trouncing of Saladin*, a wildly inaccurate version of the

Lionheart's achievements in the Holy Land. Plenty of swordplay and buckets of blood were promised. Originally there had been a female role – Pernelle had played the king's sister, kidnapped by the villain and rescued by the hero – but so far the company had had no luck in finding anyone to take her place.

Straccan settled down after supper with his cleaning gear, rags and a horn of fine sand to attend to his sword, rubbing the blade below the hilt where tiny rust spots always appeared first. David, passing, stopped to watch.

'What are the words on your sword, sir?' he asked.

'*Advocato Sancti Sepulchri*. It means "I defend the Holy Sepulchre."'

'You were a crusader?'

Straccan smiled at the child's awed face. 'Long ago.'

'Did you know King Richard?'

'Not really. I've seen him.'

'In battle?' The boy's eyes were bright with excitement.

'Yes.' Straccan smiled, remembering the Lionheart in battle, a sight no man could ever forget. And then he frowned, remembering Richard in the aftermath: morose, brooding, given to outbursts of savage cruelty.

'What was he like?' David asked.

'He had red hair,' Straccan said. 'And he was tall. Taller than me.' He poured more sand from the horn and began working on the hilt.

'Why did you go?' David asked.

'On crusade?' Straccan's hands stilled; the sword lay in his lap. 'I thought – I suppose I thought – God died for me; the least I could do was be willing to die for him, if it would do any good.'

'How many Saracens did you kill?'

'I forget.' Too many, he thought, and for an instant he was there again at Ascalon, his ears ringing with the clash of weapons, men and horses screaming, the stink of battle in his nostrils, the sun's broiling heat, the vultures circling high above; and at night the bitter cold, the stars as thick as meadow flowers and jackals yelping among the corpses. The child, of course, thought only of streaming banners and noble deeds. Pray God he'd never see the reality.

'David, come to bed now!' Roslyn called. The boy got up obediently, but looked back over his shoulder.

'Sir Richard, why do the bad men want to kill me?'

'I don't know, David. But I promise you, they won't.'

★ ★ ★

171

Later that night, half a mile from the sleeping camp, Roslyn sheathed her knife and stood up, attaching the gutted rabbit by its hind feet to her belt. For a few moments she was still, alert for any movement in the night and listening hard. Nothing. Good. The meadow was priory land – priory grass, priory stream and bushes, and this was certainly a priory rabbit – but she and David would eat from their own pot tomorrow. She dropped to one knee, tugged the snare up and slipped it inside her jerkin. Treading cautiously, she started back to the camp.

'You could lose a hand for that,' said Straccan.

She froze. Damn him, why wasn't he in bed like everyone else? What was he doing out here anyway?

He answered her thought. 'I followed you. You shouldn't go wandering off in the dark; there may be Sanctuary men about.' Criminals claiming the shelter of the Church by day, Sanctuary men frequently slipped out at night to indulge in a little free enterprise, and this close to Sempringham the chances of encountering one were probably fifty-fifty. He'd seen her slip away and was sure of her errand – Bane had told him of her wayfaring skills – but she didn't know this country, and she might run into trouble.

She was furious, with him for startling her, with herself for being caught unawares. He could have been anyone – priory bailiff, robber, even the enemy – although if *they* were near, David's dreams would give warning. She began walking again.

'I'll see you safely back,' Straccan said, falling in beside her.

'There's no need.'

'I'm going there anyway.'

Not far off a vixen yapped and screamed, and a hunting owl swooped silently over their heads to snatch up some small, squeaking thing.

Did she really stumble? Cat-footed, cat-eyed as she was in the dark. Whether or no, she fell, and he reached to pull her to her feet, and the next moment his arms were around her, her face uplifted for his kiss.

For a moment he was tempted, as any man would be with a beautiful girl in his arms; but in the distance a wolf howled and the dangerous moment passed. 'Hear that?' he said as if nothing had happened. 'It's not near, but close enough. I'll take you back.'

Chapter 31

'W e'll not be moving today,' said Giles glumly at dawn, surveying the scouring, shivering oxen. Straccan agreed. He wondered if there wasn't, after all, something in Brother Mungo's curse theory. Leaving the cowman with the beasts, he went in search of Sempringham's bailiff, and asked permission for the sick oxen to be housed in one of the cowsheds where they could be kept warm while Giles dosed them with some concoction of his own.

'They bin poisoned,' said Giles, furious and tearful.

'Are you sure?'

'Christ, can't you smell it?'

Straccan was aware of a sour, ratty smell. 'I can smell something.'

'Cowbane, that is. Scourwort, some calls it. Someone's fed it to 'em.'

'Couldn't they have got it grazing?'

'Not in these parts. 'Ere, 'old 'er, will you?'

Straccan eyed the great head with its rolling, frightened eyes and arm-length needle-sharp horns, swallowed, and clasped it like a lover while Giles shoved the small end of a hollow cow horn in the animal's mouth and poured the dose in. The ox jerked, rumbled ominously and kicked sharply, but the dose was down. They moved on to the next, the cowman lecturing as they went.

'Cowbane don't grow south of York. It's nasty stuff. Makes cows slip their calves; women sometimes use it for that, more's the pity. Someone put it in their feed last night. Saints 'elp us, these are Bishop Peter's oxen, from his manor at Draxford. If any of 'em die, my 'ide'll pay for 'em.'

'It's not your fault. You won't be punished.' Giles looked unconvinced. 'I promise you won't.'

'One bloody thing after another,' Giles muttered, crossing himself. 'First some sod tried laming 'em, and they've bin scouring on and off ever since, but never this bad. Smell that?' He thrust a handful of slime under Straccan's reluctant nose. 'They've 'ad a lot. Why?'

'I don't know, but I'll find out. Will they be all right tomorrow?'

Giles shook his head and patted the nearest flank. 'She won't be,' he said, with a fine disregard for gender. 'Nor 'er,' pointing at another. 'The rest might. They dint get so much. But we're two short already. With four, there'll be a difference.'

Sempringham's bailiff had no oxen to spare and said there was little hope of finding any between there and Temple Bruer. Going there, were they? Well, the Templars might let them borrow an ox, but it wouldn't come cheap. They were welcome to leave the two sick beasts; the priory's cowmen would take good care of them, for a price, of course. They could be collected on the way back, whenever that might be, but the size of the bill didn't bear thinking about.

The next day Giles looked the rest over and decided to carry on. The Gaudy Company was to lead a sing-song tonight and he'd been looking forward to it. Everyone looked forward to the evening entertainment. It had brought another dimension to their lives; they had their own players just like any lord, or even the king.

The camp was breaking up, ready to move out, and Roslyn was tying her bedroll and David's to her saddle when a shadow fell across her.

'Mistress Roslyn?'

Her hand dropped to her dagger hilt. 'What do you want?' She recognised the man, he was one of the players, their chief, but her hand stayed where it was.

'I, uh . . . I've got something that'll interest you,' said Piper. He was cuddling a large, cloth-wrapped bundle.

'What is it?'

He laid it on the ground, well away from the horse, and pulled back the wrappings to reveal a lute – and if he heard her indrawn breath he gave no sign.

'You're a minstrel, right? A gleemaiden. The real thing, I mean, trained and all, not just a street singer. I've heard you play your flute, but a gleemaiden ought to have other things, too. If you'd like this, well, we wouldn't ask too much. It's no use to us now; none of us can play it.'

Roslyn reached for the lute, but stopped herself before her hand touched it. 'I've no money.'

Piper's look of surprise was almost funny. 'What, none?'

'Not a penny.'

'Don't Sir Richard pay you, then?'

174

'Why should he?' Sudden and unwelcome comprehension widened her eyes. 'I'm not his whore!' She faced him, hand on dagger, eyes alight with insulted pride.

Piper blushed. 'No! I never— That's not what— I didn't mean that! But you're his gleemaiden, ain't you?'

'Oh, I see! I'm sorry. I mistook your meaning. No, I'm not in Sir Richard's service, and much as I would like to buy your lute, I truly have no money.' She clasped her hands behind her, lest, tempted beyond her control, they seized the treasure for themselves. It was a good lute – she could see that – pearwood, with ivory inlay. Some of the inlay was missing and the beautiful bulging belly scratched and scraped, but the lovely glowing thing cried out soundlessly to her to be rescued from indignity and neglect.

Piper recognised the hunger in her eyes. He'd been counting on it. 'You can borrow it, if you like.'

Get thee behind me . . . 'No,' she said sharply. 'I would only want it more.'

'Look,' said Piper. 'How about this, then?' And got down to what he'd been angling for all along. 'If you're willing, that is. We don't do plays every night, see; some nights we tell stories, sing and that. Will's got a rebec; I've got a bagpipe; Tim bangs the drum. Pernelle used to play this.' He patted the lute. 'What if you played it, eh? You'd have a share of the takings. With four of us, you'd get a quarter – after the horse, that is.'

Roslyn looked bewildered. 'After the horse?'

'Apollo.' Piper indicated the spavined, ribby, milky-eyed, swaybacked gelding that drew the players' cart. 'His share comes first, for feed and shoes and stuff. We share what's left. That's fair.'

'Yes, it is,' said Roslyn, smiling in spite of herself. 'But I don't know how long I'll be here, and I have David to look after.'

Piper looked at David, sitting on the field gate playing with more enthusiasm than skill a set of reed pipes that Bane had made for him.

'He could come too. He'll have the measure of them pipes in no time. Audiences would love him; he'd be a novelty, he'd do well— I'm sorry! Got carried away for a bit. What d'you think, though?' He held the lute against his bosom like a baby, and eyed her speculatively over its bulge.

Some folk would call it luck.

Michael recognised it as the hand of God.

Since Darley, where the man Bane had made fools of them – the damage to their girths had meant a day's delay – they'd found no spoor. There was no trace of those they sought in Derby, nor in Leicester, nor Rockingham, nor any of the miserable villages in between. If the fugitives were heading for London, they travelled like ghosts. They must have slept somewhere, bought victuals, rested their horses, bought fodder. But it was the same story at inns and hostels, stables and victuallers. A six-year-old child couldn't be hidden in a saddlebag. Yet no one remembered them. Truly, the devil looked after his own.

Until they reached Huntingdon where, at the Augustinian house of Saint Mary, God intervened.

They sat silent at the guests' table, but other travellers enjoying the canons' hospitality were disposed to gossip, and in the babel of voices, among the jests, laughter, coughing and complaining a word, a name, rang like a bell.

Straccan.

'Your pardon, sir,' said Samael courteously to the tubby pilgrim seated opposite him. 'You mentioned Straccan. Would that be Sir Richard Straccan?'

The fat man laughed. 'Aye, the chap wi' the bell. Is he a friend o' yours?'

Uriel leaned menacingly forward. 'Do you know where he is?'

Under the table Michael kicked him hard. 'We should be glad to find him,' he said. 'But what is this bell?'

'The great bell Gaudy, o' course.' The pilgrim was astonished that they hadn't heard of it. The Fenland was buzzing with it. A bell the size of a house pulled all the way from London by half a hundred oxen! 'It came through Huntingdon just last week, with a train of pilgrims like an invading army and your friend Straccan in charge, going to Saint Cuthbert at Durham. You never heard such a din in your life. They camped overnight right here in Saint Mary's meadow.'

'Where will they be now?'

'At the rate they were going?' he laughed. 'Somewhere past Peterborough, God willing.'

A light shower of rain had fallen, laying the purplish dust, to the relief of all those following in Gaudy's train. Progress had been exhaustingly slow. Despite Giles's coaxing, the oxen were in bad fettle, as touchy, ill-tempered and unwilling as any human convalescents. Straccan tipped his head back and let the welcome rain run down his face. God only knew when they would reach

176

Borninger at this rate, or when he'd be able to deliver the relic to Cerneshead. So far there'd been no sign of the Croyland bullies, and he hoped it would stay that way.

About halfway back in the line of carts David, solemn with responsibility, held Apollo's reins, with Will sitting beside him just in case. Not that anything was likely to startle Apollo. The old nag plodded steadily on, head down, a wisp of hay in his mouth and a few wilting flowers threaded in his mane. Roslyn's horse was tied on at the back of the cart, with Tim up for the ride, and Roslyn leaned back against the tailboard, the lute in her lap. She bent her head over the lute, turning the ivory pegs, tightening the strings, testing them, plucking a string here, and a string there, until, satisfied at last, she tried a scale. Each short-lived note she struck had a bell-like clarity. For the first time since Sempringham, the tight band of pain and shame around her heart eased.

'All right, is it?' Piper emerged from the bowels of the cart, a small wooden box in his hand. 'How long is it since you played one?'

'More than a year. And yes, it is all right, more than all right.'

Piper held up the box and shook it. 'Quills,' he said. 'Your fingers'll be soft after all that time.'

'Give us a tune,' called Tim.

'What would you like?'

'There's one Pernelle liked. D'you know it? "Blow, Northern Wind".'

'I know it.' Her master had written it.

The notes carried to the far end of the wagon train, and beyond, to where the man on crutches still toiled, well behind the rest. People began to hum, and sing, and whistle. Near the front, hearing them, Bane turned his horse and rode back along the line.

'Everything all right?'

'Oh yes.' She smiled at him, sitting back, the lute cradled in her lap, her slim brown hands resting on its warm, polished belly. In her eyes was a soft, loving look, like the look she kept for David. Riding slowly back to the bell wain, Bane wished she would look at him like that.

'You play better than Pernelle,' Will said as the Gaudy Company prepared for their performance. Tonight it was to be music and song, so there was no need of costume or masks, but each had donned something other than their dusty everyday clothes: Piper wore a particoloured tunic over his least-darned hose, Will had

177

coloured scarves tied round neck and arms, and Tim wore a shoulder-cape with a dagged edge, and a cap with a green feather worn at a jaunty angle.

'What happened to her?' Roslyn asked.

'She left us for a lord,' Tim sighed.

'Can't blame her,' said Will. 'It's a rough life, on the roads. And she was a looker. Not as young as she was, but she painted up good. And, well, she was a bit of a whore, Pernelle. Sang like an angel, though.'

'I hope she's all right,' Tim said. 'We thought she'd come back. She always did before. And all her things are here.'

Roslyn frowned. 'What things?'

'Her clothes, her gauds, the lute—'

'No,' Roslyn said. 'She wouldn't leave that.'

'Thought she wouldn't need it any more, I suppose,' said Piper with a sniff. 'Thought her fancy lord would give her better.' Her fancy lord would have kicked her out by this time, he was sure of it, but if she was going to come back she'd have turned up by now. 'Right,' he said. 'There's an audience waiting out there. Let's get on with it.'

Roslyn woke suddenly in the middle of the night. At her side, David slept undisturbed, but something . . . what? had woken her.

There! That was it: music, very faint and far away. She sat up, listening. A lute, and a woman singing . . . It was the song. 'Blow, Northern Wind' which she'd played for Tim that afternoon. She pulled the cover aside, letting in the warm night air and the smell of oxen and Fenland mud. The music was louder now, and it wasn't coming from outside.

It was here in the cart with her.

Chapter 32

'J esu!' said the queen.

Her jennet refused to enter the water, plunging and whinnying in terror, so that the champion had to dismount and cover the animal's eyes before he could lead it onto the causeway. After one disbelieving glance down, Isabel crossed herself and fixed her gaze on the guide's back.

'Where is Lady Maude?' she asked as they splashed their way towards Ravenser.

'Coming, my lady. My sergeant took her by another path, to confuse any who would follow.'

'Where are the rebels now?'

'Everywhere, my lady.' They passed through the gate into the bailey, and he lifted her from the saddle. 'Ravenser is a bare place, and I must beg you to pardon its deficiencies, but you will be safe here. It is Ely in little. It cannot be taken.'

She could well believe it. The surrounding marsh and mere seemed to stretch to the horizon in all directions, and anyone trying to reach the island without knowing the secret path would be sucked down and drowned.

'This way, my lady.'

Bowing, extending his hand, palm up for her fingertips to rest in, as if they were about to dance, Tyrrel led her up the steps to the door into the donjon's wing, up narrow winding steps, along a passage, and opened another door.

She stared, too amazed to speak. In this bleak place, this jewel box of a room . . .

'Isabel,' the champion said tenderly, 'this is your bower.'

Shock widened her opal eyes at hearing her name from his lips. Since leaving her father's care twelve years ago, no one but her husband had called her by name. Like the slash of a blade, it tore the protective cocoon in which her whole life, until now, had been lived: first as Count Aymer's only child, the precious heiress of Angoulême, and then, from the age of twelve, as Queen of England.

Tyrrel was smiling.

It was the first time she had really looked at him, seen more than a familiar man-shape, a handsome face, a graceful athletic body, an attractive creature like all those chosen to surround her – her knights, her squires and pages, her champion – two-dimensional figures, good-looking, witty, gallant but not real, not flesh and blood, no more to her than the puppets brought to perform for her amusement at the Christmas feast. They sang to her, love songs, of course; they danced with her, compliments fell from their lips; they postured and paraded to catch her eye, begged her favours to wear in the lists, fought one another with ferocity to win her smile. And to her they were only pretty, strutting dolls.

That they might feel – love, desire, hate, fear – had never crossed her mind, she who had never felt these emotions herself.

Now, with Tyrrel's green-amber eyes – ardent, intense – so near that she could see herself, a tiny reflection in their black centres, she knew different.

Hugh de Lusignan had looked at her like that when she was eleven years old, and asked for her in marriage.

When she was twelve, John had looked at her like that and stolen her from Hugh.

She felt Tyrrel's breath on her cheek – how dared he stand so close? She stepped back, dragging her arm from his grasp. Her bracelet of ivory plaques slid down over her hand and broke. The pieces rattled and scattered everywhere.

'I'll give you finer jewels, Isabel,' he said hoarsely.

'My name is not for *your* lips,' she said, her voice shaking. He didn't seem to hear. He stepped forward, and she stepped back. 'My lord the king will have you flayed,' she said.

'The king is dead.'

'I don't believe you!'

'It's true. All England will know soon enough. Isabel, you are free.'

Shock and sudden fear aged her face. 'My children!'

'They're in fitzWalter's care. It's all arranged. He will have Henry crowned—'

'Robert fitzWalter? Is this his doing?' She was beginning to believe it, incredible as it seemed. There had been rumours, and she knew John didn't trust fitzWalter. But what was Tyrrel's part in this? 'Sir Ralf, help me! I have to be with my children. You must take me—'

'They're safe, I promise you.' He stepped forward again.

180

'Isabel, there's no need to pretend any longer. I love you! You love me, I know you do.'

Her hands and feet were icy cold, and her legs felt tingly and weak. She mustn't faint! She must *not* faint! 'I have never, never given you any cause—'

'I saw in your eyes what your heart said . . .'

'I think you've gone mad!' He took her hand in his and her voice rose with the shrillness of panic. 'Don't touch me!'

'There is no one here to spy on us; you can follow your heart, Isabel. Say you love me!'

'Love you? Love *you*?' She tilted her head back – for his kiss, he thought – but when he bent towards her she laughed and spat in his face.

He said nothing, just drew in a sharp breath as if she'd stuck a needle into his flesh. Without a word he turned and left the room. With a sense of total disbelief she heard the key turn in the lock. Her legs gave way and she sat on the edge of the bed, shaking.

There was wine in the cupboard beside the bed, and she reached for it, then thought, *It may be drugged*, and drew her hand back sharply. She pressed her hands down hard on her thighs, to stop her legs shaking. Two tears escaped and rolled down her cheeks and she wiped them away angrily. *You are the queen*, she told herself. *Queens don't snivel like frightened serfs. There must be a way out of here.*

She got up and began to explore her prison.

A hundred candles lit the chamber, which was as rich as any in the palaces and royal castles. Instead of hangings, the walls were painted in the latest fashion, with flowering branches on which perched brightly coloured birds; on the ceiling were more painted birds, in flight. The floor was covered with a woven cloth of many colours, very costly, and the hangings of the great bed were embroidered with the arms of England and Angoulême.

There were cups and plates of silver on the table. A painted screen concealed a bath. The garderobe opened off the chamber, set in the twelve-foot-thick wall, and the clothes-poles held gowns of silk, and furred mantles in shades of blue and amethyst. At the bed foot stood a chest filled, when she looked in, with women's gauds – shoes, slippers, hose, girdles, gloves and scarves; and a small chest within the chest held jewellery.

On a bench under the window was a basket holding embroi-dery silks and a pincushion bristling with needles like a small hedgehog. The window was too small for any but a child to pass through, and anyway, looking out she could see nothing but marsh and sky.

This room had been prepared for her and no one else. Much time and labour had been spent in its preparation. Tyrrel had been planning this for a long time.

Real fear uncoiled in her belly and writhed upwards to trip her heartbeats and constrict her throat.

If John was really dead, no one would be coming to her aid.

If John was dead, little Henry, not yet five years old, was king, and whoever held him would hold the kingdom.

Robert fitzWalter would never let go.

She began to pray with a fervour she had never felt before. 'Holy Mary, ever virgin, mother of Christ, help me! Guard my sons, my daughter . . .' Sweet Jesus, baby Joan was only two. 'They are so little!'

Outside the chamber Tyrrel leaned against the door and wiped his face, staring at his wet fingers in puzzlement. His hand shook like a palsied old man's.

She had laughed at him!

It wasn't right, it wasn't meant to be like this.

She had said he was mad. She had said, 'Don't touch me!' She had said, 'Love you? Love *you*?' And laughed.

He hammered his fist into the rough stone wall, oblivious to the pain and the blood. Blood ran down over his knuckles and dripped on the floor. He groaned, but not with the pain of his smashed hand.

This wasn't meant to happen. She shouldn't have laughed.

Blindly, bumping into walls and the sides of doorways, he stumbled down passages and steps to that other chamber.

The door was locked, but he had the key.

Thought of what was within quickened his pulse and breathing. He hadn't seen this one, although it had been here for some time. There should have been no need of it once Isabel was his, but now . . . He turned the key. The steward's wife jumped up from her stool by the bed as the door opened.

'My lord, I didn't expect— She's not prepared—'

'Get out.'

She scuttled past him and ran.

He walked quietly to the bed and looked down with a sharp indrawn hiss of breath.

It was asleep. It was more like *her* than any of the others had been. He stood looking at it for some time before it opened its eyes.

He touched its cheek. It flinched.

'Oh, Isabel,' he said, tears in his eyes, 'why did you laugh?'

Chapter 33

Three riders, three knights of the White Brotherhood, three Angels of the Lord, to do his work . . . three tired, dust-caked, hungry men, moving stiffly at the end of a day's weary riding, each tending his own horse, lifting off the heavy saddle, rubbing the animal down, feeding and watering it. Not until that was done could they see to their own needs.

Swarms of gnats whined around them, drawn to their heat and sweat, and the youngest, whose task it was to get a fire going and prepare the evening meal, cursed and swatted at them as he worked, but to no effect.

Uriel loathed and despised this marsh country. It was unnatural. Day and night they were tormented by biting insects. Seemingly firm green ground quaked like jelly under-foot. And at night – it would be dark soon, and he looked uneasily around – demons lit lamps to lead Christian men to their deaths, unabsolved, in mud-holes that could swallow anything, from hare to horse.

The Angels had little or nothing to talk about. The usual conversation of travelling companions was barred to them, for they knew nothing of one another and must reveal nothing; even the names they used were not their own, although by accents and oaths each knew the others to be men of Toulouse or the country thereabouts. For various reasons they were companions in a holy quest sanctioned by the Church, and were bound by oaths to fulfil it or die in the attempt. When they knelt to pray before eating, the eldest – known as Michael – was their spokesman to God.

'*Seigneur Dieu*, we are your swords. Bring us to your enemy, that we may destroy him, in the name of Christ. Amen.'

'Amen.'

'Amen.'

They ate their meal in silence, doffed boots and belts and lay down with swords to hand, to sleep the sleep of the just.

Uriel lay awake.

The moon was almost full, but fuzzy like a ball of pale yellow

184

wool, and a mist was rising, filling the hollows like milk and spilling over. Frogs croaked and chirped relentlessly, and unseen creatures, some big by the sound of them, splashed in the mere. Uriel rolled over restlessly. At home, on summer nights there would be feasting, and the young people of the castle would dance in the meadows. Two summers ago his father had ordered rafts moored in the river, and they had feasted there, enjoying the cool evening breeze while minstrels played for their pleasure, and beautiful Marcelle, his betrothed, had turned her face aside from his kiss and slapped his hand away from her breast.

'Stop pawing me,' she said.

He couldn't understand why she didn't like him, but it didn't matter. She was his betrothed, his property, his to kiss and finger if he wished whether she liked him or not, and by God's tripes, when they were married he'd teach her obedience . . .

The faithless whore.

He'd come upon them in the orchard, Marcelle and his brother Gerard, she on her back with her skirts flung up and he in the saddle.

Murder was one thing, fratricide another.

Because his father was comrade-in-arms to Lord Simon de Montfort and a notable hunter of heretics, and because his mother was cousin to the Bishop of Toulouse, his sentence of death was commuted to perpetual imprisonment, which was worse. He'd prayed for death every day during his two years in prison. And then the miracle. The door opened to admit Maître Deil, the bishop's secretary, confidant, right-hand man, and he was offered this chance of redemption. All he had to do was kill a child.

If he'd wondered why the thought was fleeting. He'd have slaughtered fifty, a hundred, whoever they were. It had taken much longer than he'd expected to find the brat, but they were close to their quarry now. Soon he'd be free to go home, his estates and property restored to him and high in Bishop Fulk's favour.

He rolled over again, scratching at gnat bites, grunting at the discomfort, aroused by memories of Marcelle and wanting a woman.

'Be still, boy. Go to sleep,' said Michael.

Uriel scowled in the darkness. The old man treated him like a servant, quick to rebuke and even strike him. And the other, Samael, showed no sympathy. They had forgotten what it was like to be young and eager. He wondered why Maître Deil had

185

chosen such dried up old men for this task.

Larktwist was having a nightmare. He had fallen off the cause-way, and the bog was sucking him down. Someone held a stick out for him to grasp, but when he reached for it, jabbed him with it instead in the chest. 'Help!' he cried, and the muddy water ran into his open mouth. 'Help!' The stick poked him again, and he screamed and sat up.

He was in bed. Thank God! Someone was bending over him. It was the steward.

'Sir Ralf wants you. Bring your stuff.'

Larktwist got his box and followed the man through a door that had hitherto always been locked when he'd tried it, along torchlit passages into a part of the donjon that he didn't recog-nise and presently realised must be the adjoining wing.

'Who's sick?' he asked, padding in the steward's wake. The man didn't answer, but led the way up spiral steps, along more passages and past closed doors, until Larktwist had completely lost his bearings. The door they fetched up at was no different from others they had passed, and he certainly wouldn't know how to find it again.

The steward knocked. The door was unlocked from the inside and opened, and Larktwist found himself face to face with the queen's champion. He swallowed nervously, and hoped the bob of his Adam's apple had gone unnoticed. *Stick to him*, Mercredi had said, and he'd promised, but he'd never expected to get this close.

The steward followed him in and shut the door. Larktwist had never seen so fine a room as this. It was a bedchamber, painted with birds that looked as if they might fly at any moment and bright with candles, but after one swift glance around Larktwist had eyes only for the bed and the girl lying on it, beautiful, pale as a lily – and dead.

No, not dead. Her breasts rose and fell, the movement scarcely perceptible. Her silver-gilt hair, unbound, was spread over the blue silk pillows. He remembered that hair. So this was where the champion kept his bit of stuff.

'What ails her?' he asked.

Tyrrel's voice was rough-edged with panic. 'She hasn't been eating.'

She had refused to eat anything since he brought her here; at first she threw the food, dishes and all, at the unfortunate steward, but after a couple of days she just lay on the bed and turned her face away. He was afraid she'd keep it up until she died. '*Do* something!'

Larktwist had no idea what to do. 'Did she say she had pain?'

'No. Should she be bled?'

Probably, only he hadn't the faintest idea how it was done. 'The moon is waxing, a bad time to let blood.' That at least sounded as if he knew what he was talking about, and the champion didn't presume to argue. Larktwist lifted the limp wrist and felt her pulse – he'd seen quack doctors do that a hundred times; her flesh was cold as a corpse, which gave him an idea. He took up one of her hands and began rubbing it, then the other.

There was a sound, so soft he couldn't be sure he'd heard it, but he thought she'd sighed.

'Here,' he said to the champion. 'You do this. I'll do her feet.' He turned the coverlid back and began chafing her feet. Leaning over her, watching her face, Tyrrel saw eyelids flicker and colour begin to tinge the ashen lips.

'Isabel! Thank God!'

'Keep her warm,' Larktwist said. 'Better get some hot stones packed round her.'

Tyrrel rounded on the steward. 'You heard him! Get them! Go!' He thrust the man towards the door, and the sound of his running footfalls faded away along the passage outside.

Isabel opened her eyes and saw the unlovely countenance of Larktwist hovering over her.

'Who are you?' Her voice was little more than a whisper, and she spoke French, not English.

It wasn't the same voice. It wasn't the same woman. The one he'd seen in the bailey had been little more than a girl – sixteen, seventeen, perhaps. Although they were much alike, both with that wonderful pale gold hair, this one was a woman in her twenties. For a moment Larktwist wondered how many more the champion had, stowed away about the place? Was there one behind every door he'd passed? He liked them fair, obviously. Larktwist felt a twinge of envy. Nice for some!

Tyrrel said, 'He is a leech, my lady.'

She looked imploringly at Larktwist. 'Is it true?'

'What, my lady?' And before Tyrrel could stop her, she had said it.

'The king, my husband, is he dead?'

Across her body Larktwist's eyes met the champion's, and saw murder in them.

The door was flung open by the returning steward, who ushered his wife before him carrying a basket of hot stones. Animal instinct moved Larktwist while his brain was still wondering what to do. He stuck out a foot and tripped the woman, who fell, dropping the basket, stones and all. Gratifyingly, as if rehearsed, her husband tripped over the basket, and Tyrrel, reaching for Larktwist, stumbled over him and went sprawling. The steward's wife grasped Larktwist by the loose cloth of his breeches and managed to sink her teeth into his leg, but unhampered by inconvenient notions of gallantry he kicked her hard under the chin and shot through the open door like a hunted rabbit.

Behind him he heard the woman squealing, Tyrrel's shout and the thudding of feet, but he had a start. Darting down passages, round corners, down stairs, he tried a door. It opened, and he tumbled into the room, shutting the door behind him, scrabbling in vain for a bolt, praying they'd not seen him.

Feet thundered past. They hadn't seen him. His heart was racing, and every indrawn breath burned like acid. He bent forward to ease the stitch in his side, then straightened and looked around for a way out.

Moonlight coming in through the two barred windows showed this to be another bedchamber, probably directly underneath that other where the sick woman – holy saints, was she really the queen? – lay. And what did she mean about the king being dead? Could that be true?

The room was almost bare: a bench and a bed, the bed stripped to the ropes. He lifted the cover of the gong and peered down. He was a small, skinny man, and the chute looked big enough to accommodate him, but its outlet was in a covered cesspit, and all things considered he'd rather die by Tyrrel's dagger than drown in shit.

They'd be back before long.

The floorcloth was rucked up beside the bed, and caught his toe as he stepped over it. A blowfly rose, droning irritably, and alighted again, working its way busily back into the creases. He kicked at it, and more flew up, buzzing angrily at the disturbance before settling back.

Something glittered by his foot. Larktwist reached for it – beads, on a broken chain. He took it to the window. Paternoster beads, fouled with some dried gummy substance which, when he rubbed them between his fingers, crumbled into blackish fragments.

Squatting, he pulled the floor covering out flat, releasing a bad-meat reek of decaying blood and the lazy buzzing of a swarm of somnolent flies.

Shouts. Running feet. Doors banging.

Oh Christ! Here they come!

Pernelle had left everything behind, not that she had much to leave apart from the lute. When she ran off she'd been wearing a blue gown, made for some townsman's wife, that had gone through two or three more pairs of hands before coming to rest in the company's costume chest. Piper hadn't sold her other things yet; he'd packed them in a sack and stowed them safely in the cart, just in case she turned up again. Roslyn lit two candles, filched from the company's store, and unpacked them: a grey woollen gown, taken in, rubbed and worn but clean, and a pair of neatly cobbled shoes; a necklace of painted hazelnuts and a small, scratched, steel mirror.

She ran the necklace through her hands, picked up the mirror and laid it down again, touched the shoes, the gown. They added nothing to what she already knew: Pernelle was dead. Murdered.

Ghosts, earth-fast souls, whatever they were, had been Roslyn's unwanted companions since childhood. Mostly they seemed unaware of her, carrying on with their meaningless, repetitive actions as if she were not there. She remembered one young woman who kept dropping a vase and weeping for it; again and again it fell from her hands to smash, and her tears fell too, all in silence. Others re-enacted events from their former lives: meeting, parting, laughing, weeping. She had disciplined herself to ignore them, so long as they didn't trouble her.

But there were some, a few, who did – who pushed past her defences, clamouring for her help, forcing upon her their terrible memories of betrayal, cruelty, murder or self-slaughter – flooding her mind with their regret or remorse or desire for revenge; giving her no rest, who knew no rest themselves.

'Leave me alone,' she said, for Pernelle was there in the shifting shadows, watching her, imploring. She folded the grey gown carefully and put it back in the bag with the shoes, necklace and mirror. 'There's nothing I can do. In the name of the Holy Virgin, leave me alone!' She crossed herself and closed her eyes, murmuring a prayer, but when she opened them again Pernelle was still there.

She should tell the others. They were the only family Pernelle had had; they'd cared about her, worried when she didn't return.

They had the right to know; they would want to pray for her soul. But how could she tell them? She knew what they would say: How do you know?

What answer could she give? And if she did tell them, what could they do? The only one who would be able to take any action was Straccan.

She flinched. The memory of that encounter in the Sempringham meadow was like salt on raw flesh. What madness had possessed her, to stumble like that in the dark? To cling to him like a whore? How he must despise her! Since that night he had avoided her as much as was possible in the close company of the Gaudy camp, and now that she travelled with the players it was easier to keep out of his way.

No, she couldn't talk to Straccan about this.

But someone had done murder, and unless she told what she knew, that wicked one would kill again.

Bane shook Straccan awake.

He groaned. 'It can't be morning; it's too dark.'

Bane had a lanthorn, but it did little by way of light. 'It's something after midnight and getting foggy. That Mungo's asking for you. He's with Mistress Boteler and her boy.'

Straccan rolled off his pallet and reached for his boots. Morning and evening he stopped by Giles's cart to ask how the boy did, and every time expected to be told that he had died. But Lawrence clung to life, and as the dusty, jolting, tedious days passed he seemed to be getting stronger, and the ulcer on his back had begun to shrink.

'He had some sort of fit,' Bane said.

Straccan shrugged into his jerkin and ducked out of the tent. Fog was knee-high and spreading, and there was a powerful smell of marsh mud. He took the lanthorn from Bane and picked his way quietly through the clustered tents.

Dim light shone through the canvas cover of Giles's cart.

'Mistress Lucy?'

It was Brother Mungo who put aside the flap. Straccan could see into the cart, where Mistress Boteler sat by Lawrence's pallet with the child's head in her lap. By the light of the lanthorn hanging above them, Lawrence's small face was skull-like.

Mungo jumped down. 'He's still breathing. She wants to take him to the abbey at Cerneshead.'

'What for?'

'They have relics there. The girdle of Saint Audrey has cured

190

many, and a phial of the tears of Our Lady, that she shed at the cross. The Blessed Mother will surely pity another mother, weeping for her son.'

'Was this your idea?'

'I told her of the relics, yes.'

'The journey will kill him!'

'He's dying anyway,' Mungo said.

'Then in God's name, let him die in peace!'

'No!' Lucy Boteler scrambled out of the cart, tearing her gown and skinning her knee on the tailboard without noticing. 'I won't let him die! I can't! He's all I have! Sir Richard, please!' To Straccan's dismay she dropped to her knees and embraced his, clinging with a strength that surprised him. 'Brother Mungo says you mean to ride to the abbey, come morning.'

Straccan gave the monk a sidelong glance, wondering how he knew that and about to ask, but Mistress Boteler had seized his hand and was kissing it, wetting it with her tears.

'Sir Richard, if Lawrence— If he is still alive then, will you take him? I beg you, in God's name!' She raised her ravaged face, all eyes and desperation.

After a moment, and against his better judgement, Straccan said, 'Can you ride a horse?'

Larktwist let out his breath in a soundless sigh. It was quiet again, except for a faint, distant clamour in the bailey. They'd gone.

He'd had a moment of panic when he slid a yard or so down before managing to brace his feet and elbows against the slippery sides of the chute. But he'd guessed aright, thank Christ! The idiots hadn't thought to look down the gong. The chute was slimy, however, and so was he, and when he tried to push himself upwards his foot slipped and he slid further down instead, with a muffled yelp of terror, his clawed fingers leaving tracks in the clotted ordure.

Jesus! Saint Thomas! Help! I'll give you my weight in candles, I promise! His foot found some small projection – *Oh thank you, thank you!* – and after a pause to let his skittering heart steady itself, he shoved himself upwards. His fingers got a grip on the edge of the hole, and he hauled himself up and over, slithering on to the floor in an unspeakable heap. His trews and shirt would never be the same, but what was a little shit in the great scheme of things? He regarded his feet. Bugger, he'd lost a shoe down there. But he was alive! Now to find some funk-hole where he could hide until dawn, and then slip out into the bailey. As long as no one saw him, his plan of escape stood a chance. He pulled his other shoe off and tossed it down the gong to join its fellow.

It was then it dawned on him that although they might not see him, they could smell him a mile away.

Chapter 34

At dawn Lawrence Boteler was still alive, and the fog was so thick that Straccan couldn't see further than his arm's length in any direction.

'God be with you, Sir Richard.' Dirty orange torchlight smeared the fog without giving any illumination, and there was Brother Mungo suddenly at his side as if he'd sprung from the ground, torch and all. 'The bell won't be moving today,' the sub-prior observed unnecessarily.

Ruefully Straccan agreed. The fog at least could hardly be blamed on his theoretical vengeful chaplain or the chaplain's ill-used leman, although he supposed it could be a manifestation of the so-called curse. And as if the thought had winged from his mind to Mungo's, the monk chose that moment to say, 'One could be forgiven for thinking there was a curse on this journey.' He said it loudly. Straccan could have kicked him.

'The oxen will get a day of rest. We can't break camp until the fog lifts. Brother, will you help Mistress Boteler get Lawrence ready to leave? I'll carry him on my horse. She can ride my rouncey.'

'Oh, but Sir Richard, surely you won't ride out in this?' Mungo looked concerned. 'If the horses should wander from the road—'

'Apple has more sense, and I'll have the other on a leading rein.' He looked around. He had only taken a few steps from his tent, and already he'd lost his bearings. Lanthorns hanging on carts were faint smudges of yellow in the mirk. 'Hawkan? Where are you?'

A hand on his elbow made him jump. 'Here.' Bane held up a light, which might as well have been a brick for all the good it was.

'Get the people to light fires by the carts, and set torches or fires between the tents. Better have water buckets standing by, just in case. Brother,' to Mungo, 'may we borrow your novices to help?'

'I'll send them to you.' Brother Mungo vanished in the fog.

Patches of blurry light dotted the camp as torches and fires were lit. The fog held the smoke down, and it drifted, low, through the encampment. People materialised, coughing and complaining, and were swallowed up again. The fog played tricks with sound, too. Straccan could hear the oxen's bellies rumbling although they were at the far end of the camp, and a woman's voice, seemingly right in his ear, said crossly, 'Don't just stand there, Jen. Stir that pot, do!'

Bane reappeared. 'I've saddled the horses. Are you going to eat something before you go?'

'What've you got?'

'Bread and bacon.' At the word 'bacon' the dog appeared at his side as if by magic, and fixed him with a hopeful, hungry stare.

'Put it in my saddlebag, will you? Oh, and Hawkan, tie the dog up until I'm away. I don't want him plunging about like a fool in the marsh.'

'Right you are. How far is it to Cerneshead?'

'About five miles.'

'Think the boy will make it?'

'No.'

Larktwist crept along a passage and tiptoed past an open door.

'Jesus,' said a disgusted voice. 'What 'ave you bin eating?'

'What d'you mean?' snapped another voice, indignantly. 'It ain't me!'

Ever since the novices' escapade on Bankside Brother Mungo had insisted the shelter they all shared be sited apart from the rest, so that their contemplations would not be disturbed by the pilgrims' worldly doings. When he reached it, the sub-prior stuck his torch in the ground, where it burned sullenly, and sent the novices to give Bane a hand with the fires. When the fog had swallowed the two robed and cowled figures, Mungo paced back and forth outside the shelter, passing his prayer beads through his fingers, looking up sharply now and then as some sound caught his ear.

Presently he heard what he was listening for: the soft jingle of harness and the clink of a horse's hoof on a stone, and a few moments later the signal he awaited: a low whistle, just two notes. Mungo puckered his lips to return it, but his mouth was dry and nothing came. He licked his lips and tried again, this time managing two rather shaky notes.

Anyone seeing another cowled figure emerge silently from the fog would have taken it either for Aidan or Finan, but it was a stranger. They spoke together briefly before the stranger-monk shouldered the fog aside and disappeared, unseen by anyone else.

A narrow flight of spiral steps led down to another passage, with three closed doors. Larktwist hesitated. Was this the way he'd come? He wasn't even sure whether he was in the donjon now, or still in the wing.

He heard voices behind him, at the top of the steps. Nothing else for it! Praying there would be no one inside, he opened the nearest door and sagged with relief behind it, leaving it ajar.

Footfalls on the steps, and now in the passage just outside.

'Steward says he's got away.'

'Never get across the marsh. Eels'll 'ave im.'

'Christ! What's that smell?'

'I thought it was you.'

Less than a mile to the south of the Gaudy camp the Angels too had awoken to fog and an eerie silence. Usually, from first light to nightfall, the sounds of the marshland surrounded them. Birds whistled, piped and hooted, frogs croaked and plopped, gnats whined maddeningly, and the willows and reeds rustled a constant accompaniment. Uriel didn't like it, but the silence was unnatural, and he liked it even less.

'What shall we do?' Samael asked. 'Wait until it lifts?'

'It may not lift for days,' Uriel protested. 'We are close behind them; the dung of their beasts was fresh last night. In this fog we can fall upon them unawares.'

'That would be foolish. There are more than fifty people there,' Samael said.

'We're not going to fall upon them,' said Michael. 'All we want is the boy.'

'Let me go among them alone,' Uriel said eagerly. 'I will find him and kill him.' He drew his dagger and slashed at the fog as if it were a throat.

'No!' But the idea itself had merit. 'I have the most English of us three,' Michael said. 'I will go. If there is a chance I will seize the boy and bring him away.'

Less than a mile to the north of the Gaudy encampment five riders, robed and cowled and armed with staves and slings, grouped around a sixth, who came riding out of the fog.

'Brothers, rejoice! Our friend has given us the good word, as he promised. The Holy Caul is on its way to us.'

'With what company?'

'One man.'

Jubilant faces and cries of amazement: 'One man! God is with us! Saint Peter wills it!'

'He's escorting a woman and child to Cerneshead. Let them pass. He is our target. And he's a knight; he'll fight if he gets the chance, and if he does, some of us will die. So do exactly as we've planned and no one will be hurt. We are monks, remember. We may not shed blood. Now, ride! We shall wait for him at the Waystone.'

Larktwist had found what he was looking for – a trapdoor – but the bolt was so stiff that he couldn't work it loose. He drew his dagger and hammered at it, cringing at the noise, which must surely bring someone to investigate. But his luck held, and he heaved the heavy door up.

'Faugh!'

A stench billowed out. He stepped on to the ladder, and tugged the trapdoor shut after him; as it crashed down he ducked, but not far enough, and it struck him a stunning blow on the back of the head, knocking him off the ladder into the foetid darkness. But that was the least of his troubles.

He landed on something yielding, warm and irritated.

There were pigs in the undercroft.

Straccan had been gone less than an hour when a tall old man in a hooded cloak loomed out of the fog and found himself in the thick of the pilgrims, who were enjoying a protracted breakfast.

'God save you, friend,' he said politely in French-accented English to Luke Bannerman, who was on his third kipper. 'Who leads this honourable company?'

'Thass Sir Richard,' the bannerman said, spitting bones. 'Sir Richard Straccan. You've just missed him, sir, but he'll be back by evening, God willing. Would you like a word with Master Bane? Thass Sir Richard's servant.'

Bane would recognise him; he had seen all three of them at the inn at Darley.

'No, my business is with Sir Richard. I will come back.'

'He's gone to the abbey at Cerneshead, with the little boy and his mother, poor soul. Sir? Sir? Blind me, he's gone!'

Trusting to the horse's instinct to keep to the road, Straccan let

Apple have his head, and rode at walking pace, leading the rouncey through a landscape in shades of grey, although now and then the fog would thin and lift, and let colour return to the world briefly before closing in again, thicker than ever. On both sides they heard water lapping and the occasional splash of some marsh creature. Fog and imagination played tricks with sound: from time to time he even thought he heard men's voices, but it was impossible to tell from where they came – behind, before, right or left.

It was easy to pray in this shrouded world. There was no distraction. He prayed for Lawrence, for if it was God's will the boy might recover; impossible as it seemed, with God there were no impossibilities. He prayed for David, that his enemies should not find him and he should come at last to safety; he prayed for Gilla, and he prayed for Janiva. *Lord, protect her. Christ, of your mercy, watch and ward her from harm. Bring her safe out of all danger. Let me find her.*

He held Lawrence against his breast as gently as he could, fearful that the boy would never live to reach Cerneshead. In his wrappings he seemed as light and fleshless as a dead bird.

'How far is it?' Mistress Boteler asked.

'We should come to the Waystone soon – that's halfway.'

When Apple's ears cocked sharply back, he turned and wasn't a bit surprised to see the dog had managed to follow him after all.

Michael rode as fast as he dared, the mile back to the Angels' camp seeming three times as long. The others, hearing him coming, stood ready with drawn swords in case he was an enemy, but sheathed them again when they saw him.

'Mount up,' he cried. 'They are here, the boy's mother is with him after all. Straccan has taken them to Cerneshead abbey. No, leave the fire, leave everything; there's not a moment to lose!'

Chapter 35

'**D**id you hear that?'
     'What?'
'Listen!'
The Angels reined in.
'I don't hear anything.'
'Quiet, damn you! There!'
The snuffling *frrr* of a horse, the jingle of harness, a smothered cough.
Uriel spurred forward and was lost to sight. The others followed. Somewhere in the mirk ahead they heard shouts and curses. They spurred towards the noise.
The Waystone marked the boundary between Cerneshead abbey lands and those of the fabulously wealthy Poor Fellow-Soldiers of Christ and the Temple of Solomon, at their Temple Bruer headquarters. Beside the tall granite monolith the Croyland monks surrounded a writhing body on the ground. Bursting out of the fog and piling into the huddle, Michael realised it was Uriel, helpless and struggling in the bird net with which the monks had swept him from his horse. Even as he drew his sword, a staff swung by a militant – and muscular – Benedictine met his upper arm with tremendous force. The sound of bone breaking was like the crack of a whip, and a high scream jerked out of him as the pain lanced, it seemed, right to his heart. His sword fell from his hand and he reeled in the saddle.
'They are monks,' Samael cried. 'Monks! Not our quarry!' He laid about him with the flat of his sword, felling two of the party who were trying to pull Michael down. One of the unfortunates lay still, the second crawled to the shelter of the others' robes. The brethren fell back and drew together around the Waystone to blame one another.
'Whose bright idea was this, then?'
'Don't look at me! That Judas-haired monk said *one* knight, with a woman and child.'
'I never trusted him!'
'He sought us out, offered his help—'

198

'Didn't that strike you as queer? You were a fool to trust him!'

'Who are you calling a fool?'

'Stop it, both of you! I think Brother Hubert's dead!'

'No, look. He twitched, see?'

Samael dismounted, picked up Michael's sword and restored it to him. Michael, white about the mouth, took the weapon in his left hand.

'Get me out of this,' yelled Uriel. The other two took no notice.

'Why did you ambush us?' Samael asked.

'It was a mistake.' One of the monks came forward cautiously to help the fallen Hubert to his feet. 'We took your companion for someone else. Can we make amends?'

'We're looking for a man who should have come this way. He has a woman and a boy with him,' Samael said.

'Straccan!'

'Yes! You know him?'

'We were waiting for him. We thought that' – he nodded at the squirming Uriel – 'was him. We were told he'd come this way.'

'Then where the hell is he?'

Somewhere off to his left Straccan thought he could hear shouting. Someone lost, probably. He was beginning to fear he was lost too. The road had narrowed to a single-horse track and come to an end abruptly at the water's edge. Ghost-like, a barn owl whispered overhead, and somewhere in the water there was a glooping splash.

The fog shifted again to reveal a jetty stacked with fish traps, and on a low hump of solid ground, a hut with walls of woven reed and a warped and corrugated hide roof.

'I'm afraid we've gone wrong somewhere,' Straccan said. 'We should have come to the Waystone long since. We'll have to turn back.'

'Lawrence—'

'He's asleep.' He saw her face. 'Truly! Just asleep.'

'Look!' She pointed across the water.

'What is it?'

'Lights! I saw lights out there.'

They stared into the fog, but if there had been lights they were hidden now.

Like some great mythical marsh creature, a boat nosed silently alongside the jetty, one of the long, flat-bottomed fen boats,

199

propelled by a long pole in the hands of a man standing in the stern.

'God save you, sir and mistress,' said the boatman politely. He was tall and burly, his hair and beard white as the mist which beaded his slick leather cape. Fog closed again around the boat, so that he looked to be floating upon nothing, and at the same time a rift opened in the murk above, and a huge pallid sun haloed his head as if he were a painted saint on a church wall. The dog uttered a joyful bark.

'Where are we?' Straccan asked.

'This is Cernesmere, me lord.'

Straccan sighed. 'We were making for Cerneshead abbey, but we've lost our road.'

The man made his boat fast and jumped out. 'You've come a mile from the road. I doubt you'll find the way back now; the fog'll get thicker yet afore it lifts.'

'Can you show us the way? I'll pay well for your time,' Straccan said.

'Oh, there's no need to go by road; the abbey's just across the water. Perhaps you saw the fires? Father abbot lit them to guide folk lost in the fog. I'll take you over. Easier on the young un – no jolting by water. Let the mother get in, and you give me the boy, me lord, while you get down. Your horses will be safe here till you get back.'

He settled them in the boat, placing Lawrence in his mother's arms with great gentleness. Then he tied the horses to the jetty's handrail, and cast off.

The craft moved as if through cloud, with scarcely a sound, utterly cut off from the everyday world, a disorientingly dream-like journey which Straccan, who kept looking vainly over his shoulder in the hope of seeing where they were headed, began to fear might go on for ever. He sat in the prow with the dog between his knees, an absurdly joyful dog that had to be restrained from romping along the length of the boat to fawn on the boatman, and so contented itself with tail-wagging and excited whimpers.

Thankfully, at last Straccan saw grimy smudges of light and heard voices.

'Ho, the abbey!' he shouted. Immediately, in response, a horn blew, and the blurred lights became a double row of fires marking the path sloping up from a jetty to the abbey gate, where torches in cressets flared.

'God keep you, friend,' a voice came out of the fog. 'By his grace you are come safe to Cerneshead!'

The boat bumped gently against the jetty, and the boatman jumped ashore to make the boat fast, followed by the dog. Straccan got out and took the boy from his mother while the boatman helped her out.

Welcoming lanthorns bobbed towards them. Mistress Boteler held out her arms for her son, and when Straccan turned back to thank and reward their rescuer, the man and his boat were gone.

When Lawrence and his mother had been borne away to the infirmary, Straccan asked to see the abbot, and gave him the relic.

The abbot opened the case and checked that the fragile membrane was safe and undamaged within. His astonished relief at its return was obvious. He summoned the sacristan and gave him the treasure to lock away. 'And send men down the road to find those Croyland thieves,' he said. 'Tell them the Holy Caul is safely back where it belongs, and they may as well go home. Those Croyland ruffians have been patrolling the road between here and Peterborough for many days,' he added to Straccan, as the sacristan hurried off. 'Without armed men it seemed we might never get our relic back. I am pleased to see you had no difficulty on your way here.'

'I saw nothing of them, but in the fog I took the wrong road; otherwise there might have been some "difficulty", as you put it.'

'These are evil times,' the abbot said, 'when Benedictines turn to highway robbery to steal from their own brethren. But what can you expect in a realm under Interdict?' He poured two cups of wine and gave one to Straccan. 'So you lost your way. But thanks be to Saint Christopher, who watches over travellers, you found it again.'

'My lord abbot, will you tell me the name of the big fisherman who lives in the hut across the mere? It was he who found us and brought us by boat. I meant to reward him, but he slipped away before I had the chance.'

The abbot looked mystified. 'There is no hut there.'

'A flimsy affair, just reeds and hides, right by the jetty. The boatman is tall, white-haired, white-bearded.'

'I know no such man, Sir Richard,' the abbot said, his broad innocent brow creased in puzzlement. 'And to my certain knowledge – I was there yesterday – there is no hut.' He looked thoughtful and drummed with his fingers on the board before him. 'You don't think— But no, no . . . Is it possible?'

'What, my lord?'

'You bore his precious Caul. The man you describe, Sir Richard . . .' The abbot's eyes gleamed with rising excitement. 'Perhaps Saint Peter himself came to you in your need. There is certainly no hut, and no such big white-haired man among our villeins.'

Straccan, long accustomed to monastic enthusiasms often far wilder than this, crossed himself and looked suitably awed. 'It may be as you say, my lord.' Privately he thought it more likely the boatman was from a neighbouring manor, taking advantage of the fog to poach the abbey's preserves, but stranger things had happened.

The abbot walked courteously with him to the gate, his mind clearly on other matters. A splendid new miracle to add to the lustre of the Holy Caul was just what the abbey needed, and he couldn't wait to call the senior brethren together and have the wonder properly recorded.

As they reached the gate a cacophony of horns and shouts announced another fog-bound traveller's arrival. A novice with a lanthorn on a pole trotted forth to greet and bring the lost one within the enclave, returning with an undersized figure that even in the all-pervading brume had, Straccan thought, something familiar about it.

Probably the smell.

For a moment it looked as if the dog meant to lift a leg against the reeking apparition, but on second thoughts it uttered a sharp bark and bit the man's leg instead.

This was too much for Larktwist. He'd been bitten once today already; hidden down a privy, in a pigsty, burrowed in a muck heap and under the contents of a dung cart, and made his way barefoot for several miles through dense fog, every nerve and fibre taut with terror. This was the last straw. His legs folded under him; he sat on the ground and laughed until he cried.

'Larktwist!' said Straccan, incredulous. 'What in the name of God are *you* doing here?'

The apparition clambered to its feet, and then, to Straccan's horror, flung itself upon him, clasping him like a long-lost brother and enveloping him in stench.

'Oh, Sir Richard! You don't know how glad I am to see you!'

Chapter 36

Already the abbey was a-buzz with the news of the miracle; nothing was too good for the bearer of the Holy Caul, and by extension his companion, no matter how repulsive. Larktwist was handed over to the guest master, who – after one sniff – handed him over in turn to his assistant, who led him to the bathhouse and sent lay brothers in relays for hot water, food and ale.

'How can you go around stinking like that?' Straccan asked, as the attendants filled the bathtub.

'You get used to it,' said Larktwist vaguely. 'Can I have some more ale?'

Straccan poured him another cup. 'All right, spy. What's going on?'

'Do you know the queen's champion?'

'Ralf Tyrrel?' Straccan frowned. 'I saw him at Southwark, at dinner with the Bishop of Winchester.'

'Yes, well, he's got this island – Ravenser, it's called – eight or ten miles that way.' Larktwist gestured. 'Or maybe that way. God, I don't know! A bloody long walk anyhow. I hid in the dung cart—'

'Why?'

'He was going to kill me, Tyrrel was. Sir Richard, he's got the queen there. I think she's his prisoner, and I don't think anybody knows where she is. Ow!' Straccan's hand had his thin upper arm in a painful grip.

'What are you talking about? The queen? Did you see her?'

'Let go! Yes, I did. Sir Richard, is the king dead?'

Straccan blinked. 'He was very much alive at Nottingham a few days ago. No, he can't be dead; there'd be uproar. Who said he was dead?'

'The queen. She asked me if it was true.'

'What did she say?'

'She said, "Is my husband the king dead?" And Tyrrel jumped at me.'

'Then what?'

203

'I got away. Don't ask me how.'

'I can guess!'

The bath was ready, and Larktwist reluctantly shed the last of his disgusting garments. He was much the same colour underneath. He eyed the steaming tub suspiciously. 'Do I have to get in there?'

'Haven't you ever had a bath?'

'Not on purpose.'

'Get in!'

Reluctantly Larktwist stepped into the bath. 'Yah! It's hot!'

'It's meant to be. There's a stool in there. Sit down.' A smirking lay brother handed Straccan a jug, which he emptied over Larktwist's head. 'Pick up that soap-bag and wash your hair, and then the rest of you. Better bring more water,' he said to the attendant. 'He'll need a lot of rinsing.'

Larktwist unhappily rubbed the soap-bag over his head, exclaiming in alarm at the appearance of suds, 'It's frothing!'

'It's supposed to.' Straccan poured more water over Larktwist's head. The little man screamed.

'My eyes! It burns! I'll go blind!'

'Oh, shut up!'

Larktwist squeezed his eyes shut and swiped at them with the back of his hand. 'Can I get out now?'

'Not yet. Here.' Straccan passed him a stiff-bristled brush. 'Scrub your hands and nails with that, and any other bits that can bear it. Are you sure it was the queen you saw?'

'I don't know; I've never seen her before. But he called her Isabel, Tyrrel did.'

'What was she like?'

Larktwist thought. 'Beautiful.' He groped for words: 'A . . . a silver woman, all moonlight . . .' and stopped, looking embarrassed.

Straccan, surprised at Larktwist's flight of poetry, whistled softly. But he had seen Queen Isabel, and was convinced.

'That's not all, Sir Richard.' Larktwist heaved up in the tub, sending a surge of scummy water over the rim on to the towels spread on the floor around it, staining them an unpleasant shade of beige. 'You'll never guess who else Tyrrel's got on Ravenser.'

'The Pope?'

'Old friend of ours. Yours. Remember Soulis's mad Arab?'

'Abdul al-Hazred. *He's* there?'

'Tyrrel keeps him in a round tower, making gold for him.'

'*Al-Hazred?*'

204

'Who else can it be? A very old Saracen wizard. Can't be two of them. Can there?'

'Christ, I hope not! God's bones! Al-Hazred!' The rush of adrenaline left Straccan feeling oddly cold. If Tyrrel's sorcerer and Rainard de Soulis's Arab were the same, he might be calling demons out of the sky to Ravenser, as he had in Scotland. He blanched at the memory of the unholy, unearthly horror al-Hazred had summoned at Soulis's bidding. It required blood, and the Arab had slaughtered children to feed it. Gilla had been an intended victim.

He would have to do something. He was supposed to stay with the bell, but penance or no penance, Abdul al-Hazred was unfinished business. And Tyrrel . . .

'God's bones,' he said again. 'Does he mean to kill the queen?'

'Tyrrel? No,' said Larktwist. 'I saw the way he looked at her. He's sweet on her.'

'Then what—'

'Look, Sir Richard, something's been going on for some time. I've been following him – orders, you know.' Straccan nodded, he knew of Larktwist's peculiar occupation. 'First I was following Robert fitzWalter, and then Tyrrel, and there were several others, great lords, and they were up to something. My master in London knows all about it, and I have to get word to him.

'So you must,' Straccan said. 'You'd better come with me.'

The abbey's almoner supplied the spy with clean apparel and a pair of shoes which almost fitted, and when Larktwist was ready, a boat and boatman were provided to take them across the mere, and a guide, a young monk called Bartimeus, to show them the way back to the Gaudy camp. If anything, the fog seemed thicker, but their boatman poled the craft unerringly to the jetty where the horses waited, and wished them God speed before turning back.

'You're in good hands now, my masters,' he cried cheerfully as he vanished in the brume. 'Not fog nor night nor anything can lead Brother Barty astray!'

There was no hut. Straccan couldn't believe it. Brother Bartimeus waited patiently while Straccan beat about among the reeds, reluctant to give up. The fog had deceived his eyes, he decided, transforming a clump of hazel or willow into the flimsy dwelling he thought he'd seen.

Leading the horses, he and Larktwist fell in behind the young monk, who led the way at a smart pace along a track they barely glimpsed as the fog opened to let them through and closed behind them again. After half a mile or so, Bartimeus stopped,

205

head back, snuffing the wet air like a hunting dog.

'Smell that?' he said. 'Thass the sea, that is. Wind's coming. That won't be long now.' And he smiled at a point midway between his two charges. Only then did Straccan realise that he was blind.

It was all Michael could do to stay upright in the saddle. The pain in his arm was shocking, and he could feel the tension of his swelling flesh in his mail sleeve. The Croyland monks had gone home sulking after a messenger from Cerneshead, not bothering to hide his glee at their discomfiture, had found them arguing at the Waystone and told them the relic they'd planned to steal from Straccan was now and forever beyond their reach. Somehow Straccan had found another way to Cerneshead; he and the boy were within the abbey walls.

They would think themselves safe.

'We will go to Cerneshead,' he said. 'The infirmarian can mend my arm. If they have the boy there I'll find him.'

Bane greeted Larktwist without enthusiasm. 'What are *you* doing here, spy?'

'Nice to see you, too,' Larktwist muttered.

In his tent Straccan slung his saturated cloak on a peg and shucked off his wet clothes. Rummaging through his things, he found a dry shirt and chausses, talking while he dressed. 'Any trouble?'

'Quiet as a nunnery,' Bane said. 'What about Lawrence?'

'I left them in the infirmary.'

'Will he live?'

'That's up to God.'

'How did you run into him?' Bane jerked his head in Larktwist's direction. The spy sat on the end of Straccan's pallet, tenderly massaging his feet, which had blistered in his new shoes.

'Now that's quite a story. You tell him, spy.'

Larktwist took a deep breath and began at the beginning.

'You believe him?' said Bane, when he'd finished.

'I think I do, yes. Most of it, anyway,' said Straccan. 'Remember, Larktwist may not look like much' – the little man gave him an indignant scowl – 'but he's good at his job. He has to be. He's one of the king's spies, and John's are the best. I wish Blaise was here, or Miles, but we'll have to do the best we can without them. Temple Bruer's about twelve miles from here; I'd planned to stop there tomorrow night anyway. The commander there's a man called Durand – a friend of Blaise. If the king *is* dead, he'll know for certain. And he'll have heard of al-Hazred; Templars throughout the country were looking for him after he escaped. Larktwist, you and I will ride to Bruer at dawn.'

'Me?' said Larktwist. 'I've got to get word to my master.'

'You can do that at Bruer.'

'What about me?' Bane asked.

'You have to stay here, Hawkan. Just because we've seen nothing of the White Brotherhood doesn't mean they're not out there somewhere.'

'You'll look a right pair of prats if that girl turns out to be just the champion's bit of stuff,' Bane said.

'He had another woman there too – a girl, really,' Larktwist said. 'I was there when she arrived. You could take her for the queen; they were very alike, so fair. But she was younger, the other one.' He reached inside his tunic and brought out a pouch that still had a whiff of pigs or privy about it, and took out the paternoster beads. 'These were hers. She was wearing them when they brought her to Ravenser. I found them just before I got away.'

Straccan picked up the chain. 'Gold,' he said. 'A costly trinket.' He ran the smooth blue beads through his fingers. 'You found it?'

Larktwist explained.

'Blood?' said Bane.

'It looked like blood, it smelled like blood,' said Larktwist impatiently. 'And the bloody blowflies thought it was blood! I think she's dead. I think he killed her. I think there may have been others before her. I think he's as mad as a bloody March hare!'

Bane was looking at him as if he had begun to grow a second head, but Straccan said, 'Others?'

Larktwist looked closely at the gold chain, fitted the broken links together and closed them tight with his teeth. 'There were these two kids, they helped me get away,' he said, wrapping the beads round his wrist the way the girl had worn them. 'No one notices kids. Their dad's the causeway guide. They go everywhere, see everything, hear everything. They said there have been other women, all of them fair.'

'Fair?' Straccan said sharply, reminded of the missing girls at Waltham and Cromber.

'Yes. They were brought to Ravenser, the boys said, and then they disappeared. You know what I think?'

He'd thought about it a lot while he was hanging by his fingernails in the privy, while he huddled among the pigs, while he was half-suffocated under a load of dung, and while he staggered through the fog afraid every next step would plunge him into the bottomless mire.

'What do you think?' Straccan asked, wondering if the spy was thinking the same thing he was.

'I think he's been working up to the real thing – the queen. He's wanted her for a long time and made do with those others, but now the king's dead, or Tyrrel *thinks* he's dead, and he's got the real thing at last.'

Brother Bartimeus' promised wind licked tentatively at the evil mixture of fog and smoke that hung in a choking miasma over the Gaudy camp, before shredding it with gusts that carried off the all-pervading reek of oxen and latrines and revealed the camp in all its squalor. It reminded Straccan of the beggars' town outside Ludlow where Larktwist had taken him last year.

'Is there any supper left?' he asked.

'There's some here.' Larktwist peered into a pot hanging from a tripod over a flaring fire, and saw the stiff tail of a fish erect in the scum and steam. It was a fish day, and this was the Gaudy Company's leftovers. His belly growled. Piper handed him a bowl and ladled a generous helping into it, slapping a thick chunk of coarse brown bread on top.

There was a tug at his tunic. 'Who are you?'

Larktwist looked down and found a small boy at his side. 'I'm Larktwist. Who are you?'

'David. Were you lost in the fog?'

'Almost. What's that you've got there?' The child was clutching a set of reed pipes. 'Can you play that?'

The boy put the pipes to his lips and blew a few notes of a popular tune.

'David!' A girl's voice was calling. 'Where are you?'

'Don't tell,' the boy said with an impish grin, slipping behind Larktwist. 'I don't want to go to bed.' But it was too late: she had homed in on the music and found him.

'There you are.' She held out her hand for the boy's.

Piper eyed her with concern. She hadn't looked well for the past couple of days. He thought she was thinner, and there hadn't been enough flesh on her bones to begin with. Of course, unrequited love pared flesh away quicker than fever; he'd seen the way she looked at Sir Richard when she thought no one was looking. Poor lass. A pity she couldn't have taken a fancy to Hawkan Bane who, as anyone could see, was besotted with her.

Bane said, 'Will you have supper, Mistress Roslyn?'

Something in his voice made Larktwist look sharply at him, and from him to the girl; and what he saw made him arch an eyebrow and hide a smile. So poor old Bane was hooked at last! Well, he'd picked a beauty, but not an easy one. Larktwist noted the winged eyebrows, high cheekbones, cold eyes at odds with the warm, full lips, and the way her hand rested on the killing knife at her belt.

'Roslyn,' said the boy, 'this is Larktwist. He's a friend of Bane.'

'No he ain't,' said Bane. Larktwist looked hurt.

But the girl was staring at him. He smiled sheepishly and self-consciously fingered his unshaven chin. The gold chain around his wrist gleamed in the sunlight, and the beads clinked together.

'What is that?' she asked, not admiring the pretty gaud but looking at it with . . . Why, for God's sake, why the look of horror?

Roslyn felt an ice-water chill rise from her feet through her whole body. She shivered. 'What is it?' Her lips and tongue were stiff with shock, and her voice so changed that Bane, alarmed, moved to stand at her side.

'Paternoster beads,' Larktwist said.

'Where did you get them?'

'They belonged to a girl I saw on Ravenser.'

'The fair-haired girl,' said Roslyn. The bowl slipped from Larktwist's fingers, but no one noticed. 'She wore a blue gown. Oh God, her eyes are open! Her eyes are full of dust!'

They were all looking at her, some crossing themselves or forking their fingers at her as if she were one of the unholdon, the unblessed.

'Mistress Roslyn,' Straccan said, 'what are you saying?'

She was very white. 'God forgive me! I should have spoken before this. Now it's too late – she's dead. He killed her.' Her eyes darted from Straccan to Larktwist. 'Her . . . her father—' She drew a tearing breath. 'She says he sits and weeps. She cannot comfort him; he cannot see her. Someone called her name, she says. It was the middle of the night, but she had to go. He put a glamour on her. She was afraid, she was so afraid!' Roslyn's eyes brimmed with tears; she blinked, and they overflowed.

'What's she on about?' Larktwist backed away, his eyes showing their whites like a nervous horse. 'She mad or something?'

'Quiet!' Straccan grabbed his arm and held it up. 'Mistress Roslyn, have you seen these beads before? Did you know the girl who wore them?'

'Not in life, no, but I can see her now.' Roslyn's voice was barely more than a whisper. 'There she is.' She pointed, and their heads turned, but they saw nothing. 'He killed her, like he killed the others, like he killed Pernelle.'

'Pernelle?' Piper said, astonished. 'Someone killed Pernelle?'

'What did I tell you?' Larktwist cried. 'I said there were others! Those kids knew. Everyone on Ravenser knows, but they won't tell – they daren't. That steward and his wife, they know. That bloody Tyrrel!'

Roslyn reached out to touch Piper's arm, but he stepped back. 'Piper, I'm so sorry. I should have told you about Pernelle. She'll never come back. She's dead. They're all dead.'

He looked scared. 'How d'you know that?'

She'd known that's what he'd say. So now she had to answer. 'I saw her. She told me.'

They stared at her, as she'd known they would, with fear in their eyes.

Chapter 37

There were six beds in the abbey infirmary, two already occupied, one by a very old monk peacefully dying, and the other by a sleeping child. Michael's heart thumped at the sight of the boy, but as the abbot was kneeling in prayer by the dying brother's bed with half a dozen monks in attendance he could do nothing but sit on the edge of an empty bed and submit to the infirmarian's attentions.

The next hour was not pleasant. The abbey's smith was sent for to cut through the sleeve of his mail shirt, and then the padded leather tunic underneath was slit to expose the grossly swollen elbow joint and the ugly spear of broken bone jutting through the beetroot-red flesh.

'Can you repair it, brother?' Michael asked through his teeth.

'It's a bad break.' Brother Beda, the infirmarian, sucked his teeth and looked grave. Samael appeared equally worried.

'I've broken bones before,' Michael said.

'Not like this.' The infirmarian cleaned away the clotted blood as tenderly as he could, but Michael was rigid and sweating with agony by the time he had done.

'Can you mend it?' Samael needed to know.

'I can, yes, if you'll help.'

'How can I help?'

'Like this.' Beda took a stick from a bundle of kindling in the hearth. 'There's his arm bone,' he said, and snapped it in two. He held the two halves together, broken edge to edge, then slid one down past the other so that it stuck out sideways. 'The broken end there has burst through the flesh, like that,' he said. 'Left to itself it will probably go bad, which will kill him unless it is amputated at the shoulder, which would almost certainly kill him anyway. And if it doesn't go bad, the muscles will contract and drawn the limb up; it will shorten, he will lose the use of the arm, and the forearm may wither.

'But' – he looked earnestly at Samael – 'if you will grasp the arm firmly just *there*' – demonstrating with the bottom half of his stick – 'I will pull the bone above upwards and back into place.'

211

He put the stick's halves neatly together again. 'Then,' he continued, 'while we hold the bone firmly in place one of my assistants will support it with a pair of spelcs, tied at top and bottom.'

'What are spelcs?'

'Flat pieces of wood to hold the bone in place until it grows together again.'

'How long will that take?' Michael asked.

'If God wills it, many weeks, but the arm will then be the same length as before and you will have good use of it.'

Just then the boy stirred and cried out: 'Mum!'

'Hush, Lawrence,' the infirmarian called softly. 'Your mother will come again on the morrow.'

'Lawrence?' said Michael, feeling a chill of presentiment.

'Poor child,' the monk said. 'He is paralysed. He hasn't been able to move his legs for two years. His mother bore him on her back to Saint Thomas *and* to Saint Edmund, and he was no better for it. But tomorrow we shall see what Saint Peter will do. He will be touched with the Holy Caul which Sir Richard Straccan brought back to us from Peterborough.'

'His name is Lawrence?'

'Yes,' said the infirmarian. 'Lawrence Boteler. He walked and ran like any other boy until he fell beneath the wheel of a cart when he was five years old. That was two years past and more, and he looks no bigger than he was then.'

Michael's eyes met Samael's, and he let out his breath in a great sigh. 'Do your work, then brother. Mend my arm, and be quick about it. We cannot stay here.'

Beda looked doubtfully at him. 'You won't be able to ride. You will be very weak. You must keep abed—'

'Get on with it!'

'I was a fool,' Michael said when it was all done, and he found he could no more rise from the bed than spread wings and fly, so weak was he with the fever rising. His arm ached and throbbed so badly that it was all he could do to speak instead of howling. What ill fortune! Satan and all his fiends must be rolling about in hell, helpless with mirth. If that fool Uriel hadn't charged ahead at the Waystone . . . But there was nothing to gain in brooding on that. Uriel had been dismissed to the refectory to share the monks' dinner, but Samael, after a hurried meal, returned to Michael's bedside and sat there sponging his face and breast with cool water.

Loose-tongued with fever, Michael muttered apologies to

God for the folly of impatience that had caused him to make such a mistake, and to Samael for bringing them on this wild goose chase.

'God pardon my stupidity! When that man said Straccan had taken them, I never thought it could be anyone else! A boy and his mother – who else *could* it be? In the morning we will go back to their camp and kill the boy.'

'He can be no bigger than that poor sick lad,' said Samael, nodding towards the bed where Lawrence lay. It was very quiet in the infirmary; the attendants wore felt slippers so they would not awaken any sleeping patient, and in the dark, candlelit intimacy of that peaceful place his tongue too was loosened. 'One cannot help wondering . . .'

'What?'

'Can this be right?'

'We are swords. A weapon doesn't question the hand that wields it.'

'But didn't Christ say, "Whosoever shall offend one of these little ones, it were better for him that a millstone were hanged about his neck, and he be cast into the sea"?'

Michael's burning hand gripped his wrist. 'No, no, my friend! You have it wrong. He did not say that. "Whoso shall offend one of these little ones *which believe in me*." That's what he said. Believers, Christian souls, not heretics. Don't be misled by pity; it is Satan's snare.'

'Do you feel no pity?' Samael freed his hand gently and resumed sponging.

'I did at one time. I thought the heretics could not all be evil. There were children among them; they at least, I thought, might be saved. I presumed to know better than Holy Church. I have been atoning for that sin ever since. The one we seek is altogether evil. He was conceived to destroy Holy Church, to make a mockery of Christ's sacrifice, to throw Christians into doubt and panic and lead them into hell! No, my friend, I feel no pity for David d'Ax.'

Samael's hand stopped in mid-air and the sponge dripped on the bed. He took a deep breath. 'His name is d'Ax?'

'Yes.'

'You didn't tell us.'

'There was no need. What does his name matter?'

'It doesn't, of course.'

The night attendant padded to the bedside, bringing the patient a generous dose of poppy syrup to dull the high pitch of

213

pain. Presently Michael slept, and Samael was free to find his way to the guest quarters and the chamber he shared with Uriel.

Uriel was snoring.

From where he lay Samael could see a patch of sky through the window and a sprinkling of stars. After the long, colourless, claustrophobic day in the fog this sense of space should have been restful, but he was not calmed. He lay like a paralysed man, slow tears running into his hair.

David d'Ax. Amador's son. Amador.

They had been squires together. He had been groomsman at the wedding of Amador, the Sieur d'Ax, and Giraude d'Etranger. Later he heard there was a child, a son, but he had never seen him. The war came. Pope Innocent, that thwarted emperor, shocked by the murder of his legate, determined once and for all to root out the heretics who defied him from their strongholds in the Languedoc, and proclaimed a crusade. Eager for plunder, men flocked to the Church's banner, and Samael's world went up in flames and down into torrents of blood. He fought on the wrong side, though it seemed right at the time, and was taken as a heretic, and thrown into the Church's prison.

At first they kept him in a pit, an oubliette, where he lay in his own foulness and did not see another human being, nor the light of day, for half a year. Then they brought him out of the pit and offered him the mercy of the Church if he would but recant and name his fellow-heretics. When he said he knew no heretics – he was a Catholic, his friends, his family, all were obedient children of the Church – he was starved, beaten, kept from sleep, forced to walk around his cell day and night, until he collapsed; water was funnelled down his throat until it seemed his swollen belly must burst, slivers of wood were driven under his finger-nails, flame held to his feet. He couldn't remember when he had died, but he must have, for he was in hell.

When at last he broke, admitting his guilt and begging the Church's mercy, its price was the betrayal of everyone he had loved. He gave his questioners eleven names, including his sister and her daughter, and others who had been his friends – Amador d'Ax among them. A few were hanged, the rest burned, and he was offered the choice: watch them burn or burn with them. He chose to watch. Then he was released, on condition he undertook this task.

All this time, without knowing it, he had been hunting his best friend's son.

214

The sun rose in unnecessarily gory splendour, flinging sheets of vulgar colour over the marshes and turning the waters to blood.

Straccan wished he had his stallion, Zingiber. Apple wasn't a warhorse, trained to respond to the least pressure of the rider's thighs and knees, and ready and eager to do battle, to slash with lethal hooves, to rear and plunge into the thick of the fray, to bite and kill. Still, he was a sturdy, willing animal, and would have to do. Straccan had one hand on the pommel and one foot in the stirrup when Brother Mungo bore down on him.

'Is it true what Master Bane says? We're not moving on today?'

'That's right.'

'Why not? There's nothing to keep us here now, and we're many days later than we should be already.'

'I have an errand,' Straccan said. 'The bell must wait for me.' He prepared to mount again, but the monk yapped at his back like a lady's brachet.

'But surely, Sir Richard, we can proceed towards Lincoln. You can catch up with us when your errand's done.'

'*You* may proceed towards Lincoln, Brother,' *or towards hell for all I care*, he added silently. 'Any of the pilgrims who wish to go on are free to do so, but Gaudy's my charge, and she doesn't budge until I return.'

'And when may that be?'

'Tomorrow or the day after.'

Mungo flung exasperated hands into the air and stalked away in a high state of annoyance, his robe flapping round his long skinny legs, reminding Straccan of a rook done out of a titbit.

'I don't like that man,' said David, at Straccan's side. The boy had a knack of appearing silently and disappearing the same way.

'Therein you show judgement,' said Straccan.

In the players' cart Roslyn sat on the driver's seat fitting a new string to the lute. Her few things were packed in a neat bundle beside her. The cart shook as someone climbed into the back. She didn't look up until Piper's soft voice behind her said, 'Why didn't you say anything?'

She sighed. 'Because you would either think me mad, or be afraid of me, as you are now.'

He shifted her bundle and sat beside her. 'I'm not afraid of you, lass. But you must admit it's a bit disturbing. Ghosts. You may be used to 'em, but other folk aren't.' He lowered his voice. 'Is she here now? Pernelle?' He looked behind him nervously as

215

if expecting to see her phantom perched on the props basket.

'No. She's gone. She wanted me to tell you, so you would know she didn't run out on you, that she meant to come back. I should have told you the first time I saw her. I'm sorry, Piper.' She met his sad, kindly eyes. 'Look, here's her lute. I've put in two new strings, and here are the quills. You'll find someone else to join the company and play it.'

'I don't want it back,' Piper said. 'It's yours, and you are one of us for as long as you want to be.' He patted her hand, opened his mouth to say more, thought better of it and shut it again.

'What?' she asked.

'Nothing, I . . . Well, maybe it's not my place to say anything, but I hate to see you so unhappy. It's no use hoping for anything with *him* – you know – Sir Richard, I mean. Don't look daggers at me, lass; I can't help what I see. It's hopeless, you and him. He's in love with someone else.'

'How do you know?'

'Hawkan Bane told me. Her name's Janiva. He wants to marry her, but he lost her.'

'Lost her? You mean she died?'

'No, no. She disappeared. He's been looking for her ever since – oh, two years now. See, lass, he's a decent man, for a knight. Too decent, maybe. I saw how he looked at you, but he'd never forgive himself if he wasn't true to her.' He stared stolidly ahead, pretending not to see the silvery thread-like tracks of tears down Roslyn's cheeks. 'Quite like a ballad, ain't it? I should mind me own business, I know, but I thought it might help, if you knew.'

Roslyn dragged her sleeve across her eyes and picked up the lute again. Her hands shook a little. 'It is folly,' she said. 'A song, like you say. It will pass.'

'Course it will,' said Piper, secretly touching the wood of the seat. She might get over it in time, but it would be a bloody long time, if he was any judge. 'Well, then,' he said. 'Give 'em music tonight, eh? You and Will and Tim. A few songs. Keep them cheerful, that's what we're paid for.'

'Me and— Why, where are you going?'

'I'm going to follow Sir Richard and that Larktwist fellow to Ravenser, and settle accounts with the man who took Pernelle from us.'

'Oh, Piper!' She looked helplessly at him, not wanting to say, *You'll just get in the way*, and seeing in his face that he knew what she was thinking. 'You can't go! You're not a fighting man.'

'Any man'll fight for his own,' Piper said.

216

Chapter 38

Piper waited at his ease – no sense in being uncomfortable – lying on the turf at the foot of the Waystone, his head propped against it, watching the road to Temple Bruer while the sun crawled down the sky, the stone's shadow lengthened and a pair of optimistic buzzards circled overhead, waiting for Apollo to drop.

He narrowed his eyes, staring hard. That was dust in the distance; they were coming. He got up and mounted, patting the old horse's shoulder encouragingly. Apollo was half blind and breathed like a bellows, but it took a lot to stop him once he got started.

He could see them now: their leader's white mantle blazoned with the eight-pointed red cross, the black and white Beauseant banner fluttering, sunlight glinting on harness and weapons. A sight to put the fear of God – and the Temple – into any enemy. The commander rode at the head of a conroy of twenty black-clad sergeants – Piper could make out Straccan and Larktwist in their midst – and there were two servant brothers bringing up the rear.

The troop cantered straight on past the Waystone without glancing at Piper, but Straccan reined in.

'No,' he said.

'Before you say anything else,' Piper said, 'I'm coming with you. Don't you worry about old Apollo, he makes a noise but he keeps going; he won't hold you up any. You go with the others, Sir Richard, we'll follow at our own pace.'

Straccan had no qualms about saying it: 'You'll get in the way.'

'I won't. I have to see him – the man who killed Pernelle.'

Straccan sighed. 'All right, follow if you must, but you're on your own. We can't wait for you.' He touched spurs to the splendid horse the Templars had lent him, and galloped after the others.

Piper slapped Apollo's neck. 'Come on, old son.' Something else moving farther back on the road caught his eye. He paused, stared, and chuckled. 'You too, eh?' Tongue lolling, grinning like a crocodile, Sir Richard's dog loped past him.

Convincing Durand had not been as difficult as Straccan had feared. The commander, a veteran in his fifties, was still bronzed from the sun of Outremer, his hair and beard iron-grey and his features as rigid and unsmiling as the effigy that would one day lie upon his tomb. When Straccan presented himself at the monastery gate he was directed to the stables, where Durand – just returned with his conroy from Chester and reluctant to plunge back into routine administration and the interminable business of draining the order's acres of bog – was usually to be found. Grateful for any interruption, the effigy led Straccan and his distressingly below-the-salt companion to the hall, sent a servant brother for wine, called his sergeants in, and listened.

'John's not dead,' he said when Straccan had finished. 'But as for the queen, no one knows where she is. At Woodstock they say she went to Nottingham, and at Nottingham they say she should be at Corfe. When the plot came to light—'

'Plot?' said Straccan.

'Robert fitzWalter, Eustace de Vesci – they meant to murder the king when he took the field in Wales. Didn't you know? Where've you been, man? John was warned, and called the campaign off. FitzWalter fled to France, de Vesci to Scotland. John's gone to earth in Nottingham castle with his blasted mercenaries. Doesn't trust anyone else. He sent an escort to Woodstock for the queen, to take her to Corfe, but when they got there she'd gone, ridden off God knows where with just Alan de Lacy and six men-at-arms. I ask you! Vanished into thin air, the lot of them. Rumour says she's been kidnapped, raped, killed. The king's got men everywhere looking for her. But Ravenser – and Tyrrel! Are you sure it's the queen?'

'Master Larktwist is a valued agent of the king,' Straccan said. 'Very experienced. He's sure.'

For some reason Larktwist didn't look particularly pleased at this mark of confidence.

'Hmm,' said the effigy. 'What makes you think he's got al-Hazred?'

'Who else can it be?'

'Know him, do you?'

'Well enough. I was with Blaise d'Etranger' – he noticed Durand's start at Blaise's name – 'when the warlock Soulis was taken and killed. Al-Hazred got away, but I saw the body of a

218

child he'd killed.' It would have been Gilla who had died under the Arab's knife, if Hob hadn't saved her.

Durand seemed satisfied. 'Good enough. If we're to slip in without them knowing, we must wait for dark.'

'Can it be done?' Straccan asked. 'It's said the place is unassailable.'

'Men who think themselves unassailable grow careless,' said Durand. 'But we'll need something to amuse the guards so that we can get to the island without them annoying us. Brother Martin!' A sergeant stepped forward and went down on one knee before the commander. 'You know what to do?'

Martin looked up, smiling happily. 'Oh yes, my lord.'

'Get on with it, then.'

Larktwist fidgeted. 'Er . . .'

'What's the matter?' Straccan asked.

'Can I go now? I have to send word to my master.'

'No, Master Larktwist, we need you with us,' the commander said. 'You know the place; we don't. One of the brethren here will take your message.'

'Larktwist, let me have the beads.' Straccan held out his hand for them, and passed them to Durand. 'Will you send someone with these to the abbey bailiff at Cromber, Hugh Tapton? Tell him, if they belonged to the missing maid, to meet us at Ravenser as soon as he can.'

'Is this more of Tyrrel's doing?'

'I fear so, my lord.'

Durand called a servant brother over and gave him the beads and instructions, and the man hurried out. 'Let's get started, then.'

Larktwist followed them to the stable, looking around for the quickest way out, but a sergeant fell in at each side of him and hoisted him into the saddle of a splendid but frighteningly tall horse. He gathered the reins nervously and took his place beside Straccan.

'You don't think they expect me to do anything *useful*, do you?'

'You underrate yourself, Master Larktwist.' Sod it, Durand had heard him. 'You will rise to the occasion, if required.' He had one of those sonorous voices that imbue all speech with deeper meaning, but Larktwist didn't look at all impressed.

'It is time, *sayyed*.'

The slave picked up the tongs and reached into the fire to draw out a small iron chest, glowing red hot, which he set on the

219

stone hearth. The Arab shuffled across the chamber and squatted beside it, putting out his hand. The champion gasped as he raised the lid, quite unscathed, as though the fiery metal were black and cold, and with a shrill cackle took out something, something no bigger than a walnut.

To Tyrrel's disgust the old mummy spat on it and polished it on his sleeve before offering it to him. It looked like a lump of suet: yellowish-white with blood-coloured streaks and spots, and glistening, as if wet. He took it gingerly, expecting it to be hot, but it was no more than comfortably warm.

The Arab mumbled something, and the slave translated. 'It is written in the *Book of the Phoenix* that this must be dissolved in a mixture of red wine – no more than that' – he indicated the amount against a bottle on the table – 'and your own blood. When the stone is all dissolved away the elixir is ready.'

Tyrrel was turning the stone over and over in his fingers. 'How can I be sure it will work?'

The Arab tsk'd impatiently and picked the stone from the champion's hand. Rummaging in the muddle on the table, he gathered several small, misshapen bits of lead. These he dropped into a crucible with the stone, and thrust the pot into the hands of the nearer slave with a sharp word of command. As the slave put it in the fire Tyrrel started forward with a cry of protest, but the Arab, with a grip stronger than he would have dreamed possible, seized his wrist and held him back.

At last the sorcerer reached into the flames, bare-handed, and took out the clay pot, picking the stone, which was quite unchanged, from the molten metal with his unprotected fingers. He tipped the crucible and let the contents drip slowly into a small dish, solidifying as they fell into little drops and beadlets of gold. With a shout of triumphant glee, Tyrrel snatched up the stone and the gold.

As the sorcerer sank exhausted to the floor he muttered something, which the slave repeated as, 'The *sayyed* sees it is the true stone. If gold is the *sayyed*'s desire it will do that as many times as you wish, but to make the elixir you must forfeit the stone.'

Tyrrel shoved the slave aside and strode to the door, stepping across the old man's body. 'You shall make me another, for the gold.' He wrenched the door open. The Arab started up from the floor with a broken screech of rage.

'But my lord,' cried a slave, 'that will take another year! You promised to let us go!'

The door slammed and the key turned in the lock. Tyrrel's laughter floated back to them as he descended the steps.

Tears running from their blinded eyes, the slaves sank down, one at each side of the old man, and kissed his hands. He patted their shoulders, but the words he murmured made them twitch and sweat with terror.

A broad-shouldered young man in a hooded cloak, riding a tall grey gelding and leading a laden rouncey, approached the out-skirts of the Gaudy camp and stopped briefly with a whistle of astonishment when he saw its size. There must be a couple of dozen tents there at least, plus small handcarts and larger wagons, the towering bell wain, and assorted draught animals – oxen, horses, even mules. The rider shook back his hood and gazed around as he passed through the tents and the groups of people clustered round cook-fires. The savoury smells of bacon, pottage and onions reminded him he hadn't eaten since breaking his fast that morning, and that was eleven hours ago.

Was that music? He reined in, listening. Over the noise of laughter and quarrelling and talk he could hear the breathy sound of pan pipes, the rattling beat of a tabor and the clear, bright voice of a lute. The music got louder as he wound his way towards the great shrouded bell, and someone – a tuneful, pure tenor – began a bawdy popular song. Some folk joined in, while others clapped to the rhythm or tapped their feet.

He saw two carts parked end to end with planks laid across the gap between them to form a stage, and on it were the players: two young men, a girl in a Queen Mab mask – it was she who had the lute – and a small boy dressed like an elf in a dagged green tunic, playing the pan pipes and dancing around the stage with a bacchanal wreath of ivy set askew on his dark curls. The song ended, the players bowed, the onlookers applauded, and the child jumped down and took the hat round for the audience to show its appreciation. When he came to the grey horse the boy held the hat up with a grin, which changed to a look of amazement and delight when he saw the rider's face.

'Roslyn! Roslyn, come! It's Miles!'

'Where's Richard?' Miles sat between Roslyn and David by the Gaudy Company's fire, spooning beans and bacon from his bowl. 'I've news for him.'

'He's gone to Ravenser,' Bane said, refilling the bowl. 'He'll be

221

back tomorrow or the day after. How did it go at home, after we left?'

'Did the bad men come?' David asked.

'Yes, they did. We saw them off, but they killed Nicholas.'

Bane swore, and David began to cry. Roslyn put her arms round him but he broke away, swiping at his tears with the backs of his grimy hands. As fast as he wiped them, more brimmed over and fell. 'It's my fault,' he sobbed. 'If it wasn't for me, they'd never have come here.'

'No, *cher*, that's not true,' Roslyn said.

'It is! It's because I'm the *Logos*!'

Miles's eyes met Bane's, then Roslyn's. 'What does that mean, David?'

'I don't know! I don't!' The boy scrambled to the cart where he slept with Roslyn, and up the ladder, burrowing inside to weep in decent privacy.

'What *does* it mean?' Bane asked.

'I have no idea. Sorrow?' Roslyn shook her head. 'We knew *you* were all right,' Miles went on. 'Gilla scried for you every day. The trouble is, it only works one way. She couldn't let you know what was happening at Stirrup.' He shook his head at Bane's offer of another bowl, full at last. 'She scried for Janiva, too – that's what I must tell Richard.'

At the mention of Janiva's name Roslyn turned pale, but all she said was, 'You've come to take David.' Not a question but a statement.

'Yes. Blaise wrote when he got Richard's letter. He said I must take David to a man called Durand, a friend of his, at Temple Bruer.'

'The Templar? But he'll be with Sir Richard, at Ravenser,' said Bane, and told Miles what was going on.

Miles looked worried. 'I wish Blaise were here. He's the one who should deal with al-Hazred. But Durand is his friend, and a man of knowledge. We must trust in him, and God, of course.' He scraped his bowl clean. 'Have you seen anything of the Brotherhood?'

'Not since we gave 'em the slip near Derby,' Bane said. 'Not a sniff of 'em, but they'll show up.'

'Sooner than you think,' Miles said. 'I've been behind them since Huntingdon. Fog held me up at Brandleby, and after that I lost their trail, but they can't be far off. I ought to leave with David at first light, but if Durand's not there . . . Blaise said not to trust anyone else. I'll have to wait for his return.'

★ ★ ★

Isabel paced the floor of her jewelled, painted prison, raging within at her helplessness. She had abandoned her fast. Her death could not help her children, and self-slaughter was a mortal sin. If John was really dead – and she feared he was, for otherwise he would have found her if he had to drain the whole Fenland to do it, and portions of Tyrrel's flayed corpse would by now be decorating the new London bridge – if John was dead, and little Henry King of England as Tyrrel said, then she, the mother of the king, could not be kept a prisoner for ever.

If only she knew what was happening! The woman who usually brought her meals, a fat slut with skin like raw pastry and little dark eyes like currants, wouldn't answer her questions – never spoke a word. The other jailer, a man, unlocked the door to let the woman in; when ready to leave she rapped on the door and he let her out. There was no other way out of this gorgeous, cushioned cell. Even if she were able to injure the woman, knock her out, stab her, she couldn't get past the man, and for all she knew there were guards outside the door.

She still wore the same gown, crumpled now and stained, in which she had come here, rather than put on any of the clothes Tyrrel had provided. If she had a knife she would have rent them to pieces. She had thrown the jewel box into a corner of the garderobe. Expressionless, the woman had picked everything up and put it all back.

Tyrrel hadn't come back since the visit of the leech. What was he doing? Was he still at Ravenser? When would he come back? Was there anything to gain by leading him on, pretending a softening of the heart towards him? Perhaps, but her pride would not have it. Already he had degraded her with his touch, taken her hand, dared to talk – at the memory she spat – of love!

If – when – she got out of here she would need a month of daily baths before she could hope to feel clean again.

At the sound of the key in the lock – it would be that dough-faced woman, with fresh candles – she walked to the window, turning her back. The door opened and closed. Soft footfalls crossed the floor. On the table something clinked, and she heard the sound of wine being poured into cups.

'Isabel,' said Tyrrel.

She whirled. He stood not a yard from her, close enough to touch, holding a golden cup. Over his shoulder on the table she saw its fellow. Sick dread, like a bleeding wound, drained strength from her.

223

'My queen, my love,' he said, holding the cup out to her, 'I will make you immortal. Drink.'

'Would you poison me?' She struck at it and he jerked his hand back. Some of the liquid splashed on the floor, frothing and fizzing like sherbet.

'Poison? No! God's eyes, Isabel, d'you think I'd harm you? *You?*'

'What else can I think? You bring me to this horrid place, lock me up alone— Where is Lady Maude?'

'Safe, she's safe, I promise. I'll bring her to you presently, but Isabel, drink this.'

'No!'

'I swear it's not venomous. Look.'

He tipped the cup to his lips; it rattled against his teeth as his hand shook, and his eyes widened in surprise as he swallowed. The elixir was icy cold. The coldness flashed instantly from his mouth and throat to his chest and belly, and he felt his heart stop, jump, and start again. Isabel watched him warily. He was smiling, his eyes unnaturally bright, his tanned cheeks flushed. She thought he was drunk, but it was euphoria.

It was true! He could feel it in every fibre of his body! He was immortal, invincible; there was nothing, *nothing* he could not do!

'Drink, Isabel. You must!' He picked up the second cup. 'You will be beautiful for ever. We will never grow old.' She had no idea what he was talking about. 'It will make you immortal – *we* will be immortal!'

He moved swiftly, his left hand cupping the back of her head while the other pressed the goblet against her lips. She clenched her teeth and clawed at his face. Her sharp nails tore the thin skin below an eye, and the bright blood ran down. He let go of her, touching the wounds and staring at his bloody fingers in shock, and in that moment she dashed the cup to the floor. The contents soaked into the painted cloth carpet.

'No!' Tyrrel screamed, grovelling on the floor for the rolling cup. Only a drop remained, clinging to its side. 'What have you done?' he raged. 'There's no more! It was a year in the making! Isabel, what have you done?'

Chapter 39

Anyone not knowing the Dykes might easily have passed the farm village without noticing it, so perfectly did the huts, ephemeral affairs of woven willow and reed thatch, blend in with the surrounding carr. Back in King Stephen's day such camouflage had saved many a tiny Fenland community from destruction, and the inhabitants saw no reason to alter a good thing for the sake of change. The memory of the bad old days had taught them caution, and after one petrified look at the Templars they oozed back off to their various muddy, eel-oriented occupations, determined not to return until the invaders had buggered off.

Larktwist dived into one of the huts and winkled out a shock-headed boy – bow-legged from rickets, pigeon-chested and hunched from carrying too-heavy loads – his bright eyes shining nevertheless with excitement through his matted fringe.

'This is Ketil. He'll lead us across.'

Durand eyed the boy doubtfully. 'Does he understand the need for silence?'

'Oh yes, me lord. He nips in at night, sometimes, to see his dad. If the guards spotted him, they'd shoot.'

'How can he find the way in the dark?' Straccan asked.

'Search me! Webfoot, ain't he? They're different. Special.' He clapped the boy's bony shoulder.

It was moonless dark when the troop moved out at last on foot to trudge the mile or so to Ravenser, leaving the horses – including Apollo, who had turned up eventually, to Straccan's surprise – in the care of a servant brother also charged with making sure the dog couldn't follow. The way lay under a low, thin ground mist, and without Ketil they would have gone astray long before they reached the end of the road. The island was a darker blot in the darkness, but firelight flickered behind the high window in the juliet tower, and there were torches in cressets on the gatehouse roof and dim smudges of light at the windows of the donjon.

The troop halted at the black water's edge.

'What are we waiting for?' Piper whispered to Larktwist.

'Something his nibs set up.'

Presently they saw a glow on the horizon. 'Something burning?' Piper asked.

'Ssshh.'

Something cold and wet nudged Straccan's hand. With a sinking heart he looked down. 'Oh, shit! Get out of here! Go back! Go!' The idiotic dog sat at his feet and looked lovingly up into his face. 'Bloody hell!'

Someone had brought a coil of rope. Ketil took one end and started off, with the troop following in single file, each man holding on to the rope. As Straccan stepped into the water the dog plunged after him with an anxious *yip*. One of the sergeants drew his knife, flipping it over to catch by the point and throw, but Straccan knocked into him with his shoulder, and his throw missed the dog by a yard. The sergeant turned on him, but at a word from Durand he stepped back and took his place in line.

'Sir Richard,' said Durand softly, 'if your dog makes another sound, cut its throat, or I will.'

Embarrassed and furious, Straccan scooped up the wet animal and clamped it ferociously under his arm. Taking hold of the rope he tagged on behind Durand. Larktwist followed him, then Piper, and the other servant brother brought up the rear.

The night watch on the gate were bored, but were used to that. They had heard one another's dirty stories over and over, it was too dark to throw dice or play I Spy, and there was sod all to do except peer out into the rising mist and keep an ear open for any unusual sounds. So when Edric said, 'What's that?' he got everyone's attention.

'What?'

'Look, there! Ain't that fire?' They scooted over to Edric's corner of the roof, shoving and jostling one another as they peered along the line of his pointing finger.

'I don't see nothing.'

'There it is!' They stared at the small dancing glow in the distance. 'Is it the beacon?'

'Wrong place. Too far west. Thass Darrowby, surely.'

'What's burning? There's naught but the church and the vill.'

'Could be the church— Whee!' A billow of flame shot up into the black vault of the sky. 'Look at that!'

'God ha' mercy, there's another!' A second glow had appeared, south of the first, growing brighter.

'That'll be Hoppel's Foss, Cerneshead way. Nothing there but the barns. Jesus, thass the abbey's hay going up in flames!'

'There's more!' Another glow, and another, farther to the north.

'Well, it's nothing to do with us, and sod all we can do about it anyway.' They had their orders. Nobody on, nobody off the island, come hell or high water, and nobody to disturb Sir Ralf tonight unless he wanted to lose important bits of his body.

So they watched the distant fires until they dwindled and disappeared, and heard nothing, saw nothing, suspected nothing.

The time of greatest danger for the Templars was just after they reached the island, when they must pass close under the gatehouse and the guards' noses, but Brother Martin's distraction served; the men were all on the far side of the roof laying odds on what might be burning, and Ketil led the troop along below the wall until the gatehouse was out of sight and they came unchallenged to the back of the donjon, where they threw up the scaling ladders and with no more than a muffled bump or two dropped to the ground within the curtain wall.

They had gone over the layout of Ravenser with Larktwist time and again while waiting at the Dykes for nightfall, and once within the bailey the troop split into groups which went their separate ways. It was all accomplished in surprisingly little time and with very little noise. Straccan heard some stifled cries from the gatehouse, but none of the guards had time to sound the alarm before the Templars overpowered them; there were startled cries from the stable, cut short before they could arouse anyone else, and a bit of a scuffle at the foot of the juliet tower, but the Arab sorcerer's guards were no match for the Poor Fellow-Soldiers of Christ, and in the hall the sleepers awoke to blades at their throats and a fait accompli.

But of the queen's champion, the lord of Ravenser, there was no sign.

The steward and his wife were fetched trembling from their bed to the hall, where Durand, still dripping, stood on the dais with one foot on Sir Ralf Tyrrel's great chair.

'Where is the fair-haired woman?'

The couple looked furtively at each other. 'W-what woman, lord?' the steward stammered. By now, his eyes, rolling desperately to see some way out of this, had recognised Larktwist among the Templars, and he grew if possible even paler.

Durand drew his dagger and nodded to one of his men, who

227

stepped up behind the steward, caught his hair and dragged his head painfully back to bare the vulnerable throat in which his Adam's apple bobbed like a drowning mouse. His wife squawked like a terrified hen and fell to her knees at the commander's feet, quivering.

'Well? Where is she? Speak, or I'll unsoul him here and now.'

'In the south wing, lord!'

'Berta,' her husband wailed, 'Sir Ralf will kill us!'

'No, he won't,' Durand assured them with what might have been a smile which, if so, was decidedly nasty. 'I reserve that pleasure to myself. You,' to the steward, 'where is Tyrrel?'

'He went to her, to the fair woman, the new one. He said no one was to disturb him.'

'Lead the way. Move!'

The steward led them into the adjoining wing, up stairs, along passages and around corners, passing several closed doors until he came to a door set back in an alcove, hidden by shadow. 'In there,' he said sullenly.

In the room behind the door, a woman screamed.

The commander drew his sword. 'Key!'

The steward took the key from his belt and gave it to Durand.

'Straccan, come with me. The rest of you stay here until I call. God knows what we'll find in there,' he added in an undertone to Straccan. 'There are rumours already. If they're true, the fewer who know, the better.'

He turned the key, saying, 'Don't kill him. We need answers,' and flung the door open.

Afterwards Isabel recalled only isolated images of the melee that ensued when, as if her scream were a signal, the door burst open. The white surcoat and red cross of a Templar . . . another man, not of the Order . . . Tyrrel charging at them like a bull, but with only his dagger against their swords . . . blades clashing, men grunting, gasping, rolling on the floor like boys fighting . . . And then it was over: the Templar, winded by a kick, wheezed on hands and knees and the other man punched Tyrrel on the jaw. She heard his teeth snap together. Blood ran from his bitten tongue, but he lay still. It was ludicrous. It was wonderful. Isabel laughed and couldn't stop laughing. The men, her rescuers, looked at her with concern. With an effort she choked back the hysterical laughter.

The Templar was elderly and grey. He sank to one knee to kiss the hand she held out – a token gesture, his lips never touched her skin.

'Madame, I rejoice to find you unharmed. I will send word at once to the king.'

'He said' – she twitched her skirts aside from Tyrrel's sprawled body – 'that John was dead.'

'Not true, madame.'

The other man knelt too. He was younger, his face scarred, and his lips just brushed her hand. 'Your Grace.' Between them, on the floor, Tyrrel stirred and moaned. 'Your pardon, my lady,' said the scarred man, and hit him again.

There was much to be done, but such was Templar organisation that by mid-morning it was all in hand. The queen's attendant, Lady Maude, had been found locked in another chamber of the donjon's wing, terrified but unharmed, and restored to her mistress's service. Messengers had been sent to the king, to Sempringham to bid the prior prepare to receive the queen until a royal escort should come for her, to Woodstock for her women, to the Temple in London, and to the nearest Templar commanderies for reinforcements to replace the couriers and to escort the queen to Sempringham.

Templar sergeants now guarded the gate and kept the watches, Templar servant brothers manned kitchen and stables, the troop's horses had been brought from the Dykes, and Beauseant, the black and white banner of the knights, flapped in the wind on the donjon roof.

Most of Tyrrel's men-at-arms and servants had been locked in the undercroft with the pigs – and fed the same slops – and the steward and his wife had been shut in the still room to await interrogation when Durand had time for it, and hadn't been fed at all.

Straccan found Larktwist in the stable, stuffing bread and cheese in his saddlebag and strapping a wooden box to the saddle.

'What have you got there?'

'My leech box,' said Larktwist, pleased. 'I left it here when I scarpered. Can I go now? There's nothing more I can do here.'

'Yes, there is. Show me where you found the beads.'

Larktwist led him to the room where he'd hidden after seeing the queen. The dog, which had stuck to Straccan like his shadow ever since they set foot on Ravenser, stopped at the door, bristling, tail clamped under its belly and lips wrinkling back from its teeth in a soundless snarl.

The floorcloth was as Larktwist had left it, crumpled and bloodstained. Straccan knelt to examine it.

'What did he do with her body?'

'In the marsh, most like,' Larktwist said.

Straccan snapped his fingers at the dog. 'Here, boy!' It took no notice and stayed put, but when he and Larktwist left the room it ran ahead of them along the passage to the steps, turning now and then to make sure they were following.

'Let's have a word with Tyrrel,' Straccan said.

The champion was so wrapped in chains he could barely move for their weight. He lay on his side on the dais, with four sergeants on guard.

Straccan didn't bother with niceties. He seized the neck of Tyrrel's tunic and twisted the material round his fist so that the prisoner began to choke. The guards shifted their feet and watched closely, ready to interfere if things got out of hand, but so far Tyrrel was just a bit blue and they saw no reason to butt in.

Straccan slackened his hold. 'Where are their bodies, cur, the bodies of the women you killed?'

Tyrrel shrugged, and the mass of chains shifted and clinked.

'Ailith of Waltham,' Straccan said. 'You took her, didn't you?' Christina Aurifer? Pernelle the singer? How many more? Did you even know their names?' Tyrrel turned his head away. Straccan twisted the fabric again and drew his dagger. 'No one will mind if this slips, accidentally, and pierces your eye,' he said. 'Which one shall it be?' He jabbed the point towards the left eye, and Tyrrel flinched. 'Not that one? As you will. It's all the same to me.' He raised the dagger again, and Tyrrel squeezed his eyes shut, unable because of the chokehold on his windpipe to utter more than a gurgle.

'What was that?' Straccan loosened his grip again, but the champion stayed silent.

Larktwist leaned over Straccan's shoulder. 'His steward knows,' he said helpfully.

'Does he?' Straccan let go of Tyrrel and got up, sheathing his knife and wiping his hands on his thighs. 'We'll ask him, then.'

The steward had managed to hang himself from the window bar with his wife's girdle, but she, when Straccan hauled her before Durand, collapsed like a pricked bladder and told them all she knew.

Once snatched from their homes – and there was some enchantment to that, she said, of which she knew nothing – the girls were taken to Locksey. There, she and her husband drugged them and brought them to Ravenser, where they were kept until Lord Ralf came. When he had done with them her husband took them away. He didn't tell her how or where; she didn't ask.

'I always thought they were sent back to their homes,' she pleaded, eyeing her questioners slyly through her tangled hair. 'If harm came to 'em, I had no part in it, lords! I looked after 'em tenderly.'

'Write down her testimony,' said Durand, disgusted, 'and lock her up again. She can hang later.'

'Surely the people here must have known what was going on,' Piper said, when Straccan relayed the woman's confession to him.

'Some of them guessed. They may not have known for sure, but they certainly suspected.'

Shortly after noon a group of men in the livery of Cromber abbey hailed the gatehouse, and the guide trotted forth again to lead Hugh Tapton and his men-at-arms to the island. Straccan, with Piper and Larktwist, met them at the gate.

'Where is she?' Tapton asked, still in the saddle.

'Dead, I fear,' Straccan said.

'And the other? The maid from Waltham? I went there, after you told me of her. I saw her sister – she was much like Christina.'

'Dead also, by Ralf Tyrrel's hand, and God only knows how many more there may have been.'

'You've not found them, then.'

'Not yet. They are probably in the marsh. All we have are Christina's beads and a bloodstained carpet.'

'Show me.'

The dog trailed unhappily after them. When it realised where they were going it sat down at the foot of the steps, put its head back and howled. The desolate sound echoed back from the stone walls, and Tapton crossed himself. When they entered the room the dog lurked outside, as before.

'That's where the beads were.' Larktwist indicated the rucked-up floorcloth. 'The blood was still tacky.'

The dog whined. 'What's the *matter* with you?' Straccan asked.

'Maybe he knows,' said Piper sombrely. 'Dogs sometimes do. They sense where something wicked happened, when life was torn away. Give him the scent, sir.'

Straccan took the dog by its collar and dragged it into the room. It resisted with all its might, but he towed it right up to the carpet and shoved its nose into the stiff, blackened creases. It shivered violently and kept growling, a long, low, penetrating rumble. He patted its shivering flank. 'Good dog, good boy. Where is she?'

As soon as he let go of the collar the animal was out of the room, away along the passage and down the steps, with the men tearing after it. Through the connecting door into the donjon, down into the hall and out into the bailey, past kitchen and stables, towards the far end of the island, the juliet tower and the empty church.

At the church door the dog stopped, sniffed about, and ran back and forth a little before standing up on its hind legs and scratching at the door.

'Good boy,' said Straccan. 'Steady, now. Steady.' The dog's eyes rolled back to look at him, showing the whites, and it whined again, as if in pain.

The inside was just as Larktwist remembered, stacked with firewood and coals, the same dust and debris and the same dead bird. They followed the dog to the low arched doorway at the back, and down the slimy steps.

It was very cold in the crypt, and Tapton's men muttered nervously when they saw the ancient bones and coffins. The dog pissed against the stacked stone blocks, whined again, just once, then sat down and began scratching its ear as if nothing was happening.

'Here?' said Tapton. 'Those bones are old.'

'Maybe they're in the coffins,' Larktwist suggested.

At a gesture from the bailiff, his men began pulling the stone lids off the coffins, finding only more mouldering ancient bones.

'Up there,' said Straccan. They looked where he was pointing, at the saints' niches. Half a dozen had been filled in with stone blocks, and the rest stood empty. 'Get picks,' he said. 'And lights.'

Tapton's men attacked the nearest niche. Mortar crumbled, stones fell, and presently one of the wreckers cried out, flinging down his pick and backing away. The others stopped. In the dusty, damp silence their panting breath sounded loud. One crossed himself.

Straccan and Tapton moved to see. A woman stared back at them with sunken eyes. Her cheeks and chin were grey with

232

mould, pale hair hung like dead winter grass over her naked shoulders. Her milky eyes were filmed with dust.

'Fetch more lights,' snapped Straccan. He stooped for the dropped pick and swung it with all his strength at the base of the niche. 'And tell Durand he'd better come.'

Chapter 40

Michael had no secrets now. His mind wandered the dark paths of memory while he burned with the dry heat of fever, and at his side Samael listened unwillingly to the sick man's hoarse muttering.

In the far corner of the infirmary Lucy Boteler sat by her son's bed. Lawrence was keeping down the draughts and nourishing pap Brother Beda administered, and was sleeping peacefully. The Cerneshead community praised Saint Peter for the miracle of the boatman, and had lost no time in setting up a temporary shrine on the jetty, with plans for a permanent chapel to welcome pilgrims and fleece them of their offerings. Croyland was spitting tacks.

At the sound of footfalls, Samael looked up.

'Why must we stay here?' Uriel complained. He came no further than the door, fearful of contagion though the infirmarian assured him that none of the sick had anything catching. 'We don't need him to get the job done. We know where the brat is; let's go after him.'

Samael sighed. 'We can't leave him here alone.'

Uriel fiddled with his dagger, clicking it up and down in the sheath. 'Isn't that why there are three of us, so the loss of one, or even two, will not stop God's work?'

Samael didn't answer. He slipped his hand beneath the sick man's head and raised it, holding a cup of watered wine to the fever-blistered lips. Most of it trickled down Michael's neck, but a little moistened his mouth.

'Stay with him yourself, if you must,' Uriel said. 'I will go.'

'No!'

'He is like to die,' Uriel said reasonably. 'But if he recovers he can follow us.'

'We'll wait another day.'

'Another day,' echoed Uriel. 'That's what you said yesterday.'

They had brought up the bodies, out of the crypt, and laid them side by side on the floor of the church, and while someone went to fetch something with which to cover them, someone else fashioned a rough cross from the firewood stacked to hand, and hung it on the wall where the long-gone Saxon rood had left its shadow.

Durand looked down at them. One was little more than bones, another curiously changed, the flesh almost waxen. The others were still recognisable as Pernelle, Christina and Ailith although the sixth – someone's daughter, someone's young wife – remained unknown. All six had long, fair hair.

'What now?' Piper asked. 'They should have Christian burial.'

'No one may have Christian burial now,' Tapton said. 'The Interdict forbids it.'

Straccan turned to the commander. 'My lord Durand, am I right in believing that your order is exempted from the rigours of the Interdict, throughout Christendom?' Durand nodded warily. 'And,' Straccan went on, 'didn't Pope Innocent II grant you the right to bury strangers in your cemeteries?'

The effigy scratched his nose thoughtfully. 'You're right, Straccan. He did, in the bull *Omne Datum Optimum*, more than seventy years ago.' He looked sombrely at the covered bodies. 'I believe in these circumstances the order should take care of these poor remains and give them burial in holy ground. I pray their families may take some comfort in that.'

'What will you do with Tyrrel?'

'I've told him we found the bodies. He stayed mute. But while Beauseant flies over this island, I have the rights of high and low justice. His punishment will be fitting.'

They fetched the queen's champion from the hall, and brought out the people of Ravenser, under guard and reeking of pigs, that they might see justice done and profit by the horror of the example. All Durand's men, sergeants and servants, were there too, and Straccan saw Ketil and his father sitting on the steps, witnesses who would carry the tidings back to the Dykes, and to all the lord of Ravenser's other farms and holdings.

It took four sergeants to carry Tyrrel, chains and all, to the church, past his victims' bodies – he gave them not a glance – and down into the packed crypt. He said nothing until then, his handsome face fixed in its look of scorn, but when he saw the servant brothers waiting, aprons over their habits, trowels in their hands and the mortar fresh-mixed, he threw back his head and began to howl. The sound bounced deafeningly off the damp walls, and many in the crowd covered their ears.

'Shall I gag him, my lord?' a sergeant said.

'No,' said Durand.

They set Tyrrel in the niche where Pernelle had been found, and now the stones were up to his knees. He tried to hurl himself forward, but they held him fast while the masons laid another row, and another. Durand gazed into the doomed man's eyes. 'Pray, if you can,' he said. 'God in His mercy may forgive even you.'

'No! No! You can't!' Tyrrel's eyes were starting from his head, huge with horror. To win God's mercy he would have to die – but he could never die, never! 'No! Have pity!' The stones rose up the niche, level now with his thighs, his waist, up to his breast. 'No! You don't understand! I cannot die! I cannot die!'

He stared at the little patch of light remaining to him . . . a hand's breadth, a finger's . . . and it was gone! He was alone, in darkness. He would stand here, in the dark, for all eternity!

The watchers filed up the steps, out of the church, into the pale evening light. Last to leave, Straccan and Piper paused and looked back.

'What's that?' Piper asked.

'What?'

'Listen!'

They stood still, barely breathing. Magnified by the sounding chamber of the crypt, the small sound went on and on – the rasping scratch of his nails as he clawed at the stone.

Later, looking for Durand, Straccan saw him crossing the bailey and fell in beside him.

'What can I do for you, Straccan?'

'You've seen the Arab? It is al-Hazred?'

'It's him all right.'

'What are you going to do with him?'

'I've sent a courier to London, to the Temple, to tell my superiors we have him. They'll want him. The Grand Master himself is there – *he'll* want him.'

Straccan stopped and caught the commander's sleeve. 'William de Chartres? But he's King Philip's friend! If al-Hazred's power falls into Philip's hands, England will have a French king before Christ's Mass!'

They looked at each other. Their walk had brought them to the juliet's long shadow. Durand stopped, sticking his hands behind his belt buckle and gazing at the tower.

236

'How is it Tyrrel could hold him, keep him prisoner?' Straccan wondered.

'He had this,' Durand said, taking from the breast of his tunic a greyish-green star-shaped stone. It fitted the palm of his hand, and had a look of great age. Straccan drew in his breath sharply. 'He won't say how or where he got it. I see you know what it is,' Durand added softly.

'Yes. Blaise had one, but he buried it in the stone circle at Skelrig,' Straccan said, staring. Suddenly he knew where Tyrrel had got it. 'Rainard de Soulis's wife, the poor mad lady, she had one.'

'Ah,' said Durand. 'So that's it. Tyrrel was in Scotland with the king, not long after your encounter with Soulis. It is a talisman of great power. So long as he had it, the creature must obey him.' He directed a glare towards the Arab's window.

'My lord,' Straccan said urgently. 'You know what al-Hazred is! You know what he can do!'

'Yes, Straccan, I do. Like our friend Blaise, I have made a study of Saracen magic. With the consent and protection of the Church.'

Unlike Blaise, Straccan thought, *who was cast out of the Order for his studies*. 'He's a murderer,' he said, seeing in his mind's eye the boy who had died in Gilla's stead three years ago. 'There wasn't an inch of whole skin left on the child he slaughtered at Skelrig, and he would have done that to my daughter. Kill him now! Or let me! That's the only way to be sure he'll do no more harm.'

'I know what he was doing at Skelrig, and I know you have a personal score to settle,' Durand said. 'And I know what my orders will be.' He turned, and began pacing back towards the gatehouse.

'My lord—' Straccan began. Durand raised a hand to cut him off.

'I also know I won't receive those orders for at least two more days.'

The gate guards saluted the commander. Durand walked on towards the donjon. Straccan took a deep breath. 'What will you do?'

'There's a lot of stuff stored in that tower. Sulphur, cinnabar, saltpetre, nitre and God knows what else. Charcoal and wood, too. Nasty stuff if you're not careful.'

'Can I help?'

'Better not. Just get yourself and your companions off Ravenser before vespers.'

The Templars were assembling in the great hall for vespers when Straccan, Piper and Larktwist led their horses from the stable.

'What about *him*?' Larktwist jabbed a thumb towards the top of the juliet.

'The Temple's claimed him; he's their trophy.'

'After what he did?' Larktwist sounded wholly outraged. 'I saw that boy at Skelrig. I heard his mother, when she saw him. You're not going to let him go!'

'He's Durand's prisoner. There's nothing I can do.'

Larktwist checked his girth – and his tongue, with an effort – and mounted his horse.

Durand came down the donjon steps. 'God go with you, Straccan.'

'And with you, my lord. I'll return your horse to Bruer tomorrow and pick up my own.' As he spoke, Straccan leaned from the saddle to seize his dog by its scruff, and hauled it up before him.

'The king will doubtless wish to reward you for your part in this adventure.'

'Ah,' said Straccan, pausing. He wanted nothing to remind John of his existence. The king took an interest in him – one he could do without. 'As to that, I'd prefer it if you didn't mention my "part" in it.'

'Oh?' Durand's eyebrows arched questioningly.

'Just don't mention me at all. Give any credit to Master Larktwist. If it weren't for him the queen might have been the seventh corpse in that hellish place.'

Durand acknowledged Larktwist with a slight bow. 'If that's what you want.'

'It is, Commander. It is.'

In single file behind the guide, Straccan leading, then Larktwist, and Piper on Apollo plodding at the rear, they were crossing the causeway and nearly at the other side when, behind them, there was a tremendous rumbling boom, the surface of the mere quivered, and the causeway shuddered beneath them, throwing the guide on to his hands and knees.

They turned, amazed, in time to see the juliet tower leap into the air, whole and entire for a split second before it burst apart in a storm of stones with a noise like thunder that went on and on. As if hurled from siege engines, stones splashed down into the reed beds, making waves and sending waterfowl shrieking in a panicky scramble to get airborne and away; and Larktwist's horse

238

would have bolted had Straccan not caught its reins and dragged it round. A vast cloud of sulphurous yellowish dust billowed up and rolled over the marsh, enveloping them where they stood, stunned.

'God save us,' said Piper shakily. 'What the hell was that?'

The dust began to settle, coating the surface of the mere, and as the island became visible again Larktwist gaped at the destruction.

'It's gone! Look, the tower's gone! What happened?'

Flames were shooting up above the curtain wall, and they could hear a lot of shouting, punctuated with further, minor explosions and the rumble of stones shifting and settling as what was left of the juliet tower collapsed into a mound.

'There was a lot of combustible stuff in there,' Straccan said. 'Someone must have got careless.'

'But—' Larktwist said.

'Didn't I see *you* come out of there, spy, just before we left?'

'Me? No!'

'I would have to tell Durand, of course, if he should ask.'

Larktwist's voice had a panicky edge. 'You wouldn't!'

'I would. Although of course, if you leave me out of your report . . .'

Larktwist muttered something. It sounded like 'You cunning bastard' but Straccan pretended not to hear. He tipped the guide generously, and they rode on in silence for some miles before Larktwist mustered up the nerve to ask, 'Sir Richard?'

'What?'

'How did you do it?'

'I don't know what you mean.'

At Cerneshead Michael had come to his senses. He was light-headed and feeble but no longer delirious, and he recognised the other Angels and Brother Beda.

'We will leave on the morrow,' he said, stilling Beda's protest with a look.

'You are not strong enough,' Samael said. 'There will be much pain.'

'Pain means nothing. God will give me strength. You see what marvels He can do? Through the intercession of His servant Peter, He has healed that poor boy.' He nodded towards Lawrence's bed, where the child lay propped on pillows, eagerly swallowing the broth his mother fed him with a spoon. His recovery was the talk of the monastery and tidings of it were already spreading outward like the ripples from a stone tossed in a pond.

'We will leave at dawn,' Michael said sombrely, 'and slay the enemy of God.'

In the Gaudy camp the enemy of God lay asleep on his straw pillow in the players' cart, limbs flung wide in the total abandon of young children, dark curls sticking to his damp brow. One hand curled around his pan pipes, the other lay palm uppermost next to his flushed cheek.

Roslyn watched his sleeping face and gently stroked the damp hair back from his forehead. Very soon now, perhaps tomorrow, Miles would take him away, and already the ache of losing him choked her. She felt as if her heart were being ground between millstones – the upper the impossibility of her love for Straccan, the lower the loss of David. With no hope of one and bereft of the other, she would be alone indeed.

Perhaps not. If she wanted it, she had a place with the Gaudy Company. That would mean security, at least until the bell reached Durham. After that the company would be back on the roads, travelling from town to town, trusting to luck and whichever saints might be persuaded to take an interest in their fortunes. It was a way of life she had known from her earliest childhood. Piper was a good man, Tim and Will too; they wanted her, ghosts and all.

She sighed. She would say goodbye to David and Miles, and when Piper returned she would tell him she'd decided to stay.

Straccan's heart sank as he came in sight of the Gaudy camp and got the first whiff of sewage and smoke. The camp was a smelly slum, with the bell in its filthy swathings the mosque-like centrepiece of a squalid temporary village. Slatternly lines of laundry were strung between the wagons, the turf was worn bare, the latrine ditches full, and the smoke of cook-fires (the camp had just had supper) still hung in wreaths over all. The oxen had been shifted several times and were now back on their first pasture, which hadn't had time to recover. It was definitely long past time to move on.

Millie Fisher was the first to greet Straccan as he rode into camp. 'Hello, me lord. It's gettin' a bit niffy round here. Can we move on now?'

'At first light, Mistress Fisher.'

Luke Bannerman offered him a sausage.

Straccan slid stiffly from the saddle. Bane took the bridle, ignoring Larktwist. 'Where's Piper?'

'He's a bit behind us. Everything all right?'

'Sir Miles is here.'

Straccan saw Miles's face among the rest. 'Miles! When did you get here?' They clasped each other's shoulders and thumped each other's backs.

'Just after you'd left.'

'Gilla—'

'She's well, and sends her loving greetings. Richard, you look half dead. You need a wash and something to eat. Come to your tent, and I'll tell you the tidings from Stirrup.'

'That sounds good. God, I'm weary!'

Bane followed them into the tent with hot water and began easing Straccan's boots off – it felt as though they'd been welded to his feet. Straccan peeled off his sweaty clothes and dunked his head in the bowl, reaching blindly for the dish of soap. God, it felt good to be clean again! Some poor sinners, for penance, gave up washing altogether. He thanked God the bishop hadn't suggested that!

As Straccan came up for air, Miles said, 'There's news of Janiva.'

Straccan's face blazed with sudden hope. 'What? Where is she? Have you seen her?'

'No, not me. Gilla scried for her; she saw her. She says Janiva's all right, but we don't know where she is. Richard, there was trouble—'

Oh, Christ! 'What sort of trouble?'

'With the Church.'

While Straccan put on clean clothes, Miles told him what Gilla had learned. 'Janiva went to help a young noblewoman; I don't know who but she must be pretty important because of all the fuss. It seems she was sent to a convent against her will, and the prioress threw her out because she upset the other novices.'

'What d'you mean, "upset" them?'

'According to the prioress, she tore off all her clothes and made lewd suggestions.'

'*What?*'

'That's not all. She tried to seduce the other novices into what the prioress called "unseemly behaviour"; she smashed the coloured glass window in the chapel, broke the nuns' priest's nose when he tried to stop her, and then pissed on the altar! The prioress said she was possessed by a demon and sent her home, and the girl's mother sent for help to the wise woman at Pouncey.'

'Osyth!'

'That's right. Only it seems she's too old and infirm to travel now, so Janiva went.'

'Well? Then what?'

'The girl's father didn't approve of wise women. He sent a courier all the way to France to consult his bishop, and the bishop sent one of his own chaplains to cast out the demon. Only the demon was stronger than the chaplain, and he was paralysed and lost the power of speech. Janiva was able to get rid of the demon, and she also healed the priest, but he didn't thank her for it and began bleating about sorcery. But before he could do anything about it, Janiva disappeared.'

'Oh, God! Miles, where *is* she?'

'I don't know, but she told Gilla to tell you she was safe, that she has something else to do first, and when that's done she will wait for you' – he paused for a moment, to be sure to get it right, then said carefully – 'under the *Feoh* rune. Do you know what that means?'

Straccan's legs felt weak, and he sat down abruptly. 'Yes. Yes, I do.'

'When your penance is done, she'll be there.'

The vast upwelling of relief was too much to contain. Straccan leapt to his feet, flung his arms round Miles and hugged him, laughing even while tears of joy ran down his transfigured face. 'Oh, thank God! Thank God!' She was all right! He would find her at Pouncey when his task with the bell was finished. He sleeved the tears away and sat down again, grinning like an idiot.

Miles sat beside him. 'Richard, that's the good news. There's the other sort as well.' The smile faded from Straccan's face and his mouth tightened to a grim line as Miles gave an account of the events at Stirrup, the arrival of the three knights and the murder of Nicholas. 'David's taken it badly,' Miles finished. 'He says it's all his fault, because he's the *Logos*. Richard, what *is* that?'

Straccan shook his head. 'Are you sure Blaise never said anything about it?'

'No, never. He sent a message to me at Stirrup: I'm to take David to Commander Durand at Temple Bruer. They are old comrades. Blaise sent word to him; he'll be expecting us. Richard, you know him. What sort of man is he?'

'You can trust him,' Straccan answered, seeing in his mind's eye the juliet tower rising like an arrow into the air, the danger of Abdul al-Hazred gone for ever. Durand had risked much for that.

'He'll put us on a Templar ship for Berwick. Blaise will meet us there.'

'Bruer's our next halt. What about Roslyn? Does she go with you?'

Bane looked up quickly. Miles sighed. 'What would she do at Coldinghame? There's no place there for a gleemaiden.'

Straccan held out his cup to Bane for more ale. 'What about a wife?'

'What?'

'You could marry her. Then she'd have a place. She loves David; he loves her. She's as brave as a bear.' *And she'd be happy if she and David could stay together*, he thought. He very much wanted Roslyn to be happy.

'I know she's brave,' said Miles. 'The best of comrades! But . . . *marry*?'

'And she's beautiful.' Straccan lifted his cup to his lips and found it still empty. 'Hawkan?'

'*Sorrow?*' Miles sounded astonished. 'Beautiful? *Is* she?'

Bane put the ale jug down clumsily, without looking; it fell over and spilled on the ground. He blundered out of the tent like a blind man.

'Hawkan? What's the matter?'

'Richard, I can't marry anyone,' Miles was saying. 'I've no land, no money— What's wrong with Bane?'

Straccan rummaged in his pack for a pair of shoes and put them on. 'I'll be back in a minute.' But he couldn't find Bane, and after a while, puzzled, he returned to his tent. The dog, a sausage between its teeth, followed him in.

'Good God,' said Miles. 'What's that?'

'My dog.'

'A dog, is it?' The dog gulped the sausage, shoved its nose into Miles's extended hand and wagged its tail. 'Well, if you say so.' He laughed 'Another misfit?'

Straccan laughed too, remembering how Rainard de Soulis had mocked his companions, calling them 'misfits'. The dog lay down on the foot of his bed and went to sleep.

'What happened at Ravenser?' Miles asked. Straccan told him. When he came to the destruction of the juliet tower, Miles let out a whoop of satisfaction.

At Straccan's twentieth yawn, Miles got up. 'Get some rest,' he said. 'I'll see you in the morning.' The dog woke up and woofed softly.

'Quiet, you,' said its master.

'What's his name?'

'It hasn't got a name. I can't think of one.'

'I had a hound just like him when I was a boy. I called him Coy. My father said it meant rogue, or rascal, in some foreign tongue he knew.'

'Rogue, eh? Coy?' The dog jumped up and barked. The two men laughed. 'That'll do,' Straccan said.

Miles went to his bed – Bane was already in his, apparently asleep – and all around them the camp settled into the quietness of night. When at last all was silent, a dark shape slipped stealthily from cart to cart, keeping to the darker shadows, until it reached the bell wain and clambered silently up into the wagon bed. After a while it dropped to the ground again and scuttled back to its own shelter.

The Angels attacked before they had gone a mile the next morning.

Chapter 41

L arktwist left in the first pale light before the sun was up and while the camp was still half asleep. Straccan and Miles saw him off. There was no sign of Bane, who'd already ridden out to Temple Bruer to tell Durand they were bringing David.

'Go with God, spy, and watch your back.'

'You too, Sir Richard, Sir Miles.'

'And remember, if you feel the urge to mention my name, the king's law will come hard on whoever destroyed al-Hazred.'

Larktwist shrugged. King's law, God's law, sod's law, they were all one to him: guaranteed to kick a man when he was down. He'd been down, very far down, in the days before his unusual talents were recognised and won him full employment. He wasn't going to risk plumbing those depths again. He was thinking of retiring, anyway. The Widow Trygg had left an indelible memory, and with Tyrrel gone, Locksey seemed a good enough place for a man to settle down.

They watched him ride away until the turn of the road took him from their sight.

The oxen groaned and grumbled, leaning into their harness and straining to jar the bell wain from its resting place. It resisted at first, then, with a jerk, lurched forward. Aidan and Finan took their stations, one each side of the bell, and behind them the long line formed, ready for the off – a straggling procession leaving behind a large and malodorous scar on the landscape.

Straccan ranged up and down the line as each segment started off, urging folk to close up and keep together. They managed it for the best part of a mile, then began to straggle, shouting to one another over the familiar din of the Gaudy train under way; the heavy rumble of the bell wain, the earth-shaking thud of the iron-shod oxon, the creaking and screeching of wheels, the laughter and bickering of the pilgrims and Coy's exuberant barking as he annoyed Brother Mungo by running under his mule's belly and making it shy.

At the tail end as always, Wilfred crutched along, muttering to the Lord Christ as was his habit. 'Here we go again, Lord, eatin' dust, drinkin' dust, breathin' dust, but You know all about that, don't You? Carryin' that ole cross on a dusty road like you did, fallin' down an' all, the pity o' the world, and all for us sinners. What's a mouthful o' dust an' sore armpits compared to what You suffered?' He heard the hoof beats coming up behind and squinted into the brilliance of the morning sun as the rider drew alongside him.

'God save you, pilgrim.' A foreigner, but his English was fair enough. An old man with a knight's sword, skull-faced and with one arm in a sling.

'You too,' said Wilfred. 'God'll save us all if we believe in Him. He promised.'

'So He did. Are you with the company that follows the bell?'

'I am that.'

'Do you know a boy called David?'

Wilfred could hear more horses following a little way behind. He glanced back and saw two cloaked riders holding their horses in, keeping their distance. Well, if they were robbers he had sod all worth stealing, unless they were after his last night's sausage, which he'd saved for today, wrapped in a dock leaf in his pocket; and if they killed him his soul would go straight into the arms of the Lord Jesus and theirs to the lord of hell, for pilgrims were sacred.

'David? You mean that nipper as plays them pipes, one o' them players?'

Michael frowned. Had he heard aright? 'A player? Are you sure?'

Wilfred stopped, indignant. 'That's what I said. I may be lame, but I ain't daft.'

'Where does he ride in the train?'

'In the players' cart, o' course. I saw him when we set off, up on the driving seat.'

'Which one is that?'

'Got a brown patch on one side, an' a poor ole wore-out horse to pull it.'

Michael turned his horse and cantered back to the others, and Wilfred resumed his litany.

Straccan stood in his stirrups and looked ahead, then back. He couldn't see far for dust, but so far so good. They had come a mile from the campsite, and were nearly at the stone bridge over the River Slea which marked the boundary of the Templars' domain. He and Miles rode across and back again, and studied the bridge from either side. The parapet on the right-hand side had taken some knocks and was crumbling, but the bridge itself stood on massive stone piers and was sound. Straccan waved the bell wain on, while Miles crossed again and rode ahead, alert for any ambush.

Mungo on his mule trotted over to wait on the other side, out of the dust. The novices grasped ropes and swung themselves up on to the bell wain, one on either side of the bell, and hung on. The first pair of oxen trod forward on to the bridge.

By now the tail end of the train was nearly half a mile back, and the Angels, coming up behind and seeing the bottleneck ahead, spurred forward, jumping barrows and handcarts and scattering shrieking pilgrims.

At the bridge the horse-drawn carts rolled to a halt while the great wain crossed. The brown-patched cart was sixth in line behind Gaudy with Piper and Roslyn on the driving seat and David sandwiched between them, holding the reins. David had cried himself to sleep last night, sobbing into his pillow where no one could hear him, overcome with grief and guilt. So many deaths, so much blood shed, and all because of him . . . But this morning he was ashamed of his weakness, and it would take a very observant watcher to notice the occasional quiver of his lip. He was the son of a knight, and would be a knight himself. Knights didn't cry.

The deafening noise on the bridge drowned the drumming of hooves, and those in the carts were oblivious to the peril coming up from behind. As the sixth pair of oxen stepped on to the bridge, Straccan turned to start back down the line and saw the Angels coming. Hell and death! Bane wasn't here and Miles was on the other side of the bridge! With a yell he drew his sword and galloped towards them. The drivers saw him and looked back, craning round the bulging sides of their wagons to see what was happening.

Roslyn pushed David back inside the cart and started to pile stuff over him – bundles of costumes, painted scene cloths, masks.

'Roslyn!'

'Lie quiet! Be still!'

Piper had snatched the reins, but there was no point in trying to gee-up Apollo: there was no way out. They were boxed in behind, and oxen and bell completely blocked the bridge.

David struggled up. 'Roslyn!'

'Be quiet!' She pushed him down again and crouched behind

247

the driver's seat, her long dagger in one hand, eating knife in the other. At a glance, the cart held nothing but piled bales of curtains, bundles of costumes and rolls of painted cloth, but it wouldn't fool them; she knew that.

She felt the familiar frisson that lifted the hairs on her arms and heralded a presence – another woman, standing by David's hiding place. She was thin rather than slender, her hair in braids over her shoulders, dressed in a dark blue kirtle over a light blue smock and as solid-seeming as Roslyn herself; but in the dim yellowish light that filtered through the canvas she cast no shadow, no shadow at all.

'I know you,' Roslyn whispered. 'You're David's mother.'

The woman smiled and held out her hands, as if in welcome.

Sunlight dazzled Roslyn's eyes as the canvas was ripped apart and a man's huge dark shape tore into the cart, sword in hand.

Even under the bundles piled over him David could hear people screaming, and rage overwhelmed him. The bad men were here, in broad daylight, not nightmare shadows, not ogres but real men with swords, like the men who took his father away and killed him, and there was no use in screaming, no use in crying, no use in hiding and nowhere to run.

He knew what he had to do. Instead of letting his terror and fury go to waste, he must . . .

. . . pull it inside himself, like air, and let it out, like breath . . .

He knew where to focus it, and it was as easy, now, as pointing his finger.

The bell wain was on the bridge now, and not even a child could have squeezed through. Miles urged his horse into the water, but the treacherous river bed sucked at it, and his weight made it impossible for the animal to pull free. He kicked his booted feet out of the stirrups and rolled out of the saddle, and the horse dragged its feet out, sending up great swirls of mud and sand, and swam, with Miles clinging to its mane. When it reached the other side it stumbled and slid up the slippery bank, leaving him sprawled, waterlogged, still half in the water.

Michael, like the angel of death, was waiting to cut him down before he could get his footing on firm ground.

The oxen had cleared the bridge, but the bell wain was still half on it. Miles never saw what made the oxen stampede – he had eyes only for his enemy's blade as he tried to drag his own from its sheath – but stampede they did, tossing their great horned heads and turning in their tracks, dragging the wain round, bell and all, and thundering back over the bridge. The novices leapt for their lives. As the great wagon turned, it tilted to one side, tipping driver and mate off the seat to a bruising impact on the road, and teetered and scraped along the parapet. The bell swayed, snapping its lashings, and toppled quite slowly off the bridge, taking the parapet with it as it plunged down to the river.

One moment Miles was looking up at the knight looming over him – at the great sword swung one-handed in a whining circle to take off his head – the next moment something passed over him like the wing of a vast dark bird, the draught of its passing ruffling his hair, and horse and swordsman were both gone as, with a monstrous splash, the bell hit the water, rolling over as it sank and flinging, it seemed, all the river ashore with a force that knocked Miles flat on his face in the mud. In the surging water knight and horse tumbled over and over as they were borne downstream.

By the time Miles had squirmed and slid up the bank to the bridge it was all over. The carts stood anyhow, just as they'd halted, and people were clustered in small groups, shocked and oddly quiet. The oxen had not gone far; he could see them standing some way down the road, looking puzzled. Smashed pieces of the wagon bed – wheels, planks, bales of charred and blackened straw – were strewn along the bridge and the road. It looked as though an army had passed through, wreaking havoc as it went.

Straccan appeared unhurt. One of the raiders, bloody and limp, was tied to a wheel of the smith's wagon, and the other had fled, 'on fire', some silly bugger said.

'David?' Miles panted. The canvas cover of the players' cart had been slashed from end to end, and was charred, thin acrid smoke still rising from it. The dog was crouched under the cart, huddled as if injured, and trembling.

'He's all right. Unhurt.' Then why did Straccan look so grim? And what was Piper doing, and the other two, on their knees on the ground? Miles squelched forward. Piper looked up at him – the man was crying. Tim and Will shuffled aside to let Miles in, and he stared in disbelief at the bloody blanket and what lay under it.

'Sorrow? Sorrow! Oh Christ! Where's David?'

Straccan nodded towards the cart. 'In there.'

'What happened?'

'She hid the boy under the stuff inside. One of them got in – he knew David was there. She jumped on him, stabbed him in the back, but her blade must have skated off a bone. He flung her off and ran her through. And then suddenly there were flames everywhere, don't ask me how! He caught fire – his hair, his clothes – he was all flames! The oxen came thundering through, and somehow he got away.'

Miles touched Roslyn's cheek – it was still warm. She looked asleep; the blanket hid the great wound that had killed her. Straccan was right, she *was* beautiful. How was it he had never noticed, until now? He bowed his head and let his tears run unchecked.

A thin, reedy piping came from the players' cart: Miles recognised the faltering tune, 'Blow, Northern Wind'.

He started up angrily. 'What's he doing? I'll—'

Straccan caught at him. 'No, Miles, let him be. He means it for her.' They listened as the tune rose and fell, and stopped, only to begin again.

Presently Miles said, 'What was it turned the beasts?'

'The fire. Didn't you see?'

'No.' Miles sleeved away his tears. 'You know what it's like – all you see is the fight you're in. Someone tells you what happened afterwards.'

'It was the damnedest thing! It burst out of the road, right under their feet! I've never seen anything like it. They ran down Brother Mungo. It's a miracle they didn't trample anyone else.'

'Is he dead too?'

'No. He'll be all right. His lads are tending him. He saw the oxen coming and shoved Finan out of the way, then he went down under their feet like a bundle of washing.'

'What about him?' Miles indicated the bound prisoner.

'He's lost a lot of blood. If he dies, I'll have answers from him first.'

People were wandering, still in that dazed, sleepwalking fashion, to the river bank to stare at the bell. Settling into the mud, it looked smaller than it had on the wain. The river parted to flow round it, just as it did round the piers of the bridge. The churned mud smelled of decay. Presently Giles's son ventured on to the bridge and began retrieving broken pieces of harness, and Straccan sent Giles and the smith along the bank to find the bodies of the swordsman and his horse.

Straw lay in heaps all along the bridge, and hung like bleached hair over the side where the parapet had fallen away. Giles's son tugged at the buckle-end of a strap sticking out of a clotted pile of straw, and as it came free the straw broke up, releasing something dark that slid soggily over the edge and fell into the water.

'Sir! Sir Richard!' The boy's voice started soprano, broke, and ended gruff, but the note of panic got all Straccan's attention. 'Come an' look at this, sir!'

They stared down. It looked like a body. Oh Christ, it *was* a body, in a dark gown which ballooned to keep it afloat, bobbing face down in the yawning mouth of the bell. The overgrown tonsure was unmistakable.

'A monk,' gasped Luke Bannerman.

'A priest,' Aidan corrected. 'That's a priest's tonsure, not a monk's.'

'Grab it, quick,' cried Straccan. 'Before it floats away.'

Aidan plunged in, seized a handful of the voluminous gown, and towed the body to the bank. As he hauled it up, the rotted cloth tore, and something round and dull-metal grey rolled into the mud. Straccan picked it up.

It was a plain pewter reliquary, a travelling case used when a relic was borrowed or sold, transferred from one place to another. He could just span its girth with his two hands. There was a thin groove around the middle. He twisted the top and bottom halves against each other and opened it, not surprised to see the polished ivory gleam of bone within.

'What is it?' Aidan asked.

Straccan looked at the corpse, which was adding its own contribution to the smell of dissolution. 'I think that's Lady Judith's missing chaplain,' he said slowly. 'And if so, it's a safe bet *this* is Lord Joceran's head.'

The prisoner groaned and tried to move, and the master carter, who'd been minding him, shouted to Straccan 'Sir! He's come to!'

Straccan waved back. 'Coming!' To Aidan he said, 'Get some of the people to clear the bridge, will you?'

'Aye, sir. What about the corpus? The two corpuses?' For the smith and the cowman could be seen plodding towards them, carrying the body of Miles's antagonist.

Straccan surveyed the debris. 'There's plenty of planks. Get someone to knock up a couple of coffins; we'll leave them here and send someone back for them when we reach Bruer.'

'What about the bell?'

'Never mind that. It's not going anywhere.'

The prisoner was as pale as parchment. Straccan's sword had pierced him under the left arm, managing to miss heart and lung but letting out a considerable amount of his blood.

'Who are you?' Straccan asked.

The prisoner licked his pallid lips. At Straccan's word, Aidan brought a wineskin and dribbled a little into the wounded man's mouth. He coughed and spat. 'I'm called Samael. The man your bell killed was Michael, our commander. The one who ran away is Uriel. And I was not trying to kill David when you came at me – I was trying to save him from Uriel. You I tried not to harm, only to defend myself.'

Straccan squatted on his heels in front of Samael. True, the man hadn't tried to touch him, just to hold off his blade, and had done so with skill until his foot slipped and let Straccan get under his guard.

'Why have you been trying to kill the boy?'

'The bishop told that only to Michael.'

'What bishop?'

'Fulk de Marseilles, the Bishop of Toulouse, the leader of the White Brotherhood. May I have another drink?' Aidan gave him some more sips of wine, and a little colour tinged his cheeks and lips.

'Go on,' said Straccan. Miles was listening too.

'He sent us to kill the enemy of God, in the form of a child. I didn't know it was David d'Ax. His father was my friend.'

'How can a child be the enemy of God?'

'I didn't ask. It was the price of my life, and that mattered to me at the time. I am sorry for it now. But listen, Straccan, you must beware . . . Uriel will come back.'

Road and bridge were cleared at last and they were ready to move on. Samael had been bandaged and tied to a drag. It looked as if he would live. The rest of the carts and conveyances were undamaged, and the cowman had rounded up the oxen; he and his son would drive them to Temple Bruer in the wake of the others. Roslyn's body, wrapped in a curtain, lay in the players' cart, which Piper drove, with the other two gleemen walking beside. Miles took David, white, silent and dry-eyed, up before him.

Keeping well over to the undamaged side of the bridge the carts lumbered across, followed by the walking pilgrims, voluble

252

once more but solemn and subdued.

A mile further on they met Bane.

Bane emerged from the cart looking like a man who has taken a mortal wound but isn't yet aware of it.

He said nothing, but as he turned his head Straccan saw the shine of tears under his eyes before he dashed them away. When Straccan touched him, Bane jerked away with a sharp gasp, as if touched on raw flesh.

'Hawkan—'

'He should never have given her that God-damned name!'

'What?'

' "Sorrow"! Asking for grief, that was!' He wiped his nose on the back of his hand. 'Where's David?'

'Riding with Miles.'

Bane clambered up on the driving seat beside Piper. 'Let's go, then. No use hanging about here.' Piper shook the reins, and Apollo ambled forward.

Straccan followed, filled with grief for Roslyn – grief, and a burning rage at the man who had cut her down. All that beauty, talent and courage wasted and lost. Everyone who had known her, and even those who had simply flocked to listen, rapt and silent, when she sang, would mourn her. She was the one who had lived with ghosts all around her, but Straccan knew her memory would haunt him evermore.

Worst of all was that she'd died unshriven, and there could be no masses for her soul in a land under Interdict.

Chapter 42

The graveyard at Temple Bruer was within the monastic enclosure and sheltered behind high walls. Not since the last outbreak of plague had so many graves been filled in one day. Thanks to a seventy-years-old papal bull, and Durand's generous interpretation of it, Roslyn de Sorules, Lady Judith's chaplain and Tyrrel's victims were laid to rest in the blessed security of holy ground. The present Pope might not like it, but even he couldn't argue with the ruling of his predecessor.

The strictures of the Interdict had, however, been fully observed with the body of Michael, which had been shovelled without ceremony into the nearest ditch. That over, Straccan set about arranging for the retrieval of the bell.

'Certainly you may hire our great wain,' Sergeant Brother Denys, Bruer's seneschal, said, and named a fee that made Straccan blink.

'You misheard me, brother. I said hire it, not buy it.'

The seneschal gave him a pitying look. 'You seem to have been misfortunate with your own wain, and ill fortune has a way of sticking. The fee, naturally, includes a percentage to insure against loss in the event of a similar disaster.'

In the sure and certain knowledge that Bishop des Roches would not reimburse him for any of this – not even when he learned that his sister's treasure, her lord and husband's head, had fortuitously been found – Straccan settled down to serious haggling, emerging, financially bruised, just in time to keep his next appointment, with Bruer's master mason, who was willing to supervise the salvage of the bell for a price that took Straccan's breath away.

'*How* much?'

The master mason reckoned it on his fingers. 'There's use of the lifting tackle, the men, the transportation, the stone and mortar and skilled craftsmen to repair the bridge—'

'Repair the bridge? But it was falling down before we got there!'

'Thass as may be, sir, but you can't deny it was your bell as demolished it.'

Well, he couldn't, could he? Straccan reined in his temper. This, after all, was part of his penance. His sacrilege had been a slap in the face of Christ, who had died for him. He was lucky not to have been sent to the Holy Land, or barefoot to Saint James at Compostela.

He surrendered. 'How soon can you start?'

The master mason pursed his lips and considered. 'First light tomorrow, if it don't rain.'

Coldinghame's sub-prior had scarcely an unbruised inch of skin on his body, although miraculously nothing seemed broken or burst, he wasn't leaking blood from any orifice and his heart beat strongly. But nothing would convince him that he was going to live, and he had demanded a priest, made his confession and afterwards asked to see Straccan.

'There you are! I've something to tell you. That priest won't absolve me unless I do. Listen. The accidents that have troubled our progress . . . I caused them. I lamed the oxen—'

'*You?*'

'Yes, me. Giles startled me, and I swung round with the torch in my hand. I swear I didn't mean to hurt him. You must believe that! I meant no harm to any Christian soul.'

'But why?'

'I put the fire box in the bell wagon.' Straccan opened his mouth on another why? but swallowed it unsaid and listened with growing incredulity as Mungo went on. 'I told the carters that the bell was cursed, that it would bring bad luck. I cut the lynchpin; I dosed the beasts with scourwort . . .' The words came tumbling out, he couldn't say them fast enough. 'At Peterborough Prior Alrede told me about the caul. I suggested he ask you to take it, and I met secretly with the Croyland monks and told them. If they'd taken it from you this cursed journey would have ended there and then. Cerneshead would demand the bell, at the very least, in compensation for their loss'. He glared at Straccan. 'Trust you to get lost in the fog and spoil everything!' He gnawed his lip for a moment, then, with an air of triumph, brought out his final declaration. 'It was I who cut the ropes on the bell. That's why it fell today.'

'I tested the ropes!'

'Pah! Your tugging at them wouldn't matter. The bell had only to lean a little, and its weight would do the rest. But, as God sees me, I never meant it to kill anyone.'

Just as well it did, Straccan thought. And so much for his clever

255

theory that Lady Judith's chaplain, poor devil, or his concubine, were to blame for the misfortunes that had plagued the bell's journey. But *Mungo*?

'Did you hear me, Sir Richard?'

'Yes. Yes, I heard you. But . . . *why*?'

Haltingly the tale came out. When Prior Aernold died, Mungo and Radulfus were rivals for the priorship. Mungo spread sweeteners with a lavish hand, and the community at Coldinghame cheerfully took his bribes and promised their votes. Yet when the votes were counted, they were all for Radulfus; not one had been cast for him. He would never forget Radulfus' smug smirk when the result was announced. They had hated each other for more than twenty years. The others avoided his gaze, but he heard them sniggering in the cloister as he passed by. And then Radulfus had sent him on this unspeakably awful journey, riding a ridge-backed mule at snail's pace for weeks on end with only a couple of young fornicators for company. He was damned if Coldinghame would get the bell they set such store by, or the legacy that went with it!

'So that was it? Revenge? All that, and a man's death, just for spite?'

'I don't ask you to understand. I have told you because that priest ordered me to. I am dying, and I'm content to die, knowing Radulfus will never get his precious bell!'

Straccan looked at the carroty head on the pillow. He knew that to be a monk didn't necessarily make one a good man, and the personal loathings that could arise in the confines of the cloister sometimes reached murderous extremes, but it was hard to believe that a man could be so consumed by spite that he would gladly die so long as he had managed to grieve those he hated.

'I'm so sorry to disappoint you, brother. The bell will be salvaged, and you, I'm afraid, will go back to Coldinghame to face your brethren.'

Mungo smiled serenely. 'I shall be dead, and beyond their wrath.'

'Wrong again,' Straccan said. 'You're not going to die.'

Commander Durand lost no time in sending Miles and David safely on their way. By noon the escort was ready to leave, and only the boy was missing.

'I'll find him,' said Bane. David was in a corner of the hayloft, with the stable cat's kittens in his lap. 'They're waiting for you. It's time to go.'

'I don't want to.'

'It'll be all right. The commander's got men out all around, looking for that murdering bastard, and there's a whole conroy to take you to Boston.'

'What's a conroy?'

'Twenty knights.'

'Oh.' The child set the kittens down carefully. As he got up, his foot knocked against something that rattled and skittered on the boards. Bane stooped and picked up the pan pipes, smashed and splintered.

'I'm sorry,' David said. 'I don't want them any more.'

'That's all right.'

'I miss her, Bane.'

'So do I.'

'She wasn't going to Scotland with us, I knew that. She was going to stay with Piper. I was sad about it, but she'd still have been alive. I'd have been able to think about her playing the lute and singing.'

'I liked to hear her sing.' Something in Bane's voice made David look wonderingly at him.

'Bane? Roslyn said men don't cry.'

'They bloody do!'

With a great dry sob David threw his arms around the man and buried his face against him. Bane held him until the storm of weeping abated, as his own tears wetted the boy's curls.

'I'm ready,' David said at last. 'Bane . . .'

'What?'

'I'm sorry I broke the pipes.'

'It doesn't matter.'

'I wish I hadn't, now.'

'Tell you what, I'll make you another. I'll give it to Finan, and he can give it to you when he gets back to Coldinghame.'

Straccan saw them off. 'God go with you, brother.'

Miles raised a hand in salute and farewell, and the knights closed around him and David. The gate swung open and the conroy swept through, the standard-bearer with Beauseant at their head, a brave and daunting sight, all red and white and glittering steel.

'Don't worry about them,' Durand said as they walked back to the hall. 'They'll be safe on the ship by nightfall.'

'Any sign of the one that got away?'

'Not yet. He'll have to hole up somewhere, if he's badly burned. We'll find him. Now see here, Straccan, I want answers. Why were those men after Blaise's boy?'

'I have no idea.'

Durand looked hard at him. 'No? Have you asked that *salaud* you brought in?'

'All he knows is they had orders from Bishop Fulk of Toulouse to kill the "enemy of God".'

A nerve beside Durand's eye twitched. 'What does that mean?'

'I thought perhaps you could tell me, my lord.'

'Oh you did, did you?'

'We are both friends of Blaise d'Etranger. We should be able to trust each other.' And after that business with the Arab, Straccan thought, he was more than ready to trust this man. But would Durand trust him?

'So you *do* know something,' said Durand.

'No. All I have is another question, but if you can answer that it might answer yours as well.'

'Go on.'

'What does *Logos* mean?'

Durand let his breath out in a noisy exhalation. 'So *that's* it!'

Straccan waited. Durand rubbed a hand over his beard and came to a decision.

'Do you know the story of Vezelay, Straccan?'

Straccan thought for a moment. 'After the crucifixion, Christ's disciples and friends had to fly for their lives. Mary of Magdala and her brother Lazarus fled oversea to Provence. They lived many years at Vezelay, spreading Christ's teachings. There's a shrine there.'

'That's it.' Durand lowered his voice. 'But some say when Christ's body vanished from the tomb it was because He had not died. They say – and they are heretics who hold to it – that He survived the cross, and was hidden from His enemies by the Magdalene and her brother. They escaped across the sea and settled at Vezelay after much wandering, and there' – his voice was a mere whisper now – 'Christ and the Magdalene lived as man and wife, and a son was born to them.

'It is said that the bloodline has survived, generation after generation, to this day,' Durand finished.

Straccan felt cold.

'To answer your question, Straccan, *Logos* is Greek. It means the Word, the Word made flesh. The Christ.'

Chapter 43

The Templars' church was cold, clean and bare, the rood unveiled, for the order was not penalised by the Interdict. Straccan knelt on the stone floor, staring at the ivory face of the crucified Christ. The carved figure was all one piece, done from a massive tusk, and the sculptor had followed the tusk's curve to shape the tortured body, giving it a brutal realism.

Straccan thought about David d'Ax.

The thing was impossible! It was insanity, it was heresy! No wonder Fulk had sent forth his Angels of destruction. It hardly mattered whether it was true or not; if men believed it, it was an earthquake that could overthrow the Church.

He felt as though the ground he stood on had become a thin crust over a sucking swamp. If Christ didn't die on the cross, if He didn't rise from the grave, if He lived, married and begot sons, what was there to believe in? There was no reason for the Church to exist at all!

Then what would become of priests, of monks and nuns, eh? And bishops, and even popes?

If Christ had not died for mankind, the Church was as much a sham as those painted cloths the Gaudy Company used to represent castles, halls and meadows.

Samael was in a cell, with two brawny guards at his door, but the infirmarian tended him there, dressed his wound and dosed him. Though weakened by loss of blood and the slight wound-fever that made him a little light-headed he told his story unfalteringly, and candles were brought and lit before it was done.

When he'd finished he lay shaking, filled with such self-disgust that his body seemed swollen with it, like some unnatural gestation waiting to burst forth in all its rottenness. The scalding bile of remorse nauseated him. In his memory, day after day, and in his dreams, he saw his kin and friends twisting in the flames, and heard their agonised screaming. The enormity of his betrayal was more than he could bear. The Church taught that no sin was beyond pardon, no penitent beyond redemption, but there had been no forgiveness for Judas.

'Have you found Uriel?' he asked Straccan, after a long silence during which each man had suffered his own thoughts.

'Not yet.'

'He will try again. He knows Michael is dead, and that I failed.'

'Perhaps . . .' said Straccan, who was beginning to see a possibility, 'perhaps you could convince him that you succeeded.'

'What do you mean?'

'You could find him, or he could find you. If you tell him David is dead, that *you* killed him—'

'No,' said Samael. 'That wouldn't be enough. We were to take his head.'

Shit!

The idea came to Straccan in the middle of the night. They had camped in one of the Templars' stubble fields, and although some of the pilgrims had decided to leave the Gaudy train and trust to their own luck to avoid bandits, there were still five wagons and twenty-odd tents; the camp, though lacking its hub, the bell, still resembled a small, slummocky village.

Straccan got up in the dark and rummaged in his chest, finding what he wanted by touch, down in one corner. When he'd retrieved it he lit the stub of a candle and sat cross-legged, like a tailor, on his pallet, preparing his bait.

Also unable to sleep, and seeing the light, Bane poked his head in at the flap.

'Jesus!'

'Like it?'

'What is it?'

'The head of the enemy of God,' Straccan said, fitting it into the reliquary that had held Lord Joceran's contentious skull. That he wrapped carefully in his own clean shirt and put it in the chest. Then he went to find Durand. Coy *wuff*ed – a soft, eagerly expectant sound – and padded after him.

The community was at matins. He waited by the night stairs and waylaid the commander as he came up. The knights, sergeants and servants, filing back to their dormitories, heard behind them the murmur of voices and then a strange sound like a sudden sharp bark of mirth, choked a-borning. But as the commander had never been seen to smile, let alone heard to laugh, it must have come from that gangrel dog lurking at Straccan's heels.

The guards saluted Durand and unlocked the cell door.

'Are you sure about this?' Durand asked.

'As sure as you were about al-Hazred.'

Durand took the keys and dismissed his men.

The prisoner was awake and looked better. He watched in surprise as Durand unlocked the fetter on his ankle.

'Do you want to save David d'Ax?' Straccan demanded.

'I do.'

Straccan took the reliquary from his pouch. 'Then listen.'

It took the rest of the day, once they got the lifting gear set up, to raise Gaudy from the river, and it was evening when the labourers lowered her gently on to Temple Bruer's great wain. Stripped of her sodden, filthy wrappings, she shone like a gilded minaret as they swarmed over her with a cat's cradle of ropes, making her fast. Giles and his son had spent all day repairing what harness they could save, and Straccan paid over the odds to replace what was lost. They would start the next stage of their journey on the morrow. Incredible, Straccan thought, walking round the bell wain in the twilight, bats flicking past his ears, that after such chaos, order could be restored so soon.

They moved out soon after sunrise, and Bane set out for home.

Straccan wanted to say something that would make Bane feel better, something wonderfully wise and heartening, but all he managed was, 'God go with you, Hawkan.'

Bane's grin didn't reach the bleakness in his eyes. He gathered his reins and heeled his horse. 'You too. See you in a month or so.' And he was gone.

Durand saw them off, standing at the monastery gate alone until the last pilgrim, Wilfred on his crutches, was out of sight. Then, seeing the seneschal heading his way with an armful of parchments, he nipped into the stable, took a file from the hand of a groom and picked up the hoof the man had been working on. It would be monotonous around here again, now Straccan had gone.

Samael's wound throbbed, but that was just background discomfort, a dull reminder that he was still alive and hadn't yet fulfilled his task. For once, his head was wonderfully empty of thought, as if cleansed – perhaps by his cathartic confession – of the pageant of blood and fire that had haunted him for so long. He rode slowly, slack-reined, letting the horse go where it chose. It didn't matter where he went; he knew Uriel would find him.

They had given him the reliquary and a wallet of food. He gave the wallet to the first beggar he met. The man called on Christ and the saints to bless him. After that he turned his head aside when he met other travellers, not replying to their cheery 'God save you's'. They looked uneasily after him, forking their fingers at his back to avert ill.

Uriel had lost his surcoat, his sword and most of his hair, and the right side of his face and neck were raw and blistered, and hurt as if still in flames. To the pilgrim he robbed of food, purse and pack, he was a sight from a nightmare.

'P-p-please d-don't kill me! Take it, take all I have! Only have m-mercy!'

He spoke in the local dialect; Uriel didn't understand a word. He cut the purse, took the food and rifled the pack. He couldn't let the man go – he would blab at the nearest vill or convent, and a hue and cry was the last thing Uriel wanted.

He had to find the others.

What had *happened* at the bridge? He'd leaped into the wagon and something splintered under his boots as he tumbled the bundles over, looking for the brat. Someone – a woman – had jumped on him, stabbed him, but he had killed her; he was sure he had killed her. And then he was on fire! His hair, his surcoat. He had dropped his sword – dropped his *sword* – rolled over, beating at himself. He had scrambled out of there and on to his horse and ridden as if the devil was behind him – which he was.

He told himself he need not be ashamed. Any sane man would run from the devil.

God! Christ! His face hurt! Water ran continually from his right eye, the eyelid was swollen and inflamed, and he feared it would get infected.

What *had* happened in the wagon?

The boy had been there. For an instant he'd seen him, the devil, the abomination – had seen fire leap from his hands.

Samael waited. This was as good a place as any, a shrine to some local saint – a carved figure, damp-swollen and unrecognisable, not well done to begin with and now rather like a three-days corpse taken from the river, but nevertheless wreathed with wilting water lilies.

He leaned back against the image's blurred feet and watched

the path down which Uriel would come.

He was coming now.

Uriel dismounted, letting his horse graze beside the other. 'Where's Michael?'

'Dead.'

Dead. Good. 'The boy?'

'Dead.'

Uriel's heart gave a hard thump. 'Are you certain?'

'I killed him.'

'Ah!' Uriel sat down and took bread from the pilgrim's pack, offering some to Samael, who shook his head. Uriel put a piece of bread in his own mouth, but his face hurt too much to chew. He sucked at it until it was soft enough to pulp with his tongue, swallowed, and put the rest away.

'You took his head?'

Samael nodded. Uriel's hands were shaking with excitement. 'Show me!'

Samael gestured towards his saddle bag. The younger man got up and opened it, taking out the reliquary. As he lifted it, something inside shifted and settled again. He turned the top until it came off and looked inside. The coppery reek of blood and a hint of decay rose from it. He saw something round, bigger than his fist, wrapped in a blood-soaked rag with blood-caked dark hair sticking out.

Quickly he put the case together again and clasped it to his chest.

'Put it back,' said Samael. 'I shall take it to the bishop myself.'

Uriel could feel his heart shaking his body. Flames seemed to lave his face again, and his eye burned like a hot coal. 'We'll both go,' he said thickly.

'No. I killed him. The glory's mine, and the reward. Put it back.'

The reward danced enticingly in Uriel's brain: gold and silver, land, favour, advancement . . . He looped the reliquary's strap over his pommel and drew his dagger.

He took the dead man's sword and horse, and rode as fast as he could eastward, towards the coast. As he rode he wondered, briefly, why Samael had laughed as he died, but he soon forgot about it.

Tomorrow they should reach Lincoln.

Walking through the camp on his routine evening round, trailed by his dog, Straccan noticed that the pilgrims had begun

263

to recover their spirits at last: there was much of the usual bickering and laughter round the cook-fires, and twice he stopped to deal with a complaint. Things were getting back to normal. Perhaps in time, he thought, even he might think of the gleemaiden less often and with less pain.

If Bane made good time he should be home by tomorrow night. Home! Straccan longed for the day he would return to Stirrup, with Janiva as his bride. There were many miles still to drag Gaudy, between here and Durham, but as soon as the bell was off his hands he would ride like the Wild Hunt itself for Pouncey, where Janiva would be waiting . . .

God willing, the journey should be straightforward now, without a disgruntled wrecker or a group of murderous fanatics to contend with. There would be the usual hazards. He sighed. Broken axles, broken wheels, cast shoes, lame oxen, squabbling pilgrims, mouldy provisions, crumbling bridges, rutted roads, flooded roads, roads like quagmires, hills, profiteering victuallers, thunderstorms, thefts, accidents, incidents, medical emergencies – everything from nosebleeds to childbirth (Mistress Twiller, who'd joined the train a week ago, looked likely to burst at any moment). Oh yes, smooth and easy from now on, all the way to Durham!

There was a yell of outrage. 'Comebackyousonofabitch! I'll kill you!'

Something whizzed between his feet like a hairy arrow. 'Whoops!' The master carter almost knocked Straccan flying. 'Sir Richard! Your dog—'

Straccan spun on his heel. There was Coy, damn him, inside his tent looking out, and in his mouth the master carter's roast goose dinner.

'Give me that, you thieving sod!' The carter grabbed for his goose, the dog growled, retreating, the carter dived after him, bringing the tent down upon himself. Straccan saw Coy creep out under the canvas at the back, teeth still clenched upon his booty, and streak into the brambles at the roadside. Under the fallen canvas, the master carter heaved and swore.

All the way to Durham, he thought. *God help me!*

Well, with God's help and a measure of good luck, they might reach Durham in a month, although five weeks, or even six, Straccan reckoned, was probably a more realistic goal, given the nature of the oxen and the state of the roads ahead. The further north, the worse they'd be. But, God willing, they should reach Durham by Simon and Jude's Mass at the latest, and before the first snow of winter.

264

Chapter 44

S now came early that year, in October, on the eve of Saints Simon and Jude: a light fall, but a sure sign of worse to come. It would be a long winter, folk said, and a hungry one. The path up to the little stone house at Pouncey was treacherous, slick with frost under the snow, and Straccan slipped and came down hard on hands and knees more than once in the gathering dark. It was utterly silent, save for his panting breaths.

Is she there? She has to be there!

Somewhere in the stunted trees to his left there was movement, the fall of snow from branches dislodged by a heavy body. Wolf? Boar? He waited, still as stone – heard the coughing grunt of the beast as it crossed the path ahead of him and plunged into the trees on the other side – and let out the long breath he hadn't known he was holding.

Janiva, are you there? God, please, make her be there!

He had reached the rock ledge, and the cliff face towered above him. It was not yet too dark to see the vast branching quartz vein overhead. It seemed to gather light to itself and glimmered like a beacon, but no light gleamed from the tiny house at the end of the ledge, and Straccan could feel his heart thumping as he reached the door. There was a cold, sick, hollow apprehension in his belly. Out of breath from the climb, he rested one hand on the door frame and raised the other to knock.

Just as before, it opened ere he could knock, and light and warmth streamed out as if from a fairy hill. The tiny white-haired crone could have been a fairy too. He had forgotten how blue her eyes were, and how they seemed to look past his flesh and see his thoughts.

'My lady Osyth.'

She smiled. 'Back so soon, lad?'

Soon? It had been seven months. It seemed like half his lifetime.

'Where's Janiva?'

'Your hands are bleedin'.' Straccan turned them palms up and saw deep, bloody grazes. He hadn't known they were there, but now they began to smart like fresh burns. He had left a bloody handprint on the doorpost, too.

'She said to come—'

'Give them here.' The old woman took his hands in hers and blew softly on them. The smarting stopped.

He snatched his hands back and stared. The flesh was whole and unmarked. His mouth was open. He shut it.

'You just goin' to stand there? Don't you want to see Janiva?' the old woman asked, before he could speak again.

'Where is she?'

Osyth stepped out of the door and pointed back along the ledge. 'See that path there, runnin' behind the garth? She's gone to the spring for water. Go along past the wall. You'll meet her comin' back.'

Darkness pooled under the trees where the snow hadn't fallen. She was wrapped in a dark mantle and walked like a shadow, soft-footed on the pine-needled path, the jug of water swinging in one hand while the other clasped the mantle at her neck.

His throat felt so tight that his voice could hardly emerge. 'Janiva!'

She saw him and stopped. 'Richard?'

'Oh, my love, are you really here? I was so afraid—'

She dropped the jug – it smashed to pieces – and ran into his arms.

Chapter 45

The wayfarers, a man and a young woman, came to the nunnery at Bedesdale on the last day of October, Saint Quentin's feast day, on the wings of the worst snowstorm in living memory, living memory being Dame Ada, who claimed seventy winters, if such a thing were possible.

The woman stood in the crook of her companion's left arm, leaning against him, his cloak around them both, and he looked down at his treasure with an expression so nakedly vulnerable in its tenderness that Prioress Brigid felt a wrench at her own heart, cured leather though she thought it.

He was a knight, he said, although he had no servant with him. Sir Richard Straccan, of Stirrup, a place the prioress had never heard of although she had heard that name, Straccan, somewhere. Barely were they welcomed in, the lady seated by a roaring fire with one of Dame Lovisia's hot possets, than this Straccan demanded to see the nuns' priest. The prioress sent a novice to fetch Father Thomas from the mews, where he was, as usual, fiddling with his sparrowhawk.

The priest looked up, blinking, from the delicate task of imping his bird's broken wing-feather. 'Ah, Hilda, just put your finger on this knot, will you? That's it.' He pulled the thread taut and snipped it. Hilda, who was afraid of the hawk, stepped back quickly as it stretched its wing and shifted its taloned grip on the perch. Father Thomas made kissing sounds and gave it a scrap of raw meat, wiping his hands on the skirt of his gown.

'Please father, will you come at once?' Hilda panted. 'It's urgent, mother says.'

'Is someone dying?'

'I don't think so. They looked all right to me.'

'Who?'

'The knight and his lady.'

'Visitors? In this weather?' The priest hurried to his room for his satchel with the viaticum, just in case, and followed Hilda to the guest parlour, where the prioress, looking flustered, met him at the door.

'He insists on seeing a priest. His name's Richard Straccan, a knight, so he says.' She opened the door. Father Thomas took a deep breath and followed her in.

The young woman, flushed with the fire and Dame Lovisia's posset, was clad in rough brown homespun, with clumsy wooden-soled shoes such as villeins wear in winter; her hands, clasped round the warm cup, were chapped and marred by work. The knight, a tall grey-eyed man with a scarred face, swung round as the door opened and got straight to the point.

'Father, will you hear our vows? We wish to marry. Now.'

The priest's mild, curious gaze sharpened. Runaways? It was by no means uncommon for some enterprising rogue to steal an heiress from her father or guardian. Sometimes she was willing, more often not, but priests had been known to comply at sword's point if necessary, and this man – that was a very big sword – looked formidable. The girl, however, showed no sign of fear, and besides what knight would steal a girl such as this – so poorly clad – a villein, surely?

Father Thomas swallowed. Sword or no sword, this was irregular. It was his duty to enquire further.

'Is this with your consent, my lady?' He hoped the quaver in his voice would not be noticed. 'Answer freely. If there is force used here, I won't permit this.'

She smiled. 'I am full willing, father.' That was not the accent of a villein.

'Is there any impediment? Kinship? A prior contract?'

'I'm a widower,' the knight said. 'We are both free to marry, and no kin. I give you my word, father.'

After a searching look at their faces, the priest nodded. 'I will hear your vows. But you know I can't say a Mass for you. The Interdict forbids it. I'm sorry.'

'Never mind the Mass,' the knight said. 'So long as we are wed, with you and my lady prioress to witness.'

He unbuckled his sword harness and laid it down, then took a ring from his little finger, a silver band with a single green stone, and put it on the third finger of his bride's left hand. It was loose but would serve for now. He'd give her a better one when he got her safe home.

'Janiva, before these witnesses I take you as mine. All that I have is yours.'

For an instant a cold worm of fear uncoiled and twitched within him, fear that even now, her hand in his, the ring on her finger, the witnesses watching, even now she might draw back.

She had refused him three times before.

'I take you as mine, Richard,' she said. 'Though I have nothing to give you but myself.'

He felt light-headed with relief and an overwhelming joy that made him want to shout aloud. 'You are all I want,' he said. Still holding her hand, he took the purse from his belt and gave it to the priest. 'Thank you, father.'

Mother Brigid relieved Father Thomas of the purse and tucked it away in her voluminous gown. 'This marriage will be entered in our record, Sir Richard,' she said, still wondering why the knight's name was familiar. 'We will make you and your lady as comfortable as we can, while the snow keeps you here.'

The snow would keep them for some days, and if it drifted deeply they would have to await a thaw before he could take his wife home.

It had been nothing like his first wedding. The road to the church that day, fifteen years ago, had been strewn with flowers. He remembered Marian, shy and proud in her red dress and silver girdle; his father's hall hung with garlands and ribbons, the table laden with borrowed silver, and the bedchamber resplendent with hangings – also borrowed – and candles, real beeswax candles. The room had smelled of honey.

There were no ribbons this time, no flowers, no silver, no guests; the bride wore the next-best thing to sackcloth; no laughing, tipsy friends to see them to the bride bed in the priory guest house which, thanks to the snow, they had to themselves. But there were candles, clean sheets, well aired blankets and a feather bolster from the prioress's own linen chest; and some dear romantic soul among the nuns – Straccan blessed her with all his heart – had braved the snow to gather glossy trails of ivy and sprays of berried holly to garland the bedposts.

He'd dreamed of this so often, for so long – Janiva asleep in his arms, her breath warm on his shoulder – that now he feared to sleep, lest on waking he should find it just another dream.

He watched her sleeping face in the light of the summer-scented candles. Her hair was spread across his breast like a shawl, her head lay on his arm, and as the night hours passed, marked at intervals by the nuns' sweet high voices singing nocturne and matins, his arm grew numb, but he didn't move. God had been good to him beyond his deserts. Against all odds, she was his at last, and now that he had been absolved from his sin, there was no shadow over his marriage.

★ ★ ★

269

Three days of rain had washed away the snow, leaving the roads muddy and treacherous, but the fourth morning dawned clear and pale with a relentless ice-edged wind that promised lasting frost and easier travelling: the knight and his young bride would have cold faring.

The prioress loaned them a palfrey for Janiva, to be left at the convent's sister house in York, and all the community – nuns, novices, lay sisters and even the servants of the house – gathered on the frosty steps to see them off. It was an infraction of the Rule, but a minor one, surely, and all had agreed: each would perform some private penance or repeat a hundred paters to atone for this lapse in discipline and indulgence in worldly pleasure.

They watched until their guests were out of sight, then, some dabbing at sentimental tears, took up the interrupted pattern of their lives. Mother Brigid and Father Thomas were the last to go inside, she leaning on his arm to climb the frost-slick steps and still rummaging her memory for the reason why the name Straccan seemed familiar.

'I wish I knew who he was,' she muttered.

'But surely you know? Whoops!' Father Thomas steadied her as her foot skated; only his wild grab at the door knocker saved them both from an undignified tumble.

'Sir Richard,' he panted, shimmying through the doorway with his arm about the prioress's waist – a sight that made her daughters-in Christ stare in surprise – 'is the man Prior Reginald spoke of when he stopped here on his way to Hexham: the relic dealer.'

'*That* man?' The prioress stared at him, appalled. 'Old fool, why didn't you tell me?'

Father Thomas deposited her on a bench and closed the door behind them, thankful to be out of the wind. The chilly entrance hall was warm by comparison; his nose began to run and he wiped it vigorously on his sleeve. 'I thought you knew.'

'By our Blessed Lady, I wish I *had* known! That's the man who got the Holy Foreskin back after it was stolen from the nuns at Sheppey. And didn't he find the Pendragon Banner? If I'd known who he was, I'd have asked him to find a good relic for us.' *Something better than the Virgin's tears the nuns of Saint Clement's claim*, she thought sourly, *which everyone knows are just rain water in a phial*. 'Oh, Blessed Mother, to think he was here, and I never knew!'

★ ★ ★

270

On the eve of Saint Brice's Mass the kitchen at Stirrup looked like a battlefield after the battle, with exhausted bodies slumped in ungainly positions just where they had collapsed; but these bodies were all female, and still breathing – one or two were even snoring – and woe betide any scavenger who dared trespass on *this* scene of carnage and bloodshed.

True, the blood belonged to pigs and sheep, chickens and ducks, geese and rabbits; the knives lying about were not weapons, though they could serve that purpose at need; and the unmoving bodies were resting after a long day's labour, for this was the calm before the storm.

Sir Richard and his lady would be here before nightfall.

Adeliza and her conscripts, manor workers' wives and daughters, had been hard at it since dawn, and not just today. The orgy of preparation had begun a week ago, when Sir Richard's messenger rode in with tidings of the wedding. Today was the culmination of their culinary labours.

The entire manor was involved. Small boys with slingshots had been set to killing waterfowl, older boys to snaring rabbits, cottars to butchering pigs and poultry, and their womenfolk to mending, sweeping and scrubbing. Not that the place was dirty – Adeliza, who had cooked and kept house for Sir Richard for seven years now, took pride in her job – but they were all devoted to their master, and all wanted the manor to look its best to welcome Sir Richard's bride, now he had got her at last.

It had taken him long enough.

There was a flat, tinny clanking. The watchbell! They had been seen from the tower. Everyone not engaged in preparing the feast or decking the hall trooped out to meet them, led by the master's daughter Gilla, who'd been like a cat on hot bricks all day. The kitchen hands jerked awake and sprang into action again. Time to slide the last-minute dainties, the pies and tarts, into the ovens; time to put on clean coifs and aprons; time to carry the jellies and sweetmeats across the yard, and thanks be to God that it wasn't raining!

Evergreen branches had been cut and laid in the road, and the gateway was festooned with ivy. Indoors the hall was ablaze with candles, and hung with garlands of winter greenery and strings of brightly painted nuts and gilded fir cones. The tables creaked under the weight of roast pork and mutton, chickens and ducks and geese, sides of bacon, hams, bowls of pottage and porreys, dishes of sweet wrinkled apples, custards, pears and plums preserved in honey, pickled eggs, great wheels of cheese, platters

271

of dried fruits and piles of soft white loaves, jellies studded with almonds, and trays of savoury pies and sweet tarts.

No one, from the oldest granny to the youngest child, was going to miss the fun, and the bride-ale feast went on half the night, with people slipping from the benches to sleep in the straw under the tables as the hours wore on. They weren't strangers to Janiva; she'd guested at the manor once before and knew them by sight if not all yet by name. Their splendid welcome more than made up for the hasty wedding, and she would always love them for their joy in Richard's happiness and hers.

When at last they retreated to the bedchamber they found the floor and bed strewn with dried rose petals and lavender, and a dozen extravagant beeswax candles filling the chamber with the scent of honey.

As Janiva unlaced her gown, the lambent golden light slid over her hair, turning it to amber, and gilded her shoulders and breasts. Straccan put his arms around her and kissed her, holding her against him, wanting to pull her inside his own flesh and bones, where she would always be safe. He couldn't keep her from danger, he knew that. She would go where she was needed, when she was called; but she was here now. Now she was his. Tonight and tomorrow, and all their tomorrows, she would be his.

He picked her up and carried her to the bed. Laughing, she said, 'You've forgotten the candles.'

'No, I haven't,' he said, and kissed her again. Ten thousand tomorrows, ten thousand tonights. 'Let them burn.'

Chapter 46

'My lord! My lord bishop!'

Fulk stirred under the coverlid and grunted.

'My lord, wake up! He's here! He's come back!' In his agitation, Maître Deil let the candle he was holding tilt, and drops of hot wax fell on the bishop's shoulder, causing him to yelp and surge up from his bed, fully awake in the instant and after blood.

'Imbecile! Clumsy dog! What d'you mean by this, eh?'

His secretary set the candle down and stood at the bishop's bedside, hands folded as in prayer. 'My lord, the Angels—'

'The Angels? Here, now? Why didn't you say? Where's my gown?' Fulk emerged, naked, from his heaped quilts, fumbling his arms into the dressing gown his secretary held ready, his feet into furred slippers.

'Only one has returned, my lord. The one you called Uriel.'

'Uriel? Which is he?'

'The youngest.'

'What of the others? Your cripple and the heretic?'

'Dead, my lord.'

'Did—' The bishop could hardly frame his question, so vital was the answer. He tried again, hoarsely: 'Did they succeed?'

'He says so, my lord. He has proof.'

'God and the saints be praised!' The bishop clasped his secretary in his arms, then fell on his knees. 'Mighty, mighty art thou, Lord, God of Hosts! Thou hast put down thine enemy and made safe the foundations of thy Church!'

Uriel swung round as the bishop entered, followed by Maître Deil, who hurried round lighting candles. As the waxing light illuminated Uriel's face, the bishop gave an involuntary gasp.

'What happened to you?'

'It was the devil, the boy. He threw fire and burned me. He killed the others. They failed, and he killed them, but I killed *him.*'

The bishop sat behind the table and clasped his hands

273

together in his lap to still their trembling. 'You have the proof?'

Uriel undid his satchel and offered the reliquary. Fulk opened it, recoiling from the gush of decomposing flesh. He glimpsed the crusted, stained wrapping and the lank, clotted hair as he hastily clapped the case together again and reached for his pomander.

'Well done, well done indeed, my son. Your name was . . .'

'Ernaut de Troyes.'

'Sir Ernaut, you have performed a great service for the Church, and the Church will show her gratitude. But now it is the middle of the night; you are travel-weary, hungry, thirsty, I am sure. Maître Deil will take you to a private chamber. I will send food and wine to you. Rest now, my son. Tomorrow we shall discuss how to reward you.'

Ernaut bowed, and followed the secretary.

When Deil returned, the bishop was sanding a hastily written letter. 'Wax,' he said curtly. Deil lit the candle stub under the wax boat. Fulk folded his letter, poured the black wax and pressed his signet ring into it.

'I will summon a courier,' Deil said.

'No! We take no chances with this. An escort of knights – pick them yourself, Deil – they must leave for Rome at dawn. Have you . . . *dealt* with that creature? I remember something of him – murder, wasn't it? His own brother? His wife?' The bishop's nostrils flared with disgust.

'His betrothed,' Deil corrected.

'It seems you chose them wisely, our Angels, after all. So . . . have you taken care of him?'

'He was drinking the wine when I left him, my lord. In the morning, *helas*, he will be found dead.'

The bishop picked up the reliquary again. Nauseating though it was, he would look the enemy of God in the face. 'Fetch some towels, Deil, and hot water and a basin, and clean that thing up.'

He leaned forward cautiously, pomander to nose, as his secretary opened the reliquary and shook the thing in it into the basin.

Sprawled on the floor, where he had fallen, Ernaut de Troyes convulsed again. The agony in his belly was like a wolf trying to eat its way out. The room stank of vomit and excrement and blood. He wallowed in unspeakable slime. He had screamed his throat raw; he had no voice left with which to scream again and could only whimper, begging uselessly for help.

Suddenly there was a face over him, a mouth bawling at him, hands shaking him. 'Help me,' he mouthed silently. 'Please!'

'Where is he? The boy! The boy! Where is the boy?'

But although he would suffer for a long time yet before he died, Uriel, the Flame of God, was past speech and could tell Maître Deil nothing.

In his chamber, Bishop Fulk, white with shock and rage, was still staring at the thing in the basin, and the monkey's shrivelled black eyes, like currants, stared back at him.